W9-AVH-979

DATE DUE

MAY 2 6 2015		
JUN 1 5 2015		
JUN 29 2015		
JUL 1 8 2015		
AUG 1 9 2015		
JAN 4 2016		
JUL 2 6 2016		
JUN 2 3 2017		
JUL 3 2017		
NOV 2 8 2017		
JAN 1 1 2018		
JUL 2 0 2018		

F   Tucker, K.A.   2015
TUC   Burying Water

SWISHER CO LIBRARY
127 SW 2ND STREET
TULIA, TX 79088

BURYING
WATER

ALSO BY K.A. TUCKER

Ten Tiny Breaths
One Tiny Lie
Four Seconds to Lose
Five Ways to Fall
In Her Wake

BURYING
WATER

A NOVEL

K.A. TUCKER

SWISHER CO LIBRARY
127 SW 2ND STREET
TULIA, TX 79088

ATRIA PAPERBACK

NEW YORK   LONDON   TORONTO   SYDNEY   NEW DELHI

ATRIA PAPERBACK

A Division of Simon & Schuster, Inc.
1230 Avenue of the Americas
New York, NY 10020

This book is a work of fiction. Any references to historical events, real people, or real places are used fictitiously. Other names, characters, places, and events are products of the author's imagination, and any resemblance to actual events or places or persons, living or dead, is entirely coincidental.

Copyright © 2014 by Kathleen Tucker

All rights reserved, including the right to reproduce this book or portions thereof in any form whatsoever. For information, address Atria Books Subsidiary Rights Department, 1230 Avenue of the Americas, New York, NY 10020.

First Atria Paperback edition October 2014

ATRIA PAPERBACK and colophon are trademarks of Simon & Schuster, Inc.

For information about special discounts for bulk purchases, please contact Simon & Schuster Special Sales at 1-866-506-1949 or business@simonandschuster.com.

The Simon & Schuster Speakers Bureau can bring authors to your live event. For more information or to book an event, contact the Simon & Schuster Speakers Bureau at 1-866-248-3049 or visit our website at www.simonspeakers.com.

Interior design by Meryll Rae Preposi
Jacket design by Anna Dorfman
Cover photograph © Vilde Indrehus/Room/Getty Images

Manufactured in the United States of America

10 9 8 7 6 5 4 3 2 1

Library of Congress Cataloging-in-Publication Data

ISBN 978-1-4767-7418-3
ISBN 978-1-4767-7419-0 (ebook)

To Lia and Sadie

And the truth pushed to the surface.
Like water, buried.

BURYING
WATER

JESSE

NOW

This can't be real . . . This can't be real . . . This can't be real . . .

The words cycle round and round in my mind like the wheels on my speeding 'Cuda as its ass-end slips and slides over the gravel and ice. This car is hard to handle on the best of days, built front-heavy and overloaded with horsepower. I'm going to put myself into one of these damn trees if I don't slow down.

I jam my foot against the gas pedal.

I *can't* slow down now.

Not until I know that Boone was wrong about what he claims to have overheard. His Russian is mediocre at best. I'll give anything for him to be wrong about *this*.

My gut clenches as my car skids around another turn, the cone shape of Black Butte looming like a monstrous shadow ahead of me in the pre-dawn light. The snowy tire tracks framed by my headlights might not even be the right ones, but they're wide like Viktor's Hummer and they're sure as hell the only ones down this old, deserted logging road. No one comes out here in January.

The line of trees marking the dead end comes up on me be-

fore I expect it. I slam on my brakes, sending my car sliding sideways toward the old totem pole. It's still sliding when I cut the
rumbling engine, throw open the door, and jump out, fumbling
with my flashlight. It takes three hard presses with my shaking
hands to get the light to hold.

I begin searching the ground. The mess of tread marks tells
me that someone pulled a U-turn. The footprints tell me that
more than one person got out. And when I see the half-finished
cigarette butt with that weird alphabet on the filter, I know Boone
wasn't wrong.

"Alex!" My echo answers once . . . twice . . . before the vast
wilderness swallows up my desperate cry. With frantic passes of
my flashlight, my knuckles white against its body, I search the
area until I spot the sets of footprints that lead off the old, narrow
road and into the trees.

Frigid fingers curl around my heart.

Darting back to my car, I snatch the old red-and-blue plaid
wool blanket that she loves so much from the backseat. Ice-cold
snow packs into the sides of my sneakers as I chase the trail past
the line of trees and into the barren field ahead, my blood rushing
through my ears the only sound I process.

The only sign of life.

Raw fear numbs my senses, the Pacific Northwest winter
numbs my body, but I push forward because if . . .

The beam of light passes over a still form lying facedown in
the snow. I'd recognize that pink coat and platinum-blond hair of
hers anywhere; the sparkly blue dress that she hates so much looks
like a heap of sapphires against a white canvas.

My heart freezes.

"Alex." It's barely a whisper. I'm unable to produce more, my
lungs giving up on me. I run, stumbling through the foot of snow
until I'm on my knees and crawling forward to close the distance.
A distance of no more than ten feet and yet one that seems like
miles.

There's no mistaking the spray of crimson freckling the snow around her head. Or that most of her long hair is now dark and matted. Or that her silver stockings are torn and stained red, and a pool of blood has formed where her dress barely covers her thighs. Plenty of footprints mark the ground around her. He must have been here for a while.

I know that there are rules to follow, steps to make sure that I don't cause her further harm. But I ignore them because the sinking feeling in my stomach tells me I can't possibly hurt her more than he already has. I nestle her head with one hand while I slide the other under her shoulder. I roll her over.

Cold shock knocks the wind out of me.

I've never seen anybody look like *this*.

I scoop her limp body into my arms, cradling the once beautiful face that I've seen in every light—rage to ecstasy and the full gamut in between—yet is now unrecognizable. Placing two blood-coated fingers over her throat, I wait. Nothing.

A light pinch against her lifeless wrist. Nothing.

Maybe a pulse does exist but it's hidden, masked by my own racing one.

Then again, by the look of her, likely not.

One . . . two . . . three . . . plump, serene snowflakes begin floating down from the unseen sky above. Soon, they will converge and cover the tracks, the blood. The evidence. Mother Nature's own blanket to hide the unsightly blemish in her yard.

"I'm so sorry." I don't try to restrain the hot tears as they roll down my cheeks to land on her mangled lips—lips I had stolen plenty of kisses from, back when I was too stupid to realize how dangerous that really was. This is my fault. She had warned me. If I had just listened, had stayed away from her, had not told her how I felt . . .

. . . had not fallen wildly in love with her.

I lean down to steal a kiss even now, the coppery taste of her blood mixing with my salty tears. "I'm so damn sorry. I should never have even looked your way," I manage to get out around my sobs, tucking the blanket she loved to curl up in over her.

An almost inaudible gasp slips out. A slight breeze against my mouth more than anything else.

My lungs freeze, my eyes glued to her, afraid to hope. "Alex?" Is it possible?

A moment later, a second gasp—a wet, rattling sound—escapes.

She's not dead.

Not yet, anyway.

ONE

ALEX

IN BETWEEN

A fire.

The fragrance calls to me.

I cannot see, for my eyes are sealed shut against the wicked glow in his stare.

I cannot hear, for my ears have blocked out his appalling promises.

I cannot feel, for my body has long since shattered.

But, as I lie in the cool stillness of the night, waiting for my final peace, that comforting waft of burning bark and twigs and crispy leaves encases me.

It whispers to me that everything will be okay.

And I so desperately long to believe it.

———

Beep . . .

". . . basilar skull fracture . . ."

Beep . . .

". . . collapsed lung . . ."

Beep . . .

"... ruptured spleen ..."

Beep ...

"... frostbite ..."

Beep ...

Beep ...

"Will she live?"

Beep ...

"I honestly don't know how she has survived this long."

Beep ...

"We need to keep this quiet for now."

"Gabe, you just showed up on the doorstep of my hospital with a half-dead girl. How am I supposed to do that?"

"You just do. Call me if she wakes up. No one questions her but me. *No one*, Meredith."

———

"Don't try to talk yet," someone—a woman—warns softly. I can't see her. I can't see anything; my lids open to mere slits, enough to admit a haze of light and a flurry of activity around me—gentle fingertips, low murmurs, papers rustling.

And then that rhythmic beep serenades me back into oblivion.

TWO

JANE DOE

NOW

I don't know how I got here.

I don't know where here is.

I hurt.

Who is this woman hovering over me?

"Please page Dr. Alwood immediately," she calls to someone unseen. Turning back to look at me, it takes her a long moment before she manages a white-toothed smile. Even in my groggy state, there's no missing the pity in it. Her chest lifts with a deep breath and then she shifts her attention to the clear-fluid bags hanging on a rack next to me. "Glad to finally see your eyes open," she murmurs. "They're a really pretty russet color." The hem of her lilac uniform grazes the cast around my hand.

My cast.

I take inventory of the room—the pale beige walls, the stiff chairs, the pastel-blue curtain. The machines. It finally clicks.

I'm in a hospital.

"How—" I stall over the question as that first word scratches against my throat.

"You were intubated to help you breathe. That hoarseness will go away soon, I promise."

I needed help *breathing*?

"You're on heavy doses of morphine, so you may feel a little disoriented right now. That's normal. Here." A cool hand slips under my neck as she fluffs up my pillow.

"Where am I?" I croak out, just now noticing that bandages are dividing my face in two at the nose.

"You're at St. Charles in Bend, Oregon, with the very best doctors that we have. It looks like you're going to pull through." Again, another smile. Another sympathetic stare. She's a pretty, young woman, her long, light brown hair pulled back in a ponytail, her eyes a mesmerizing leafy green.

Not mesmerizing enough to divert me from her words. Pull through *what* exactly?

She prattles on about the hospital, the town, the unusually brisk winter weather. I struggle to follow along, too busy grappling with my memory, trying to answer the litany of questions swirling inside my mind. Nothing comes, though. I'm drawing a complete blank.

Like she said, it must be the morphine.

A creak pulls my gaze to the far corner of the room, where a tall, lanky woman in a white coat covering a pink floral shirt has just entered. With quick, long strides she rounds my bed, drawing the curtain behind her as she approaches. "Hello."

I'm guessing this is the doctor whom the nurse had paged. I watch as she fishes out a clip from her pocket and pins back a loose strand of apricot-colored hair. Snapping on a pair of surgical gloves, she then pulls a small flashlight from her pocket. "How are you feeling?"

"I'm not sure yet." My voice is rough but at least audible. "Are you my doctor? Doctor . . ." I read the name on the badge affixed to her coat. "Alwood?"

Green eyes rimmed with dark circles search mine for a long

moment. "Yes, I operated on you. My name is Dr. Meredith Al-wood." I squint against the beam of light from her flashlight, first into my left eye and then my right. "Are you in any pain?"

"I don't know. I'm . . . sore. And confused." My tongue catches something rough against my bottom lip and I instinctively run my tongue along it, sensing a piece of thread. It's when I begin toying with it that I also notice the wide gap on the right side of my mouth. I'm missing several teeth.

"Good. I'm glad. Not about the confused part." Dr. Alwood's lips press together in a tight smile. "But you'd be a lot more than 'sore' if the pain meds weren't working."

My throat burns. I swallow several times, trying to alleviate the dryness. "What happened? How did I get here?" Someone must know something. Right?

Dr. Alwood opens her mouth but then hesitates. "Amber, you have your rounds to finish, don't you?"

The nurse, who's been busy replacing the various bags on the IV stand, stops to look at the doctor for a long second, her delicately drawn eyebrows pulled together. They have the same green eye color, I notice. In fact, they have the exact same almond-shaped eyes and straight-edged nose.

Or, maybe I'm just hallucinating, thanks to the drugs.

Kind fingers probe something unseen on my scalp and then, with the sound of the door clicking shut, the doctor asks, "How about we start with the basic questions. Can you please give me your name?"

I open my mouth to answer. It's such a simple question. Everyone has a name. *I* have a name. And yet . . . "I don't . . . I don't know," I stammer. How do I not know what my name is? I'm sure it's the same name I've had all my life.

My life.

What do I remember about my life? Shouldn't *something* about it be registering?

A wave of panic surges through me and the EKG's telltale

beep increases its cadence. Why can't I seem to recall a single scrap of my life?

Not a face, not a name, not a childhood pet.

Nothing.

Dr. Alwood stops what she's doing to meet my gaze. "You've had a significant head injury. Just try to relax." Her words come slow and steady. "I'll tell you what I know. Maybe that will jog your memory. Okay? Just take a few breaths first." She's quick to add, "Not too deep."

I do as instructed, watching my chest lift and fall beneath my blue-and-white checkered gown, cringing with a sharp twinge of pain on my right side with each inhale. Finally, that incessant beeping begins to slow.

I turn my attention back to her. Waiting.

"You were found in the parking lot of an abandoned building nine days ago," Dr. Alwood begins.

I've been here for nine days?

"You were brought into the emergency room by ambulance with extensive, life-threatening trauma to your body. Your injuries were consistent with a physical assault. You had several fractures—to your ribs, your left leg, your right arm, your skull. Your right lung collapsed. You required surgery for a hematoma, a ruptured spleen, and lacerations to . . ." Her calm voice drifts off into obscurity as she recites a laundry list of brutality that can't possibly have my name at the top of it. "It will take some time to recover from all of these injuries. Do you feel any tightness in your chest now, when you inhale?"

I swallow the rising lump in my throat, not sure how to answer. I'm certainly having difficulty breathing, but I think it has more to do with panic than anything else.

"No," I finally offer. "I think I'm okay."

"Good." She gingerly peels back pieces of gauze from my face—some over the bridge of my nose and another piece running along the right side of my face, from my temple all the way down to my chin. By the slight nod of approval, I'm guessing she's happy with whatever is beneath. "And how is the air flow through your nose? Any stuffiness?"

I test my nostrils out. "A little."

She stops her inspection to scribble something on the chart that's sitting on the side table. "You were very fortunate that Dr. Gonzalez was in Bend on a ski trip. He's one of the leading plastic surgeons in the country and a very good friend of mine. When I saw you come in, I called him right away. He offered us his skill, pro bono."

A part of me knows that I should be concerned that I needed a plastic surgeon for my face, and yet I'm more concerned with the fact that I can't even imagine what that face looks like.

"I removed the stitches two days ago to help minimize the scarring. You may need a secondary surgery on your nose, depending on how it heals. We won't know until the swelling goes down." Setting the clipboard down on the side table again, she asks, "Do you remember *anything* about what happened to you?"

"No." *Nothing.*

The combination of her clenched jaw and the deep furrow across her forehead gives me the feeling that she's about to deliver more bad news. "I'm sorry to tell you that we found evidence of sexual assault."

I feel the blood drain from my face and the steady beeping spikes again as my heart begins to pound in my chest. "I don't . . . I don't understand." She's saying I was . . . raped? Somebody touched me like *that*? The urge to curl my arms around my body and squeeze my legs tight swarms me, but I'm too sore to act on it. How could I possibly not remember being *raped*?

"I need to examine the rest of your injuries." Dr. Alwood waits for my reluctant nod and then slides the flannel sheet down and lifts my hospital gown. I'm temporarily distracted by the cast around my leg as she gently peels back the bandages around my ribs and the left side of my stomach.

"These look good. Now, just relax, I'll make this quick," she promises, nudging my free leg toward the edge of my bed. I distract myself from my discomfort with the tiled ceiling above as she gently inspects me. "You required some internal stitching, but everything should heal properly with time. We're still running some tests and blood work, but we've ruled out the majority of sexually transmitted diseases. We also completed a rape kit on you."

I close my eyes as a tear slips out from the corner of one eye, the salt from it burning my sensitive skin. Why did this happen to me? Who could have done such a thing?

Raped . . . STDs . . . "What about . . . I mean, could I be pregnant?" The question slips out unbidden.

True to her promise, Dr. Alwood quickly readjusts my gown and covers. Peeling off her gloves, she tosses them in the trash bin and then takes a seat on the edge of my bed. "We can certainly rule that out from the rape." She pauses. "Because you were already pregnant when you were brought in."

The air sails from my lungs as she delivers yet *another* harsh punch of news. My gaze drifts to my flat abdomen. I have a baby in there?

"You were about ten weeks along."

Were. Past tense.

"Do you not recall *any* of this?" Dr. Alwood's brows draw together as she watches me closely.

A soft "no" slips out and I can't help but feel that she doesn't believe me.

"Well, given your extensive injuries, it is not at all surprising that you miscarried. You're lucky to be alive, as it is." She hesitates before she adds, "I don't think that whoever did this to you intended for you to survive."

A strange cold sweeps through my limbs as I take in the ruined body lying on this bed before me. I've been lucid for all of five minutes—the long hand on the clock ahead tells me that—

and in that short time, this doctor has informed me that I was beaten, raped, . . . and left for dead.

And I lost a baby I don't even remember carrying, or making. I don't know who the father was.

I don't even know who *I* am.

"I'm going to send you for another CT scan and MRI." I feel the weight of her gaze on me. "Are you sure there isn't someone or something that you remember? A husband? Or a boyfriend? Or a sibling? A parent? Maybe a city where you grew up? The hospital would like to find your family for you."

Her barrage of questions only makes my heart rate spike and the annoying EKG ramp up again. I can't answer a single one of them. Is anyone missing me right now? Are they searching for me? Am I from Bend, Oregon, or do I live somewhere else?

Dr. Alwood sits quietly, waiting, as I focus on a small yellow splotch on the ceiling. That's water damage. How can I recognize *that* and not my own name?

"Even a tiny detail?" she presses, the urgency in her voice soft and pleading.

"No." There's nothing.

I remember nothing at all.

THREE

JESSE

THEN

There are a lot of things I don't like about Portland.

The rain tops the list.

Scratch that. *Driving* in the rain tops the list. It's usually just a dreary never-ending drizzle, but once in a while the skies open up for an especially heavy downpour. The shitty old Toyota I bought for five hundred bucks doesn't deal well with that weather, the engine randomly sputtering and cutting out like it's drowning. I don't know how many times I've tried to fix the problem.

September was a heavy month for rain. It looks like October is competing for a record, too, because it's pouring again tonight. It's only a matter of time before the car gives out on me, right here in the middle of this deserted road. Then I'll be just like the poor sucker on the shoulder up ahead, his hazards flashing.

Even though I've already made my mind up to keep moving, when I realize it's a BMW Z8, my foot eases off the gas pedal. I've never seen one in real life before. Probably because there are only a few thousand in the entire country and each one would go for a pretty penny. It's rare and it's fucking gorgeous.

And it has a flat tire.

"Nope." Changing tires in the rain sucks. That rich bastard can wait for roadside assistance to come save him. I'm sold on that plan until my headlights catch long blond hair in the driver's side. Twenty feet past, my conscience takes over and I can't help but brake. "Shit," I mutter, pulling off to the shoulder and slowly backing up.

No one's getting out, but if she's alone, she's probably wary. With a loud groan, I step out into the rain, yanking the hood of my gray sweatshirt up over my head. I jog over to the passenger-side window. Growing up with a sheriff as a father, you learn never to stand on the road, even if there isn't a car in sight. People get clipped all the time.

I knock against the glass.

And wait.

"Come on . . ." I mutter, my head hung low, the rain pounding on my back feeling like a cold hose bath. It can't be more than 40 degrees out here. Another five seconds and I'm leaving her here.

Finally the window cracks open, just enough for me to peer through. She's alone in the car. It's dark, but I'm pretty sure I see tears. I definitely see smeared black makeup. And her eyes . . . They glisten with fear. I don't blame her. She's driving a high-priced car and she's sitting alone out here after eleven at night. And now there's a guy in a hoodie hanging outside her window. I adjust my tone accordingly. "Do you need help?"

I hear her swallow hard before answering, "Yes. I do." She sounds young, but it's hard to tell with some women.

"Have you called Triple-A?"

She hesitates and then shakes her head.

Okay . . . not very talkative. She smells incredible, though, based on the flowery perfume wafting out of her car. Incredible and rich. "Your spare's in the trunk?"

"I . . . think so?"

I sigh. Looks like I'm changing a tire in the pouring rain after all. "Okay. Pop your trunk and I'll see what I can do. Stay in here."

I round the car. Beneath half a dozen shopping bags and under the trunk floor, I find the spare tucked away. Running back to get my jack and flashlight out of my car—I use my own tools whenever I can—I settle down by the back corner of the Z8, happy for the dead roads. Not one vehicle has passed since I stopped.

The BMW is jacked and the lug nuts are off when the driver's door opens. "I'll have this changed in another two minutes!" I holler, gently pulling the rim off. "You should stay inside."

The door slams shut—I cringe, you don't slam anything on a car like this!—and then heels click on the pavement as she comes around to stand next to me. The rain suddenly stops pelting my back. "Is that better?" she asks in a soft voice.

I don't need to glance up to know that there's an umbrella hovering over me. "You're not from Portland, are you?" I mumble with a smile. Neither am I, technically, but I've learned to adapt in the four years that I've lived here. Part of that is knowing that no guy in Portland would be caught dead using an umbrella. Neither would most women, actually. We'd rather duck our head and get wet than be labeled a wuss. Smart? No.

"No, not originally."

I yank the tire off and roll it to the side. That's when my eyes get caught up in a pair of long, bare legs right beside me, covered in goose bumps from the cold. Forcing my head back down with a low exhale, I grab the spare.

"Thank you for stopping. Most people wouldn't have."

Most people, including me. "You should really get a Triple-A plan."

"I have one," she admits somberly and then, after a second's hesitation, adds, "My phone died and I can't find my car charger."

So, she was *totally* stranded. As much as this sucks, I'm glad I stopped. This should give my conscience something to feel good about, seeing as I've tested it plenty over the years. "I can't find my phone charger half the time. It's usually under the seat. I finally went and bought a second cord that I keep in my glove compartment."

I hear the smile in her voice as she says, "I'll have to remember that."

"Yeah, you should. Especially in a car like this." The spare is bolted in place in another minute.

"You're very fast."

I smirk as I lower the car. "I've been changing tires since I could walk." Well, not really, but it feels like it. Grabbing the flat tire with one arm, I intentionally step out from the umbrella so I don't get her dirty with it on my way to the trunk. It's too late for me, but I'm used to it. I go through more clothes than the average guy. "Do you have far to go? These aren't meant for long distances."

"About ten miles."

"Good. I can stay behind you until you get off the highway, if that makes you feel better," I offer, wiping my wet, dirty hands against my jeans. "I'm headed that way anyway."

"That's very kind of you." She doesn't make a move to leave, though. She just stands there, her face hidden by the darkness and that giant umbrella.

And then I hear the stifled sob.

Ah, shit. I don't know what to do with a rich girl crying on the side of the road. Or crying girls in general. I've made plenty of them do it, unintentionally, and felt bad about it after. But other than saying, "I'm sorry," I'm at a loss. I hesitate before asking, "Is everything okay? I mean, do you have someone you can call? You can use my phone if you want. I'll grab it from the car."

"No, I don't have anyone."

A long, lingering silence hangs over us.

"Well . . ." I really just want to get home and catch *The Late Show,* but I didn't get soaked so I could leave her standing out here.

"Are you happy?" Her question cuts through the quiet night like a rude interruption.

"Uh . . ." *What?* I shift nervously on my feet.

"In your life. Are you happy? Or do you ever wish you could just start over?"

I frown into the darkness. "Right now I wish I wasn't freezing my ass off in the rain," I admit. What the hell else do I say to that? I wasn't ready for deep, thought-provoking questions. I generally avoid those, and God knows the idiots I hang out with don't toss them around. Is this chick out of her mind?

She steps in closer, lifting her umbrella to shield, granting me part of my wish. "I mean, if you could just start over fresh . . . *free* yourself from all the bad decisions you've made . . . would you do it?"

Obviously this woman's shitty day started long before the flat tire. "Sounds like you have some regrets," I finally offer. It's not really an answer to her question but, honestly, I don't know how to respond to that.

"Yeah. I think I do." It's so soft, I barely hear her over the rain hitting asphalt and the low rumble of her idling engine. I startle as cool fingers suddenly slide over my cheek, my nose, my jaw— covered in fresh stubble—until they find my mouth, where they rest in a strangely intimate way. I feel like she's testing me. What's going on in this woman's head right now?

Though I can't stop the steady climb of my heartbeat, I don't move a single muscle, more curious than anything. Very slowly, the shadow in front of me shifts closer and closer, until her mouth is hovering over mine and her breathing is shaky.

And then she kisses me.

It's a tentative kiss at first, her lips lightly sweeping across mine without committing entirely, but it gets my blood rushing all the same. I can't say that I've ever kissed a woman without seeing her face first. It's both unnerving and strangely liberating. If she looks anything like her lips feel, then I'm kissing a super-model right now.

Finally she finds her place, her lips slightly parted as they gently work against mine, each one of her ragged breaths like an intoxicating spell as they slip into my mouth alongside her tongue. I don't even care about the rain or the cold or getting home anymore, too busy fighting the urge to loose my hands on her. But I don't know why the fuck she's doing this and I'm a suspicious person by nature. So, I ball my fists and keep my arms to my sides while her mouth slowly teases mine and her hand grasps the side of my face.

Just when I'm ready to give up on my mistrust and pull her into me, she suddenly breaks free, her short, hard pants dispelling her calm. She steps back, taking the shield of her umbrella with her. The cold rain is a semi-effective douse to the heat coursing through my body.

"Thank you."

I smile into the darkness. "No big deal. Tires take me no time."

"I wasn't talking about the tire." She's smiling too. I can hear it in her soft words.

With my mouth hanging open, I watch her silhouette round the car. In one fluid motion, she folds her umbrella up and slides into the driver's seat.

And I'm left standing here, wondering what the hell just happened. She doesn't know what I look like either. We could pass each other on the sidewalk and we'd never know.

Maybe that's the point.

Shaking my head, I dart back to my car, my clothes soaked and my mind thoroughly mystified. She may be sweet but if she goes around kissing strange men on the side of the road, no wonder she has regrets. I hope regrets are the worst thing she ever has to deal with.

True to my word, I tail her for eight miles, my fingers testing my lips as I recall the feel of hers against them, until she signals toward one of Portland's richer areas. A big part of me wants to turn off and follow her the rest of the way. Just so I know who she is.

I have my hand on the turn signal. But at the last minute, I pull back and keep heading straight. Regrets have a tendency to spread when you tie yourself to the wrong kind of person. I've learned that the hard way.

I hope she finds what she's looking for.

FOUR

JANE DOE

NOW

"I told you already; she's not lying. She doesn't remember *a thing*! Anyone who looks into the poor girl's eyes can see that!"

Dr. Alwood's harsh tone pulls me out of a light sleep. She's standing next to my bed, squared off against a man with an olive complexion and wavy chestnut-brown hair—peppered with gray at the temples—and a grim expression, dusted with day-old scruff.

"I have to do my job, Meredith," the man says, his dark eyes shifting to catch me watching. With a nod in my direction, he clears his throat.

Dr. Alwood turns and her scowl vanishes, replaced by a soft smile. Today she's wearing a baby-blue blouse tucked under her white coat. It doesn't do much for her pallid complexion, but it's pretty all the same. "I'm sorry to wake you," she says, her voice returning to its typical calm. A life jacket for me these past few days, while submerged in this ongoing nightmare. "The sheriff would like to speak with you." With a gesture to the man, she introduces him. "This is Sheriff Welles, of Deschutes County."

The man offers me a curt smile before dipping his head

forward and squeezing his eyes shut. As if he has to regroup; as if facing me for more than that short period of time is difficult. Maybe it is. Based on what the small parade of nurses coming in and out of my room have told me, the swelling has gone down and the deep purple bruising has faded. You can even see my high cheekbones again, whatever that means. I have yet to even glimpse myself in a mirror and no one seems to be in a rush to bring one to my bedside, not even to see if it may trigger my memory. They keep telling me that we should wait "just a few more days."

"He's going to ask you a *few* questions." She casts a glare his way. "Right, Gabe?"

His heavyset brow pulls together as he lifts his gaze to meet mine again. Such penetrating eyes—not a single fleck of gold or brown to break up the near-black color. They draw me in and make me hold my breath at the same time. He must do well in interrogations. "Right."

Gabe Welles. Of course, the sheriff knows what his name is. Everyone knows what their name is. I'm the only clueless one around here. "I don't know how much help I can be," I say, my voice much smoother than when I first regained conscious-ness . . . my eyes flicker to the clock to calculate . . . forty-two hours ago. I've regained nothing else.

I still have no idea who I am and I certainly don't remember being raped and beaten. I imagine most victims like me would do anything, take any sort of pill or potion, to forget the traumatic experience. But I've spent every conscious moment grappling with the recesses of my mind, hoping to find a thread to grab on to, to tug, something that will unravel the mystery.

Nothing. I remember nothing.

"You seem to be doing much better than the last time I saw you," Sheriff Welles says in a rich, gravelly voice that demands attention.

"Gabe—I mean, Sheriff Welles—was the one who found you," Dr. Alwood explains.

My cheeks heat with color. "How bad was I? I mean . . . ?" *Was I on bloody, naked display for him to see?* Do I even want to know if I was? It should be the least of my worries, and yet the thought churns my stomach.

"I've seen a lot in my thirty-five years in the police force, but . . . you were in rough shape." He pauses to clear his throat. "Dr. Alwood has already informed me that you don't recall anything. I have something that I thought may help." From a canvas bag, he pulls out a clear plastic package marked "Evidence," followed by a case number, and holds it up. Electric-blue sequined material stares back at me. "You were wearing this dress when I found you."

Where would I be going in that? A wedding? A disco? Based on the reddish-brown stains and tears, I won't be wearing it ever again. The sheriff and doctor watch me closely as I admit, "I don't recognize it."

He dumps it back into the canvas bag and pulls out another plastic evidence bag, this one with a light pink coat and very clearly covered in blood. "You were wearing this over your dress."

Was I? "It's not familiar," I answer honestly. The steady pulse from the EKG begins to increase again. I've noticed that it does that every time Dr. Alwood begins questioning me, as my agitation rises.

He pulls out a third bag, with only one silver dress shoe in it. It has a heel so high, no sane human would choose to wear it. "Just like Cinderella," I murmur half-heartedly, adding, "I don't even know how I could walk in that."

Without a word, he holds up a small bag with a necklace in it. Even in the muted fluorescent lighting above, the stones sparkle like stars. "We had these diamonds inspected. Whoever bought this isn't hurting for cash," Sheriff Welles says.

"I don't know who that would be," I answer honestly. Is that person me? Am *I* wealthy? Or is the person who gave that to me rich? Who would have given that to me? The father of my lost child, perhaps? Where is he *now*? I instinctively glance at my hands. At the fingertips that reach out from one end of my cast, the remnants of my red nail polish still visible though my nails are badly broken. Half of my pinky nail has torn off. If I look very carefully, I *think* I can make out a tan line on the third finger of my right hand. "Was I wearing a ring?"

"Why do you ask? Do you remember wearing a ring?" His voice has dropped an octave, almost lulling. As if he's hoping to coax an answer out of me.

I frown. "No. I just . . . If I was pregnant, does that mean I'm married?" Did I walk down an aisle in a white dress and profess my love to someone? Am I even old enough to be married?

"This was the only piece of jewelry that we found on you," Sheriff Welles confirms.

"Could my ring have been stolen?"

"I can't say for sure, but my experience tells me that, had this been a robbery-motivated attack, they would not have left this necklace behind."

Not robbery.

If not that, then *why*?

Why?

Why would someone do this to me?

Dr. Alwood and Sheriff Welles sit and wait while a thousand questions flood my mind and tears of fear and frustration burn my eyes. I gather they're waiting for me to be struck by an epiphany thanks to a couple of plastic bags stuffed with bloody clothes and jewels. They don't seem to understand, though. My memory—my life—isn't simply riddled with holes. It has been sucked into a black hole, leaving nothing but this battered husk behind, my mind spinning but unable to gain traction.

Finally, I can't take it anymore. I burst out with, "I'm not lying! I don't remember who I am!"

A wisp of a sigh escapes the sheriff as he drops the jewelry

back into the bag, his gaze touching Dr. Alwood's eyes in the process, an unreadable communication between them. "Okay, Jay—"
He cuts himself off.

"It's okay; you can call me that," I mutter through a sniffle.
I've overheard the nurses referring to me as "JD" a few times and,
when I finally asked Dr. Alwood about it, she admitted with a grimace that it stands for "Jane Doe." Because that's who I am now.

Jane Doe.

Apparently that's not just reserved for people with toe tags.

He pauses, settling his stern gaze on me. "I wish I had more
to tell you about what happened, but I don't. We believe that you
were dumped in the location where we found you. Where you
were attacked, I can't say. We've canvassed the area for clues, but
nothing's come up. We don't even have good tire tracks to work
with; the fresh snowfall covered them. No witnesses have come
forward yet and no one has filed a missing person's report that
matches your case. I have my men scouring the database."

He sighs. "The rape test returned no results. There were no
DNA matches in there. Dr. Alwood was able to order a DNA
test on your unborn fetus. Again, results did not match anything
in the database."

I guess that means that the father wasn't a criminal. At least
there's that. "So . . . that's it?"

His jaw tightens and then he offers me only a curt nod.

My eyes drift away from both of them to the window across
from me, the sky beyond painted a deceptively cheerful blue. The
small television mounted on the wall is still on—I fell asleep
watching it—and showing a news broadcast. Yellow caution tape
circles a gas station. A caption flashes along the bottom, calling
for witnesses.

And a thought hits me. "Was my story on the news?"

"No." Sheriff Welles's head shakes firmly. "I've kept this story
away from the media." He adds in a low mutter, "God knows
they'd love to have it."

"But maybe it would reach my . . . family?" The family who hasn't filed a report yet?

"Yes, maybe. Maybe it'll also reach the person who attacked you. Do you want him to know that you survived?"

A cold wave rushes through me as Dr. Alwood snaps, "Gabe!"

His mouth purses together but he presses on. "Reporters will sensationalize this story. They'll want pictures of your face. They'll want to post details of your attack. Do *you* want that all over the news?"

"No." My eyes dart to the door as a spark of panic hits me. "You don't think he'd come here for me, do you?" Maybe he already has. Maybe my attacker has already stood there, watching me as I've slept. I shiver against the icy chill that courses through my body with the thought.

"I think he assumes you died and your remains would be dragged off by a mountain lion or wolves before they were discovered," he assures me, his words offering little comfort. "That old tannery building probably hasn't had a visitor in over a year."

"How'd you find me, then?"

"Sheer luck," he answers without missing a beat. "I have a police officer stationed outside your door just as a precaution. We'll keep you safe. If you do remember something, no matter how small, please let either Dr. Alwood or me know immediately." The way he names himself and the doctor—slowly and precisely—I get the distinct impression that he meant to swap "either" for "only."

With my reluctant nod, he heads toward the door.

"I'll be back in a moment," Dr. Alwood says. I watch her trail Sheriff Welles out to stand behind my door. Thanks to the window, I can see them exchanging words, their lips moving fast, their foreheads pulled tight. Neither seems happy. And then Sheriff Welles leans forward to place a quick peck on Dr. Alwood's cheek before disappearing from my view.

Suddenly the slips of "Gabe" and the terse tone you wouldn't expect a doctor to use with the sheriff make sense.

"Are you two married?" I ask the second Dr. Alwood pushes back through the door, glancing down to see that her fingers are free of any jewelry.

"For twenty-nine years. Some days being married to the town sheriff is easy, and . . ." she collects my chart from the side table and hangs it back on the end of my bed, a corner of her mouth kicking up in a tiny smirk, "other days, not so much."

I think about that extravagant necklace I was wearing, and the ring that I was not. "I guess I wasn't married to the father of my baby." Had I been happy when I found out I was pregnant? Was the father happy? Did he even know?

Is he the one who did this to me?

Dr. Alwood heaves a sigh as she begins pushing buttons on the heart rate monitor. The lights dim. "Your heart is strong. We don't need this anymore." With cool hands, she peels the various electrodes from my chest, my arms, and my thighs, as she explains, "It isn't uncommon to see patients with amnesia after a brain injury. It's more commonly anterograde versus retrograde, but . . ." She must see the confusion on my face because she quickly clarifies, "You're more likely to struggle with your short-term memory than long-term memory. And, when it is retrograde, the gaps are usually spotty, or isolated to specific events. It's *extremely* rare to see a complete lapse in memory like yours, especially one that lasts this long. Your tests have come back showing normal brain activity and no permanent damage."

I feel the pull against the raw scar on the side of my face as I frown. If it's not brain injury, then . . . "What does that mean?"

"I think it may be psychological."

"What does *that* mean?" Is the doctor saying I'm crazy?

"It means that whatever happened was traumatic enough to make you *want* to forget everything about your life." Her eyes drift over my body. "Given what I've seen, I can believe it. But on a positive note, you're more than likely to overcome this. Brain injuries tend to have long-lasting effects."

"So you're saying I'll remember something soon?" I hold my breath, waiting for her to promise me that I'll be fine again.

"Maybe." She hesitates. "Unfortunately, this is not within my expertise. I've referred you to an excellent psychologist, though. Hopefully she can give us some answers."

"What if she can't? What if I never remember anything?" What if I simply . . . *exist* in the present?

"Let's meet with Dr. Weimer before you worry too much," she says, reaching forward to rest a hand on my leg cast. Given that her interaction with me up until now has always been friendly but on the extreme professional level, this feels both foreign and welcome. Dr. Alwood may be the only person in the world right now that I trust.

That's probably why the question slips out in a whisper. "Did I do something to deserve this?" It's a rhetorical question. She can't answer that, any more than she can tell me who attacked me, who raped me, who left me for dead next to an abandoned building. But I ask it anyway.

She shakes her head. "I can't believe that there is anything you could have done to deserve *this*, Jane."

Jane. I don't like the name. Not at all. That's not Dr. Alwood's fault, though. What else are they going to call me?

"Thank you." I sound so small, so weak. So . . . insignificant. Am I? "*Someone* must be missing me. Even just *one person*, right?" I can't be all alone in this world, can I?

Dr. Alwood's face crumbles into a sad smile. "Yes, Jane. I'm quite certain that there is someone who misses you dearly."

FIVE

JESSE

THEN

"Tell me again why I'm *here* tonight?"

Outside of sharing an apartment and working together, I make an effort not to spend my time with Boone, for my sanity and the survival of our living arrangement. We're just too different. Most days I'd take his bulldog, Licks, over him, and that damn dog ate two pairs of my shoes.

The handful of times we've gone out together over the years, it's been with college friends, the destination local pubs and the odd club. But The Cellar isn't even a club. It's a "lounge," in the underground level of a downtown Portland office building, full of pretentious people in dresses and suits holding martini glasses, while sparkle-framed mirrors and black see-through curtains hang where there aren't any windows. Slow-paced trance music beats in the background, the kind of music that punk kids listen to at raves after they've dropped a hit of Ecstasy. Totally out of place here, and yet no one else has clued in and changed the channel.

Boone leans back in the booth, his eyes roaming over the crowd. "Told you already. Because Rust asked."

Rust, also known as Boone's Uncle Rust, also known as the owner of Rust's Garage, where we work as mechanics. And Rust's Garage is known around Portland as *the* place to bring your car if you've got a problem, you don't want to pay the inflated prices at the dealership, and you don't want to get ripped off by some hack with a wrench. It's not cheap by any means, but Uncle Rust keeps the rates at 10 percent below the dealers' book price and he keeps highly skilled staff in place.

Except for Boone.

Boone spent the first two months after mechanics school shadowing the others and handing them tools. He's bitched about it behind closed doors but he bites his tongue around the garage, knowing he has no right to complain. Every other guy there has had to put in at least ten years of legit experience elsewhere and jumped through flaming hoops before being considered. Boone only has a job thanks to nepotism. So do I, technically, because Boone got me in. At least what *I* lack for in years, I more than make up for in skill.

"He could have just come to the shop," I mutter, tugging at the wide collar of Boone's gray dress shirt that he made me wear, along with the only pair of black dress pants that I own, which I've worn exactly two times—to both of my grandpas' funerals. I certainly would have stuck out in the faded T-shirt and jeans I had on earlier. Hell, the bouncers wouldn't even have let me through the doors. I would have been happy with that.

I'm just not a lounge kind of guy.

A server with long, jet-black hair and tanned skin approaches our table, a round serving platter of empty flutes and wineglasses balanced in her hand. Five minutes in this place proved that all the servers are young, thin females, smoking hot, and full of themselves. This one's no exception. I'd love to see the hiring process.

"Hey, Luke, what brings you up here tonight?" She reaches out with her free hand to adjust a strand of hair that curls out at the nape of his neck.

He throws his arm over the back of the bench, all relaxed-like. He's a natural at charming women. I don't get it. I guess maybe his baby-blue eyes camouflage the fact that he can be a dog. That, or they see it and just don't care. "Just chillin' for a bit. How're things with you?"

Her eyes roll over the customers as she says, "Oh, you know." She taps his watch. "New?"

He twists his wrist to give everyone a better look at the Rolex his uncle just gave him, a proud smile on his face. "Just got it last weekend." Gesturing my way, he says, "This is my friend Jesse. Jesse, this is Priscilla."

I manage to pry my eyes off her fake tits and move to her face a second before crystal-blue eyes lined with heavy black makeup flash to me. She offers me a tepid smile with those bright pink-painted lips. "Nice to meet you, Jesse." Nothing about that sounded sincere.

I'm surprised I even got that much out of her. Must be the clothes. If she saw me on the street tomorrow, I doubt she'd bat an eye my way. It's not that I've ever had trouble attracting girls. Granted, they lately tend to be of the hood-rat variety. The "classy" ones have outgrown their need to rebel against their parents and the smart ones are just plain nervous around me. And girls like this? She's not the type to be satisfied with a guy who lives under a hood and comes home with grease under his fingernails.

And I have no plans to change.

"The usual, Luke?"

"Yeah, make it two." He jerks his chin toward me. "And he's paying."

I watch her ass sway as she stalks back to the bar with those spikey four-inch heels. While I may not be interested, I can appreciate a tight body when I see one.

"Women here are sweet, huh?" Boone says.

"They're not women. They're gold-diggers. Entirely different breed." There was a time when we preferred the same type—local

college girls. The kind you might see heading to a nine a.m. class
in pajama pants and a messy ponytail; the kind who wear tight
T-shirts and cut-off jean shorts and will get stupid-drunk on
beer bongs with you before slurring about how hot you are and
dragging you to their dorm room. But over the last year, Boone
has started hanging out a lot more with his uncle and his tastes
have become more refined. Now he prefers the kind of girl who
will duck out of bed to fix her makeup before waking him with a
morning blow job.

He gives me a "yeah, I know" shrug. "I'll bet you could hit that
for a night, now that you're not dressed like a gearhead."

"I *am* a gearhead. And so are you, *Luke.*" I struggle to get that
out with a straight face. He hates anyone but women calling him
by his first name. And he *despises* being called a gearhead. In truth,
he doesn't exactly fit the model.

I still laugh every time I think about the first day of class.
In a sea of Columbia sportswear and baseball caps, Luke Boone
stuck out like a shiny new Porsche in a junkyard, strolling in in
his pressed pants and dress shirt, the sleeves rolled high enough to
properly display his gold watch. That wasn't a first-day-of-school
look, either. That's how he *always* dresses. The only time he and
I ever look like we may tread in the same water is when we're
wearing our navy-blue coveralls at work.

I shake my head for the thousandth time. How did a preppy
boy like Luke Boone and me, a guy who's been questioned for
attempted murder, end up sharing an apartment? There are really
only two reasons I can come up with: we both live for cars and
neither of us gives a fuck about anyone else, including each other.

Boone loves looking at cars, knowing about cars, talking
about cars. He sure as hell loves driving them, and fast. But he's
more interested in following in his uncle's enterprising footsteps
than actually getting his hands dirty. Rust actually *made* him
take the two-year mechanics program after finishing a four-year
bachelor's degree. He wants the future manager of his garage and

whatever else he has in store for Boone—possibly a managerial job at the car sales company he owns—to know the ropes from the ground up. While Boone wasn't at the top of our mechanics program at college—I was—he's a natural with people and meticulous about details. He'll probably do well in an office setting.

I get a middle finger in response before Boone's attention shifts to the crowd, looking every bit a socialite with money and class, and not the guy who stocks our cupboards with cans of Chef Boyardee and snaps when the DVR messes up and doesn't record an episode of *American Idol*. What he does have is a rich bachelor uncle who throws him nice things here and there—cash, gift cards to high-end stores, the watch around his wrist, the cufflinks holding his sleeves together. When Boone's not rolling out of bed to come into the shop, he looks like he's heading to a photo shoot, dressing in clothes I'd reserve for weddings and gelling his hair—taming those curls into something females can't help but start playing with.

The guy's *hair* picks up women.

"Do you *seriously* like this place?" I ask.

"Rust likes it here and I like hanging out with him, so . . . yeah."

Priscilla comes back with two rocks glasses full of colorless liquid. That was fast. That tells me these aren't complicated mixes. Her hand settles on my shoulder, giving it a friendly squeeze before a sharp fingernail grazes behind my ear. "Did you want to run a tab?" Of course, now that she knows I'm the one paying, she's spreading the charm on thick.

"Yup, and you can bring us another round when you have a sec, doll," Boone answers before I can, a smirk plastered on his face. "Cheers!" He clinks my glass and sucks back his drink.

I follow suit, gritting my teeth against the slight burn of hard liquor. It slides down my throat without too much bite, though, so I'm guessing it's not the four-bucks-a-shot bar-well vodka. Still, I'd rather just have a beer.

"How can you afford coming to places like this?" I hold up my glass. "Drinking *this*." Boone makes the same amount as me and it's nothing to brag about. Sure, our cost of living is low, renting in southeast Portland, but living like Boone isn't cheap. I don't even want to think about the bill this asshole's going to stick me with tonight.

Boone answers with a one-shouldered shrug. "I buy one, two drinks max. Rust always picks up the tab. I'm his favorite nephew."

"Aren't you his *only* nephew?"

Another middle finger answers me.

Three vodkas later, I'm feeling tingles coursing through my limbs. Boone slaps the table and slides out of his chair. "Come on. Don't say anything stupid around these guys, all right?"

I roll my eyes at him as we abandon our seats and head through the growing crowd, toward the back of the club. The crowd thins the farther we go, until we've reached a section with five alcoves and one roped-off area. Very VIP. Boone stops at the last one, a large, round leather booth with dim crystal pendants hanging from above and heavy black curtains around the sides to add to the secluded feeling. Four men are seated within.

"There he is!" Rust slides off the end to throw an arm around Boone's shoulder. "Thought you weren't coming tonight." I've met the tall blond man exactly twice before, for two minutes apiece. He's the money behind the garage but he leaves the actual garage operations to his manager, Steve Miller, a 250-pound man with a long, scruffy beard and abysmal people skills.

Boone jerks his head back the way we came. "Just hanging up front with Jesse for a bit."

Rust's sharp blue eyes land on me—the same blue as his nephew's. He reaches out to offer me a firm handshake, his gold watch catching a glint of light from above. "How are things going at the garage, Jesse?

"So far, so good."

He gestures at the two empty chairs pulled up to the outside of the booth. "Top-ups?" He reaches for the bottle of vodka—the label in some foreign language with a weird alphabet—that sits in the middle of the table. I can't say I've ever seen an entire bottle of hard liquor sitting on a table at a bar before, but I guess that's how the rich roll.

And these guys stink of money.

As we take our seats and Rust pours, I scan the three other guys sitting around the table. Two are talking quietly on cell phones. The third, a lean, blond guy with angular features, dressed all in black, in his late thirties by my guess, gives the glass in front of him a hard glare while he rolls what looks to be a wedding band around his ring finger.

Now I know why Boone likes hanging around with these guys. He loves the stink of money.

"From what Miller tells me, my nephew's not full of shit. Miller's never seen anyone work so fast before." Rust pushes my glass—almost overflowing—to me. "And I hear you might have my Corvette running again soon? No one's been able to get that lemon working."

I'm unable to smother the proud smile. I've been fiddling with engines since I got my first wrench and a dirt bike at nine years old. I used to sit on the bench in the garage and watch my dad work on his '67 Mustang. The car *I* ended up finishing before he sold it. It was just a hobby to him. To me, it was a calling. The guys in high school shop used to call me the engine whisperer because I can fix anything; it doesn't matter how complicated or how broken.

Regardless, I try not to act like a douchebag about it, so I play it off with a shrug. "I like classics."

"Luke was telling me. You're looking to get a . . ."

"'Sixty-nine Barracuda. Black." No hesitation with that answer. It's what I've wanted since I was seven years old and saw one race through Main Street back home on rodeo weekend, its black paint glistening after a car wash. It's what I've been saving for. It's the reason I'm driving a piece of shit now. Another year and it'll be mine.

"Huh. That's a good one." Rust nods slowly, seemingly impressed. He lifts his glass in a toast and then gestures to the man in black across the table. "Well, my business partner here, Viktor, may have some extra work for you."

I turn to find steely blue eyes already fixed on me from across the table, in a hard face that doesn't appear accustomed to smiling. He sure as hell isn't smiling now.

"Yes . . ." This guy, Viktor, pulls out a single cigarette and lighter from his shirt pocket and proceeds to light it up. "Perhaps first you could tell me about yourself. Rust has not shared much." An accent touches his words, though I can't identify where it's from. Either way, he doesn't sound particularly friendly. He must not be from America. That would explain why he thinks it's okay to light up in a public establishment. That or he's just ballsy as fuck.

I shrug. And then I hear my dad's voice inside my head, ordering me to stop shrugging. *Criminals and half-wits answer with shrugs.* "Not much to tell. I just love working on engines is all." There's not much else Rust could tell this guy because there's not much his nephew knows about me. Despite Boone and I living together and going to school together, we stay out of each other's personal lives. He's too self-involved to ask and I'm too private to offer. He knows I'm from mid-state but he doesn't know I'm from a small town northwest of Bend, called Sisters. He knows my parents still live there and he's overheard enough arguments over the phone to know that our relationship is rocky, but he has no idea that my dad's the sheriff and my mom is a reputable surgeon. He knows I have a twin sister named Amber who's a nurse, but I sure as hell am never introducing him to her.

I glance at Boone, not sure what else this Viktor guy expects me to divulge. Boone's unusually quiet, though, his eyes bright and curious as he watches the man. In awe. Probably memorizing his style. If Boone starts smoking in our apartment, I'm going to kill him.

When I turn my attention back to Viktor, I see that he's no longer focused on me, but on a spot behind me. Through a puff of smoke, two words laced with anger emerge. "You're late."

The guy to Viktor's left slides out of the booth just as a waft of perfume catches my nose. It's a nice enough smell and somehow familiar, but it's way too heavy. I like a hint of perfume, where you're not sure you caught it the first time, and you have to lean in closer, maybe dip your head into her neck, to catch it again.

A young woman in a flashy dress and too much makeup slides into the booth. Her side profile makes me think she might not be legal. Maybe a head-on look would change that assumption, but she hasn't turned her face from the guy for one second. "My hair stylist took longer than expected," she explains evenly.

"And you were incapable of calling?" It's not even anger in his voice now. It's ice.

"My cell phone battery died."

"Of course it did," he mutters, picking up his glass and swirling the clear liquid around, his jaw visibly clenched. "Why is charging your phone battery so difficult for you to remember?"

She sighs, like she's tired. "I don't know, Viktor. But I'm here now, at your demand."

He butts his cigarette out on a plain white plate sitting on the table. And then his hand shoots up and slaps her cheek so fast that I almost miss it. It's not a big slap—more of a sharp tap—but he does it, all the same. "Thirty minutes late."

I shift uncomfortably in my seat as I watch this domestic scene unfold in front of us. If anyone else is bothered by it, they're hiding it well, carrying on their own conversations.

She hesitates and then, when she speaks again, it's with a more contrite tone. "Yes, Viktor. I know. I'm very sorry."

"You complain that I don't spend enough time with you, and

then when I ask you to meet me somewhere, you make me wait and accuse me of being demanding."

A gaudy diamond band sparkles on her delicate hand, catching my attention as she touches her long, straight hair. The color makes me think of Boone's giant tub of peanut butter back home, as odd as that is. "Do you like it?"

"No, not particularly."

I can't keep my eyebrows from jumping at that one. I may be only twenty-four, with minimal relationship experience, but isn't there a golden rule that you lie with these kinds of questions if you want to get laid?

"Do I look fat?" "No."

"Am I ugly without makeup?" "No."

"Are you attracted to my friends?" "No!"

Viktor takes a sip of his drink and then, staring at the liquid within, murmurs, "What am I going to do with you, my beautiful wife?"

Five long seconds pass, where I watch her watch him without blinking, her right hand balled into a white-knuckled fist on the table, and then Viktor leans in and lays a slow kiss on her lips. Despite her stiff demeanor, I feel the air shift around me with the affection, as if she just avoided a catastrophe. Hell, *I* feel like I just avoided a catastrophe.

His finger twirls a strand of her hair. "At least you did not cut it."

She gives a half-hearted smile and then shakes her head. "Just wanted to try something new."

"Viktor . . ." The thick-necked blond guy to the right nudges him, covering his phone with one hand while he spews off a bunch of words in a foreign language. It allows his wife's attention to flicker over the other faces at the table. Striking reddish-brown eyes suddenly land on me. They rest there for one . . . two . . . three quick seconds, before she shifts her gaze to the vodka bottle in front of her.

And I realize that I've been staring at her for way too long. I quickly swing my attention to Rust and Boone's conversation.

"How much longer before I can start running the garage?" Boone asks.

"Not until you learn how to balance a tire properly," Rust throws back. "Don't think I didn't hear what happened with the Cayenne."

"Ah, fuck. That wasn't my fault! Miller distracted me with . . ." I wonder how long it's going to take Boone to figure out that Miller is gunning for him. He knows that Rust has no use for two managers. Once Boone's ready, Miller's out. The forty-eight-year-old—who's as abrasive as a Brillo pad against your cheek—is in no rush to let that happen.

Either way, I've heard this story before and I don't need to hear about Boone's dumbass mistake again. My eyes drift back around the table. The guy to Viktor's right is off his phone now and leaning in to tell Viktor something. I can't hear what they're saying but both of them look agitated, Viktor's finger tapping the table repeatedly. His attention seems fully occupied.

Maybe that's why I hazard another glance at his wife.

Maybe that's why I find her blatantly staring at me.

Her expression is hard, disinterested. She's probably bored, sitting in this booth with a bunch of men and no one to talk to, no drink offered, nothing to do but twirl that flashy wedding band around her finger and fiddle with the top of her sparkly blue dress. She certainly put effort into her appearance, a dark layer of blue swiped across her eyelids and bright red lipstick painting her full lips. She has perfect, high cheekbones. The entire package looks impeccable and rich, and yet also somehow cheap.

A sudden hand on my shoulder makes me jump. I look up to find Priscilla hovering behind my chair. "Did you want another drink?" She obviously hadn't even checked the glass in my hand; otherwise she'd know it's full and that question was stupid. Given her eyes are on Viktor, it's safe to say I'm only an excuse for her visit here, anyway.

"No, thanks. Can I grab my check when you get a chance?" I'd like to say "close the tab and get me the fuck out of here ASAP," but with my employer here, I hold myself back.

"Priscilla," Viktor calls. She managed to grab his attention, after all. To his wife, Viktor utters an abrupt word in that other language, pushing her out of the booth with a hand on her slight upper arm.

Reaching out to touch Priscilla's shoulder with a degree of gentleness that he didn't show his wife just a moment ago, Viktor rattles off something to her. She answers him with a coy smile and a nod, obviously understanding him. I don't miss the smirk she throws toward his wife before turning and leaving, her hips swaying *way* more than they did when she walked away from our table earlier. I'm guessing a guy like Viktor would be right up her alley.

I'm also guessing Viktor's already been up her alley. Something about this guy—and what I just witnessed between him and his wife—tells me he's not above fucking around on her, no matter how beautiful and young she is.

And, I'll admit, Viktor's wife is definitely beautiful.

"It was good to meet you."

It takes an elbow from Boone in the bicep to realize that Viktor's standing over me, looking down at me, talking to me.

"Uh, yeah. You too." Not really, but what the hell else do I say?

"Perhaps we can discuss my business proposition another night."

I shrug. "All right."

That cold, steely gaze weighs down on me for a split second and then he leaves, dragging his preschool trophy with him by her wrist.

Fucking weird people. And fuck Boone for bringing me here.

Boone leans in and whispers, "Are you an idiot? Do you know who that guy is?"

"A rich, foreign asshole?" I don't do well with arrogance or authority. Probably why having a sheriff for a father hasn't worked out well for me. Then again, maybe it's *because* I have a sheriff for a father that I don't do well with arrogance or authority.

Boone's eyes flash as he scans around us, a hiss of warning sailing through his teeth. "That's Viktor Petrova."

"That name means exactly nothing to me."

"Whatever." Boone rolls his eyes. "The dude just picked up your tab."

With a frown, I glance over my shoulder. Priscilla is already at the bar, collecting drinks for someone else. "How do you know he grabbed my tab?"

"Do we even know each other? I'm part Russian. I understand some."

My face screws up. "Really? 'Boone' is Russian?" *Russian.* So, that's what that sharp-sounding language is.

"No, my mom's side. Her father didn't speak a word of English. I learned from him."

I seek out Viktor and find him standing with Rust and another well-dressed, middle-aged man. Whatever had him heated earlier seems to have blown over, because he's smiling.

But why the hell would he pick up my drink tab? He's either trying to butter me up for this "business proposition" or he's just showing his money off. Rich people and people who want to pretend that they're rich like to do that. "What did you say he does again?"

"I didn't say." Boone's focus shifts to the glass in his hand, pausing for a moment. Like he's making a decision. "Officially, him, Rust, and two other guys own an international car sales company together." Then he leans in, dropping his voice to a low murmur. "Unofficially . . . if you want a car—*any* kind of car—Viktor is the guy who can get it for you. Well, not him. But he'll arrange it."

"So he sells stolen cars. Is that what you're saying?" My dad would go ballistic if he knew I've been sitting at a table with a guy like that.

"Jesus, Welles!" Boone barks, scanning the area around us again. "Don't *ever* bring that shit up with anyone. I'm only telling you because it looks like he wants to make some sort of deal with you."

"Like I would." I glance over my shoulder at them again. A blue sparkle catches my eye. His wife is standing in a corner now, released from Viktor's ironclad grip. She's much taller than I would have guessed. And thin, her curves subtle and delicate. That dress of hers barely covers her ass, making her long, slender legs that much longer. "How old is his wife?"

"Dunno. Old enough to land herself a rich husband who buys her all kinds of stuff. She's been in here before. Never says a word to anyone. I think her face might crack if she smiled."

"If I were married to someone who slapped me around, I probably wouldn't be smiling either."

Boone helps himself to another drink from the bottle on the table. "Slaps her . . . fucks around on her . . . and she's not going anywhere. I guess the diamonds and fancy clothes are hard to walk away from."

"Yeah." I turn my back to her and dump the rest of that smooth-tasting free Russian vodka down my throat.

SIX

JANE DOE

NOW

"A psychological amnesia with a global loss." I repeat what the hospital psychologist—a tall, thin British woman who wears glasses on the bridge of her nose—told me as Dr. Alwood takes a seat in the chair next to my bed. "She said she wants to do further assessments, but that is what she suspects. And it's extremely rare."

"Yes, I spoke to her this morning," Dr. Alwood admits, hitting the automatic button on my bed's handrail. The upper half of my body slowly rises. "I know it doesn't sound like it, but this is very good news. It gives us hope that you'll remember something."

That's what the psychologist said. But she also said I may not. Or I may remember just bits and pieces. I may remember them next week. Or next year.

Or not at all.

And until then, what do I do? I'm stuck in this hospital room for now, my bones mending as my muscles go into atrophy. The nurses come to shift my body several times a day to help avoid bedsores, telling me that they'll be forcing me out of bed to move around soon. Next will come rehab. All of this is

government-funded because I have no identification and therefore, no insurance. And then what? If I never regain my memory
and no one comes to claim me, where will I go? What will I do?

How will I survive?

"I want you to remember that there is still some bruising and
swelling, especially around your nose area. That will change the
look of your face," Dr. Alwood says, cutting into my silent worries,
the handle of the blue-framed mirror gripped in her hand.

I eye it warily. "You really didn't have to do this. Reid or
Amber would be willing." Or any other nurse, for that matter.
Anyone but "the best surgeon in the hospital," on her day off, sitting at my side in jeans and a red sweater, her long hair normally
tied back now cascading over her shoulders.

"Also, the redness in the scar will fade. I'm hoping for a fine
line," she says, ignoring me. She pauses to smile. "Really. It could
have been so much worse, Jane. Remember that. Okay?"

I nod slowly, my adrenaline spiking as she raises her arm,
angling the mirror just right, so I can set eyes on a face I'm sure
I've seen thousands of times.

A complete stranger stares back at me.

"Breathe," I hear Dr. Alwood remind me and I inhale sharply,
as if I wasn't able to gather air in my lungs before. She waits patiently, quietly, while I study this battered stranger who I do not
recognize.

"So, that's what russet looks like." I zone in on my deep reddish-brown irises while I try to ignore the purple bags hanging
beneath. Most of my face is puffy and mottled with yellow and
purple bruising, the worst of it around my nose. If this is what I
look like and this is a vast improvement, I understand why no one
would hand me a mirror before now.

There are so many details to take in, I don't know where to
focus first. I run my tongue over the dark mark across my bottom lip, where Dr. Alwood confirmed it had been split open.
The stitches have since dissolved. My long, straight hair—a light

blond color with dark roots and hanging limp from grease—is partially pulled back to reveal a shaved patch and dark scab on the side of my scalp.

But it's the glaring red line running vertically down the side of my face from my temple to the underside of my chin that holds most of my attention. I flinch as I take it in, wondering what caused it. Was it accidental?

Probably as accidental as the rape.

"It will fade with time," Dr. Alwood reminds me as I stare at my reflection.

"And what if I still don't recognize myself then?" I ask with a hollow voice, my gaze catching the gap on the top side of my mouth. Three teeth. I'm missing three teeth. Was I pretty once?

I certainly wouldn't call myself pretty now.

Maybe that's why, when there's a knock at my door followed by the squeak of a hinge, I instinctively duck my head. For all the weeks and all the nurses who have strolled in and out of here, I've never felt the instinctive need to conceal my face. But now that I know what I look like, I'm suddenly desperate to hide.

"Jesse, you can't be in here!" Dr. Alwood hisses.

"I need to head back to the city, Mom." A masculine voice— deep like the sheriff's, only smoother—answers.

Despite my distress, I find myself hazarding a glance, curious what the offspring of Dr. Alwood and Sheriff Welles might look like. I find a young guy standing in the doorway, his face a stony mask.

His intense gaze riveted to me. A wave of familiarity washes over me as I take in the eyes he shares with his father—set with striking eyebrows and so dark they could be mistaken for black. He holds my gaze steady, even takes a step closer. He's curious, I'm sure. He's probably never seen a face this bashed up before.

A police officer pokes his head into the room. "He told me it was okay."

"Of course he did," Dr. Alwood mutters, shooting her son a dirty look before standing.

The officer seizes Jesse's bicep and gives it a tug.

With a scowl, Jesse jerks his arm free. "Get your fucking hands off me, Crane!" He obviously has no qualms about swearing at a police officer. I assume it's because he's the town sheriff's son and can get away with it.

Dr. Alwood intervenes. "It's okay, Officer Crane. We don't need a scene in here." She turns her attention to me. "This is my son, Jesse. He drove me in to work today. Car troubles. I'm sorry for his rudeness." I feel her weighty gaze on me as I can't help but steal another glance, quickly evaluating him from head to toe—his short ash-brown hair, his strong jaw, the way his blue-and-black checkered shirt hangs nicely off his body.

Yes, the good doctor and the sheriff certainly created a handsome child.

I duck my head again, knowing that my battered face can't possibly earn the same appraisal from his end.

"I'll leave this here for you, okay?" Dr. Alwood sets the mirror down on the nightstand. With a slow smile, she adds, "Don't worry. It will all work out."

Hiding my right side, I watch Dr. Alwood stroll toward the door. "Come on, Jesse. It's time for you to go." She loops her arm around his waist. He's still staring at me as she tugs him out.

Back to their lives.

And I am left completely alone, waiting to remember mine.

SEVEN

JESSE

THEN

"Not bad, kid." Miller hovers over the open hood of Rust's '78 red Corvette, the low rumble of its engine filling the six-bay auto shop. "Get working on the Enclave." And then the burly man ambles toward his office, a greasy rag hanging from the back pocket of his ratty jeans.

I shoot a glare Boone's way. *Is that all I get?*

Boone shrugs and smiles lazily. "What do you expect?"

I've got the boss's car purring in under an hour, when it wouldn't give more than a hack and a cough before stalling for everyone else. I know that our shop manager can be a dick, but this is fucking ridiculous.

"A bended-knee proposal, that's what," I mutter as I kill the engine and slide out of the driver's seat, wiping my hands on a cloth. For all the good that'll do. My fingernails have been stained black with motor oil since I was fourteen.

Boone wanders over to slap the frame of the car, as if he's the one who fixed this beast. Given it's his uncle's, he'll probably be driving it anyway. "You want a bended-knee proposal, come out to The Cellar with me tonight and maybe you'll get one from Viktor."

"No thanks," I mutter, heading over to the Enclave, already up on the hoist. "I'm done with that place. If this Viktor guy wants to make a deal, he can come talk to me here."

"Nurse Boone, will you please hand me that torque wrench?" Tabbs hollers from beneath the hoisted Cadillac.

Snickers fill the shop as Boone drags his boots along the concrete floor to meet the mechanic. He slaps the tool into his greasy hand none too gently.

"Hey! Didn't they teach you how to pass tools gently in nursing school?"

Zeke, a heavyset black mechanic with a Louisiana accent, explodes with a roar of laughter.

"Just keep it up . . ." Boone pops a dirty middle finger in the air and marches over to join me under the Enclave. "I'm fucking sick of this."

"What's your problem? You had those brake jobs and that timing belt." I guess his complaints to Rust at The Cellar reached Miller, because he's been giving him some work.

"Yeah, but these guys are never going to stop busting my balls. Not until I'm running this place and I fire their asses."

"Just smile and ignore them until then."

"Easy for you to say." He wanders over to a table covered with tools and begins wiping them down. Miller may look like a bum off the street, but he's meticulous about how he keeps this place. I don't know if that's his rule or Rust's, but every tool is cleaned and put in its rightful spot each night or there's hell to pay. Unfortunately for Boone, that job normally lands in his lap.

I've managed to make a good impression on the other mechanics. I got a lot of smirks when I strolled in here the first day. And then I overhauled a Volkswagen W8 engine in record time and they all shut up pretty quick. Some of them have even asked for my advice when it comes to an engine problem. I've been here for only six months.

"You're the one who wanted me here so bad." I wait for him

to glance back so he can see the wide grin on my face. I know Boone's not jealous of me. Well, maybe a little. But he hasn't been a dick to me about it.

"So . . . The Cellar tonight?"

I shake my head. Any place that requires I borrow clothes from Boone isn't my style. Plus, I can live without another vodka-induced hangover, especially when I have to be inhaling fumes here at eight a.m. sharp tomorrow. Miller docks pay by the hour for latecomers.

"You sure, man? Priscilla's friend, the redhead at the bar, was asking about you."

"Sure she was." Boone can be relentless. And a liar. "For what, exactly?" It's fair to assume that she's exactly like Priscilla. I picture a girl like Priscilla waking up on the double mattress lying on my bedroom floor—no frame—and I burst out laughing.

Turning back to work on the wheel alignment, I listen to the guys chirp harmlessly back and forth. I like them. They're all a little rough around the edges, but they know cars. Just like me.

I'm finished with the Enclave about half an hour later and lowering the hoist when a loud grumble approaches outside. We had the bay doors open all summer, but now, with the cool fall temperatures, Miller makes us keep them closed.

Tabbs peers through one of the windows and drawls, "She's baaaack. Wonder what the missus did this time."

Any half-wit would know it's coming from a wrecked muffler.

I glance out the small panel window but can't make much out besides drizzle from this distance and angle. A whistle sails through the garage as Tabbs punches the button on the wall, and a door begins its noisy ascent along its tracks.

My attention immediately zeros in on the rare silver BMW Z8 parked just outside. There's little doubt that it's the same car. But can it possibly be . . . ? A woman steps out of the driver's seat and pops a zebra-striped umbrella open.

No way. It's the gold-digger from The Cellar. The one with the peanut butter–colored hair.

Her hair isn't peanut butter–colored anymore, though. It's back to the platinum blond that my headlights caught that night in passing. In black dress pants and a fitted leather jacket, her hair pulled back in a ponytail, she still screams money, only now there's something less trashy about her, something decidedly more sophisticated.

Maybe it's because she's not attached to her middle-aged Russian sugar daddy.

Her husband. The car thief.

Who she technically cheated on, with me.

Holy shit.

"I hope that chubby's for the car, because nothing good can come of it otherwise," Tabbs warns in a low voice as he passes by me and steps out into the rain to meet her, his polite mechanic mask firmly affixed. When the doors are closed and we're working, there's nothing polite about Tabbs. He's five-foot-four, balding, and tests new combinations of every cuss word I've ever heard, plus some new ones.

"Sounds like you have a problem there, little lady."

Boone guffaws and I know exactly why. The top of Tabbs's head comes up to her chin.

Her eyes don't veer from Tabbs as she sighs. I hear the slight shake in it. "I must have hit something on my way home from class. Viktor said to bring it right over and someone would take a look at it."

I do a cursory glance at the six bays—all being used. There's a line of cars waiting to get in, too. I don't see how this is going to happen.

"Zeke! Clear Bay Two for me, will ya!"

I guess our boss's business partner has a lot of pull around here.

"Thank you." At least she remembered her manners.

"Of course. It's no problem, Mrs. Petrova."

She glances at her watch. "Will this take long?"

"Depends on what's wrong. Hopefully you just lost a clamp. If we need a replacement part, that'll take time." Tabbs gestures with one greasy hand toward the waiting room. "Come . . . Have a cup of coffee. It's on me."

I roll my eyes at Tabbs's cheesy line. The customer lounge has one of those coffeemakers that does everything but sing and dance. There are over thirty types of coffee to choose from, including the organic stuff that most people in Portland would be happy pumping into their veins intravenously, and it's all free.

A faint smile curls the girl's lips. Her heels click along the pavement as she rounds the car, using her free hand to open the passenger-side door and pull out a messenger bag. She struggles to sling it over her shoulder, the corner of what looks like a textbook popping out.

Though I should turn my focus back to the car, I can't pry my eyes from the zebra umbrella as it passes each bay door, heading toward the customer entrance to the lounge.

It isn't until someone bumps into the back of my knee, buckling my legs, that I snap out of it. "I thought you weren't into her *breed*," Boone says.

"I'm not. It's just . . ." She disappears from sight. Is that really her? It's got to be her, but how are my mystery woman and Viktor's trophy wife one and the same? "Shut up and open the bay. I've gotta test this."

Shaking his head, he reaches up to slap the button on the wall.

———

"Gotta admit, it's impressive," Boone says to the group standing under the car, staring up at the gaping crack in the muffler.

Tabbs doesn't look impressed. "Was the broad off-roading

through the ass-splittin' mountains? How in the hell did she manage this?"

"It's a low car. She probably punched a speed bump," I offer as I pass by, the Enclave's keys swinging around my index finger. Miller likes us to report in as soon as the work is done.

"Well, we need a new part and we won't get it in today. She may as well go home. Hey, kid!" Tabbs hollers, and I know he's talking to me. "Let her know, seeing as you're going that way?"

I was hoping he'd ask.

"And watch your manners."

I shoot him a glare on my way to the sink to scrub the dirt and oil off my hands. The lounge is the only truly clean room in the entire shop and everyone, including Miller, gets pissy if there's so much as a fingerprint left on any of its white surfaces.

I push through the service doors and into the brightly lit hall as a ball of nerves hits me. Which girl am I going to get when I walk in there? The stony gold-digger from The Cellar or the sweet kissing bandit from the side of the road? She may not even recognize me from the club. In my mechanic's coveralls, I sure don't look like I did that night.

Rounding the corner to enter the spacious lounge, fully equipped with leather chairs, a flat-screen television, and inspirational pictures of mountains, I see her sitting in a chair with her jacket and heels off and her bare feet pulled under her ass. She's twirling the end of her ponytail in her fingers, her long, blood-red nails such a contrast against her pale hair.

She's relaxed and casual, her attention focused on a textbook.

"You're muffler's mangled." I didn't inherit my mom's bedside manner, like my sister, Amber, did. I figure this is as good an opener as any.

She must have been deeply engrossed in her studies because she jumps at my voice. The textbook slips off her lap and lands on the ground. I feel her staring at me as I stroll over and pick it up, silently praising myself for spending extra time on washing my hands. The last thing I want to do is be the dirty mechanic who left grease marks on all her stuff.

When I lift my gaze again, I sense recognition in her eyes. But does she *really* recognize me? I match her stony expression with one of my own. Two can play at this game. "*Anatomy and Physiology?*" I read out loud, handing the textbook back. "My favorite."

Finally, a small smile touches her lips. "Maybe you can tutor me." So she has a sense of humor. That or she's propositioning me.

Remembering Tabbs's warning and who her husband is, I clarify, "I know engines, not science."

"Mechanics is a science to some degree," she counters, setting the textbook down on her lap, closed. "You have to fix cars made by all those manufacturers, all designed differently. Not everyone can do that."

I know that she's paying me a compliment, but I don't take compliments well. So, I do what I always do. I play it off. "Are you saying Boone is smart, then? Because there's a garage full of guys out there who may argue with you on that one."

She grins at that. A real, dimple-cheeked grin that makes her eyes sparkle as she watches me. And then a long, lingering silence hangs between us.

I clear my throat. "What are you going to school for?"

"Nursing. It's my first year."

"Huh. Really?" When her perfect, thin eyebrows shoot up, I explain, "My sister's a nurse, so . . . small world." Amber works long hours with sick and hurt people, some of whom can be real ass-holes, from the stories I've heard. Honestly, you couldn't pay me to handle the kinds of bodily fluids she's had to deal with. You have to be a special type of person to want to do it. A giving, kind person.

I've never been accused of being giving or kind. Except by the woman on the side of the road.

And this woman in front of me now? I can't picture her rolling up her fancy sleeves to help with an enema.

"Is she here in Portland?" she asks, those pretty eyes watching me.

"Nah. Bend."

She nods once and then begins biting the side of her mouth, her gaze drifting over my coveralls.

"That's a really nice car out there," I say.

"It's too flashy." The diamonds on her wedding band glitter in protest as she smooths her hand over her hair. "Viktor bought it for me as a wedding gift." I don't feel the love when she says his name.

Veering over to the coffee machine, I offer, "Want one?" I know I need one. Plus it gives me an excuse to stay a little longer.

"I'm fine, thanks." She watches me quietly as I make mine. "I remember you."

"Yeah?" I stifle my smile as I suck back Colombia's finest. *Do you, really?* Because I remember her. I remember the way she smells, the way her lips taste, the way her mouth moved against mine. The way that single kiss held my thoughts long after my head hit my pillow that night. I assume that's what thirteen-year-old girls act like after their first kiss.

This woman made me act like a thirteen-year-old girl.

"Yes. You're Jesse, right? We met last week."

I pause. I never gave her my name at The Cellar. Which means she made an effort to know my name.

I stall as I decide on my answer. *Hell, yeah, I remember you* sounds a little too forward. *You're the one married to that asshole who slapped you across the face* would probably be considered offensive. True, but offensive. I settle on, "I think the word 'met' is a stretch, but, yeah, I was there. I don't remember us meeting, officially."

"Luke talks about you a lot," she says, adding, "and I remember your face. I mean . . . your eyes. They're very dark and intense." Her cheeks flush red, wrecking her whole calm and sophisticated persona. In a good way.

"Boone talks a lot, period." I choose not to address the comment about my eyes. I've heard it before; I know they're dark, even darker than my father's. I've had girls tell me that it makes them nervous when I look at them. I kind of get it. There was a time when I was afraid of my dad, for no other reason than what it felt like to have his dark eyes settled on me.

She nods, smiling. It's getting harder for me to look away from her. I should be walking out of here and moving on to Miller's office before he finds me. My feet seem to have planted themselves, though.

"You've only come once," she says.

So you were keeping track of that, too. I shrug. "Not really my thing."

Her gaze slides over my navy mechanic's coveralls, heating my blood a few degrees. "No. Not really mine, either."

I'm hit with a mental image of the sparkly dress, the killer heels, the slathered makeup. "Sure looks like your thing."

"It does, doesn't it?" That smile, that glow, flickers and fades with my words, until it vanishes. She glances at the clock on the wall as she swallows. "Are you guys able to fix my car?"

I wish I had a time machine to go back ten seconds. I don't want to lose that smile. "We need to order a part. You can either leave your car here or bring it back when we call. Depending on how far away you live, the cops may ticket you for driving with a faulty muffler." I know my dad would. He can be an ass like that. I also know that the rich area she turned off the highway to that night is twenty-five miles from here. "Or I could give you a ride home." Did I just say that out loud? Miller will have a fit. *Fuck it.* I don't care. She needs a ride home and I want to know 100 percent if she's the girl who kissed me. The one who wants a new life and—this is just a wild guess—to leave her husband. "My car's not as nice as yours, though," I warn. Understatement of the century. That '05 Toyota Corolla has been through hell and back with me. It's clean, but it's definitely past its prime.

I'm expecting a "thanks but no thanks." So when she tucks her textbook back into her bag and looks up at me, her full lips stretched wide, her eyes dancing with nervous excitement, and says, "I'd really like that," it takes me a moment to answer.

"Okay. Let me just get my keys and—"

Heavy footsteps behind me cut my words off. "Viktor is outside, waiting for you," Miller's sudden gruff voice calls out from behind me.

Her back stiffens. "Viktor's *here*?" Immediately she's unfolding her legs and sliding pretty feet into her heels, her wide-eyed gaze passing by me to search the hall through the windows. Reaching up, she yanks the elastic out of her ponytail, letting her hair fall down over her shoulders and back. It looks silky soft. I want to reach out and touch it.

Because that would go over well.

"I'm sorry if Jesse was bothering you," Miller mutters, and I roll my eyes.

"He wasn't, at all. Thank you, Mr. Miller." Standing, she pulls her jacket on and begins smoothing her pants and adjusting her clothes. It's becoming glaringly obvious to me that her appearance is very important around her husband. "Where is he?"

"Out front, talking to Tabbs."

She rushes past me, her eyes sliding over mine for the briefest of seconds before she drops her gaze, heading toward the door. No "bye," no "thanks for the offer." I watch her go, and see her feet falter just as her hand touches the handle. But then she lifts her head high, pushes through the door, and is gone.

I feel my body slump with disappointment.

"I don't care if you can turn a Pinto engine into a flying spacecraft. I don't pay you to stand around here and chat with pretty *wives*."

"I was just telling her that we need to order a part for her car," I retort, annoyed by his insinuation. I'm not after anyone's wife.

I'm after the girl who kissed me on the side of the road one rainy night.

His chubby finger pokes the air. "I like you, Welles. But don't grow an attitude problem."

Great. It's like I'm working for my father.

"Now, get back to that Enclave before I dock your pay. And stay the hell away from Alexandria Petrova."

I toss him the keys and don't bother to hide my dry tone when I say, "It's done."

His frown eases. "Already?" Shaking his head as he walks back to his office, I hear a mutter of, "Damn fast, kid."

Alexandria.

Knowing her name makes me smile.

EIGHT

JANE DOE

NOW

"She sleeps like the dead."

I crack an eyelid at the unfamiliar voice. A thin woman with short, dove-gray hair occupies the bed next to me, a square piece of fabric in hand, a glower pulling her brow down as she threads a needle through the material. There's no one else in the room, so I assume she's talking to herself. I really don't care, though.

Because I finally have a roommate.

When they moved me from critical care to this ward, Dr. Alwood warned me I'd probably have to share the room. She made it sound like that would be a bad thing. I guess for most people, it might be. They'd rather have privacy while they visit with friends and family.

But for me, I'm desperate for the company. For human interaction.

I'm sick of being alone.

I've been here for three months. *Three months*. No one besides the nurses, Dr. Alwood, and occasionally Sheriff Welles comes by. Peace is a myth when I'm lying in bed all day and night, drowning my time with sitcoms, thinking about everything . . . and nothing.

Because to think about something, you need to *know* something, and most days I feel like I know nothing at all.

Sure, I know how to tie shoes and how to get the television remote to work. I know how to feed myself and how to read. The hospital psychologist, Dr. Weimer, explained that there are different types of memory, and my "semantic memory"—how to do things—remains intact. It's my "episodic" memory—events of my life—that is impaired. If by "episodic" she means my *entire life*, then I guess she's right.

"What time is it?" I stretch my arms, reveling in the freedom from the uncomfortable plaster cast they removed two weeks ago.

"Did you forget how to tell time?" The woman jabs one long, wiry finger toward the clock up on the wall that reads nine thirty. There's nothing playful in her tone.

"Right, sorry." I know that clock is there. I've spent ample time staring at it. I don't know why I asked. To keep the conversation going, perhaps.

The door pushes open and Amber walks through with a tray of small paper cups. "Hey, Jane."

I return her warm smile, even though that name grates on my nerves. At first it was just another part of my reality, the fact that I arrived at the hospital half-dead and without identification. But somewhere along the line, it ceased to be simply a label.

I now answer to it without hesitation.

Amber rounds my neighbor's bed. "How are you doing, Ginny?"

"I'd be better if your mother would hurry up with this surgery so I can get outta here. I don't know what's taking so damn long," the woman mutters, her eyes never leaving her quilt work.

The first time I heard Amber call Dr. Alwood "Mom," I was sure I misheard. Even though I had picked up on the similarity in their features the first day that I met them, I was too distracted to make the connection. It wasn't until weeks later that I learned Amber was Dr. Alwood and Sheriff Welles's second child, a twin sister to the son who stormed into my room that day.

"I'm sorry, Ginny. There was an emergency and they needed that OR. You know how these elective surgeries can get bumped. They should have you in shortly."

"Good, 'cuz I'm not coming back again, so we'd best be getting this gallbladder out today."

"Yes, Mom's working on making that happen." Amber offers her a tight smile as she sets the tray down on the adjustable bed table. "We thought you could use something to calm your nerves while you wait."

Ginny's fingers pause and one sharp eye lifts to study the cups. After a long moment, she says in a slightly softer tone, "Well, go on, then. Leave them there and move along."

So far, my new roommate isn't the most charming person.

Amber does as asked and steps back to give the woman space. I catch the small eye roll as she turns around to face me. Otherwise, she doesn't seem the least bit perturbed by the woman's frosty temperament. "How are the pajamas?"

I toss off my sheet, displaying the pink two-piece set that she left on my nightstand yesterday. The second pair that she's given me. These ones still had a tag on them. "They're perfect. Thank you."

She smiles. "I figured the flannel would be getting hot, now that spring's here."

Spring. I have no actual memories of spring and yet when Amber says the word, I'm immediately hit with the smell of fresh dirt, the tickle of warm rain against my skin, the sight of tulips and daffodils poking through the ground. The ever-present weight on my chest lifts slightly. Do I like spring? Is it my favorite season?

"You want some help getting to the bathroom?" She holds out a hand as I swing my legs over the edge of the bed and step down carefully. Though my leg cast is off, I still have to wear a brace around my knee for support.

I slowly limp my way to the small, uncomfortable bathroom

with my cosmetics case in tow. Another gift from Amber. It's filled with basic toiletries and some nice creams that I keep finding on my nightstand when I wake in the morning, little gifts from the nursing staff that I both appreciate and despise. Appreciate because their kindness for the lonely, deprived Jane Doe has ensured that I'm never without; despise because I'm at everyone's mercy. I can't take care of myself.

"I'll be out here. Holler if you need me," Amber says, shutting the door behind me.

I smile. Knowing that there are people like Dr. Alwood and Amber in the world to balance out the malicious monster who put me here is comforting. Even the sheriff is nice. Quiet, but nice. The only one in that family I can't speak for is Amber's brother. I haven't seen him since that day he barged into my room.

I let the shower warm as I undress, avoiding the mirror. Even under the dull fluorescent lighting, it reveals too much. My eyes immediately search out the round tribal tattoo on my pelvis. My fingertip traces the wavy lines. The moment I first saw it, I knew that it stood for "water," though I don't remember getting it and I certainly don't remember why.

All I know is that it's the only visible tie to my past.

Dr. Weimer said that, following the general "rules" of my condition, I shouldn't remember what it means. She said that something like that would be a part of my episodic memory. I don't speak in tribal symbols, after all.

I have no answer for that, except that I know what it means.

But I don't know *what* it means.

My palm rests against my abdomen, as it does every day, taking a few minutes to imagine what the tattoo would have looked like with a swollen belly, had I not miscarried. A hollow ache fills my chest. It is becoming more obvious, as the rest of my body heals, that the loss of my baby isn't merely one of many injuries earned with the attack. I may not remember its conception but somehow, it still exists in my heart.

The X-rays of my pelvis confirm that I've never given birth before, so there is no motherless child standing by a doorway in tears, wondering why mommy hasn't come home yet. That's good news, at least.

Still, the existence of an unborn child means the existence of a man who I've shared at least one night with. Perhaps many nights. A man who doesn't seem to be looking for me now.

No one seems to be looking for me.

In the shower, the warm, soothing water takes some of the edge off, as it does every day. Unfortunately, when it comes time to brush my teeth and comb my wet hair, that edge reemerges with a vengeance. It's impossible to avoid my reflection. It's not completely monstrous anymore. My skin is no longer Technicolor and my nose has healed to a narrow and small centerpiece that Dr. Alwood says turned out better than she expected. But, besides the patch of short hair where my head was shaved for stitches and the drainage tubes, the missing teeth that I hide by not smiling, and the swollen purple spot on my lip that I'm told will fade, there's nothing to distract my attention from the unsightly line running down the length of my face. It's still red, though not as bright and puffy as when I first saw it. Dr. Alwood keeps reminding me how lucky I am that a renowned plastic surgeon was here to help; how lucky I am that my attacker didn't slash diagonally, cutting into an eye or across my nose. She says that within a year, some concealer and foundation will make it almost vanish.

Almost.

And yet I will see it every time I look in a mirror, from now until my last day, whether it is through the eyes of who I once was or who I have since become. Or, more likely, a jaded combination, because that original girl will never truly return.

When I'm dressed again, I emerge from the bathroom. Amber is gone.

"When was the last time you went outside?" Ginny asks, her tone not as harsh as it was earlier. The drugs must have kicked in.

"Amber took me out last week, but it was too cold to stay long." I drop my things in the drawer by my bed and then make my way over to the window. Round shrubs stand in a solitary row outside. Beyond them is a blanket of manicured green grass and, beyond that, a parking lot filled with cars. It's not much to look at and yet each time I venture over to the glass, both my impatience and my fear swell. I've been confined to these dreary walls for months now and I'm ready to see the world beyond that parking lot. Yet, that will mean I've been released into the world. Released to go . . .

Where?

I have nowhere to go.

Here, within these walls, I have people. Paid staff, mind you, but people.

Out there . . .

I have no one.

"Tell Meredith to take you out today. It was mild this morning, on my way here. Finally. What a long winter it's been! They're calling for a cool summer with more rain than normal. We don't get much of that in the interior, so that'll be nice. I'm sure the folks in Portland will be complaining even more than usual, though."

I finally venture, "It sounds like you know Dr. Alwood well."

"I've lived next door to the Welles family all my life. I used to babysit Gabe, back when he was making mud pies and throwing frogs at girls. Why some idiot gave him a gun and let him run the town is beyond me."

I glance over my shoulder at her, still focused on her needlework. She's definitely older than Sheriff Welles but by how much, I'm not sure. Maybe the gray in her hair is deceiving me. It looks like she cut it herself. With hedge clippers. Though I shouldn't judge, given my own hair right now.

And what she lacks in her hairstyle, she makes up for in her complexion. Her face is relatively wrinkle-free. Maybe never smiling is the trick to smooth skin.

"Does amnesia make you forget basic manners? Don't stare at me, girl!"

My mouth drops open. Dr. Alwood told her about me? Why?

Noise at the door distracts us before I have a chance to speak. A tall male nurse pushes a gurney into the room. "Good morning, Miss Fitzgerald . . ." He lifts the chart from Ginny's bed. "I see we're taking your gallbladder from you today."

"You most certainly are not!" she retorts, her eyes flashing as they size him up.

His brow spikes with surprise, but then he chuckles as he approaches the side of the bed. "Don't worry. It's just a routine—"

"Where are Amber and Meredith? Find them, now!" she barks.

The guy reaches for her, saying, "They're waiting for you in the OR. We'll see them in—"

She slaps his hand away and then wraps her arms around her chest, hugging herself tightly. "Don't you dare touch me!"

I'm definitely staring now, and rather rudely. Is this all an act or is Ginny Fitzgerald crazy? But then I see the quilt square bunched tightly in her shaking fist. Crazy isn't the right word. The woman is terrified.

The nurse appears wary now, but he has a job to do. He holds his hands up in a sign of surrender. "Okay, Miss Fitzgerald. I won't help you get up on this gurney. But I'll need you to climb up on—"

"I'm not going anywhere with you!" she manages to get out, her entire body trembling now.

I may not know a lot, but I know that this is not normal, nor is it good. Did Amber expect this reception when she gave her those drugs? Whatever they were, they don't seem to be helping. "Excuse me. I think you should go find Nurse Welles and Dr. Alwood."

The male nurse seems to notice me for the first time. His eyes automatically settle on the side of my face, on my scar. Heat flushes my cheeks and I instinctively turn my head so I'm not directly facing him. I imagine I'll be doing that for the rest of my life.

Shoes pound against the tile floor somewhere in the hall and then a moment later, both Amber and Dr. Alwood round the corner, panting. "We'll take it from here," Dr. Alwood says, practically pushing the male nurse away to wedge herself in next to a shaking Ginny.

The confused nurse seems only too happy to spin on his heels and dart out.

"You . . . you promised me!" Ginny stutters, her pointed finger stabbing the air in front of Dr. Alwood.

"I know, Ginny. I'm sorry. We had to switch ORs and things got scrambled." A pause. "Do you think you can still handle this surgery today?"

Ginny's chest puffs out and deflates with several deep breaths as her eyes shift between the door and her doctor, and back again. And then she tosses the crumpled quilt material onto her side table and mutters, "I'm not coming back again, so let's get this over with."

Amber rolls the gurney next to Ginny's bed. Before they can help their neighbor out of her bed and onto it, Ginny's finger comes up again. "But if I see that *man* in there . . ."

"It's an all-female staff, just like I promised, Ginny." Dr. Alwood's eyes drift to mine. "Hi, Jane. How are you feeling today?"

I glance over at their patient, who's scowling as Amber adjusts the bedsheet draped over her body and begins pushing her gurney toward the door. "Curious."

Dr. Alwood laughs. "I'll bet. Well, I suspect your roommate won't be nearly as pleasant post-op."

Now Ginny shoots a scathing glare at the back of Dr. Alwood's head.

Great.

With that, they wheel the cantankerous woman into the hall, leaving me with plenty of questions.

And all alone. Again.

———

"You touched my stuff, girl."

The groggy accusation cuts through the darkness, startling me. Ginny hasn't spoken since Amber wheeled her back into our room several hours ago.

"I thought maybe if I stuck that square in a heavy book, it'd flatten the pattern for you," I explain, clearing my throat several times, suddenly nervous. I wait, staring at the parking lot light outside my window. I never draw my bed curtains fully at night. The space feels too small, too confining, and, with each creak of the door, a part of me fears the person who might enter my room.

Finally, I hear a low mutter of, "I don't like people touching my stuff. You can't be doing that."

"I'm sorry. I was just trying to help." I dare add in a light tone, "It looks like it's going to be a beautiful quilt when it's done." Okay, I could be lying about that. I have no idea what that square was. All I could see were patches of red and orange and yellow. But her needlework is tidy and precise.

The sound of metal rings scraping across a rod fills the dark hospital room, revealing the old woman from the chest up, her eyes narrowed to slits. "Is this an act?"

"Excuse me?"

"This memory thing of yours. Are you lying?" I can't tell if she's asking or accusing.

"I wish I were," I answer honestly.

"Don't wish that, silly girl," she snaps. "You should be happy."

"Happy?" I burst out in shock. People have given me a lot of pieces of advice over these past few months. This has not been one of them.

The way I must be glaring at her now doesn't seem to dissuade her. "Yes, happy. Happy that you can spend the rest of your life in ignorant bliss. That you don't have to lie in bed with your memories—the smell of his breath, the feel of his weight on you, the sound of his voice when he yells at you to stop crying. Because those memories are like demons. They'll chase you, and when they grab on, they hold on tight. They break you. You get to relive them over and over and"—her voice drops to a hiss—"*over* again."

"But what about . . ." My voice trails off. She's not talking about forgetting my entire life.

Just a very specific part of it.

My stomach drops as understanding slams into me. It would explain her reaction to the male nurse today. "You were . . . it happened to you, too," I stammer.

"And I've spent almost fifty years wishing I could forget it. So be happy, girl, because if you ever wake up to your reality, I promise you'll be wishin' you could forget all over again."

The curtain abruptly closes. Clearly, our conversation is over.

The first hints of blue appear in the sky when I finally manage to drift off, the old woman's words a dark shawl of unease hanging over me.

Wondering what kind of demons may be lying in wait for me.

NINE

JESSE

THEN

"You changed your mind awfully quick."

"I'm allowed." That repetitive, irritating thrum of music hits me as we step around a group of guys in suits.

"If you're gonna make this a habit, you'd better go buy some new shirts. Guys aren't supposed to swap clothes like this. It's weird." Boone flicks the collar of a black button-down that I borrowed from him.

"It won't be a habit. I just feel like hanging out with you tonight is all."

He snorts. "Bullshit." I trail him to the bar, where he waves down Priscilla. "Two of the usual, babe," Boone orders, flashing her a suggestive smile. I caught him practicing that smile in the mirror once.

When she lays them on the counter, I throw down cash to cover it. I don't want Alexandria's husband paying for my drinks tonight.

Alexandria.

Since she climbed into a Hummer with her husband this afternoon, her name's been dancing through my head, followed quickly by her smile. And then a strange tingle skitters down the back of my neck and through my body.

The only reason I came tonight is because I'm hoping she's here.

With a salute toward Priscilla—promising myself that this is the only drink I'm having—I head with Boone to the same alcove at the back of the lounge. The way Boone walks toward it, I know that Viktor and his friends own this table.

Sure enough, they're already here.

And so is Alexandria.

My heart jumps when I see her. She's sitting next to Viktor, her hands folded on the table, the relaxed air she had earlier today traded in for the hard mask. Instead of a blue sparkly dress, this time she's wearing red, to match her bright lips, and her long, white-blond hair has smooth waves in it.

She definitely doesn't look cheap now.

She looks like a damn movie star.

And her husband has his back turned to her, in deep conversation with the same big blond guy as last time.

"Rust!" Boone dispenses with the pleasantries as I stand slightly back, watching Alexandria's eyes lift to meet the newcomers.

They find me.

And the veil drops for just a second, long enough to reveal a glimmer of surprise.

I smile at her and she dips her head. I have enough common sense to pull my attention away from her and move it to Rust before anyone notices the exchange. If they did and they asked me what it meant, I'd have no idea what to say because I don't understand it myself yet. All I keep thinking is that she made a point of finding out my name.

"Good seeing you here again, Jesse. How're the guys treating you?" Rust asks.

"They haven't mistaken me for a nurse yet, so there's that."

That earns loud laughter from Rust as he slaps his nephew on the back. "Here, sit." He gestures at the same chairs as last time. I get the impression that we need the invitation. Not just anyone walks up to *this* table.

I take my seat.

Viktor breaks free from his conversation to regard me with an even look. "Jesse. I missed you at the garage earlier, when I was picking up Alexandria. I was hoping we could talk."

"Sorry. I was probably on break." I wasn't. I was lurking in the window, avoiding conversation with him while I could study her.

Viktor snorts and then mutters something in Russian before saying, "I should have bought this woman a farm truck, the way she drives." Alexandria's lips purse together but she says nothing. "Do you know how many women would love to have that car?"

"I didn't ask for it, Viktor," she answers in a low, cautious voice, her eyes on her hands in front of her. "I would have been happy with a farm truck."

I'm somehow not surprised to see Viktor's jaw tense. "You seem happy spending all of my money, too. Maybe I should stop giving you cash to spend?" Reaching out, he grabs her chin and forces her face up to meet his. "See how happy you are then."

Well, that escalated quickly.

I glance around the table to see everyone busy with their own conversations. Are they truly oblivious to this? Or am I just too in tune?

Viktor lets go of her chin, the simmering storm in his eyes dissipating as fast as it came. He drifts back into his private conversation with the guy next to him as if nothing happened at all, leaving Alexandria to sit like a statue, doing her best to keep her eyes on the tall glass of water in front of her. I can't help but suck back the vodka Boone and Rust keep pouring from the bottle in the middle of the table.

Finally, she slides out of the booth without a word to her husband, her eyes grazing me as she goes. I fight the urge to watch her glide toward the restroom. The urge to get up and chase after her is even stronger. But that would be too obvious. So, I pull my phone out and pretend to go through my messages, when I'm really just watching the clock. I decide six minutes and twelve seconds is long enough and then I slip away. I need to hit the can and grab a water anyway so I'm not an idiot at work tomorrow.

My timing couldn't be more perfect. Alexandria is gliding down the long, narrow hall from the restrooms, her long red dress flowing around her legs, the material parting dangerously high up her thigh. I struggle not to stare as it spreads open with each step. *Damn*, Viktor's a lucky son of a bitch.

Her eyes lock on me immediately and they don't let go as we close the distance between us.

And then I realize that she's not going to stop.

I react without thinking, reaching out to slip my hand around the far side of her waist. "Hey." I've never been shy, but I'm usually smarter than this. Must be the alcohol.

"Jesse." My name sounds breathless on her lips. I like it. Her eyes dart behind me for a split second before returning to mine, her hand reaching up to gently retrieve my hand from her body. She's radiating that same nervousness that poured off her the last time I was here, when she was late and Viktor was pissed. It's so palpable, it's making *me* nervous.

"Are you all right?"

"I'll be fine. I just . . ." Her brow furrows as something that looks a lot like recognition swirls behind those beautiful irises.

I asked her that exact same question the flat-tire night. "What?"

She gives her head a small shake. "Nothing, I just . . . nothing." Her eyes drop to my mouth before stealing another glance behind me. "I have to go." I watch her bare, delicate back as she walks away, her heels clicking fast against the wood, that heavy dose of perfume clinging to my nose. It's starting to grow on me.

I pick the farthest urinal in the men's room, closing my eyes and letting my head tip back as I consider my options. Should I tell her I'm the guy who saved her that night on the side of the road? Would she want to know? Especially given the way her husband treats her. Obviously the guy's a douche. But she married him. She *is* married to him. I don't know what the hell I was thinking, coming here. Roadside kiss or not, nothing is going to happen.

The door squeaks open. A moment later I sense someone take the urinal next to me and I sigh. "Five other spots available. Just saying." Normally, any conversation at the urinal is not cool by me, even to cuss someone out. But I'm in a bad mood.

"Then I would have to yell to talk to you."

I recognize that slight Russian accent and the smooth voice.

"So, about my business proposition. What do you know about Aston Martin DB5s?"

Something tells me blowing off Viktor Petrova right now would be a bad idea. Even if that means I have to talk over the sound of piss hitting porcelain. "They're hard to fix."

"Yes." I hear the smile in the word. "And they are apparently even harder to rebuild. I have wanted one all my life and have finally found the perfect one. A 'sixty-four model. It is sitting in my garage. Would you be interested in bringing it back to life for me?"

Found. I wonder if that's code for *stole*.

It takes a moment for me to realize that I'm still standing there with my dick in my hands while he has already finished and is moving to the sink. Quickly fixing myself, I head over to join him. *No, I wouldn't. You're an asshole.*

"I'll make it worth your while."

You're an asshole who thinks you can buy me like you probably buy everything else, including your wife.

"Certainly enough for that car you wanted. What was it, again?"

Fuck. The guy knows which carrots to dangle. "'Sixty-nine

Barracuda." Now he has me interested. "I'd have to see it, see what shape it's in."

Viktor smiles at my reflection in the mirror. "That is fine. Mr. Miller will tell you where to go. Have a good night." He strolls out of the washroom, leaving me staring at his tall, lean form in his tailored charcoal suit as he exits.

I'll be *told* where to go. I'll bet that's how Viktor operates. Well, fuck him. I don't operate like that. Still, rebuild a '64 DB5 *and* make enough to get myself my car? I'm going to have a hard time turning that one down, even if he's an asshole.

When I reach the table, Viktor and Alexandria are gone. There's really no need for me to be here. I grab my jacket off the back of my chair.

Boone frowns at me. "Where are you going? Priscilla and her friend are getting off soon. They want to come by for a drink."

"I'm out." I tell him what happened in the bathroom. By the time I'm done, his mouth is hanging open.

"Rust tells me he's got one helluva vintage car collection. You'll blow your load if you get to see it."

"We'll see," I say as I head out, wondering if blowing my load over Viktor's cars will be more acceptable than wanting to blow it over his wife.

TEN

JANE DOE

NOW

"There's no reason to keep you here longer, Jane."

Dr. Alwood sits on the empty bed beside me, stripped of sheets after Ginny's departure early this morning, delivering the news that I knew was coming. Nausea bubbles up inside me.

"We'll want to continue some outpatient physio and your visits with Dr. Weimer, of course, but hospital administration won't approve the additional medical bills for keeping you here. You don't *really* want to be stuck in a hospital, staring at these same beige walls, do you?"

I bob my head absently, the desire to wrap my sheet around me in a cocoon overpowering. The little that I know in life is about to be taken away from me. I get it, though. Dr. Alwood, Amber, the hospital—they've done all that they could for me. I'm not their problem anymore. Now I'm my own problem.

If my chest were still hooked up to the heart monitor, that beeping would be going wild right now.

What the hell do I do next?

"Jane? Are you okay?"

Pain shoots through my jaw as I clench my teeth. *I really hate that name.* "I just . . ." Hot tears begin rolling down my cheeks. "I don't know where I'm going to go."

Understanding takes over her face, followed by a look of sympathy. "Did you think we'd just open the doors and kick you to the curb?"

I feel a salty droplet reach my top lip.

She clears her throat. "I've been looking into a few options and I see two. The first is a shelter. There are two *all right* ones in the Bend area. You'd have to share space with the other single females, so there's really no privacy. Administration has already called them. They can accommodate you."

I wipe away the tears with the back of my hand. "Are you trying to sell me on this shelter?"

A soft smile touches her lips. "No. I'm not a fan myself of option one."

"Okay. So what's option two?"

She pauses. "What did you think of Ginny Fitzgerald?"

"I . . . uh . . ." The sudden change of subject has me stammering. And what do I say? The woman is her neighbor, after all. "She's not the friendliest person I've ever met, but my sample size is rather limited."

She grins. "Fair enough. She was a bit crotchety, wasn't she? When she's on her own turf, she's not *that* bad. Coming in here was a big deal for her. It took me months of convincing and making special arrangements to get her to have the surgery done."

"You told her about me." I don't mean for it to sound like an accusation, but that is exactly what it is.

"Yes, I did. I realize that is not only a complete violation of my professional position; it's also a violation of your trust." Dr. Alwood has the decency to look sheepish. "But it was important that I tell her. You see, Ginny lives alone on an old ranch next door to us. She's been there all her life. Her parents both died years ago and she has no family to speak of. She keeps to herself. As I'm sure you can guess, she doesn't make friends easily." I chuckle. Thankfully, she joins in. "Anyway, she has an apartment above her garage that I thought might work well for you. For now, at least. It'll afford you some privacy and quiet. You'll have us right next door, should anything happen; you can keep an eye on Ginny—she's nearing sixty-five—and help her out with the horses. God knows she needs the help and she won't let anyone step foot on her property besides Gabe, Amber, or myself."

I note that she doesn't include her son, Jesse, on that list of acceptable trespassers.

"Have you already talked to her about this? Because I'm not so sure she's going to like this idea." I'm not sure *I* like this idea.

"She has already agreed to it." She adds after a pause, "She likes you. A lot."

"What?"

All Dr. Alwood does is shrug and smile. But then she frowns. "She says she had a good talk with you last night? About your . . . similar pasts."

The ball of fear that's taken up residence in my chest since our conversation swells. What if Ginny's right? I've been sitting in this hospital room for months now, hoping and praying that one morning I'll wake up and feel *whole* again. I'll know what my parents' names are and whether I look more like my mom or my dad; I'll know if I went to the prom like the girls on television and, if I did, who my date was. I'll remember my first kiss, my summer vacations, my best friend's name.

I'll remember *my* name.

But what if I can never be whole again?

What if all those little bits that make up me get lost, over-shadowed by one dark memory? My last memory, the one that made me want to forget everything else in the first place. Will I be able to escape the kind of damage that experience can cause? "Do you think that I'll turn out like Ginny?" I finally whisper. Bitter and cowering in the presence of men.

Eternally afraid.

"Ginny's always been a little bit 'off,' from what Gabe remembers of her, even when he was a young child. Part of it is just her. Her little 'eccentricities.'" She pauses and then admits, "But part of it isn't."

"She didn't tell me much. What happened to her?"

"She's never talked to me or anyone else about it. I only know because Gabe knows. If it hadn't been especially traumatic, I'm guessing no one would ever have found out." She pauses. "That she actually brought it up with you says something. Maybe one day she'll tell you the rest."

Maybe. There's only one reason I can think of for her to divulge her own dark secret. It would be on the day that I remember mine.

ELEVEN

JESSE

THEN

I doubt this driveway has ever seen the likes of a shit box like mine. I was kind of hoping the automatic gates at the entrance would malfunction and crush my car as I edged through.

That didn't happen, though, and now I'm navigating the long, winding landscaped drive to the sprawling estate home ahead, rubbing the sleep out of my eyes, my head pounding from all the vodka last night. Wondering for the hundredth time what the hell I'm doing here. Not that I had an option to say no. The second I stepped into the garage this morning—still half asleep thanks to thin walls and listening to Boone and Priscilla until three in the morning—Miller shoved a slip of paper into my hand and ordered me to follow the directions to "Mr. Petrova's" residence for a ten a.m. meeting. And to call him Mr. Petrova, unless he tells me otherwise.

I pull up alongside a gold Hummer just as Viktor and a man I haven't seen before step out of the double-story brick house, golf bags slung over their shoulders, gold watches catching rays from a rare day of blue skies and sunshine. Next to their tailored pants and collared golf shirts, I look every bit the broke-ass kid mechanic in my ripped jeans and worn T-shirt.

If the way I look right now bothers Viktor, he doesn't let on. With that stone-cold mask, he doesn't give much away, period.

"Hello, Jesse. I am glad you could make it." Not giving me a chance to respond, he hands his clubs to the guy beside him and begins walking toward the four-car garage, calling out behind him, "Follow me, please." No friendly urinal-side chatter. This guy's all business today. That's fine. I don't have much to say.

When he punches a code into the garage door and we step inside, all I can manage is a low whistle. The garage may have only four doors, but it extends far enough to accommodate eight cars and Viktor has used the space wisely, lining the back wall with a '62 fire-engine-red Ferrari, a '65 Shelby Coupe in metallic blue, a black '68 Porsche 911, and a green '55 Mercedes Coupe. The four together have to be worth a couple million. Easy.

Boone's right. I may blow my load in my pants right here, standing next to Viktor Petrova.

"As you can see, I, too, have a passion for classic cars. These have all been completely restored." Prying my eyes from the Shelby with difficulty, I glance over at Viktor. Genuine excitement dances through his eyes as they slide over his collection: all rare, all expensive, and all in mint condition, their coats of paint gleaming under the fluorescent lighting.

With a nod toward the far left, he says, "I would like to add my Aston Martin with your help." A mixed collection of boxes and loose car parts surround the classic, a dull navy blue in need of some serious body work, a small rust hole eating through the back panel. Still . . . it's a fucking DB5! This guy already has the polished but hardened appearance down pat. Throw him in a suit and this car, finished, and someone might cast him in the next James Bond movie. More likely as the villain, though.

I watch as he pulls a cigarette and a lighter from his shirt pocket. The pack has the same strange alphabet on it that I now recognize as Russian. Through the first inhale, he murmurs, "The engine has seized. I expect it will need plenty of new parts. If you provide me with a list, I will appropriate them quickly."

I find his precise dialect and tone off-putting. He says "I will" instead of "I'll"; he uses words like "appropriate" instead of "get"; and though he isn't lacking in manners, he speaks with stern authority, as if he expects everyone to listen.

I cross my arms over my chest as the first swirl of tobacco touches my nostrils. My eyes scan the corners of the room, looking for cameras. From what I could see coming in, the entire property is surrounded by black wrought-iron fences. With four mint cars in the back, and one in pieces, there's no way this garage isn't heavily watched. I can't find any cameras, though.

"Rust told me you are somewhat of a . . ." He searches for the word and ends with, "virtuoso."

I've never heard anyone use that word before, but I have a general idea of what it might mean. "I know a few things." I feel the smirk touch my lips. Unlike Boone, I'm not one to brag. And because I have a friend like Boone, there's no need. The guy does plenty of it for me. "I don't know how long this will take. I mean, I can swing some evenings and weekends, but—"

"I want you to start right now."

My fingertips scrape against my stubble—no time to shave this morning—as I ponder how to handle what is basically an order. "No offense, Mr. Petrova, but I can't lose my full-time job because you want to fill your garage with expensive rides."

His lips press together in a tight smile, and I can't tell if he's annoyed or sincerely amused. "Call me Viktor, please. Fair enough. After your regular hours. And weekends. Until you're done."

That won't be exhausting at all.

"It's not going to be cheap." He said he'd make it worth my while but we have yet to talk actual figures, and if he's going to demand my time, then he can pay for it. I'm no sucker.

His hands lift in the air, palms up, cigarette hanging between two fingers. "Does it look like I'm concerned?" The way he says that—with that condescending smile—should annoy me but it doesn't, because it's the truth. I expect him to say, "Name your price," so I start crunching numbers in my head—how much I get paid at Rust's times how many hours this may take me, plus travel and gas, plus overtime plus extra padding, just because.

Basically, how much I can tally up to earn enough for a decent '69 Plymouth Barracuda, which is why I came in the first place.

"You put this car together for me and I will hand you the keys to *your* car." He takes an extra-long haul of his cigarette, then leans down to butt it into the cement floor.

"You serious?"

Viktor smiles, but it doesn't reach his eyes. "There are two things I never joke about, Jesse: cars and my debts."

"And all the papers to go with it?" The last place I want my dream car taking me is to jail for grand theft auto.

A frown zags across his forehead. "Of course."

"And it'll run?"

"Does it matter? You can fix anything, right?" He gestures ahead of us. "As you can see, I have plenty of tools, an engine hoist. I can get whatever you need for my *expensive rides*. I am not home much, so I will make sure that my wife is here to let you in."

Mention of Alexandria has my eyes drifting to the steel door in the corner. I assume that leads into the house. Is she in there right now? Or did she take another car and go out? Tabbs had her BMW on the hoist this morning, affixing a new muffler that had miraculously appeared overnight.

"So? One Aston Martin for one Plymouth Barracuda?" Those cold blue eyes penetrate mine. Does he hope I'll say yes? Or does he simply expect it?

Strolling over to the frame, I slide my hand over the hood. This hunk of metal in front of me was once a beautiful car that purred and raced. If I have any clue what I'm doing, it will be again. And I get the distinct impression that if I say yes to him, I sure as hell better know what I'm doing and fast.

"It's a deal."

"Good." His dress shoes scrape against the concrete as he approaches my side, a smooth, manicured hand extended. He's not one for dirty work; that much is obvious. I guess the manly garage is just for show. "So, you'll be here tonight to take a better look." It's more a statement than a question. "I'm eager to drive this car."

"Viktor!" his friend calls from the doorway. It's followed by something in Russian, the words sounding quick and harsh.

"If you will excuse me now, Jesse. I need to be on my way." He stands by the door, his arm gesturing out. Clearly sending me a message to hit the road.

"I guess I'll see you tonight, then." I could argue with him, reject the timing. I'm good at negotiating. I've had years of experience doing it with a dad who thinks the world should bend to his will because he's the almighty sheriff. But Viktor's dangling something that I'm willing to jump through hoops for and he knows it.

I throw my shitty-ass car—I can't wait to park this ball-less hunk of metal for the last time—into reverse to follow the Hummer out when something catches the corner of my eye. Alexandria, leaning against the window next to the door.

Watching me.

I check my rearview mirror to see the Hummer's brake lights by the end of the drive, waiting for the gate to open. So I wave at her. Not really a wave. More like four fingers lifting into the air, my thumb still hooked on the steering wheel. I hold my hand there, wondering what she'll do.

At first I think she's not going to acknowledge me. But then her own hand lifts to press against the glass. She keeps it there as I roll away.

TWELVE

JANE DOE

NOW

Dr. Alwood's black sedan chugs along the bustling main street of Sisters.

My new hometown.

It's only twenty-one miles northwest of Bend, but it already feels like a lifetime away from the only other place in the world that I remember.

Dr. Alwood sighs, coming to a dead stop in front of a hair salon as someone up ahead waits to make a left turn. The sight makes me reach up and touch my own hair, now colored a nice golden blond and cut to my shoulders. We just left the stylist in Bend. She showed me how to set the part so the patch where they had to shave my head is covered.

"If the town would just build a bypass for the highway, we could avoid this daily traffic jam," Dr. Alwood murmurs.

"I don't mind the traffic." With the sun beating down on us and the windows rolled open, the warm spring air carries with it the hum of *life*. My eyes skim the pedestrians and the storefronts along both sides, many of which appear to be galleries. "A lot of people like art around here, don't they?"

Dr. Alwood nods. "The town has become something of a tourist destination. That's the intention, anyway. They did some major restorations, trying to bring the old frontier-town feel back to it."

"Frontier. Yes . . ." The boxy buildings with angular faces *do* remind me of an old black-and-white western movie I watched the other night in my hospital room, when entertainment options were slim. While western films don't seem to be my thing, I like the feel of this place. It seems small.

Safe.

"How many people live here?"

"About two thousand. Just the way Gabe and I like it. After a stressful day at work, it's nice to come back to something more simple."

I press up against the window to see the top of a tall, narrow tree on the corner, its needled branches like pipe cleaners.

"That's called a ponderosa pine," Dr. Alwood explains. "We're known in these parts for them. You'll see them all over Ginny's ranch. Our place, too."

"Dr. Alwood—"

"Please, call me Meredith," she interrupts me. "You're no longer in the hospital. Same with Gabe. I'd like to think we know each other well enough to use first names now."

I nod and try it out for the first time. "Meredith—I want to get a job and earn money. What is there to do around here?"

Her brow pinches together. "We'll think of something. Gabe's family has lived in these parts for generations. I'm sure someone would be willing to help us out if we ask. Maybe a small retail store." She points to one with a scrawling sign hanging at the front of it. A quilt dangles in the window, with swirls of blue and white in the background and the black skeleton of a tree standing prominently in the center. "That's actually one of only a few original buildings that didn't get burned down in the 'twenties. Still, Sisters has survived and thrived."

Surviving and thriving. Maybe this town is perfect for a person like me. I have the first part down pat.

We continue the ride in relaxed silence, leaving the bustling town behind for a series of side roads, each one bumpier and more remote. Soon the houses disappear altogether. Ahead of us is nothing but wide-open straw-colored fields, peppered with those ponderosa pines. And looming like a curtained backdrop, three mountain peaks ahead.

"Those are the Three Sisters," Meredith explains, noticing my riveted attention. "They're actually volcanic peaks. Low risk, though."

"They're really high," I murmur, taking in the white caps they still wear, even when everything below is a lush green.

"Yes. Over ten thousand feet."

We make a left down a slightly narrower dirt road. "That's our house, back in there." We pass a long drive that disappears into a screen of tall trees. About a hundred yards over sits a rusted and dented blue mailbox that reads "Fitzgerald," its flag raised. Meredith pulls the car up and empties it of a thick stack of flyers and envelopes. She hands them to me. "Can you sort these for me? Remove anything not addressed directly to Ginny or we'll have to listen to a ten-minute rant about a government conspiracy."

I filter through the pile, wondering yet again what I've gotten myself into. It took me a night of contemplation, lying in my dark, lonely hospital room, to realize that this is actually a great thing. One cranky old lady with a bucket of issues and my own space to live in is definitely preferable to a shelter full of nosy strangers and no privacy. Besides, the Welleses live next door, and they're as close to family as I have right now.

Meredith's car dips and bumps as we slowly make our way over the potholes. "As you can guess, getting trash to the curb on collection day can be a real pain. We're about a quarter of a mile off the road. She has an old truck that she uses to take out the bags, but it's still tough. Doing that and getting the mail are some things that you can do to help Ginny out, as long as you feel up to it physically. But you'll just have to start doing it. She won't ask. She's stubborn like that."

We round a bend of trees and I get my first look at the Fitzgerald ranch, complete with three mismatched buildings—a small white clapboard house to the far left, a brown two-door garage ahead, and a sturdy-looking red barn to the right. Wooden fences trail along the property as far as my eye can see, creating a maze of corrals. Some sit faded and falling apart, while others stand secure, lighter beams of wood telling me that they've seen some repair.

"Is that Amber?" I watch the rider atop a black-and-white horse gallop toward a striped wooden beam erected in between two stands. The horse sails over it with ease.

"Yes, that's my Amber." Meredith's eyes gleam with joy. "She used to ride competitively. She retired a couple of years ago, but she keeps Ginny's horses active. Back when Gabe was young, the Fitzgeralds had many horses on this ranch. They've died off over the years. There are only two left." Meredith's head nods toward the field where a second horse grazes in the distance, its brown-and-white coat shining in the sun.

"You said she's lived here all her life?" I can believe it. The house looks old and in some need of mending, the shingles lifting, the siding stained by weather and dirt. But those details are less striking than the black iron bars on the first-story windows.

Meredith must see my frown. "Ginny likes to feel secure in her home. That's all that is."

We come to a stop in front of an oversized covered porch—judging by its newer and mismatched shingles and wood beams, clearly a later addition to the house—and I immediately spot the gray-haired figure sitting on a bench, her lap covered by a large quilt, needle in hand. A mottled brown dog of no identifiable breed lies on the worn wood floor next to her, its tail flopping up and down at a leisurely pace.

Meredith climbs out of her car with the ease of a woman who hasn't touched a potato chip in ten years, bikes the old roads twice a week, and swims at the Y every Saturday morning that she's not working. Once, when we were having a conversation about age—mine, in particular—she told me that she's forty-eight. That after I guessed forty, tops, and she laughed at me.

"Hello, Ginny. How are you feeling today?" Meredith calls out.

Shrewd hazel eyes regard us. "Like you stole an organ from me a week ago."

"A terrible organ, at that. Would you like it back?" The bitterness in Ginny's voice seems to simply roll off Meredith.

Setting her quilt down next to her on the porch swing, Ginny slides off the bench and takes the three steps down to the grass slowly. The dog trails her like a shadow. By the white beard dusting its chin and the cloudy eyes directed my way as its nose twitches, I can see that it's old. "So they've finally let you out of that godforsaken prison? That's good."

I swallow, not really sure how to answer that. After all, the hospital doesn't have bars on the windows. I finally decide on, "Thank you for letting me stay here."

"Well, of course. Come on now, girl."

I've noticed that she has yet to call me "Jane" like everyone else. I wonder if that's a conscious choice on her part or if she can't be bothered with names, fake or otherwise.

Throwing my small duffel bag over my good arm, filled with a collection of donated items from the nurses as well as a goodbye card from the hospital staff, we trail Ginny and the old dog as they lead us away from the house and toward the garage.

"If you ever need anything, we're just a hop over the fence away." Meredith points to the other side of the garage, past a dilapidated farm fence and through a thin line of those ponderosa pines, to a much more modern but small gray bungalow with a sloped red roof and big bay windows. For all the wide-open fields around us, I find it odd that the two houses are practically side-by-side.

"Yes. So close that when that damn boy of hers shows up with that damn car, it'll rattle your teeth!" Ginny grumbles.

The mention of teeth has me running my tongue along the new wall in my mouth, where dentures have filled the gap. Given everything else that was broken and battered on my body, a few missing molars should have been the least of my worries and yet, when a dentist from Bend offered his services as part of a good-will gesture a few weeks ago, I started to cry.

With a patient smile, Meredith answers, "I know, Ginny. I asked him if there was anything we could do about it. Unfortunately, that's just the type of car it is. It's supposed to sound like that."

"Why? So it can wake the dead?" Ginny rounds the corner and begins climbing a steep, narrow set of wooden stairs. The dog, who hasn't strayed more than two feet from its owner since we arrived, now hunkers down on the concrete landing, forcing us to step over it to follow the old woman up and through a plain white door.

It leads into a long, narrow room with sloped ceilings meeting in the center and sparse, mismatched furnishings throughout. Running along the left side is a kitchen with a white speckled countertop, old, compact appliances, and a small, worn wooden table. To the right is a seating area with two wicker armchairs flanking a simple woodstove, a tidy small pile of wood next to it. A brown-and-black tube television sits atop a faded blue dresser; the screen can't be more than eleven inches. In the far corner is a twin bed with a simple white iron headboard. The smell of bleach and fresh paint permeates the chilly air, telling me that, though old, the bright white walls are freshly painted and the place was recently cleaned.

"I lived in this little apartment for nearly thirty-seven years." Ginny's eyes roll over the place. "It's just been sitting here, doing nothin'. I thought it may as well be put to use."

I struggle to keep the burn in my eyes from developing into

full-blown tears. "This is perfect." I turn to face her. "Thank you."

She peers at me with her lips pursed together, as if deciding whether to say what she's thinking. I get the impression that Ginny doesn't censor herself much. Finally, she points a thin finger to the corner opposite the bed. "Bathroom's over there. Nothing but a few old tractors and a mouse or two down below. But Felix just had young'uns, so they'll take care of those quick. She's a good mouser."

I lift a brow. *A female cat named Felix?*

"I've left you a spare set of keys for the truck, in case you want to drive yourself into town. It's old, but she'll get you there. You know how to drive, right?"

Good question. I shrug. Maybe? "I don't have a license." I don't have any sort of identification. "Sheriff Welles . . . I mean, Gabe . . ." I frown. Calling him by his first name just doesn't settle well. I decide on a middle ground. "I mean, Sheriff Gabe is going to help me get one."

She dismisses my words with a wave. "No matter. I guess we'll find out soon enough. There ain't no people out on these roads anyway. And if you get pulled over, just give them Gabe's name. It's the least he can do for not finding the person who hurt you. Dinner'll be ready at six p.m. on the porch. Don't be late."

The way the old woman strings together thoughts—bouncing from the mundane to the serious, and back to the mundane—is mind-boggling.

I listen to the stairs outside creak as Ginny leaves.

"Last week was the first time I've ever been up here in my life," Meredith, who has remained quiet since following me into the apartment, admits. "Not bad, right?" She takes slow steps through the space, her boots clomping over the faded plank wood floors. "It's a little sparse. We'll get some more comfortable furniture in here as soon as we can."

"It's more than enough for me." I don't know how I'm used to living, but right now I don't care about fancy furniture. I've been in limbo for months. I'm finally standing in a place that I can begin to call home.

She makes her way over to open the old, round-edged refrigerator. "Good. Amber got some fruit and yogurt . . . juice . . ." She adds absently, "If it had been Jesse stocking this, you'd be living off frozen pizzas and Coke."

"So both your children live with you still?" I ask as casually as possible. She doesn't ever bring her son up in conversation.

She pushes the door shut slowly before shifting over to the stove, turning this knob and that as if testing it. "No. Only Amber. Just for now, and she's rarely home, she works so much."

"And your son?"

"He lives in Portland. He'll come for the odd weekend, though. He stays in the apartment above the garage." Tapping the back left burner, she adds, "Gabe says this burner is temperamental, so just avoid it when you cook." Much lower, she mutters, "Because I'm sure you'll need a break from Ginny's cooking sooner rather than later."

Me? Cook? Do I cook?

I wander over to the bed to take in the colorful spread. And my feet falter. "Hey, this is . . ." My voice drifts off as my fingers trace over the red and yellow and orange swirls. It's the quilt Ginny was working on last week in the hospital. The one she crumbled and I smoothed out. The bright colors are merely a backdrop for an enormous black tree, the obvious focal point. Just like the quilt hanging in that store window in town. "Wow, she finished it already?"

"Ginny's known around town as the 'Tree Quilt Lady.' I swear half of Deschutes County has one of her creations in their house. That store I pointed out to you? It sells them on consignment." Meredith's brow furrows. "It may be worth talking to the owner, actually. I thought I heard her say that she needed some help this summer."

I nod slowly. A quilt store. I could handle working in a quilt store. I think? My attention shifts back to the beautiful piece stretched out over my bed. "These must take her a lot of time."

"Ginny *has* a lot of time." There's a pause, and I turn around to find Meredith gripping the back of a rickety whitewashed chair with her skilled surgical hands. "Look . . . Ginny takes some getting used to. Don't take anything she says personally, especially in the next little while. This is a big change for her and she doesn't adjust well. To anything. If you haven't figured it out already, she isn't a fan of people. She much prefers to be alone. And she doesn't like anyone in her space."

"Right. Don't touch her things." I remember her words from the hospital. *You can't be touching my stuff,* Ginny had said. Was that a warning? Did she already know that she'd be taking me in?

Meredith cringes. "Well, yes. But it goes beyond that. Until last week's hospital trip, Ginny hadn't left this property since she buried her father, almost *ten years* ago. I pick up her groceries and drop her mail off, to pay her bills. The veterinarian comes to check in on the horses. *No one* besides Gabe has stepped foot inside her house in over seven years, and that's because the only toilet backed up and she refused to let a plumber in the door." She snorts. "Gabe didn't know a thing about fixing toilets. He spent all weekend there, with a manual and a new set of tools, cursing. The porch is the only common space under that roof. So, don't be offended when she doesn't invite you in. Ever."

"Okay . . . So she's a bit territorial."

"And paranoid. And frugal. You also won't find a television or phone anywhere in her house. She disconnected all the lines after her father died."

I walk over to study the television on the dresser with a curious frown.

"That was her father's," Meredith confirms. "She noticed that you liked having a television in the hospital room, so she dragged it out of her storage cellar. Apparently all of her parents' things are stowed in there. Ginny's a bit of a pack rat. An extremely tidy and organized one."

"But . . . does it work?" I turn the knob on the top right. Gray static fills the tiny screen.

Meredith shakes her head. "She's making an extraordinary effort for you, believe me. But that's as far as she got. We can see about getting you a newer one."

I smile at the thought of the old woman setting this up here. For me.

"Gabe arranged for a cable company on Monday morning to install a line for you. You may want to be on the lookout. Ginny's liable to change her mind and chase them away with her broom. Amber has a cell phone and an old laptop for you that she'll bring over. You'll be able to pick up our wireless router signal from here. Just keep it out of Ginny's sight so you won't have to deal with her grumbling."

"Okay. Thanks. That's . . . great." Not that I have anyone to phone. And will I know how to use a computer? I saw plenty of them at the hospital, but I never actually sat down in front of one to see how much of a "learned behavior" it is for me.

She sighs. "Well, I've got to get ready for work. Are you okay here alone?"

"Of course." I've been completely alone for three months now.

"Like I said, Amber will be over soon. I'm sure you two will be spending a lot of time together." A warm smile stretches across her face as she squeezes my shoulders. "Open some windows and enjoy the fresh air. Everything will be just fine. You were meant to survive. I firmly believe that."

With those final words, she strolls out the door, pulling it shut behind her. And I frown at the peephole, the two deadbolts, and the latch lock that can't possibly be necessary out here, in the middle of nowhere.

Unless you're the victim of a rape that still haunts you almost fifty years later.

I close my eyes against the rising panic. Will this be me one day? Will I find comfort in the locks and chains, will I wish for bars across my windows?

I told Dr. Weimer about my talk with Ginny and the growing fears that sprouted from it. She didn't make any sugarcoated promises or predictions. *It will be difficult*, she said. *You will wish you didn't remember that part*, she said. *You may never remember that part, depending on how lucid you were at the time*, she also said. I found myself praying for that possibility. I'd like to know who did this to me, but I don't need to relive it. It's not like I'll ever forget that it happened. All I have to do is look in the mirror to be reminded that it did.

But Dr. Weimer also reiterated that I am not alone and I do not have to live like I am.

I can choose not to live like Ginny.

I survey my space again. There are two dormer windows facing the driveway and one overlooking the side of the property, and a glass door at the other end of the long room. I slide it open and step outside. For an apartment this long and spacious, the wooden balcony is tiny. More a perch than anything. A green-and-blue woven lawn chair that has seen better days sits in the corner. There isn't room for much else.

I rest my hands on the wobbly railing and take in the smell of clean, crisp air; the vista of land and trees and the three peaks beyond. It's a view more beautiful than . . . well, I don't know if I've seen anything like this before. And, except for the occasional chirp of a bird, I hear nothing but the creak of the wood under my weight and my own pounding heartbeat.

A blue canopy hangs over me, the clouds fleecy and white. I imagine that it's a dome, enclosing me in this peace, separating me from my turmoil, which continues to swirl outside.

Motion in the grass catches my attention. A black-and-white cat creeps along the green expanse, its attention zoned in on something unseen, its body hovering low to the ground, its ears flat. I assume that's Felix, out to earn her reputation. A string of frisky kittens in varying mixtures of all black, all white, and everything in between come bounding up behind her, oblivious to their mother's endeavors. Whatever Felix was hunting must have been scared away, because the cat eases into a stand and shoots what I surmise is an annoyed glare the kittens' way.

I can't help myself. I burst out laughing. It's a low, uncontrollable sound that begins in my belly and sails from my lips with abandon.

And I realize that it's the first time I've ever heard my laugh that I can remember.

Was I a person who laughed a lot? Did I laugh at myself? At others?

I make a silent promise to learn how to laugh freely because that little burst felt like a release.

But the sound must have startled the kittens because they have scattered, two bolting under the fence between Ginny's and the Welleses' properties. From this vantage point, I have a perfect view of the Welleses' garage that sits to my left and farther back—a long structure that matches in color scheme the house, with a steep roof that allows for that room above, and a double garage door. It's open, and the tail end of a shiny black car sticks out.

And Jesse is beside it.

Watching me.

The rest of my body jumps with my heart as I take him in, leaning against the back wall, legs crossed at the ankles like he's been standing there for some time, tapping a silver tool methodically against his jeans. Even from here, those eyes feel like they're penetrating my skin.

A strange sensation washes over me.

One I can't identify. One I can't say that I like.

But also one that I can't say I don't.

One . . . two . . . three . . . Who will win this staring contest? He doesn't seem to be letting up. I let my hair fall forward a bit, in case he can see the red line from that distance, though I doubt it. This is just ridiculous. This is Dr. Alwood and Sheriff Welles's— no, Meredith and Sheriff Gabe's—son. Why would I not say hi? I hold my hand up in a tentative gesture. It's not really a wave. And I wait.

Wondering.

For some reason, not breathing.

"Hey," a panting Amber calls out, stepping out onto the cramped patio in her tall riding boots, startling me enough that I jump yet again. I never heard her come in. "How do you like it so far?"

I drop my hand. "It's perfect for me." And it truly feels like it is. Maybe this is similar to my previous life, after all. The horses, the mountains, the fresh air, the quaint little apartment . . . it feels like it fits me.

Amber grins—her typical wide, white-toothed, flawless smile. "Good. We had cleaners and painters come in this past week to fix it up. You wouldn't believe the fuss Ginny made."

If it's anything like that day in the hospital, I think I can picture it. Which makes my heart instantly soften for the old woman, because that couldn't have been easy. She really does mean well.

I can't help but glance over at the garage, but I try to do it covertly. My smile falters when I see that Jesse is gone.

"That's my brother. He barely comes out to say hi. He's so in love with that stupid car." She turns inside. I hear her mutter under her breath, "It's probably stolen."

My eyes flash as I trail her in. This is the *sheriff's son* we're talking about, right? "Really?"

"No . . . not really." She sighs as she opens the laptop resting on the table. "My brother just does things that I don't understand. Things that have made my parents' lives harder than they need to be."

"Your mom said he comes home on weekends sometimes?"

She starts hitting a bunch of keys, her fingers moving fast. "Yeah. Over the last few months, he's been doing it more often. Before that, I hardly saw him." *Click-click-click.* "I think something happened, with a girl he was dating. He told my mom that he was going to marry her, which is weird, coming from Jesse, who's never gotten serious with anyone. I guess it didn't work out."

So he was in love with a girl. Is he still in love with her? "What was she like?"

Amber sighs as she scribbles some letters down on a pad of paper lying next to her. "Don't know. Never met her, and good luck getting any information from him. Jesse isn't much of a talker. All I know is that she was from Portland."

Portland. "How far is that?" Have I been there before?

"A few hours. I did my nursing program there. Here . . . I used this laptop for school, but I have an iPad now so I don't need it." She pushes a scrap of paper forward. "I wrote the passwords and some basic instructions down, in case it doesn't come naturally." She stands and stretches her arms over her head in an exaggerated yawn, her checkered shirt riding up over her taut belly. "I've gotta run now. I picked up an extra shift tonight."

"You work a lot, don't you?" When I was in the hospital, there was hardly a day that went by when she didn't stroll into my room with her scrubs on.

Her hands slap against her thighs as she drops her arms dramatically. "For now, yeah. I don't have a boyfriend, most of my friends moved away from this town, and my father's the almighty sheriff, so . . ." She throws her hands up in the air. "What else am I going to do?"

I wonder what it's like to have Sheriff Gabe as your father. He's only ever been pleasant toward me, but if being married to the sheriff is sometimes difficult, as Meredith said, then I can't imagine what being his child must be like.

"Bamboo," Amber suddenly fires at me. It takes an arched brow for me to clue in.

"Panda?" I finally answer, feeling silly. Dr. Weimer has me playing word association games with Meredith and Amber. They say a word and I say the first thing that pops into my head. It's part of my therapy, to see if something will trigger a memory. I'm supposed to keep a journal of all the word combinations and bring them with me to my weekly sessions. "Why bamboo?"

Lifting the small fabric-bound notebook that Dr. Weimer gifted me—the cover smattered with colorful hummingbirds—off the table, she opens it and scribbles down the words for me. "Because the end table beside your bed is made of bamboo." That's how this game usually goes. Random, meaningless words plucked from my surroundings as much as out of the air.

So far, I have half a journal's worth of words that have enlightened me about nothing.

Except that apparently I'm aware of a panda bear's dietary preferences.

When Amber's gone, I head back out to the deck. I take a seat in that rickety lawn chair and simply absorb the peace and quiet while I wait. Because I have nothing better to do.

And, in the back of my mind, I admit that I'm waiting for Jesse to come out of hiding. Imagining what kind of girl he would have fallen in love with. She's beautiful; I'm sure of it.

I'm also sure that I'm jealous of her.

He doesn't poke his head out again.

———

The round white-wicker table is already set for two, the cutlery and glasses lined up tidily on either side.

"I hope you like chicken." Ginny slaps a rectangular casserole dish in the center of the table. The dog, who was lying on the old whitewashed porch floor with its eyes closed and seemingly not a care in the world when I first arrived, leaps to its haunches, its nose twitching at the scent of meat.

"Chicken's great," I confirm, pulling the zipper on my fleece jacket all the way up. It's April and, with the sun well on its way behind the mountain ridge, it's far too cold to be eating outside on the porch, screened in or not. "Can I help you with—"

"Nope." She waves an oven-mitted hand my way as she passes me. "Go on and make yourself comfortable, girl." When I reach for the closest chair, she quickly adds, "Not that one."

Of course. I take the other seat as she disappears into the house, the door slapping shut with a clatter so quickly that I can't even sneak a glance inside. It's as if she intentionally removed the hinges on it.

"Hey . . . dog." Reaching down, I snap my fingers twice to catch its attention. "What's your name?" It swings its head toward my hand and I see its nostrils twitch a second before it leans in and places a wet-tongued kiss on my wrist. It really is a mangy thing, the fur along its back in matted tufts. "I'll give you a brushing tomorrow, how about that?" Its tail wags twice, as if it knows what I'm saying.

Ginny returns with two more dishes—one full of mashed potatoes and the other filled with brown beans—and the dog instantly forgets my existence, sliding forward on its haunches, facing Ginny. "It's nothing special, but I've never been much of a cook," she admits, her chair scraping along the wood boards as she takes her seat. Pushing the dishes forward, she ushers, "Well . . . go on, then!"

"This is my first meal out of the hospital," I murmur, loading up my plate. At one point, I was twenty-five pounds underweight for my five-foot-eight stature. That was mainly due to muscle loss. I've slowly regained some of that, but my charts still say I have more to go. "I saw the quilt on the bed, by the way. It's beautiful. You're very talented."

I get a grunt in response.

I don't let that dissuade me. "My psychologist said I should consider finding a hobby. Maybe you could teach me how to quilt." A hobby would be a good start in embracing this new, "fresh" person I've become, she said.

"I've never been much for teaching anyone anything," Ginny grumbles, stabbing her chicken with her fork as she saws away at it with her butter knife.

Another minute of silence passes. "I saw Felix out hunting in the field with his—I mean, *her*—kittens today. They're cute."

"They'll likely get eaten by coyotes."

That stalls my tongue. Ginny's a real ray of sunshine.

Taking a deep breath, I do what Meredith said to do and just ignore it. "Two went running into the Welleses' garage. I can ask Jesse to fish them out and bring them over if you think—"

"That damn boy isn't to step so much as a pinky toe on my property, do you hear me?" she bursts out. There's a flash of rage in her eyes. "He's a *bad* egg." She waves her fork at me. "You stay away from him."

"What did he—"

"You gonna chatter my ears off all through dinner?"

An uncomfortable silence hangs over us as we eat, the clang of our metal cutlery against the old porcelain plates ringing through the quiet evening. That and the dog chomping at pieces of chicken that Ginny tosses its way. It has yet to catch one, too blind to see the flying meat before it bounces off its nose.

The temperature must have dropped 10 degrees by the time we finished dinner, leaving my hands pink and stiff from the cold. All I want to do is go back to my apartment above the garage and start a fire in that woodstove. My instincts drive me to stack our dirty dishes and bring them to the sink, which I start to do. But then I look at that door and the metal bars across the windows and I stall. I'm not sure what the right answer is here. Am I even supposed to notice Ginny's eccentricities? Do I bring it up? Do I—

"Just leave it be."

"I'd like to clean—"

"I'm fine!" Patting the dog's head, she tempers her tone. "Me and Felix have been on our own for years now. Haven't we, boy?"

I frown. "I thought Felix was your cat."

"What's your point?" She swipes the plates from my hand to stack on top of hers. "I like the name. Ain't nothing wrong with naming your pets by the same name if you like it."

"But . . ." I feel my frown deepen. "How do you distinguish them from each other?"

"Because *I* know which Felix I'm calling when I call them. That's how."

"It's a good name," I agree, slowly, pressing my lips together to keep from smiling. Because something tells me she wouldn't find my amusement . . . amusing.

Narrow eyes size me up. "You think I'm strange, don't you?"

I blush, afraid to say anything to offend her. She may banish me from her property yet. "I think . . . you're very kind."

Her mouth twists up, like she doesn't believe me. "Well, Felix is better than Jane Doe, I'll tell you that much. Why on earth are you answering to that ridiculous name anyway? You can't possibly like it."

I can't argue with her on that. It's the first time anyone has even asked what I think about the name. "I feel like I belong in a morgue," I admit. "And I need to find something else if I want a new ID." Sheriff Gabe already has the judge and paperwork lined up.

"Well, then, give yourself a new name! It's not hard. I don't know why you haven't done it already."

She doesn't get it. I don't just want a new name. "I want *my* name."

"Well, it doesn't look like you're getting it anytime soon, now does it? So maybe you need to let go of that idea." She outright glares at me. "Count your blessings, girl. You get to be whoever you want to be, without the burden of your past."

"Count your blessings" sounds an awful lot like "You should be happy." I don't feel blessed or happy. Relieved, yes. Standing out on that balcony of my new home, overlooking kittens running

in the meadow, I felt a degree of comfort that I had yet to experience. But none of this overshadows the fact that I don't have a *life*.

"But maybe I want to know who I was *before* I choose to start
over," I argue.

"Do you, really?" She pushes her chair out and stands
abruptly, an annoyed air swirling around her. "The girl you were
had her face sliced up, her teeth knocked out, her body violated.
Do you want to remember all *that*? Because I'm pretty sure that
brain of yours has decided it doesn't want anything to do with
the girl you *were* anymore. And if your brain is telling you that,
then maybe you ought to listen." She starts loading her arms with
dishes, muttering, "Just give yourself a damn name and that will
be your name! Who's going to argue with you?"

Deep inside, I know she's right.

Louder, she demands, "Now go home and start a fire. Your
shivering is making me cold." She stalks away, her arms full, her
hip holding the door open just long enough for Felix the dog to
scamper in behind her.

Great. First night and we're already at odds. With a sigh, I
tuck my hands beneath my arms and leave the porch, limping
as quickly as my healing leg can carry me, her words weighing
heavily on my spirit.

THIRTEEN

JESSE

THEN

"You remind me of a surgeon," comes the accented voice behind me as I stand in front of the table, the various wrenches and socket sets lined neatly; boxes ready for the clamps and bolts and fasteners to the right, rags for my hands and the tools to the left, sealers and lubricants waiting to be grabbed. The Aston Martin manual open to the table of contents.

I've heard this before. The guys in shop class used to break my balls about it. I glance over my shoulder to see Viktor at the garage door, dressed all in black. "It helps the work go faster when you know where things are."

"I see the hoist worked?" He eyes the seized engine now sitting on the ground.

"Yup. Easy." It's a good one. Not one an ordinary person would have access to. I don't want to know where he got it.

He drops a notebook and pen on top of the tools. "Write down everything you need on here. The sooner you get the list to me, the sooner I can appropriate the parts." He turns with the sound of the entrance gate opening.

An adrenaline rush hits me as the silver BMW pulls up. I

can't help but watch Alexandria's long legs as she climbs out of her car, pulling her messenger bag out with her.

"Where have you been?" Viktor snaps.

"I had a midterm. I told you that." Her tone is soft, but it only seems to anger him more.

"And I told you that I will not pay for these courses if they interfere with our lives."

Obviously, Viktor isn't too keen on the idea of her in school. That doesn't surprise me. What's going to happen when she actually becomes a nurse?

She dips her head and seems to force "Yes, Viktor," through gritted teeth.

"Excuse me?" Ice slides into his words as he closes the distance. "Have you forgotten? Do we need to talk more about this when I get home later?"

She lifts her head, her jaw set defiantly. "No, Viktor."

He pauses, his hand twitching at his thigh. "I don't know what has gotten into you lately but I don't like it, Alexandria. I didn't marry a defiant girl and you are becoming defiant. Get inside."

I turn away just as she storms past, her heels clicking fast and hard against the stone walkway.

"I give her everything she could possibly want and she is still not happy!" he mutters, and when I glance over, I realize he's talking to me.

"They never are, are they?" It's the only response I can think of. She definitely isn't happy, I can say that much. I'm guessing he wouldn't be either, if he knew what happened between his wife and me. Would he slap me like he did her? How would he react?

He smirks, as if that's the answer he was hoping for from me. "I will be late. Remember the list."

Five minutes later, Viktor already gone, the interior door at the back of the garage opens and Alexandria steps out. She's still dressed the same, though she's traded her heels for slippers and her white blouse is untucked and hanging out. All the flashy jewelry has been stripped off her body. "Are you hungry?" She holds up a plate and two bottles of beer.

My stomach grumbles at the sight. The last thing I stuffed into my mouth was a Hot Pocket at breakfast. "Starving, actually." I hold up my filthy hands.

She smiles and points to the door she just came out of. "Inside and to the left."

I follow her instructions into a mudroom that is separated from the rest of the house by a heavy door on the opposite end and is the size of Boone's and my living room. When I return to the garage with clean hands, Alexandria has set up a blue folding chair next to the table and cleared some space for my dinner. She's standing in front of the engine, her arms folded across her chest, a beer in one hand. "So Viktor hired you to fix this?"

I stroll over to the plate. "Yup. Last night, standing in front of the urinal." Stabbing a piece of stew meat, I shove it into my mouth. "Wow," I mumble around a mouthful. "Did you make this?"

"One of my duties as Viktor's wife." There's no missing the bitterness.

"Viktor's lucky to have a wife who cooks like this." I wonder how often she hears that. Because all I've heard is ridicule. Sure, he kissed her. Once.

But so have I.

I feel her eyes on me as I shovel in hunks of meat and potato like a man starved. Growing up with a surgeon and a police officer for parents, I didn't get a lot of home-cooked meals, and the few I did weren't memorable. My mom may be a genius in the operating room, but in the kitchen she's limited to a box of spaghetti and a jar of pasta sauce.

Before I can place the plate on the table, she's diving for it. "Let me get that."

"Thanks." I try her name out on my tongue. "Alexandria."

"It's Alex. Call me Alex." She pushes a loose strand of hair back behind her ear. "When it's just us."

"But not when it's not?"

"Viktor prefers Alexandria."

Of course.

She looks down at the plate in her hands. "Did you really enjoy that?"

"Yeah, it was fantastic. Why?"

"Because you left half of it."

"No I didn't. I ate the entire—" *Oh* . . . I grin sheepishly. I've been picking vegetables out of my food for so long, it's second nature now. "I ate all the good stuff," I offer, hoping she isn't offended by the tidy pile of peas and carrots I left behind. God knows I've heard enough about starving children from my mother for the past twenty-four years.

She smiles. "So, not a big fan of vegetables. What about fruit?"

"Tomato sauce."

"That's not . . ." Her voice drifts off with a sigh, her eyes flickering with amusement. "You must have driven your mother nuts."

"Maybe if she cooked more, I would have better eating habits."

"You're blaming your mother?"

"Exactly." I suck back the rest of my beer and hand it to her. "Thank you. You don't have to serve me, though."

"I know." She bites the inside of her mouth. "Viktor wouldn't like me in here with you."

"Aren't you worried about being caught on camera?" And why is she telling me this at all?

"No. There aren't any cameras in here. Or anywhere in the house. Viktor thinks that people can hack into them and watch us. There are cameras around the perimeter of the property, as well as an alarm system, though."

"You probably shouldn't tell people those sorts of things," I warn. "You don't know me."

"You're right. I don't, but . . ." Those pretty eyes regard me for a long moment. "I feel like I do."

I can't keep my gaze from dropping to her mouth as I murmur, "I think I know what you mean."

She stands across from me in front of the engine. "So . . . how long do you think it'll take you to finish this car?"

"Not sure. Depends on how many distractions I have." Like right now, I'd rather be looking at her than playing with this engine. And I love nothing more than playing with engines.

Her beer bottle pauses at her lips. She clears her throat and begins to move away. "Well, I should probably get back to studying. I have another midterm next week."

She misread my words. She thinks I'm trying to get her to leave. "Bring your books out here," I suggest casually, testing the bolts on the manifold. They're corroded. Not surprising.

"Yeah?" A hint of something in her voice pulls my attention up. Excitement, perhaps. Is it excitement about spending time with me or just a warm body in general? I wonder how often they have people over here. And how often Viktor is actually home with her. Something tells me she spends a lot of time alone.

"Yeah." I scan the front of her shirt, the outline of her bra underneath just barely visible. "You may want to change out of anything nice, though. Things tend to get dirty out here." That could be taken in an entirely different way. I don't normally say shit like that, but she seems to bring it out in me.

She gives me a small smile. "Okay. I'll be back."

Even with her shirt hanging long, I can see her hips sway as she strolls toward the door. And then I remind myself that that's Viktor's Petrova's wife, I'm in his garage and working on his car, and I don't believe for one second that this place isn't under some kind of surveillance.

I dive back into the engine, keeping my attention glued to it until I hear the door open again and Alexandria's slippers pad across the concrete floor.

"Here." I look up to find another beer in her hand. "It's this or vodka, and you don't like vodka much."

"How do you know that?" I frown as I take the bottle. Our fingers graze and I temporarily forget my question.

"Because you looked like you were forcing it down at The Cellar."

"You were watching me?" Now I can't help but stare openly at her—changed into jeans, a fitted T-shirt stretched over what I'm guessing is a B-cup chest, her hair pulled into a bun, reminding me of Amber when she used to get dressed up for ballet on Saturday mornings. Except it's Friday night and Alex can't be mistaken for a nine-year-old. "You kept your head down the entire time."

Her cheeks flush. "Well, how would you know unless you were watching me the entire time?"

Caught. I go back to my engine, a smile now affixed to my face. She has a confident streak in her.

"Viktor doesn't let me drink," she admits. Then she leans her head back and, closing her eyes, pours the beer down her long, slender throat.

A confident, rebellious streak.

"You don't talk much. It's too quiet in here. Do you mind if I put on some music?"

"Go nuts." Inviting her in here might have been a bad idea after all. I can't keep my eyes off her ass as she strolls over to the radio on the back wall. She punches in a few buttons and an alternative rock station comes on. "Thank God," I mutter, turning my focus back to my task.

"What?"

I shake my head. "I was afraid you were going to put that trance shit on, from the club."

"Oh, no." She shudders. "I can't stand that music. Or that place. The people there are all phony and vapid. I hate when Viktor makes me go." She walks back over to stand near the engine, leafing through the manual. The silence lasts for only a minute before she asks, "Do you have a girlfriend?"

"Nope."

The hesitation swirling around her is palpable. "Why not?"

"Guess I haven't met the right girl yet." I broke up with Shyanne six months ago, after dating on and off for close to a year. It was never serious—not to me, anyway—and I can't say that I miss her. I certainly don't miss being accused of looking at or talking to or flirting with another girl every single day. And I never was—not knowingly, anyway. Which made it ironic when I found out she was screwing around with her brother's friend.

"My husband is sleeping with that waitress, Priscilla." Alex just throws it out there, so matter-of-factly, that I take a moment to process it. Not because I'm shocked that he's doing it. I pretty much knew.

"I'm sorry."

"I found out a few weeks ago." She sets the manual down. "I was taking his dry cleaning in and I found her pink lipstick all over the collar."

"Maybe just an innocent hug?"

"On the inside of his dress pants, too. And a receipt for a hotel in his pocket."

You're busted, Viktor. I can't lie—I'm glad Alex knows, even if it hurts her. That was a few weeks ago, she said? Around the same time she got a flat tire. Is that what sparked the tears, the questions . . . the kiss? "And you know it's her?" I should probably warn Boone, in case Viktor's the type of guy who gets territorial about his mistresses.

"People think I'm just some stupid money-grubbing wife, that I don't know what he's doing. Or that I should just look the other way and go shopping." A bitter chuckle escapes her lips. "I don't even like shopping. I'd take a husband who loved me over all the money in the world."

I hardly know her, but I believe that she's telling the truth. "And what'd he say about it?"

She pauses. "Nothing. I haven't mentioned it."

"Are you going to?"

I almost miss her head shake, it's so slight. But then she touches her cheek, her eyes drifting.

And it clicks.

"You're afraid of what he'll do."

"Viktor doesn't take well to accusations."

Has she made that mistake before and learned her lesson? Do I want to know? I chew on that question until the words crumble in my mouth. "If he's screwing around on his beautiful, young wife, I'd hate to see what life's going to be like for you down the road."

There's a pause and then she asks, so faintly I almost miss it, "You think I'm beautiful?" Somehow I can tell it's not a fishing expedition; somehow, she hasn't figured out that she is.

I keep my head down, quietly taking notes in my notebook.

After a while, when Alex doesn't say anything else, I hazard a glance over my shoulder to find her sitting cross-legged in the folding chair with her textbook in hand, watching me. Her eyes drop to her lap instantly.

"How did you and Viktor meet?"

"My mother owned a small cleaning business. I worked for her, scrubbing strangers' toilets and washing floors, before and after school and on weekends, long before I was legally old enough to do so. Viktor was a client; he has a condo in Seattle. I was seventeen when I met him." A sad smile curls her lips as she reminisces. "I was terrified of him at first. Sometimes, I'd prepare meals and leave them in the fridge. I love to cook and he'd leave me extra cash for having dinner ready for him. Then, he started leaving roses for me every week, with the cash. One day, he offered to treat me to dinner and I said yes. He was kind and handsome and made all kinds of promises about taking care of me, paying for me to go to college. He said I'd have nothing to worry about." She shrugs. "I was naïve, and I had too many memories of waking up cold and hungry because we couldn't pay the bills. The last thing I wanted to do was follow in my mother's footsteps, working my fingers to the bone and collapsing in bed from exhaustion every night. I wanted more for my life and he was offering it. So, I took it. We got married just after my eighteenth birthday." Her chin dips down as she focuses on a spot on the ground, her voice soft and mocking as she admits, "He seemed like Prince Charming and I felt like Cinderella."

"And now?"

"And now . . ." The two simple words crackle over her rising emotion. She pauses, her chest puffing out with a deep, slow breath that she releases with her eyes closed. "Now I don't believe in fairy tales. Or at least, not in the happily-ever-afters that Disney brainwashed us all with."

I open my mouth, the urge to tell her that the night at The Cellar wasn't the first place we met overwhelming. But I rein it back as a new thought springs to my mind. Maybe she doesn't want to remember that night. Maybe she regrets that night. Maybe she'd be too embarrassed to sit out here with me. That would suck, because I'm enjoying getting to know her, as depressing as the topic of her marriage is.

When her eyes lift, there's a hopelessness in them that she's kept firmly veiled until now. She stares at me, through me, beyond me to somewhere I can't reach. But I hold her gaze, trying to follow.

In slow motion, she shuts her book. "Neither of us is going to get any work done. I should get going." At the door she stops. "Good night, Jesse." The tone of her voice is so soft, so sad, and yet so unbelievably sexy, I can't even form the simple words to answer her.

Thirty minutes later, struggling to focus because every slight noise has my eyes darting to the door, I finally pack up and leave.

FOURTEEN

JANE DOE

NOW

A stranger stands before me in the dark, only the outline of his jaw visible. He is faceless, nameless. And yet I know that I know him.

I reach up, my fingers gliding over his masculine features, reading them like a blind woman. Regardless of what my eyes cannot confirm, I know that he is beautiful. I find his lips, soft and parted. I marvel at the feeling of air drawing through them, at the quickening of his breath.

Like a cord severed by a swinging axe, our connection breaks, leaving me cocooned in cold dread.

"No one will ever touch you again," he hisses.

That voice belongs to another faceless figure hovering over me.

And I know I am about to experience pain like I have never felt before.

I bolt upright in bed, the whispered promise swirling around me like a suffocating smoke, making me gasp and cough and claw at my throat for air. I will myself to breathe in and out as my surroundings come into focus, my heart hammering against my chest. What was that? Just a bad dream?

Or . . . was that a memory?

Because I can't deal with any more memories like that.

I fold my arms around my stomach and clutch myself until my breathing calms, rocking back and forth, the creaky springs in the mattress producing a rhythmic sound that slices through the night's silence.

Sliding out of bed, I pad over to the woodstove, pulling my pajamas tight to ward off the cold. The fire that Sheriff Gabe helped me light earlier now burns low. I chuck two more logs in and then head to the kitchen for a glass of water, my eyes drifting toward the window and a spotlight shining from the front of the Welleses' garage. I peer out and see a lean but solid frame pass through it, several pieces of wood cradled within his arms. It's Jesse and he's heading toward the property line. He throws a leg over the rickety old fence.

Definitely more than a pinky toe. Ginny would be freaking out.

He disappears from view just below my window. Only for a few seconds, though, and then he reappears empty-handed. Climbing back over, he collects more wood from the neatly stacked pile against their garage before repeating the trek.

Sheriff Gabe warned that nights would be cold for another two months and I could use whatever I need from their stock. I figured I'd be the one collecting tomorrow. I definitely didn't think that meant his son would be doing it for me at . . . A glance at the clock shows me that it's after three in the morning! I ease myself up onto the counter, curling my good leg under me to get comfortable, while my injured one hangs free.

And I watch Jesse Welles, the boy who somehow earned Ginny's wrath, bring me my firewood in the middle of the night.

———

"One of these days I'm going to learn how to ride you . . . Felix," I murmur, curling the massive horse's crimped brown mane of fur around my fingers. And then I start giggling.

"I know. Ginny's a bit eccentric, isn't she?" Amber says, running a brush against the black horse's mane as it drinks from the stream that runs through the corral, just behind the barn.

"If she had her way, *I'd* be named Felix, too." Meredith wasn't kidding about Ginny's peculiarities. It isn't enough that her cat and her dog are both named Felix. When I heard the barn doors rattle open this morning at precisely eight a.m., I rushed down to see how I could help. I found Ginny at the far end, standing in front of a stall, wearing rubber boots and a stern frown, a pitchfork in her hand. It took some convincing her that my limpy leg, as she called it, wouldn't hinder my ability to "muck the stalls." Then she had to teach me what "mucking the stalls" meant.

Nothing about these horses—the smell of their stable, the sound of the millet filling their trough, the sheer size of them as I stand next to them—feels second nature to me. I have to assume that I don't have a lot of experience with these sorts of animals. I do know that I was exhausted after cleaning out just one stall. If all sixteen stables were filled . . .

It was while changing out the buckets for fresh water that I noted the horseshoe hanging above the stable door. And the name "Felix" etched into it. Stifling my laugh, because Ginny was busy in the black-and-white horse's stall, I glanced over to see a matching "Felix" above that one, too.

Sure enough, both horses are named Felix.

"I can teach you how to ride if you want," Amber offers, reaching over to slap the brown-and-white Felix's side. "This one's more tolerant of riders." He answers by nuzzling against her neck, making her giggle.

"Was the barn ever full?"

"Yeah. It was really something to watch. The horses would run laps around the corral." She waves her hand, tracing an imaginary path in the air. "Ginny's father, Mr. Fitzgerald, loved horses. When I was eight, he convinced my parents to get me my own. He let me stable her here for free. I named her Pegasus."

I nod, remembering seeing that name etched into one of the horseshoes above an empty stable. All of the stables still have names above them, except for one giant one on the end, which Ginny says is for foaling. There are five more Felixes—I know who named those—along with a myriad of others, some names cute like Licorice and others more stately, like Triumph and Retribution.

"What happened to her?"

"She died of colic when I was eighteen. I cried for a week straight. I'll get another horse one day. When I'm back from traveling. If Ginny's father had been alive when Pegasus died, he would have convinced me to get another one right away." She sighs, switching brushes for a round one to begin rubbing the horse's body in a circular motion. "I was so sad when that man died. He was like a third grandpa to me."

I copy Amber with a second round brush, running it around Felix the Brown's midsection. "What was he like?"

"Fat and jolly," she says with a wistful air. "Ginny's mom was nice too, but much quieter. I don't think they knew what to do with Ginny. I used to be afraid of her, growing up. I didn't understand why she is the way she is. I still don't, really."

We groom the horses in silence, until their coats shine and Amber has shown me how to clean their hooves.

Tossing the tools into the wooden box we carried out with us, I reach down to clean my hands in the stream, my fingertips going numb within seconds of being submerged in the cold water. Still, it's refreshing. I don't pull them out, watching the current as it flows freely over a bed of smooth stones.

"Water."

I smile, catching on right away. "Tattoo." I'm sure she could have guessed that that would be the first word to pop into my head. What neither of us knows—what no one knows—is why I have a tattoo of "water" on my pelvis. Was it an arbitrary choice? It certainly isn't a common choice, like a bird or a butterfly. So there must be a reason for it. Something important enough to permanently mark myself with a symbol representing it.

That's what I want to believe, anyway.

"This stream runs off the snow from the mountains. It'll be bone dry by midsummer."

I frown. "But it's, what, six feet wide?"

"Summers get dry around here," she laughs. "We also have a lake about a half mile back, that way." Amber points into the wilderness. "You should take a walk out there one day."

"I will." My leg can certainly use the exercise. It's bad enough that I have a giant scar running down the length of my face. I'd really like this limp to go away, and the only way that's going to happen is by strengthening it.

"We'll go camping by the lake when it's warm enough. I haven't done that in a couple of years, but I miss it. The stars are unreal."

Have I ever gone camping?

Her eyes roll over the field to our left, covered in pale yellow flowers. "In another month or two, everything will turn brown."

"It'll still be beautiful, though."

"Yeah." She nods in agreement. "Sisters may be small but it's a great town, with lots of nice people. Just wait until the summer. We have a big rodeo, and a quilt fair. Lots of tourists come through for the mountains . . . If you drive up there, you'll see the wildflowers. There are literally *hundreds* of different kinds."

I inhale the fresh air, Amber's words drifting off as my thoughts wander. Will I still be here for all of that? I hope that I am. This place feels like it fits me somehow.

I pull my fingers out of the stream, red from the brief exposure, and stand. "This water is freezing!"

"Yeah, and it doesn't warm up much. Jesse and I used to swim in it as kids. We'd be blue when we came out, even in the middle of summer."

Jesse.

"Hey, Ginny doesn't seem to like your brother much, does she?" I play my curiosity down by picking up a stone and tossing it, creating a small splash.

"You think?" she mutters wryly. "Why? What'd she say?"

"She didn't. She just called him a 'bad egg' and told me to stay away from him."

"That's probably not bad advice." I feel her eyes on me. "When we were in grade school, we still hung out together a lot. Had some of the same friends. But then we got to high school and Jesse started hanging out with trouble. The 'riffraff,' my dad called them. The kids who got arrested for drugs, and stealing, and vandalism. Two of them are in jail now." I look over to see her face twisted in disgust. "Can you imagine how that looked for my dad? Everyone knows our family around here. Some of the stuff that happened . . . I've never seen my mom cry like that over anything before."

"So Jesse did all that stuff too?" The guy who brought me all that wood might also steal from me?

Amber shrugs. "I mean, he smoked pot, but not the other stuff. It was just bad enough that he was around it. Stupid teenage boy syndrome. I know he got teased a lot about being the sheriff's son. People were always nervous around us, thinking we'd rat them out if they did something wrong. It wasn't as hard on me, though. Probably because I'm a girl.

"Anyway, my dad and Jesse have been butting heads for years, but they haven't been too bad lately. Jesse's got problems with being controlled and my dad has problems with not being in control." Giving Felix the Black a gentle slap on the hind, Amber starts walking toward the house, box of grooming supplies in hand. "I have to get going to work."

I follow, leaving the horses to graze.

"I think my dad wanted to talk to you about that new ID."

Yeah, I want to talk to him about that too. "I need to give him a new name before he can finish up the paperwork."

Amber yanks a flower from the ground, twirling it between her fingertips. "I can't imagine naming myself. It'd be weird. What were you thinking of?"

"I have no idea. But I should come up with something soon. I'll be meeting new people, hopefully getting a job. I don't want it to be as Jane anymore."

"My mom mentioned something about asking Dakota for a job."

That art store that takes Ginny's quilts. "She said Dakota went to school with you?"

"Yeah . . ." Amber hesitates, and I can tell she wants to tell me more.

"What is it?"

"It's just, she's *nice* enough, but . . ." She cringes. "No. I'll let you form your own opinions. But if she offers you brownies, just say no."

I frown. "What's wrong with eating her brownies?"

Amber shakes her head but doesn't answer that. "Just remember to keep the information about yourself to yourself, okay? She grew up in this town, so knowing everyone else's business and spreading it is in her blood. Figure out a story about who you are to Ginny and stick to it. God knows the whole town will be buzzing when they learn the Crazy Tree Quilt Lady has someone living with her."

"So lie?"

"Yes. Pretty much. Otherwise everyone will come up with their own stories about you." I turn to catch her eyes on the side of my face, on my scar. Amber and Meredith are just about the only two people I'm not self-conscious around. They've both seen me at my worst. But the idea of new eyes—so many new eyes—on my face for the first time makes my shoulders tense up.

We're just passing the barn when a slam cracks the quiet, followed by the low rumble of an engine. An inexplicable warmth flows through me. Somehow I know that's Jesse's car. *It has to be.*

Ginny was ranting about how loud it was yesterday. I don't mind the vibration deep in my chest, though. I actually like the feel of it. It's somehow . . . comforting.

We round the side of the barn to find Ginny hanging off the edge of her porch with a quilt grasped in her fingers, a scowl on her brow as she glares over at the Welles property. Her lips are moving fast, to no one in particular. Complaining to the mangy dog behind her about Jesse, probably.

The black sports car pulls into view with Jesse in the driver's seat, his crisp white shirt a stark contrast to his olive complexion and short, ash-brown hair. I can see both Meredith and Gabe in him, though he has certainly acquired his father's bottomless gaze.

A bottomless gaze that's settled on me. Even from this distance, I can feel its intensity.

He raises the hand that's on his steering wheel. It's not exactly a wave, but it's as close to a "hello" as he has given me so far.

I instinctively look toward Ginny and find her glaring at me now.

When I turn back, Sheriff Gabe is standing next to Jesse's car, in his uniform. He slaps the roof of his son's car and points in the direction of the road. As if he's kicking him out.

With a flat glare toward his father and one last quick glance my way, Jesse guns the car, his tires kicking up rocks and dirt. The engine tears into the silence as he speeds away, and I watch the rectangular taillights disappear past the house.

"Guess I'll be seeing ya, brother," Amber mutters. She reaches out to pinch my elbow. "I'm working an afternoon stretch this week, so you won't see me much. Text or call if you need anything." I watch her leave, intentionally avoiding the glower I can feel boring holes into my back from the porch. I didn't do anything wrong! Maybe if I stand here long enough, Ginny will forget.

Not likely.

"I thought he moved out!" Ginny's reedy voice hollers.

Sheriff Gabe has thrown a leg over the fence and is headed my way, his boots crunching the gravel. I don't really know him, not the way I know Meredith and Amber. He made a total of three visits to the hospital simply to say that there was nothing new to report about the investigation. For a man who deals with politicians, the media, and citizens, he's not much of a talker. But his very presence—strong and controlled—must make up for it.

"Good morning, Ginny." He reaches up to tip his hat toward her, ignoring her comment, making his way over to me. "How are you doing?"

"I'm good. How are you?"

His lips purse together and he nods once. I guess that's his answer. Glancing back over his shoulder toward the house, where Ginny's settling back down into her porch swing, he says, "I see Ginny's in fine form?"

That makes me smile. "She's okay."

"I saw you in the barn earlier today, helping her with the horses. That's good. She appreciates the help, even if she won't *ever* say it."

Now it's my turn to nod. "You do a lot for her, don't you?"

"I try to. Before her dad died, I promised him that I would. Our families go way back." He pauses. "I'm glad you chose to come here. It was smart."

"I didn't have many options," I admit, then quickly add, "but I'm glad, too. It's beautiful here."

He offers a small smile. "You'll be safe here."

Safe. That word. What does it really mean? Did I think I was safe before, too? Before I wasn't? "Any news on my case?"

His frown returns. "No. All of the evidence is catalogued and I'm waiting for a break. I'm still watching the missing persons reports, but nothing fits." Every time Sheriff Gabe talks about the investigation, he makes it sound like he's taken on all the work himself. "There've been no inquiries of any kind coming across my desk."

"So . . . what does that mean?"

He begins fumbling with the badge on his chest. "It means I don't think whoever did this is actively looking for you. It was probably a guy driving through, on the way east or west, putting as much distance between your body and himself as he could. It's not the first time I've heard of a body being dumped in the wilderness. He probably didn't realize you were still alive. And with no DNA match to the criminal database, no witnesses, and no information about you, I'm aiming at targets in the dark. In outer space."

I frown. "But didn't you say the place was just outside town? That's not really the wilderness, is it?"

"It is for city folk."

"So, you're saying he's just going to get away with what he did to me." The faceless man in my nightmare, his promise still weighing heavily on my mind, will walk free. Unpunished.

"I'm saying you're safe here and you can put all of your focus on getting better. You don't need to be afraid. As long as the guy thinks you're dead, he has no reason to come back. So let's keep it quiet. The people in Sisters don't need to know the truth."

He's telling me to lie. Just like Amber did. I nod slowly.

Still grazing in the corral, Felix and Felix suddenly take off, the brown horse chasing the black one as they gallop through the stream, their powerful legs sending water splashing in every direction.

Water, splashing.

Water . . . splashing . . .

My eyes widen.

"What's wrong?" Sheriff Gabe asks, sudden panic in his deep voice.

"I don't . . ." My deep frown tugs at my scar. "I'm not sure . . ." There's something . . . A feeling.

Is this what Dr. Weimer warned me about? A fragment of a memory?

"What is it?" Sheriff Gabe pushes, moving to stand in front of me to block my view of the stream, his stern, authoritative tone now in full effect, eyes black as coal sinking into me.

I don't want to get anyone's hopes up, especially mine. It's so vague, I couldn't even describe it if I wanted to, except to say that it made me feel . . . happy.

"Jane?"

Ugh. Ginny's right. Even Felix would be better than Jane. "I don't know. It's probably nothing. I was hoping it was something, but . . ." I shake my head slowly, watching the horses as they disappear over a crest. I guess that's the only clue they're going to give me and it's not enough. "It's not."

Sheriff Gabe's shoulders sag, almost with relief. "Amber gave you my direct line, right?"

I nod. The cell phone she dropped off yesterday came fully programmed with all of their numbers. Except for Jesse's. For some reason, I noticed that straight away.

"Also, Jane, I need a name. The judge will sign off on the paperwork and we can get you temporary identification quickly, but I *need* a name."

"How about Felix?" I joke half-heartedly.

He lets out a loud snort. It's as close to a laugh as I've ever heard from him. "Listen, you can't drive that truck off this property until you have a license. I don't care what Ginny tells you. I'm still the sheriff."

"Got it," I agree solemnly. He tips his broad-rimmed hat, and then strolls away.

FIFTEEN

JESSE

THEN

"Jesse?" Her voice peels my attention away from the engine block I've been staring at for the past half hour. She's standing in the doorway, her blond hair hanging damp around her shoulders, a bowl in one hand and a glass of orange juice in the other.

"Hey." It comes out scratchy. It's the first word I've said to anyone today, aside from Licks. I had to drag myself out of bed this morning to get here. Normally, I sleep until at least noon on the Saturdays that I'm not working. "Thanks for letting me in." I assume it was Alex who opened the gate when I buzzed and rolled open the garage door when I pulled up to the house. Her car is the only one in the driveway. "I guess Viktor's not around?"

"No. He didn't come home last night. He just texted to see if you were here. He's on his way." A look of resignation passes across her face but she says nothing more about it. Maybe her candor about her husband last night was on account of the beer she chugged in front of me. She herself admitted that Viktor doesn't let her drink. "I figured you could use breakfast." My heart picks up its pace as she takes the three steps down, her blue jeans tight around her long, slender thighs. She's wearing another

T-shirt, but this one's oversized and sliding off one of her thin shoulders.

"How'd you know?"

"That you don't take care of yourself? Lucky guess."

"I told you, you don't have to do this."

"I know I don't *have* to."

I start laughing when I look down to see the blue balls floating around the creamy yogurt.

She cocks her head playfully. "Not even blueberries? They're my favorite."

"Not even blueberries."

She shrugs, still smiling, taking several steps toward the door. "I figured it was worth a shot. I'll leave the bowl here, in case you feel like impressing me. More than you do." She adds quickly, "With the cars, I mean." Her cheeks flush with red.

I watch her take another step and bump into the boxes with the brake parts. One tumbles, hitting the ground with a rattle. Her eyes widen with panic. "Oh, no! I'm so sorry!"

I chuckle at her sudden shyness and her clumsiness. She's cute when she's awkward. "It's fine. They're car parts, not china."

Her bottom lip slips between her teeth and then she bursts out laughing. It's an infectious sound and it lights up her entire face. I'm pretty sure she's laughing at herself.

I hope so. Because I love a girl who can do that.

———

A slew of Russian words fly from Viktor's mouth as he marches past the open garage door, a phone in his ear. I try to keep my focus on the engine that's now sitting on the floor, a mess of cylinder caps and valves and bolts, but it's hard, especially when I hear who he's talking to.

There's a pause, and then in English, "I am a busy man, Alexandria. You should know. You are out spending my hard-earned money right now! . . . I do not have time to chauffeur you around . . . No . . . Maybe waiting two hours for roadside assistance will teach you to watch your gas levels after this. Or, you can always walk the five miles."

Oh Jeez. What is with that woman and cars?

He jabs at the "end" button and then to me, he raises his index finger. "When you marry a woman, Jesse, make sure she has some common sense. This one?" He holds up his phone, as if it represents his wife. "I married her for her youth, her beauty, her obedience, and her ability to suck my cock. I should have also looked for common sense. All she does lately is cause me headaches." Shaking his head, he slides his phone in his pocket. "You are on your own here until she gets back. How much longer for that list?"

"I should be able to get it together in another couple of hours."

"Good. And, just remember, the longer you take on this car, the more time you will need to work on yours." With that thinly veiled threat, he climbs into the passenger side of his Hummer. The big blond guy from The Cellar is behind the wheel.

What a dick.

And I'm not even talking about my Barracuda. He's going to just leave his wife sitting on the side of the road, in the rain, because she made a mistake? We've all made mistakes. Hell, I've made more than my share. I watch the gate close behind the Hummer and wonder if he's just shooting his mouth off, acting tough. If he's actually going to go get her.

Twenty minutes later, I still feel convinced that he's not.

And now I can't concentrate. Finally, I throw the wrench down and run out to my car, hitting the garage door button on my way out. He said she's five miles out and she was shopping. The mall's to the west, but I'm guessing she doesn't shop at malls. So, she's likely coming in from the trendier part in the north.

But if she's not?

I look at the gate across the driveway . . . If I leave, I won't be able to get back in to finish what I was working on. Viktor will be pissed.

I crank my engine.

The rain hits my windshield in sheets, the pools of water across the road pulling at my steering. Normally, all we get is a drizzle. Yet this is the second time she's been stranded and it's pissing rain. I've heard enough stories from my dad to know that drivers can get confused in heavy rain and plow into cars on the shoulder. I bite away at my thumbnail, speeding down the road, keeping my eyes peeled. What if I'm wrong and she *is* a mall girl?

I crest a hill to see the silver sports car pulled over on the opposite side. My chest swells with relief. And nostalgia. Even though it's mid-afternoon, this is all too familiar.

I can just make out a single figure sitting behind the steering wheel, the windows fogged up with her breathing. Making a U-turn, I park directly in front of her. That way she can see me. Ducking from the rain, I run to her driver's-side door and rap against the window.

There's a long delay. And then a delicate hand wipes the fog away and Alex's face appears. She cracks open her door, wiping the tears from her wide, red-rimmed eyes. "Jesse?" She frowns, glancing at the back of my car. "What are you doing here?"

"Getting soaked." My sweatshirt's drenched and clinging to my body. "So I hear you ran out of gas?"

"I was trying to make it to the full-serve near our house, but obviously I didn't."

"You're not the first to ever admit to that." I pull the door open and offer my hand. "Come on."

"But I've called Triple-A."

"And how much longer do you want to sit out here, waiting for them?"

She considers my callused palm, then slides her smooth one into my hand. She squeezes tight as I pull her out. "I have an umbrella," she offers.

I laugh, switching hands to rope my arm around her waist and keep her close to me as we run on the shoulder. Her body tenses against me. I can't tell if it's from the cold or the proximity. I usher her into the passenger side and stand in the rain, waiting for her to buckle up—another by-product of being raised by a police officer and a surgeon who have seen too many ejected bodies—before I shut her door and circle my car, my fingers grazing across the rain-splattered hood.

I shiver as I climb in. "Sorry it's not as nice as your ride."

"Does it have gas? Because if it does, I'll take it over my car right now," she jokes, pulling a tissue out of her purse to blow her nose. "Did Viktor send you?"

I grit my teeth and pull onto the road. "No. I caught the conversation. Figured I'd come find you."

"I didn't think so." She leans forward to inspect the heavy gray sky. "It hasn't let up all day, has it? It's depressing. I much prefer the sun."

"You're living in the wrong city, then."

She chuckles. "Tell me about it. I grew up in Seattle. Rain is what I know best." There's an awkward pause. "So, where'd you grow up?"

"In the interior. Small town called Sisters. Way more sun there."

"So you're a small-town boy in a big city."

"I guess you can say that."

"Do you miss it?"

"Yeah," I admit. "I'll move back again, one day." When I can buy my own piece of land so I'm not living under "the sheriff's" roof. Hopefully by then, he won't run the town anymore.

"I've heard it's stunning out there, all those wildflowers in the mountains. And horse ranches, right?"

"Yeah, my parents live right next door to one. Well, former ranch. The old woman who lives there now hasn't kept it going."

She sighs. "I've never seen a real horse up close."

"Really?"

"Yeah, really. My mom was terrified of them. Of their size.

She thought I'd be trampled to death. I've never been swimming in a lake, either."

Horses and lakes are what *I* know best.

"I think I'd like to live somewhere like that. One day. Lie out under those stars that you can't see here." She pauses. "I guess I'm a city girl who *should* have grown up in a small town. I feel like I've been living in the wrong life all these years."

I try to picture Alex—in her sparkly blue dress and exotic sports car—pulling up to Poppa's Diner in town, where three generations of families stuff their faces with grits and sausage every weekend, and every single person sitting in there has not only seen a horse but has probably grown up riding them. The image makes me smile. Then again, I know that these clothes, this car . . . it's not the real Alex. It's what Viktor has made her out to be.

"Your husband's an asshole. You should leave him." *Shit*. I didn't mean to say that out loud.

Her gaze drops to her hands resting in her lap, her fingers tugging at the thick diamond band. "I wish it were that easy."

Fuck it.

"He left you sitting on the side of the road."

She clears her throat. "He's right; it's my fault. I should have filled up twenty miles ago."

"No, Alex. I hope you don't believe that. If you do, then he really is right and you have no common sense." I catch the hurt flash across her features and immediately regret my words. "I'm sorry. I didn't mean that. Not that way. It's just . . . he's an asshole. He talks down to you. He was out fucking some bartender last night; we both know that." She flinches. "Hell, I've seen him slap you around!"

"I know," she admits in a whisper.

I sigh. "How much older is he than you, anyway?"

She turns away from me to look out the window. "He's forty-two. Twenty years older than me."

"You're only twenty-two?" I'm two years older than her. For some reason, I assumed she just looked young. I try to picture an eighteen-year-old Amber bringing home a guy like Viktor Petrova to meet my parents. To tell them that she's marrying him. My dad would have his gun out in under five seconds. Where the hell were her parents in all this? Who was there to say, "Whoa! Hold up. This guy is all wrong for you!" For all that my parents are and have been, they've always made sure I know where they stand on my choices and my mistakes.

"Do your parents like him?" I can't imagine *anyone* wanting their eighteen-year-old daughter to marry a man twenty years older.

She sighs. "I never met my dad, so I guess I don't need his permission."

"And your mom?"

"My mother would have married him for herself if he was willing." Her lips press together. "She worked right up until the day that she collapsed from cancer. Twenty-five years of working with cleaning chemicals. She died before the wedding. I have nothing, no one, without Viktor."

"And he knows it, Alex. Buying you expensive cars and jewelry doesn't give him any right to treat you like this."

"Well, what should I do, Jesse? Just pack a bag and leave?" She stares at her hands in her lap. "I want to finish school so I can get a real job first."

"So you're just going to put up with a cheating, abusive husband for how many more years? And what if he wants kids?"

"He doesn't, believe me." There's venom in her voice, and I can tell there's more to this topic of kids that she's not telling me. "He doesn't want me in school anymore. He said he's not paying the tuition. My job is to take care of him. That's why he married me. Apparently I haven't been doing that well enough since school started."

"I assume you signed a pre-nup?"

She shakes her head.

"Seriously? Well, hell! Take half his money and run!"

Another quick head shake. "I wouldn't even know how to ask for a divorce from Viktor. Besides, it's his money. He earned it."

"What do you know about that, anyway? About how he *earns* his money?" It feels like the wrong word to use in relation to Viktor Petrova.

She shrugs. "He owns a company with a few business partners. They sell all kinds of cars . . . trucks . . . even boats and stuff . . . for companies and for the public. They have sales offices all over the world."

"And you think it's all aboveboard?"

She pauses. "It's a publically traded company. They sell cars for insurance companies, dealerships, banks. It's all on his website."

So she's looked into it. I wonder if it was due to curiosity or doubt. I rephrase my question. "Do you think everything he's involved in is aboveboard?"

I get a look. A look that tells me she at least suspects that Viktor isn't necessarily on the straight and narrow with everything.

The gas station is seven miles up the road and we close the rest of the distance in silence. I make her wait in the car as I fill up a can I keep in my trunk.

The rain has eased up by the time we get back to the BMW twenty minutes later. She rolls down the window as the engine purrs again, tapping the gas gauge. "Do you think this is enough to get me to the gas station? The needle hasn't moved."

With my arm on the roof, I stick my head into the car to check it. "Yeah . . . It'll climb up in a second. But I'll follow you to the gas station and then home, just in case."

"Okay." Her breath tickles the side of my neck.

With only a second's consideration, I do what I shouldn't. I turn toward her parted lips. Her face is mere inches from mine, so close that I can see the red and gold flecks that give her eyes that unique color. So close that I barely have to lean in to kiss her.

I know that she is Viktor Petrova's wife.

But I don't care right now.

Because I want her to know who I really am.

Before I can change my mind, I lean in and let my mouth skate over hers, mimicking her own bold move from that night, a memory that I can't shake. It takes everything in me to pull away. When I do, I see the recognition in her eyes.

"Oh my God," she whispers, and her fingers find their way to my mouth. Her mouth is still hanging open, her own chest heaving.

This can't happen.

I slap the roof and sprint back to my car before I do something even more stupid than I already have.

———

The garage door closes softly behind her.

I should acknowledge her, say something. Not just stand there like an idiot, staring. But I can't help it. She's changed into a sweatshirt and track pants and washed all her makeup off. She looks like any other ordinary twenty-two-year-old, like a girl my sister might hang out with.

Or a girl I might want to wake up next to every morning.

Is this her attempt to make herself look less attractive? If so . . . it's not working. I finally manage, "You look comfortable."

"You don't." With hesitation, she practically tiptoes over to hand me the plain white T-shirt dangling from her fingertips.

I give her a pointed stare as I catch it. "I'm going to ruin that in sixty seconds." I haven't worn anything but black, gray, or navy blue in years.

"That's okay. He won't miss it, I promise." She pauses. "Besides, white will look good on you."

I'd already peeled off my soaked sweatshirt. I reach up over my head to pull my T-shirt off. And then I stall. She's watching me. Common sense tells me that undressing in front of Viktor

Petrova's young, hot wife in his garage—especially after what just happened out on the road—would be really stupid, not to mention disrespectful. Even though I'm shivering.

And the dickhead would deserve it for the way he treats her.

And I've already kissed her, so worrying about disrespecting him really should be the least of my worries.

Still . . . she's vulnerable and confused.

I drop my arms back to my sides.

"I should let you get back to work." The girl who babbled on about small towns and starry nights is gone with one simple kiss, leaving this one behind, who has crossed and uncrossed her arms three times since stepping out here.

She's nervous. I don't want her to be nervous around me.

She turns and takes five steps before her feet falter. "How long have you known?"

"Since the day you came into the shop with that damaged muffler."

"Hmmm . . . I hit that speed bump really hard, didn't I?"

That makes me laugh. On impulse, I scrawl my cell phone number on a sheet from Viktor's notebook and hold it out for her. "Here. In case you're ever stuck again."

"Do you think that's a good idea?"

"Probably not." *Definitely not.* "It's just a friend's cell number, Alex. Use it whenever you need to. For anything." She can read whatever she wants into that last part.

She quietly accepts the paper. Not until she's on the steps does she speak again. "When I saw you that first night at The Cellar . . ." Her words drift off. "I imagined that it was you on the side of the road. I hoped it was you."

I'm left standing in the middle of the garage, staring at a closed metal door.

My heart racing.

Placing Viktor's long list of parts on the table, I get in my car and take off for home, before I do something crazy.

SIXTEEN

JANE DOE

NOW

"It's most likely a memory. Or a hint of a memory. It could mean that the man who hurt me was also someone I once trusted. Maybe I loved him. Or . . ." I hesitate. "Maybe I was involved with two men, and one of them didn't take too well to it." When Dr. Weimer suggested that to me, I shook my head vehemently.

Would I have done something like that?

Meredith remains quiet, waiting for our left turn out of the hospital driveway, as I fill her in on the details of my appointment with Dr. Weimer. I suppose some people might not feel comfortable reciting the private conversation they had with their psychologist. The ideas they tossed back and forth about what a certain dream could mean.

I don't balk at telling Meredith, though. Maybe it's because she—the one who pieced my shattered body back together—now knows more about me than anyone else. Or maybe I've just come to value her opinion that much.

"I might not ever remember more than that." But I also might fall asleep one night and find myself trapped in a nightmare, reliving every painful second of my attack. A scary thought to have when you're closing your eyes at night.

"Only time will tell, I guess." She smiles warily at me as she pulls into the midday Bend traffic.

"Thank you for carting me back and forth like this. I know you must be tired." Meredith came home at seven this morning from a thirty-hour stretch at the hospital.

"It's really no problem. It's not like I was awake for my entire shift. I had a few hours off to sleep yesterday evening."

"Still, you and Sheriff Gabe, you keep treating me like . . ." Like I'm their child. Whose child am I? Is my mother even alive? I have to think not; otherwise she'd be looking for me.

Wouldn't she?

"You're good parents."

Meredith chuckles softly. "Tell that to my kids." The smile fades. "People think learning how to restart hearts and set bones and reattach blood vessels is hard, but let me tell you, it's nothing next to learning how to be a parent. And I've spent many years feeling like a horrible one. I can't tell you how many times I wished I was around more for my son."

"He's gotten into some trouble?"

A grimace touches her lips. "He made some bad choices, that's all. Nothing you need to worry about." She reaches out to tap the journal in my lap. "Chicken."

We pass a giant waving chicken—someone dressed in a costume—standing outside a fast-food restaurant. "Scary."

She chuckles. "Yes. That one certainly is. Both of my kids used to scream at anything in a costume when they were young."

"Well, I actually already used that word." I flip to the page where I tested myself one night after dinner with Ginny and read out loud. "Chicken equals *dry*. Potatoes equals *dry*."

Meredith's chuckles turn to full-fledged laughter and she glances at the page. "Beans equals *knuckles*?" That one didn't make much sense to me. The confusion on Meredith's face tells me it doesn't make much sense to her either. "What did Dr. Weimer say about that?"

"'That's *very* interesting,'" I say, mocking the British woman's lovely accent.

Several minutes of silence hang between us before Meredith suddenly says, "Baby."

Baby . . . baby . . . "Impossible."

"No." Meredith's stern gaze alternates between the road and my face. "I can tell you for certain, Jane, because I checked all the scans. You lost the baby due to the overall trauma to your body. It is *not* impossible for you to become pregnant again, when you're ready."

I quietly scribble the words down as Meredith drives along Highway 20 toward home, rambling on about my uterus and how protected those organs are, even in situations of rape. The truth is, the thought of me not being able to have children again never even crossed my mind. So why would that word be the first one to hit me? Why not "want," or "love" or "hold" or "protect"? Those are the emotionally loaded words coming to me now when I imagine cradling a baby, but they're so different from that first, instinctual response.

Why do I think a baby is impossible?

———

"Why don't we go to town together?"

Ginny's answering glare should be enough, but she tacks on a "What the hell for?" just in case I didn't get the message.

"I don't know. Something to do."

"*I've* got something to do." She drops her attention to her quilt, as if to prove a point. I can already see that this one—with blended shades of pink and purple forming a contrasting sky next to the snowy ground—will be entirely different from the one lying across my bed. Except for the giant black tree in the center. Ginny's signature.

I can see how someone might *think* she wants to just sit out here all day long. Ginny does. Literally. From the crisp early mornings to the twilight hours, she sits here, talking to herself and her dog, making quilts.

No wonder she's batty.

"Take the keys, go on into town," she says.

"I need my license."

"You don't need a damn license to drive around these parts. Just stay on the road and stop when the sign says 'stop.' Two lefts and two rights and you're there. Even a girl with amnesia can't get lost."

"I can't. Sheriff's orders," I admit with a sigh.

"What's he going to do, arrest you?" She snorts. "Gabe's always been a stickler for the rules, even when he was a little boy. He used to hang out by the stables in his cowboy hat and tattle to my father if I didn't spend enough time cleaning out each stall. I think the brat came out of his mother's womb wearing a badge."

I smile and try a different tactic. "You could see your quilt in the store window."

"I remember what it looks like just fine. I made it."

"Okay, well . . ." I drum my fingers across my knee. "Don't you want to see how the town has changed in the last ten years?"

"It hasn't changed. That's the problem. Still a bunch of whispering, gossiping fools who want to declare me unstable so they can steal my land."

"Have you always been so jaded?" I blurt out. I haven't spent much time in town yet, so maybe she's right, but . . . still!

"I guess you'd better get that license, fast. Or you'll be stuck here . . . with me." Shrewd eyes lift to offer me a look that says she's not any more excited about that prospect than I am right now. "Why don't you follow the stream and go down to the lake. Take the horses with you. That limpy leg of yours could use it." I'm halfway down the stairs when she calls out, "Just don't be fallin' into any gopher holes out there. *Jane*."

Ugh. That was *so* intentional.

———

My leg is throbbing by the time I reach the lake, but it was worth it. The cold blue water serves as a reflection pool, duplicating the picturesque backdrop of trees and mountains. I simply stand there, mesmerized.

"Come on," I say to the horses, waving a carrot in the air. Both are big fans. Their steps speed up at the sight of the treat. "Good boys." I pick my way through the longer grass to reach a sandy clearing by the water's edge. Though I haven't seen any, the last thing I need to do is step into an animal hole and break another bone.

Evidence of Amber out here with her friends sits in a circle in the sand—a man-made stone pit with a pile of ash nestled within. It's small. If it gets as dry as she says it does during the summer, then I guess nothing larger than this would be safe.

I crouch to test the shallow edge of the water with my fingertips. Ice cold, just like the stream. A person would die of hypothermia, diving in here right now. How much warmer does it get? Making a seat for myself on a nearby boulder, I look out over the water, trying to imagine myself growing up here. But it's hard. I have no experiences to draw from.

If this brain of mine doesn't want anything to do with the girl I was—as Ginny puts it—then I guess I'll have to let go and move on, make new memories. I need to meet new people, get a job. Maybe jump in this lake this summer. And camp under these stars. I tip my head back and take in the vast sky, closing my eyes to absorb the sun's rays that kiss my skin. We've hit a spring heat wave and, though the nights are still in the low 30s, the temperature has reached highs of close to 80 degrees.

I need a new name.

"I don't know why it's so hard," I say to both horses. "Ginny's right. Just pick a name and that'll be my name!" Rubbing Felix the Brown's muzzle, my gaze wanders over the lake again. "But that's the final straw, then." A new name is the official reset button. I'm abandoning the girl I was, everything about her, including hope that I'll find her again.

Leaning down, I skim the pebbles for a few small stones. I toss one stone, a second, a third, listening to the faint plunking sounds as they hit the water.

The *water*.

The idea blooms inside my mind, growing, sending a ripple of excitement through me.

It's been there all along.

———

"What's that smile for?"

I hold out the temporary ID.

Ginny scowls. "Don't be testing my patience now. Hand it on over."

I do, and then ball my fists under my armpits and hold my breath as she squints at the temporary driver's license that the nice man from the DMV issued me this morning. Sheriff Gabe had my identification papers finalized with the judge last week. Then he used his position to cut whatever red tape was required to get me a driver's license test. I earned a perfect score. The petite, dark-haired woman said that she would have thought I'd been driving for years.

I know when Ginny reaches the line that shows my new name because her scowl fades. "Water *Fitzgerald*?"

"I hope you don't mind, but I figured if we're going with the whole cousin story, then it might make sense." That's the official explanation that Meredith and I came up with. Second cousin, once removed, from Pittsburgh. I got hurt in a car wreck. It may keep the gossips at bay.

"Hmm . . . Smart thinking," she offers in an unusually soft tone. I wait for her to make some snide comment about my choice of first name. When she doesn't, I exhale in relief.

"So, if you don't mind, I'd like to take the truck out for a drive. I won't go far, I promise." I pat my phone in my fleecy pocket. "And I have my phone on me, just in case." I've left Ginny's ranch several times with Meredith and Sheriff Gabe, but now I'm desperate to wrap my hands around the old yellow truck's steering wheel and just drive off, with no destination in mind.

Ginny makes an unintelligible noise in response and then turns her focus back to her quilt, her slippered foot pushing off on the wooden floor to get the bench swinging again.

I don't wait another second. I walk as fast as I can and climb into the big truck. I've driven it up and down the driveway for mail a few times, so I'm ready to hear its struggle as I turn the key. Finally the diesel engine relents, kicking in with a slight rattling sound.

With a wave toward Ginny, I ease it into drive and give it gas.

She watches me roll by, her quilt resting on her lap, a slight smile on her lips.

SEVENTEEN

JESSE

THEN

"Jesse?" There's something about the way she says my name. It gets my blood pumping hard through my veins in an instant.

"Uh . . ." I roll my head to check on Boone, stretched out on the other side of the sectional, remote in hand. "Hey. What's up?"

"Were you planning on coming over to work on the car tonight?"

I check the digital numbers on the cable box. Nine thirty. I've done exactly what I planned on doing all day today. Sweet fuck all, while nursing a hangover. I went out to shoot some pool with a couple of buddies last night. I ended up drinking too much and comparing every woman who approached me to Alex. They all fell short. Needless to say, I came home alone. "No plans on it." It'll take Viktor a week or two—at least—to "appropriate" the parts, I'm sure. I pause. "Why?"

"Oh, I was just going to tell you not to bother. The power's out with the storm."

"Really?" This is the worst November I've seen in Portland yet. I'm surprised we haven't lost our power too. "It'll be back up soon, though, right?" Back in Sisters, when there's a good storm and it knocks our power out, it can be down for an entire night. But Viktor and Alex live in a rich neighborhood. I'm sure the rich get priority service, even with the electric companies.

"It was out for hours the last two times."

"So . . . what are you gonna do until then? Too early to go to bed, I guess?" There's not much else to do in a power outage except sleep and . . . well, I'm assuming Viktor isn't there.

"I've checked into a hotel. I can't sleep when the power goes out and I'm in the house alone."

"And you were going to be alone all night, weren't you."

"Yeah." I hear the hurt in her voice. I have a good idea why he's not coming home and I'm guessing she does, too.

Fingers snap to my left. Boone, mouthing, "Who's that?"

I answer him with a middle finger. Last thing I need is for him to know that Viktor Petrova's wife is calling me and it has nothing to do with a car. I'm guessing she just wants to talk.

Or maybe not.

I go out on a huge limb and ask, "You want company?"

There's a moment of hesitation, then, "Yes."

I spend all of three seconds evaluating whether this is a good idea. It is 100 percent *not* a good idea.

"Where are you?"

———

The second she opens the door into her dimly lit hotel room, the second I see her long, shiny blond hair, I feel the urge to tangle my fingers in it.

"Hey." She steps back just far enough to let me pass through, close enough that our shoulders brush and I catch her perfume. Much milder than what she wears to the club. From this vantage point, I have a good view down her loose purple top and I try not to stare.

"You look good. I mean . . ." Even in the shadowy entryway, her cheeks glow with a blush. She scans the soft, navy V-neck

I grabbed from Boone's closet while he was huddled under the small overhang outside on our balcony, having a smoke. It's better than anything I have. And tonight, I wanted to look good.

I let out a low whistle as I step into the room, my eyes taking in all the abstract patterns and dark colors. When I pulled my shitty Corolla into the lot of the RiverPlace Hotel, I knew the rooms would be *way* out of my price range. "How much does a night here cost?"

"Close to eight hundred for this room."

Jesus. "Nice view." I push back the black-and-white curtains to take in the dark silhouettes of docked sailboats along the river.

I sense rather than see her close the distance to stand right behind me. "Well, I figured that Viktor should at least pay for me to be in luxury while he's cheating on me." Her bitterness is palpable. Which explains what motivated her to pick a place like this.

"Is he? For sure?"

"I called the hotel he stayed in last time—when I found the receipt—and asked for them to put me through to Mr. Petrova. He answered on the fourth ring."

"He's not going to stop. You know that, right?"

"I do." So much resignation in those two words.

"So what are you going to do?"

She doesn't respond right away and when she does, it's not an answer. "Why am I not good enough, Jesse?" I can't imagine what it's like—to be twenty-two, beautiful, and married to a guy who has no intention of being faithful. He sure as hell doesn't go out of his way to hide it, either.

I admit, I knew what I was getting myself into when I scribbled her room number on a scrap of paper; when I stuck a couple of condoms into my wallet. Since hanging up the phone, I've felt like a live wire, exposed: just waiting to make contact with her so I can pass this current through me, so she can feel it too.

And when I turn around to meet her eyes, I know that she's

waiting for it. "You're plenty good enough, Alex. He's the problem. Not you."

The second my tongue touches her lips, she responds, opening to let me taste the inside of her mouth. There's no doubt she wants it. But when I slide my free hand under her shirt and up her back, pulling her tight into me, I can't ignore how stiff her body is. I break free to look down at her, at the wild mix of thrill and fear and nervousness dancing within her wide eyes.

What she said to me last night in the garage . . . I can read a lot into that, but I don't want to. I shouldn't. She's trapped in a shitty marriage with an asshole, she's kissing strangers on the side of the road—the girl's a head case right now. I don't want to confuse her, make things harder for her than they already are. "Is this *really* what you want?"

She lets go of my arms and takes three steps back to the bed. Turning off the one lit lamp in the room, leaving us with only the glow from the city lights outside the window, she pulls the hem of her shirt over her head and tosses it to the bench at the end of the bed. Her bra follows quickly, giving me a glimpse of a set of small but firm breasts, with perfect pink nipples. And then, gripping the waist of her pants, she shimmies them off, underwear and all.

A bare and trembling Alex sits down on the end of the bed and stretches her hand out for me. As if I wasn't hard enough, the rest of my blood rushes downward and I feel myself strain in my jeans. I don't think I could stop myself from going to her even if I tried. Still, why does this not feel right? I mean, I'm dying to get inside her, but something is setting off alarm bells inside my head right now.

Her hands immediately go for my belt and I yank my shirt off, tossing it onto the floor. Her eyes skate over my chest as adept fingers unbutton and unzip, pushing my pants and boxers down to my thighs. Her hot, wet mouth takes me in immediately.

"Damn." I close my eyes as my head falls back, remembering that arrogant asshole's comment yesterday about Alex's talents.

Now I know what's bothering me. Well, aside from the fact that we shouldn't be doing this, period. And that I'm thinking about her husband.

"Stop." I groan as I ease her mouth away from me. It takes me a few moments to slow my breathing. "You've never been with anyone other than Viktor, have you?"

She bows her head. When I slide my hand under her chin to lift her face and she twists away, I clue in and mentally kick myself. She thinks I'm rejecting her. She thinks I wasn't enjoying that.

That's not the issue at all.

The issue is that all she knows is an egotistical, demanding husband who has probably never even considered what she may want or need. I won't claim that I'm not a selfish person. Right or wrong, I want this. But I don't want it to be all about me. I drop to my knees in front of her and say, "Alex. Look at me."

Dejected eyes meet mine. "That's not what I meant by that question." I slip my hands around either side of her jaw. "What do *you* want? Right now, from me."

Tentative fingers reach up to touch my lips. "I want you to just kiss me for a while. A long while."

She wants to go slow. I pull her face down into mine, sliding my tongue past her lips, quickly losing myself in her mouth and her eager response, letting time tick away, fighting every urge I have to let my hands wander. Ten minutes, an hour, an eternity passes—Alex's lips are red and swollen—and then she eases herself back on the bed, her hands pinning mine to her face, pulling me with her, until we're both lying down. I can't help myself anymore, my fingers memorizing the firm, smooth curves of her breasts and the insides of her thighs.

And how ready she is for me.

She gasps against my mouth as I touch her for the first time, and then releases a soft, shaky breath before kissing me again, letting her legs fall apart.

If she told me that he's never bothered to touch her like this, I wouldn't be surprised.

But she won't be saying that about me.

When I try to break free from her mouth and move, her hand on the back of my head tightens and a soft "no" escapes. "Don't stop kissing me, please."

I smile, dropping my mouth into the crook of her neck. "I won't. I promise." Her body tenses only slightly when I start sliding down, her fingers gently digging into my back as my mouth leaves a wet trail the length of her body. She squirms lightly when I dip my tongue into her belly button.

And when I push my hands between her thighs and slide my tongue inside her, I'm pretty sure she stops breathing for a moment. But I don't stop, not until her muscles strain within my grasp, and her fingers tug at my short hair, and her pelvis bucks against me, and her entire body shudders.

I stretch out on my back alongside her, watching her chest heave with each ragged breath, her body lying limp. Wondering what's going on inside that head of hers as she stares up at the ceiling.

Finally she rolls her head to meet my gaze, her lips red and raw and so damn tempting, and my mouth is on hers again, and my body is covering hers, her thighs wrapped around my hips.

"Shit." I pull back just before I slide into her. It would be so easy to—she's so ready. "Hold on." I hang off the bed to grab my pants and fish a condom out of my wallet. I've never had issues opening one of these, but now I struggle to rip the foil open with my teeth as Alex's hot tongue slides up and down my throat. "Fuck," I groan, finally getting the package open and the condom on.

Locking eyes with her—because I need to know that she wants this as much as I do—I slowly push into her. My name escapes her lips, followed by a low moan that makes me swear under my breath. With parted lips, she watches me expectantly as I pull out and push back in again, deeper, earning another moan. She curls her hand around the back of my head and pulls me down to kiss her again. We keep that slow rhythm, our mouths breaking apart just long enough to let her little moans out, her arms and legs wrapped around my body, her thighs squeezing me tight, her nails dragging along my shoulders and back.

Until I can't hold out anymore.

"I didn't know it could feel like that," she whispers, her hands cradling the back of my head.

Neither did I. I rest my forehead against hers, both of us struggling to steady our breathing, our chests rising and falling together. Enjoying the intimate silence.

Until a tear touches my nose.

"Oh God. What have we done?" I feel the tension start to course back into Alex's limbs.

Pulling out of her, I yank the condom off and toss it to the floor—something I normally wouldn't do but right now, I don't want to let go of her long enough to find a trash can. I roll onto my back and scoop her into my chest, holding her tight.

"I'm sorry, Jesse. I don't know why I'm crying. I'm just . . ."

I kiss the top of her head. "You're just a good person."

"No, I'm not. Not after that."

"Do you think Viktor's lying in bed right now, crying over what he's doing?"

"It doesn't matter. I'm no better than he is."

I shut up and let her cry against my chest, watching the minute and hour digits on the clock change as her breathing grows slow and heavy with sleep and my own guilt sets in. I really like Alex—talking to her, laughing with her, just being around her.

Feeling her.

But tonight, I took advantage of this girl, even though I was trying not to. And I feel like a complete dickhead.

The sky begins to lighten when I carefully roll her off me. I pull my clothes on and after watching her sleep for a long moment—I don't know when I'll see her again—I leave, needing to get home to change before work.

I hope she doesn't hate me after this.

EIGHTEEN

WATER

NOW

The scent of lavender and sandalwood announces Dakota as she places a tall black coffee and a pastry in front of me.

"What a wonderful morning it is!" she exclaims with a broad smile, dropping her suede fringed purse onto the counter. In the three weeks since I started working at The Salvage Yard, the twenty-four-year-old shopkeeper has greeted me with those exact words every single day, rain or shine.

You would think that it might have gotten old by now. And yet it's a daily reminder that every morning *is* a wonderful morning. Because I shouldn't be alive to see it.

Short, natural fingernails curl around the top of a box. "Oooh! I've been waiting for Ms. Teal's jewelry. Is this it?"

I nod through a sip of coffee as she reaches in and pulls out several copper-colored bracelets made from guitar strings, her big doe eyes sparkling with excitement as she slides them onto her wrist. The shop is tiny and jam-packed with all kinds of recycled merchandise, from jewelry to clothing to furniture. And, of course, Ginny's quilts, which I found out are made from discarded scraps of fabric from a local sewing store.

"What do you think, Water?" She holds up her arm to display the various pieces.

"They're beautiful." Especially against her naturally dark Native American skin. She says she's only one-quarter Chinook, but it must be an awfully big quarter, given her exotic dark features, thick black hair, and svelte figure. I would describe her more as hippie by choice, though, opting for flowing maxi dresses and Birkenstock sandals and a makeup-free face.

She drove back to Sisters from San Francisco in her 1982 VW Beetle seven months ago after the great-aunt who raised her and owned The Salvage Yard died, leaving her the shop. Dakota expects to head south again one day, but right now she's enjoying "being back with nature."

I think that's why, the day I walked in here with Meredith and introduced myself as Water, she offered me a job on the spot, saying something about the stars aligning and a kismet connection, her slightly glazed eyes getting this dreamy look in them.

The rumor that Dakota smokes a lot of weed is not so much rumor as fact.

Luckily for me, my hippie boss believes in things like gut feelings instead of résumés and references. She also doesn't believe in paying taxes, so I'm handed cash every second Friday.

"They'll go fast with the tourists. Just you wait." She slides the jewelry off her wrist. "All of this stuff will."

I help her cut open the rest of the boxes delivered over the last week, pulling out hemp-woven bags, log lamps, and metal sculptures, until my fingertips grasp a coarse fabric.

This feels . . . I pull the material out and find a red-and-blue checkered blanket. I rub one corner between my fingertips, the strange blend of soft and rough textures pricking my skin.

"Those are wool, from the McMillan farms, about twenty miles south of here. We get a dozen each spring and they're snapped up within weeks."

An eerie tingle runs through my body, holding the blanket in my hands. When it comes times to pull them all out and lay them on a table, I find I can't let the red-and-blue one go. But the price tag Dakota just stuck on one is more than I make in a week! "Is there any chance I can set one of these aside until I have enough money to buy it?"

She smiles. "Why don't you take it home tonight and I'll just deduct a quarter from your next four pays. At cost for you, of course."

"Thank you." I know I'll have to remind her or she'll forget. I tuck it under the counter with my purse and then continue my work, hanging the rest of the bracelets.

Dakota hums to herself, reviewing a small notebook she keeps tucked in the old cash register. She doesn't believe in computers. "How's Ginny doing with her quilts?"

"She's been working hard." I set to break apart the cardboard box.

"And you? How is your new hobby?"

"I think I need to come up with another one." Ginny showed up at my door one night two weeks ago with a bag of scrap material, a ruler, and a "cutter." She started me off by showing me how to make basic squares. That was easy. Last week, she showed me how to stitch the squares together.

I've learned that I'm not the most patient person.

Apparently I also stitch like a drunk, according to Ginny.

The bell hanging over the door jangles and my stomach tightens just a little. I automatically shift my stance and shake my hair forward. I do this anytime someone walks into the shop. That's the problem with having a long scar line running down the length of your face. The concealer provides marginal help, but it can't hide the creases when I smile. At least I don't have a giant gap in my teeth anymore.

"Dakota Howard. Well, I'll be damned. Look at you!" the tall dark-haired guy who just walked in announces, straightening the collar of his black coveralls, a tag that reads "Fanshaw Electrical" sewn into the breast pocket. "When Dad told me you called for some wiring issues, I had to take the job."

Her face pinches up with recognition. "Chuck?"

He grins. "You bet! How long has it been?"

"You were a couple of years ahead of me in school, so . . . maybe eight years, I guess?"

That's the thing about a town like Sisters: everyone knows everyone. And everything about everyone. It's a miracle I've kept my own situation under wraps.

Chuck stops in front of the counter and throws me a wink. "Who's your lovely coworker?"

"This is Water. Ginny Fitzgerald's cousin, who moved here a few weeks ago from . . . ?" She squints in thought.

"Pittsburgh," I fill in. I feel bad for lying to Dakota, as nice as she is.

Chuck's eyes widen. "Crazy Tree Quilt Lady?"

"The one and only." I force a smile. Yes, she may be crazy, but she has her share of reasons and it bothers me that people call her that so openly.

"Dad says he saw Old Fitzgerald's yellow truck driving through town but figured Ginny had sold it, given she hasn't been seen in years. She still have those horses?"

"Just the two."

"She's nuts for not selling off some of that land, or at least taking in some boarders. My pops drove out there one day to suggest it to her." He chuckles. "That didn't go over too well."

"Let me guess. She chased him away with a broom?" He's right—renting those stables would be great for her, financially. But that would mean people coming onto her property, and *everyone* knows how Ginny feels about that.

"You should talk her into it. I know lots of people who'd be interested."

"I'll mention it to her," I offer, though I'm not sure I will. That will earn a thirty-minute rant about nosy Sisters townspeople.

"She's got over a thousand acres, last I heard. It's worth a mint, so close to the mountains. Get on her good side and maybe she'll leave it to you when she kicks it."

"Uh . . ."

"What's it like, living with that old nut, anyway?" They're both looking at me as if they expect me to pull up a chair and start listing all of Ginny's quirks.

"It's great. She's been very kind to me." I begin rearranging the jewelry rack to make room for the new bracelets.

I guess Chuck gets the hint. "So, Dakota . . . you called about a problem with your stereo system?"

Dakota throws her hands in the air. "Please! It just stopped working one day and this silence is driving me insane!" She leads him back through the beaded curtain, giving him a chance to do a once-over, his gaze lingering on her ass.

"No wonder it quit. How old is this thing?" I hear Chuck exclaim from the cramped storage room/office. The stereo system hasn't been working since I started here. Neither has the security camera, which Dakota says is just a dummy anyway, to scare off thieving thirteen-year-olds.

The bell jangles over the door and Amber walks in with a quilt folded over her arm. "Hey! Why aren't you sleeping?" I ask. Amber's been working a stretch of night shifts. Her red Mini usually pulls into the Welleses' driveway around the same time that I'm filling the horse trough with grain and fresh water each morning.

"I picked up a day shift tomorrow, so I need to stay up until tonight." She hands me the quilt.

I shake my head. "I don't know how you do it, Amber."

"Reminding myself that I'm going to be traveling the world next year with ease. That's how I do it." She hands me the quilt— the blue-and-green one Ginny's been working on all week. "Ginny said to put it in the display window."

I can't help but smile. The woman doesn't own this shop, but she acts like she does. I lay the quilt out over the table of wool blankets. The token tree is there, as always, with gold and green fields stretching into the horizon.

It's just like all the others—except this one has two tiny horses in the far distance, one black, one brown.

Amber digs into her pocket and pulls out a piece of paper. "The artist sent this with me. You forgot the grocery list on the porch."

"Let me guess . . ." Sure enough, the same three things top the list. "When will she stop doing this!"

"When she's six feet in the ground, and knowing Ginny, that won't be for another fifty years."

After *two weeks* straight of dried-out chicken legs, mealy instant potatoes, and beans from a can, I politely offered to cook dinner one night, as a thank-you to her. I wasn't even sure I knew how to cook, but I figured it was worth a shot.

Ginny grumbled but then relented—admitting that she hated cooking—and I set out, borrowing a cookbook from Meredith, getting ingredients for a beef stew that looked easy enough and using my '70s kitchenette for the very first time.

I may not remember ever cooking, but it turns out I'm pretty good at it. By Ginny's second helping, she agreed.

I suffered through a few more days of "Ginny's Classic" and then, when it was time for Meredith to go grocery shopping, I insisted on doing it. Ginny gave me two folded twenty-dollar bills and a grocery list with three items: two pounds of chicken thighs, five boxes of instant mashed potatoes, and seven 14-ounce cans of Heinz baked beans in tomato sauce.

I humored her by picking them up, but I also used my first paycheck to grab ingredients for several recipes I wanted to try. When I dropped her groceries off at her doorstep that day, I asked if I could cook again that night.

That was almost three weeks ago. We've since fallen into this routine where she hands me a list on Thursday night and I go grocery shopping on Friday after work. In that time, I've happily cooked every night and brought the dishes down to her front porch. And yet she still gives me a list with chicken, potatoes, and beans, even though I've now stopped buying them.

Amber glances at her watch. "I've gotta go. I have a hair appointment."

"So, movie this weekend, right?" We try to go for coffee or out to a movie at the Bend theater at least once a week, if her crazy work hours permit it. She even took me horseback riding on Felix the Brown a few times.

"No, better." Her eyes lights up. "A couple of my girlfriends are coming back into town for the Memorial Day long weekend. We'll all go out, okay?"

"Maybe? I guess?" The same nervous blip of excitement and trepidation stirs inside me as it does every time I'm around new people. Which is everyone.

She reaches out and squeezes my shoulder, a gesture that she's obviously learned from her mother. "It'll be fine. I promise."

A sudden blast of rock music spills out of the speakers and we both jump.

"Have fun," Amber whispers wryly and heads quickly out the door.

Dakota pushes through the bead curtain a few moments later. "So are you going to charge me seventy-five dollars for being stupid, Chuck?"

"Lucky for you this is a small town and I'm related to my boss. I'll see what I can do about waiving the fee. Just make sure you check the plugs next time, okay, Dakota?"

She salutes him, her face a picture of chagrin.

"And tell Ginny that the Fanshaws say hi," he says to me as he walks past, throwing me another wink before passing through the door. I guess he's a winky kind of guy.

"Oh, wow! How'd this get here?" Dakota traces the edge of the black horse on the new quilt with her finger.

"Amber Welles."

"Hmmm . . . sheriff's daughter, right? I remember her." Dakota's even tone and calm demeanor don't give much away. "She was one of the popular girls. Honor roll. Rodeo Queen. Really into sports. On all the school councils, running all the dances. You know the kind, right?"

"Right," I lie, pulling down the other display quilt. *Rodeo Queen?* I haven't heard about that.

"Some of her friends were a bit much, though. Very self-absorbed. A few ranch princesses, too. They're a nice family, though, aren't they? The Welleses, I mean."

"Yeah." I can't explain just how nice they are without divulging information I don't care to share, even with someone as seemingly harmless as Dakota. So I simply say, "They're great."

"Have you met her brother?"

"Jesse? Yeah. Well, not really. I've met him, but he hasn't been around much." Actually, I haven't seen Jesse since the middle of April, when he waved at me and then peeled out of the driveway. Every weekend, when I wake up and go down to feed and groom the Felixes, I check the garage next door, tucked in amongst the trees. He's never there.

"He's cute, that one. Looks like his daddy."

"He is," I agree. Except, when I hear "cute," I think of Felix's kittens bounding after their mother, their hinds tipping and spilling because they haven't grown into their feet. But Jesse, with his dark eyes, his strong jaw, the way his body moves . . .

Jesse is gorgeous.

I think somewhere deep inside, I knew that the first moment I saw him.

"What a troublemaker, though."

"I keep hearing that. What do you know about him?" I ask casually.

"Oh, you know how it is. The smaller the town, the bigger the mouths. I don't know what's true and what's rumor. Being the sheriff's son, people loved talking about him and he seemed to love giving people something to talk about." She takes a sip of her coffee and waves at Ms. Milliken, the florist from down the street, her eyes glazing over slightly.

"Dakota?"

"Hmm?" She turns to look at me. "Oh, right. Jesse. Well, he used to hang out with these two hooligans—Ian and Dirk—and everyone knew them as a trio of trouble. Anytime something happened in town, you could guarantee that those three were involved. But . . . Jesse always seemed different from those two. They were loud and obnoxious and . . . rude. Jesse wasn't. He was just there, usually hanging back, more cool and composed." She pauses to take a gulp of her coffee. Dakota drinks her coffee fast. "So when Tommy Myers was stabbed at that party—"

"What?" Stabbed?

Dakota nods. "Yeah, that was a big deal for this town. I don't know exactly what happened, but there was this house party and Tommy got stabbed on the street after a fight. Sheriff Welles threw Ian, Dirk, and Jesse behind bars. Ian and Dirk said it was Jesse who stabbed Tommy. There were no other witnesses except them, and Tommy was in a coma."

Jesse *stabbed* someone? "What about fingerprints?"

"It was winter. They all had gloves on. But Tommy survived. Whatever he told the sheriff got Jesse off and put Ian and Dirk in jail, like the dirt bags they are."

My face twists with horror.

"I know, right? Tommy's fine now. Living in Bend and married, the last I heard. Likes to show his scars at parties." Her eyes flicker to the side of my face. I quickly turn to the window display, setting the old quilt gently on the floor.

"What a mess, though. Jesse's father almost lost the next election, and everyone knew it was because of that whole fiasco with his son. I can't imagine it was easy for Jesse being at home after that."

I think I now know why he stays in that apartment above the attic.

"It could just be coincidence, but my uncle's neighbor's friend owns a security company and he said that Ginny had bars put up on her windows not long after. Apparently, she didn't feel safe with Jesse living next door, even out there in the middle of nowhere."

I sigh. So *this* is how rumors spread in a small town.

"I think I slept with him at a party."

What? My jaw drops and my stomach begins to churn. "You *think* you slept with Jesse Welles?"

Dakota cocks her head. "What? No! Chuck." She points out the window. There's Chuck, leaving Poppa's Diner across the street.

Relief swells in my chest. But why do I care who Jesse may have slept with?

"In fact, I'm pretty sure I did. My junior year? Or maybe sophomore?" Amber suggested that the "Dakota stories" extended beyond laced brownies and five-leafed plants in her backyard and into the beds of many guys, both in high school and older, both married and not. Dakota has called herself a "free spirit" on more than one occasion, so this shouldn't surprise me.

It certainly doesn't sway me. I still like her. Plus, who am I to judge? Maybe I was a "free spirit" too. Thanks to the baby that I lost, I know that I wasn't a virgin when I was attacked, though I may as well be for all I remember. And given that no one seems to be looking for me, I must not have been in a relationship. But who have I slept with? Just the father of my child? Was there anyone else before him?

"Water? Are you okay?"

I realize that I'm standing in the window like a mannequin, and two elderly ladies are staring at me. "Yeah. Fine." With a brief wave to them, I pick the quilt up off the floor. "So what was wrong with the stereo?"

"Oh! It was unplugged. I must have bumped it somehow." She disappears behind the curtain once again to begin flipping through the stations. "So, what kind of music do you like?"

I frown. "I don't know." There aren't any radios at Ginny's. She prefers complete silence and curses Sheriff Gabe when she can hear country music playing from his car. Meredith always has talk radio on. Amber likes pop music. I heard alternative rock coming from the garage when Jesse was there. If I had to pick, I'd probably go with that.

Dakota's head pokes out from around the beaded curtain. "What do you mean, you don't know?"

I smile. "I'm easy. Pick whatever you want."

"Good. Call me weird, but I'm really digging trance lately." A hypnotizing electronic sound pumps through the speakers.

It slides down my spine like a cold, wet finger.

And now I know what kind of music I definitely don't like. Not at all.

NINETEEN

JESSE

THEN

"Welles!"

I peer out from the engine I've been buried in all afternoon to see Miller approaching me. "Mr. Petrova wants you at his house."

My face screws up. "What for?" I left him a full-page list on Saturday night. I'm guessing some of that stuff will take weeks to get in.

Shit.

Did Alex come clean with him? A guy like Viktor would probably beat the hell out of her and then come after me.

I get no answer from Miller. Slipping my phone out of my pocket, I tap out a text to Alex, leaving greasy fingerprints on the screen.

V wants me to come over tonight. Do you know if he got parts?

I don't want to put much more in writing, in case Viktor ever snoops through her phone. I drop it into my breast pocket and stare at the engine I've been working on, wondering if I need to be worried, while I wait.

Ten minutes later, my phone vibrates. I hold my breath.

Some boxes arrived today and he had them dropped in the garage.

"Thank fucking God," I mutter, hanging my head, my chest suddenly lighter. It shouldn't surprise me that the guy can get impossible-to-find, incredibly rare parts in less than forty-eight hours.

A second text comes in a moment later:

I won't ever say anything. I promise.

Guilt swells for doubting her. I answer:

I'll see you tonight, I guess?

It's a full minute before I get a response.

I can't ever do that again. I was hurt and wanted to do something hurtful. It was wrong.

I sigh and type out:

I know. It's okay.

It's not okay. Because it's only been seven hours since I left the hotel and I miss her. Because I already want her again. And because I want to believe that what happened between Alex and me was more than simply her getting even.

———

The Shelby sits in front of the garage when I pull up to Viktor and Alex's house.

"Jesse!" he exclaims, waving at me from the walkway. It's so unlike him, I wonder if he's drunk on a Monday at six p.m. "I am glad Miller gave you my message."

"So you got the parts already?"

He smiles. A snakelike look. "Connections, my friend."

I'm not his friend, but what the fuck ever. The sooner I'm done with this job, the better.

"I am waiting on a few more, but you should have plenty to get started on. Now, if you will please excuse me, it is time for me to enjoy one of my babies. It has been too long since I have taken her out." He cracks open the front door and bellows, "Alexandria!" Shutting it, he strolls toward me. "My wife hates going for rides with me. She complains that I drive too fast. It scares her." He climbs into the Shelby and cranks the engine, the sound of it coming to life a thing of sheer beauty.

I'm in the garage when I hear the front door close and the clicking of heels on concrete. Moments later, she appears in a cotton-candy pink coat, black pants, and ridiculously high shoes. Just the sight of her back gets my blood roiling, because I know what she looks like, what she feels like, what her skin smells like, under all that.

"Hurry up, Alexandria!" Viktor barks and her heels immediately click faster, until she's practically running. That's probably why she drops her keys. She stoops to pick them up.

And her fat bottom lip stares at me. She tried to cover it with makeup, but it may as well have a spotlight on it.

I walk to the Aston Martin, gritting my teeth as rage boils inside me, ready to take a wrench to the car. I don't know how she got it, I remind myself. But I do know that she didn't have it when I left her in bed this morning.

She'll probably lie to me anyway. Tell me she walked into a wall or something.

And regardless, I can't say a damn thing. It would probably only earn her a few more punches and cause me some definite problems. For one, I could kiss my job goodbye, given Viktor's close connections with Rust. I'd also lose any chance of getting paid for the work I've done so far, not to mention my Barracuda.

But I don't really care about me right now.

A door slams and then the Shelby peels out of the driveway. An angry horn blast at the bottom makes me think Viktor probably cut someone off as he jumped onto the road.

If Alex doesn't like his driving, she's probably terrified right now.

"Fuck!" I throw the wrench against the concrete floor.

———

Why do you have a fat lip?

Viktor and Alex came racing back up the driveway about an hour later, Alex's face as white as a blank page of paper. She ducked her head and ran inside. I didn't see her again to ask, but I have to know. Even if she gives me a lame answer.

I'm beginning to think she's asleep when my phone dings.

I let my phone die last night and Viktor couldn't get ahold of me.

"You've got to be . . ." I want to launch my phone at the wall. Instead, I type out:

He was worried about you so he hit you?

No. He wanted his pinstripe suit laid out for a breakfast meeting and he expected his wife to be home to do it for him.

A second text comes through quickly after:

You can't say anything, Jesse. It won't end well for either of us.

Tossing my phone on the far end of the bed, I storm across the room, pushing Boone's door open. "Do you know that the fucker beats his wife?"

Boone, on the floor in nothing but shorts, pauses mid-crunch. He never misses his daily workout, even on days when he hits the gym. I've seen him come home from the bar annihilated and drop for a hundred reps. "Who?"

"Your man crush, Viktor Fuckhead Petrova."

He flops to the floor and reaches back to give Licks a belly rub. By the muscles straining against his abdomen, I'd say Boone's already done most of his reps for tonight. "Are you surprised? You saw him slap her at the bar."

"So . . . what? You think it's okay?"

"Of course I don't, but what the hell am I supposed to do?" He scowls at me.

"You should have seen her lip tonight."

Boone just stares at me.

I throw my hands in the air. "What?"

"Nothin', man—I've just never seen you get heated about anyone before. You usually don't give a fuck." He starts in on his crunches again. "Why doesn't she leave him?"

"She's twenty-two, Boone. She thinks she's trapped."

"Trapped with a whole lot of fancy shit," he puffs out.

"The guy treats her like a servant and he hits her. She made a mistake, marrying him."

He pauses, resting on his elbows, regarding me with recognition in his eyes. "And are you making an even bigger mistake? Because fucking with Viktor Petrova's wife will not end well for you, my friend . . ." He shakes his head, his mouth open like he's holding back from saying something. "Just make sure it's worth it."

"I'm not doing anything with Alex," I lie.

His brow pops up. "She goes by Alex now?"

"Alex, Alexandria. Whatever. The point is . . ." What is the point? Viktor beats his wife and . . . what? "The point is don't ever repeat any of this to Rust or anyone else because he will probably hurt her for it."

"Repeat what? I didn't hear shit." He rolls over onto his stomach for his push-ups.

I head back to my room, slightly more calm. Checking my phone, I see that Alex hasn't texted again and I don't know how to respond to her just yet, other than to say, "Call the police and leave the asshole." My gut tells me Viktor would get off and Alex would pay for reporting him.

Reaching over my head, I peel my shirt off. Kicking off my jeans, I drop to the ground for my own set of push-ups. I have no specific rep number, though. I figure I'll just keep going until I can work this shit out in my head.

I wake up at some point in the middle of the night, facedown on the floor beside my bed, having pushed myself to exhaustion.

And having no answer.

TWENTY

WATER

NOW

The old Chevy truck comes to a sputtering halt on the now familiar dirt road.

I check the dashboard. All needles point down.

This isn't good.

A glance in the rearview mirror confirms that I'm alone. I'm not surprised. I'm about seven miles from home, surrounded by fields and trees. I rarely ever pass anyone out here.

Reaching down, I turn the key to "off" and then try to crank the engine again. All I get in return is a clicking sound. I flop back against the bench with a heavy sigh.

Ginny's truck is dead.

And I've got the week's groceries sitting in the back. It's too far to carry them, especially with an arm that's still weak, although my leg has been better lately. I check my watch. A quarter after five. There's no way I can get home and get dinner in front of Ginny in time, and I can't even call her to warn her, because she doesn't have a phone. Thank God for neighbors.

I dig my cell phone out of my purse to call Amber. It isn't until I see the blank screen that I remember I forgot to charge it at work earlier. "Dammit!" I cry out, slapping my steering wheel in frustration. I've been so good about plugging it in for the afternoon.

Until today.

Because today, all I could focus on was that low, hypnotic rhythm over the stereo system and the ball of anxiety sitting in my stomach.

It's a clue. I know it.

I lied to Dakota. I told her I loved trance. I pleaded with her to keep it playing all day, desperate for a bigger sliver of insight—a flashback, a clearer feeling.

But all the incessant music did was grow that ball of dread bigger and stronger, making it impossible to ignore.

And now I'm stuck on an old dirt road with a broken truck and no phone.

I rest my head on the worn steering wheel. Ginny's going to freak. When she says she wants dinner at six o'clock sharp, it's not just an expression. It took me a few weeks to realize that her eyes are actually glued to the minute hand of her watch and if her meat dish—because there's no such thing as dinner without meat in Ginny's eyes—doesn't hit the table on time, she starts pacing and fidgeting.

It's not my fault. She knows as well as I do that this old thing was running by the grace of God and nothing more. On the way home from work last week, it started making a rattling sound, like something was loose in the engine. I mentioned it to her. She merely shrugged and asked me if it got me where I needed to go.

Up until now, it has.

How am I going to get to work tomorrow? Dakota needs me there. It's the first Saturday that the farmers' market is open, so the shop will be busy.

How am I even going to get home?

I'm not, until someone comes by and I wave them down. Someone I know. Otherwise, what will I do? Get into the car with a stranger? "It's okay, Water," I coach myself through slow breaths—like Dr. Weimer told me to do whenever I feel panicked. "You're in Sisters, Oregon. You're perfectly safe. Your truck just broke down. It's a normal thing. It can happen to anyone."

Except, I'm not just anyone. I'm the girl who was dropped off in an abandoned building parking lot not far from here and left for dead.

A low rumble in the distance, like thunder, and a dust cloud marks the approach of a car. A few seconds later, black paint shines in the late-day sun.

Relief slams into me. I know that car. It's Jesse. He'll recognize me. He'll stop.

Won't he?

With a hint of trepidation, I scurry out of the driver's side and round the truck to stand next to the tailgate, butterflies in my stomach as I watch the car near. I don't really know this guy at all. Sure, he's Gabe and Meredith's son. Sure, he waved at me. Once. Sure, he brought over all that firewood. But he's also the black sheep of the Welles family, of the entire town.

The sports car comes to a stop about ten feet away, its engine grumbling.

I hazard a slight wave. Not really a wave. More a tentative hand held in the air.

He kills the engine and slides out of the car, his body lean and muscular in a pair of jeans and faded black T-shirt.

"Hi . . . Jesse, right?" I've never actually talked to him directly, and yet it feels so natural to use his name.

"What're you doing out here?"

With my panic at being stranded and the subsequent thrill over being rescued, I temporarily forgot about my face. Now, though, standing in front of him, I casually brush my hair forward. Gesturing over my shoulder with my thumb, I explain, "Ginny's truck just died. I don't know what happened."

He smirks. "You didn't run out of gas, did you?"

"No! I mean . . . I don't think so." It sounds like he's teasing me. I hope I didn't do something so stupid. Then I remember stopping at the local full-serve on Wednesday. "No. It's at least three-quarters full."

I follow him as he moves to the front of the truck and lifts the hood, his arms straining against the weight until he has it propped open. A chill is settling with the early evening. I fold my arms across my chest to ward it off as I study Jesse from the side, while he tests various wires with the ease of an expert.

I would never guess he and Amber are twins. He's definitely Sheriff Gabe's son, though, with that same olive complexion, the strong jaw, and the tiniest cleft in his chin. He really is a good-looking guy.

And I'm staring at him.

"You look like you know cars," I blurt out.

"I know a little bit."

He doesn't seem overly chatty, and yet this strange, giddy feeling inside compels me to say *something*. "You haven't been back for a while."

"You noticed?"

"Yeah. I mean . . . no. I mean . . . Meredith said you come home on weekends but you didn't, so . . ." And now I'm rambling.

Jesse disappears behind the driver's-side door. Seconds later, I hear that clicking sound again. He reappears, pulling the prop down and letting the hood slam shut. "It's your alternator," he informs me, lifting his hands to inspect them. "And a dozen other things."

Alternator? "I don't know car-speak. Is that a big deal?"

"Could be worse." Jesse turns to face me, his dark eyes boring into mine. I automatically turn to give him my better profile. "Come on. I'll give you a ride home." He starts pulling the grocery bags out of the truck bed and carries them to his car in one arm, the muscles chording beautifully. He uses his free hand to pop his trunk. When I reach the passenger side, he's already standing there, holding the door open.

The scent of leather and mint fills my nostrils as I slide into the passenger seat. Jesse waits for me to buckle my seat belt before he pushes the door closed—that's rather nice, and unexpected—and then strolls around the front, his fingers sliding across the hood as he passes.

The gesture is familiar.

I'm momentarily distracted by the car's interior—the soft black ceiling, the chrome gear stick, the wide backseat that now holds two large duffel bags—but that familiarity lingers. In fact, as I reach forward to skim the dash, it's even stronger. Could this car be reminding me of some part of my life?

It only intensifies when Jesse cranks the engine and the vibrations reach deep into my chest.

"You all right?"

I smile. "Yeah, I'm good."

He shifts into first gear and the car lurches forward. I instinctively brace myself, one hand grabbing the door while I reach for the console with the other, and accidentally grab his forearm, his skin hot against my fingertips. I pull back immediately, feeling my cheeks flush. "Sorry."

He says nothing, throwing the car into second and then third gear, before reaching up to tune the radio. "Any preference?"

"No." I quickly correct, "Just no trance music."

Jesse swerves to avoid a pothole, tossing me back and forth a little. "Why not?" He sounds wary.

"I'm not sure, honestly." How much has Jesse's family told him about me? He knows I was in the hospital, but what else does he know?

Drums and guitars fill the speakers and I sigh with relief. I keep my eyes on the mountain range ahead as I absorb the beat, feeling Jesse's gaze flicker between the road and my face several times. Thank God he can only see my good side.

"You saved me from a very long walk, so . . . thanks."

He's quiet for a moment. "No problem."

I keep my eyes forward until he turns into the Welleses' driveway. "Ginny doesn't want my car in her driveway," he explains.

Or you. "Yeah, she might have mentioned that before, once or twice."

"Or a hundred times, I'm sure," he mutters.

When we pull around to the back of the Welleses' house—which they use as the front, with a giant sliding glass door off the kitchen—Sheriff Gabe is standing next to his cruiser, watching us. He doesn't look happy.

What would it have been like, throwing your own son in jail? Being told that he had stabbed another teenager? No wonder they seem to have a strained relationship. I can't imagine either has recovered completely from that experience.

Jesse hops out of the car to meet his dad head-on. No fear.

"I thought we agreed," Sheriff Gabe says in a low, ominous tone.

"Ginny's truck broke down," I blurt out, pushing open the heavy door, feeling like I need to jump in and protect Jesse from his father's anger. "Jesse, can I get my groceries, please?"

He pops the trunk and grabs the bags before I have a chance to reach for them.

"Where do you think you're going with those?" Sheriff Gabe hollers after his son.

Jesse doesn't bother stopping. "You want her to carry them all by herself?"

"I can make two trips," I call out. Jesse ignores me and keeps heading toward the fence. I'm forced to speed walk—awkwardly—to catch up.

"I should probably bring these up to your place," he says, throwing his long legs over the old wooden rails.

"That's fine. I cook dinner there anyway." Except for a few

toiletries, a bag of oatmeal, and a tub of Nutella for Ginny's daily breakfast and lunch, I would have brought it all up here.

He slows, allowing me to pass and head to my stairs, which are on the back side of the garage and not visible from any part of Ginny's house.

My skin begins to tingle as I lead Jesse into my apartment. If he feels at all uncomfortable, he doesn't let on, walking right in until he's standing in the very center, his eyes taking in the little that I have.

"I'll pick up a new alternator and get the truck running again for you," he offers, setting the bags down on the floor by the fridge.

"You know how to fix it?" I ask, grabbing a pot to fill with water for the pasta, hoping it'll come to a boil by the time I've put the groceries away.

"Yeah, I think I can handle it."

I glance over my shoulder to find him pulling out the blue-and-red plaid wool blanket. "I just got that today. It's so nice and—"

"Warm," he finishes for me. I can see his Adam's apple bob from here. "I used to have one exactly like this."

"Well, Dakota got a dozen in this week, so you can always pick up another one." I pull out the small saucepan of pasta sauce and throw it onto the stove, fumbling with the dials. "Thank you for your help with the truck. I'm sure Ginny will appreciate it." In her own unorthodox way. "Cars are complicated, aren't they? All those parts to figure out. It's like science."

I hazard another glance over my shoulder and find Jesse staring at me, his head cocked to the side and a strange look on his face. What is it, exactly? Wonder? Curiosity? His attention shifts to my scar and I duck my head back toward the stove, letting my hair fall to veil it. "Any chance you'll be able to fix it before ten tomorrow morning?" I ask, half-jokingly, as I stir.

"You've gotta be somewhere by then?"

"Yeah, at The Salvage Yard. I work there."

"How do you like it?"

"It's good. Dakota's really nice."

"She is. I remember her from high school. I don't know if she actually ever went to class, though. She just sat up on the hill, smoking weed most of the time."

"I think she still does that, just not on a hill," I joke.

The floor creaks with his approaching footsteps until he's standing directly behind me, setting my hair on end.

"How are you liking it here, Water?" he finally asks.

"It's great. The mountains, the town, your family. Even Ginny. It's all great." What must he think of me? I keep my eyes on the stove as I ask, "How much do you know? About what happened to me?" I still get a lump in my throat when I talk about it. I don't even have to get into specifics.

"I know enough." Sizzles sound from the stove as water begins bubbling and spilling over. "It smells good." Jesse takes a step closer and reaches around me to lift the lid. I glance up to catch a wistful smile touch his lips. "I should go. God knows Ginny will skin me alive if she knows I'm in here."

"And me too, for letting you in," I agree.

I watch his back as he strolls out, a pang of *something* curling around my heart.

Wondering why I reacted to his proximity like that.

Wondering if it should have bothered me.

Wondering why it doesn't.

———

"Where have you been?" Ginny's voice gets exceptionally screechy when she's upset. It's not pleasant.

I check my watch. "I'm only two minutes late, Ginny. Come on."

She swats the air. "I don't care about dinner. I've been sitting here, waiting for the truck to pull up for forty-five minutes. I thought something had happened to you!"

"Oh." I sigh with relief. And then I smile. Ginny was *worried* about me.

Someone is *worried* about me.

"What the hell are you so happy about?"

"Nothing, it's just . . ." I stifle my smile. "The truck broke down. It just *died*."

"Oh." She pauses, and then turns to the empty driveway, puzzled. "How'd you get home then? Did Gabe come get you?"

I open my mouth to answer, wondering if it's better to lie. But lying to Ginny just doesn't feel right, with all she has done for me. "Actually, Jesse was driving by so he gave me a ride."

The way Ginny gasps, you'd think someone had just informed her that a loved one had died in a fiery plane crash.

And I start to think I should have lied.

"I knew I heard that car of his!"

"He's going to fix your truck and bring it back for us, Ginny. He was *really* nice to me."

I can hear her teeth grind against each other. "I told you to stay away from that damn boy. He's trouble."

"Would you rather I still be walking home alone right now, carrying all those bags?"

"You could have called Gabe and Amber."

"My phone died."

"Well, what's the point of having a phone then, huh?" she barks.

"He was really nice, Ginny, and he's going to fix the truck for us," I repeat calmly, adding a smile. That's how I've noticed Meredith deals with her. I think it's the *only* way to deal with Ginny. "I'm guessing it wouldn't be cheap to fix. And tow to a mechanic." I know I can't afford to fix the truck on my nine-dollars-an-hour cash wage. From what Meredith has said, Ginny lives on a modest monthly budget, thanks to an inheritance from her parents and her quilt sales.

"No . . . I suppose not," she mutters, scooping up some of

the pasta. The words carry their usual snip, but there's no heat in them anymore. She allows me to ladle the sauce onto her plate, though her fingers twitch the entire time. "I don't want to see him on my property."

I nod. There are just some things Ginny's better off not knowing. She didn't see him on her property anyway, so technically it's okay.

Wanting to steer her away from the topic, I say, "So I met Chuck Fanshaw today. He said to tell you 'hi' from his family."

"Oh, I'll bet he did," she grumbles. "His grandfather showed up here a month after Papa died, trying to scam me out of this place. Chased him away."

My gaze shifts to the straw broom resting by the door. She was ten seconds away from swatting the cable guy with it that day he arrived to hook up my cable. I know it's not just a figure of speech for Ginny.

Though I know I'm going to regret this, I bring it up anyway. "He mentioned boarding horses in the barn. Have you ever considered that?"

"And have people traipsing all over my property? Over my dead body." She shovels a mouthful of pasta into her mouth.

I shrug. "You'd also have horses running in the corrals. Wouldn't that be nice to see again?"

I get a harrumph in response, but it's better than a litany of cursing, so I leave it alone.

"What else did the little Fanshaw say?"

Her reference to Chuck being "little" makes me smile. He's at least six feet tall and two hundred pounds. "Basically that I should swindle you out of your vast fortune by getting on your good side."

Her hand freezes midway to her mouth for one . . . two . . . three seconds. And then Ginny does something I've never seen her do before. She starts to laugh.

We eat the rest of our dinner in comfortable silence, with no more mention of "that damn boy" next door.

TWENTY-ONE

JESSE

THEN

Heels click against the garage floor, pulling my attention from the engine. I swing around.

And suck in a mouthful of air.

She's wearing the same short, sparkly blue dress that she wore the night I met her at the lounge. I remember thinking she looked cheap then. I'm still not crazy about the dress, but I'd never call her cheap now.

"Hi, Jesse."

With her bright red lipstick, the fat lip she had three nights ago isn't visible. But I know it was there, and I'm still angry about it.

Viktor's been around the house for the last two nights, so Alex has stayed away. Or maybe she would have anyway. It's probably best. If I had to look at that lip while working on this engine of his, I probably would have taken a blowtorch to his Shelby. Still, three days without seeing her has only emphasized for me how much I like being around her.

"The door into the mudroom is unlocked if you need to use the bathroom. The gate is set to open automatically from the inside. Just remember to shut this door when you leave, okay?"

"Where are you going?"

"The Cellar."

I glance at my watch. "It's only nine thirty."

She shrugs. "Viktor called. He wants me there earlier, so I have to go earlier."

"Just like that?"

She smiles sadly. "Just like that." She hasn't been sleeping well; I can tell by the makeup caked on around her eyes, which does a poor job of masking the dark circles.

"That getup . . ." I jut my chin toward her dress. "I know that's not you." I know it's all part of her façade for her husband.

She shakes her head, her hands stretching out the hem to show me even more of her long, lean legs. "I hate this dress, but wearing it makes things easier for myself."

"I wouldn't make you wear that shit," I hear myself say. I don't know where that came from but now that it's out, I can't stop. "I'd let you dye your hair whatever color you wanted. I'd let you shave it off, I'd let you wear men's sweatpants. I'd do anything I could to keep you in school. I'd never leave you alone in the dark." My eyes settle on that lip again, the truth hidden by a streak of red. "I'd never lay a hand on you. Not like that, anyway."

Alex's chest rises and falls with deep, shaky breaths as her eyes turn glassy. I glance down at my hands to confirm the grease. As much as I want to, I can't touch her right now. But she can touch me. And she does, lifting her hand to graze the back of my cheek with her knuckles. "I know you wouldn't, Jesse," she whispers. "If I don't see you when we get home, then have a good night."

I watch her walk toward her car, her calf muscles straining against the height of those heels.

I'd kill to be back in that pricey hotel room again.

———

Time escapes me.

Really, it's the thrill of turning the key in the ignition for the first time, the satisfaction that I've put all these pieces of metal and rubber together in just the right way, that has kept me here so late. That's why I'm sitting in the driver's side of the Aston Martin in Viktor's garage when I hear Alex's engine revving. Her headlights hit me as she races up the driveway.

I hold off, wanting to see her face when I start this car, curious about what she'll say. Unfortunately, the engine cuts off and Viktor climbs out of the driver's seat. My disappointment swells. It's stupid, really. This is his car. He's the one who needs to be excited.

"Jesse! What are you still doing here?"

Though it's not obvious with his accent, I'm pretty sure he's slurring. I answer him by turning the key. The engine fires instantly.

Viktor's mouth drops open and a stupid grin stretches across his face. Behind him, Alex steps out of the passenger seat, her face pale, her eyes lined with smeared makeup. Stumbling forward, Viktor slaps the roof of the car and nods slowly. "You are a hard worker."

Not sure what to say to that, I simply shut the engine off.

"So, is it done?"

"Just about. It'll be ready to go to your body shop by tomorrow tonight."

"Perfect. I can send it away just before I leave for St. Petersburg. Did you hear that, Alexandria? My car is almost finished."

Viktor is going to Russia. That's news to me. Is Alex going with him?

"That's wonderful, Viktor." She gives him a weak smile.

He looks back at me and rolls his eyes. "Tomorrow, then." Without waiting for my answer, he walks back out, grabbing the back of Alex's neck on the way. There's nothing about it that looks gentle or loving.

I take a step forward but her hand lifts, palm out, quietly telling me to stay put. "Come, my wife. Your husband works so hard for you. Time to make him happy."

I grit my teeth as I watch them disappear around the corner. The front door slams a few seconds later. I can't pack up my shit fast enough. Slapping my fist against the garage door button, I'm gone in under two minutes. I have a good idea of what's happening upstairs right now.

And I hate it.

TWENTY-TWO

WATER

NOW

I wake with the loud bang outside my open kitchen window. A sinking dread takes over as I lie frozen, not breathing.

And then the yelling starts.

"That's what an agreement is, Jesse!"

"This changes everything!"

"No, it hasn't. Not for her."

"I've changed my mind."

"You . . . you can't just change your mind!" Though Sheriff Gabe's voice is naturally commanding, he has always kept the volume of it in check. Until now. "This was your idea."

"And it was a fucking stupid one, Dad." A car door slams. "I can't do it."

"You don't have a choice."

"You're right! I don't. I've already quit my job and moved out of my apartment. I've got nowhere to go."

Jesse's *moving back*? A small thrill spikes in my chest with the prospect of seeing him every day, even as I wonder what caused it. Maybe it has something to do with that girl in Portland that Amber mentioned.

My curiosity pulls me out of bed. I run on tiptoes across my apartment to the kitchen window that offers a perfect view of the front of the garage. Jesse and Sheriff Gabe are facing off behind Ginny's truck, the tail end peeking out from inside the garage. That means he got it working again. I don't care as much about that right now, though.

"After all I have done . . ." Sheriff Gabe is saying. "Your sister's in the dark! I've lied to my *wife* and when she finds out . . . I could lose *everything* with the things I've done for you. Things I *still* can't believe I ever did. Have you forgotten?"

"How could I ever forget *any* of this?" Jesse launches the tool in his hand at the wall. Even from here, I can see the split in the plaster from the impact. He turns to rest his hands on the truck's tailgate, his head bowed.

Sheriff Gabe finally reaches out to place a hand on his son's shoulder. Jesse brushes his face against his own shoulder.

He's crying. The cool, quiet guy who's been in all kinds of trouble is crying.

Jesse steps away from his father and, grabbing a tool from the counter, moves inside the garage, out of view. Gabe follows him in.

I'm wide awake now. But if there's any more conversation, it's too quiet to catch. Sheriff Gabe walks back to his house, a flashlight guiding his way, leaving Jesse to toil on Ginny's truck and me perched on the counter, watching. For hours.

At about three a.m. I catch myself nodding off in my sitting position and have to give my spot up, afraid I'll fall asleep and tumble. I crawl back into bed, the image of Jesse wiping his tears away lingering as I drift off.

———

I drag my feet to the landing outside my front door just before eight, wishing I could sleep longer. It's the first time I've actually lazed around in bed upon waking since coming to Ginny's. Normally, reality hits me like a splash of cold water seconds after my eyes open and I have to get out of bed before I dwell too long on the bad stuff.

Maybe I'm finally settling in.

The horses are already kicking at their stable doors, eager to be free of their confines. I have exactly four minutes before Ginny heads down to the barn and sees that I don't have them out and fed. I don't want her to think I'm slacking.

Peering over at the Welleses' house, I see that Sheriff Gabe's cruiser is gone, which is normal by this time of day. Even on a Saturday. Amber's and Meredith's cars are parked. Amber would have already left for work, and Meredith is no doubt still sleeping. The sleek black car sits next to the closed garage, and the small window hidden within its steeply peaked roof is pushed open just enough to let the fresh air in. Will he be angry if I wake him up in an hour, to get my truck out?

I'll admit that I'm more excited by the prospect than worried. Taking the steps down—much faster, now that I'm barely limping—I round the corner and discover that I won't be knocking on Jesse's door.

Ginny's truck is already sitting beside our garage.

Jesse must have driven it here early this morning. Or maybe Sheriff Gabe did. That would be better for all involved, given Ginny's issues. I don't know how I didn't hear it, though.

Inside, the keys dangle from the ignition and a small plastic container of blueberries sits on the seat, a piece of paper tucked beneath it. "Blueberries?" I frown as I unfold the paper.

In case you're ever stuck again

Below it is a phone number. I run my fingers over the digits, my focus jumping back and forth between the words and the numbers, that constant weight in my chest lifting higher with each breath as a shiver simultaneously runs down my spine.

Because something tells me Jesse is the kind of guy that I can always count on. My gut must be telling me that I had someone just like him in my previous life. Someone I trusted.

I tuck the paper into the back pocket of my jeans, promising myself to program it into my phone as soon as I can. Then I turn the key. The truck comes to life instantly, the engine a low, smooth rumble, sounding better than it ever did before. Other things are different, too. The signal indicator has an actual plastic cover over the metal lever again. The missing heat vent has been replaced. And the radio . . . it's completely new.

I sink back against the stiff, tan-colored bench. Jesse stayed up most of the night working on this truck, when he didn't have to. And then he drove it up Ginny's driveway in the wee hours of the morning. I shake my head. Sounds like he enjoys poking a wasp's nest.

I'll have to thank him later.

I get to the barn to take care of morning chores, receiving amorous nuzzles against my cheek in greeting from the Felixes. Though technically I could have both stalls cleaned and horses groomed faster, I take my time with the horses each morning and I think they appreciate the attention.

I know I do.

I'm just finishing up with their water buckets when Ginny's rubber boots scrape against the barn's dirt floor. Felix hobbles in, the old dog's limbs stiff with arthritis. "So, the truck is working again?"

"Yup. Better than before, too." She's half an hour late. She's never late. Even though I've taken over all of the work, she's always still here. Out of habit, I've assumed. But something feels different today.

She wanders along one side of the barn, gazing over each stall and each name that hangs above it. She would have known each one of those horses—fed them, cared for them, bonded with them. While Ginny's connections with other human beings are limited and awkward, I've watched the way she is around the animals, and how they are with her in turn. She has the dog at her heels all day long; I've seen the cat perched on the porch railing on more than one occasion and, though she verbally condemned the kittens to death-by-coyote, the colorful balls of yarn that she tosses them to play with tells me she doesn't really want that. Even the horses will leave their patch of grass and trot over to greet her when she takes short quilting breaks and steps into the corral.

"I thought about what you said. You know . . . boarding horses." She clears her throat heavily, as if getting these words out is difficult. "And having more horses in the pasture. It might be nice."

I stand stock still, a mixture of surprise and excitement flooding through me.

She adds, "I still have to think about it some more." Then she walks out quietly, her ever faithful canine companion at her heels.

Leaving me whistling a tune to myself as I finish up.

I'm freshly showered and heading down my stairs when I notice that the Welleses' garage door is open again. A man's voice over the radio is announcing concert dates.

A glance at my watch tells me I have maybe five minutes to spare.

Before I can talk myself out of it, I head for the property fence. The garage is set back about 150 feet from the house and surrounded by trees. By the time I reach it, I have full-on, ready-to-pee-my-pants jitters.

A guitar plays softly on the stereo as I step in. The garage itself is extremely tidy, all the tools lined up on a rustic wood table that stretches the length of the room. The concrete floors—painted a silvery blue—are swept clean. Posters of fancy old cars plaster the walls and a calendar with a curvy woman in a white string bikini hangs in the corner. Peering closer at it, I see that it's from 2007. I guess Jesse either really likes those particular women or he doesn't have much use for calendars.

My nose catches a sickly sweet smell as I pass by a giant jug of transmission fluid. Behind it is a shelf of various jars and containers, all neatly labeled with fractional numbers, filled with little nuts and bolts and metal rings.

There's something oddly comfortable about the space. I could see myself sitting here, watching Jesse work. If he was here.

The ceiling creaks. He must be upstairs. I stop in front of the brown door at the back of the garage, deciding whether I should just leave a thank-you note or wait and talk to him in person. Footfalls sounding on the other side of the door, coming fast and hard, make my decision for me. The door flies open and Jesse barrels out, tugging a shirt down over his chest, giving me a quick glimpse of a sculpted body beneath.

He stops dead in his tracks, his eyes—lined with dark circles—widening with surprise. A drip of water runs down his cheek. I inhale the smell of soap, so masculine and clean. He just had a shower. "Ah . . . Water, what are you doing here?"

My cheeks are on fire. "Sorry, I was just here . . . I mean, I wanted to say thank you for the truck . . . for fixing it, I mean." I'm suddenly stammering and I don't know why. "It runs great now."

He steps out of the doorway, pulling the door closed behind him. Though I know I should, I don't step back. I hold my breath as he passes me, the smell of him stirring something deep in my belly.

There's no point denying the fact that I'm attracted to Jesse. The heat that's crawling up my thighs has confirmed that. But, what would it be like, being with a guy again after being raped? Would I enjoy it? Would it feel at all familiar? Would it trigger memories of what I don't want to remember? How can something that intimate not?

And then I think of the unsightly thin line running down my face and I almost laugh. Besides, Jesse obviously has problems right now. Some of those problems may involve that girl he broke up with, but there must be more. The fight between him and his father last night was about something more serious than a bad breakup.

"How much do I owe you for the parts?" I ask, trailing him out of the garage.

"Nothing."

"Seriously, Jesse."

He stops with a hand on the handle of his driver's-side door, his back to me, his head dipped forward. "Seriously, Water. It was nothing. A few cheap parts from the wreckers. I've gotta head out now, though." He adds a soft, "Okay?"

"Sure, of course." I hesitate and then ask, "Why blueberries?"

A long pause hangs between us and then he shrugs. "Because they're my favorite."

I watch until the back of the car disappears around the house and then I head back to the yellow truck. Ginny's standing beside it, narrow eyes on me. "Did I just see you over next door with that boy?"

"I went to thank him for fixing the truck. I've gotta go, Ginny. I'll be late for work." I'm in no mood to appease Ginny's foul temper.

The little container of blueberries still sits in the middle of the seat. With a shrug, I open it and pop one into my mouth, puckering against the pleasant tangy flavor. Pulling out my word association journal, I scribble down the word and say out loud, "Blueberry," as if I'm quizzing myself. My pen curls around the letters of his name as I write down my one-word response. And then I shake my head and strike it out. I toss the book back into my purse.

On my way in to work, I devour the entire container. And I decide that blueberries are my favorite fruit, too.

TWENTY-THREE

JESSE

THEN

"Welles!" Miller's booming voice pulls me from my brake job.

"Uh-oh . . . Teacher's pet's in trouble," Zeke mumbles from beneath a hood.

I'd believe it, the way Miller is lumbering toward me. But for what, I have no idea. I've been here on time every day, even with the late nights over at Viktor's. "Here." He shoves a slip of paper at me. "You're needed here before heading over to Mr. Petrova's house."

I frown at the address on the paper. "For what?"

"Do I look like your fucking secretary?" Miller snaps, turning around. "Boone. You're busy with your thumb up your ass. Go finish up this car for him."

Normally Boone would shoot a finger to Miller's back, but right now he's more interested in what I have in my hand, snatching it out of my grasp. "NoPo? What's over there?"

"The hell if I know . . ." I mutter.

"All right, well . . ." He hands it back and then slaps my hand. "Call me later."

———

I can safely say that I've never been to this part of Portland.

Checking the address one last time, I pull in next to a row of old model cars with bright pink numbers scrawled across their windshields. A couple of new Ford trucks line the opposite corner, but I'd say the sign on the white brick storefront that reads "Boris's Used Cars" is aptly named.

I climb out of my Corolla and walk through the double doors into a clinical reception area with cheap industrial floor tile, chalky walls, and a cheesy poster of a blue Porsche racing down a road pinned to the wall with tacks. A gumball machine sits in the corner, and I'll bet the colorful balls came with it when it was bought twenty years ago. The smell of cigarette smoke lingers in the air. Not the kind that clings to someone who just came in from a smoke. The fresh kind, where someone said "fuck you" to the state laws and lit up. Like Viktor did, that night at The Cellar.

A middle-aged man with a receding hairline and trim beard sitting behind a desk lifts his bored gaze to meet me. "Yeah?" He loves his job, I can tell.

I hold up the scrap of paper between two fingers, as if that tells him something. "I was told to come here."

"And *who* told you to come here?"

"Miller, from Rust's Garage."

The guy's flat stare tells me that means nothing.

I try another name. "Viktor Petrova?"

Recognition flashes in his eyes. He picks up an old-school phone, hits a few buttons, and then holds the receiver, mumbling something in what I now easily identify as Russian. Hanging up, he slides off his chair and instructs, "This way."

More than a little wary, I follow him through a side door and down a long, narrow hallway lit with weak incandescent bulbs. I saw the plain gray building that stretched out behind the small used car store. I just didn't realize it was connected.

My escort shoulders open a door on the left, marked number six, and leads me into darkness. I hear him hit a switch. "The keys are inside. Come around front and I'll finish up the paperwork." Daylight streams in as a garage door on the opposite end slowly crawls up, illuminating the small storage space.

And the 1969 Plymouth Barracuda sitting within.

He moves to leave.

"Whoa." I grab onto his forearm to stop him. "What do you mean?"

He looks down at my hand and then back at me, and I instinctually remove my grip of him. "I mean, drive your car out front and then come in to sign all the ownership papers."

"And then I can leave?"

"Yeah?" He's looking at me like I'm an idiot.

"What do I do with my car?"

He shrugs. "I'll take a look at it. See if it's worth a couple hundred. Otherwise, I don't care what you do with it." The door slams shut behind him.

And I'm left scratching the back of my head, adrenaline coursing through my veins as I climb down the steps and approach the car. Viktor actually kept his end of the deal. He bought me my dream car.

Well, she *will* be my dream car by the time I'm done with her. She's navy blue and needing a fresh coat at that. The driver's-side door squeaks as I open it, and the quarter panel has a dent in it. I wonder what shape the engine's in. The interior's all leather and looks almost as good as new. Someone has obviously cared for it.

The question is, who?

Did he legitimately buy this car? From what Alex has told me about the company Viktor co-owns, he probably has the connections to get hold of this car by legal means. Maybe it was repoed. Maybe someone was lawfully selling it. But, from what Boone told me, he also has the connections to get hold of this car without ever paying a dime.

I'll assume the former.

Though deep down, I know it's likely the latter.

I stick the key in the ignition and then, with a deep breath, I crank the engine. It chugs twice before it finally turns, the loud rumble reverberating off the metal walls. A little rough, but nothing that can't be tuned.

I throw it into first gear and release the clutch.

The car leaps forward with even more power than I imagined.

And I let out a whoop.

———

Viktor is standing by the open garage when I roll through the gates, a large suitcase sitting in the back of the Hummer. He's got a rare, genuine smile on his face, like he's happy to see me behind the wheel of this thing.

And me? I've been running on a natural high since I signed the papers and drove off the lot. I cut the rumbling engine and climb out, reveling in the feel of that simple motion.

"So? Do you like it?" Viktor calls out.

"It's . . ." I step back to admire it again. "Yeah. I like it."

"I have been told the engine needs minimal work. Nothing you cannot handle."

And new brakes and shocks. I don't even care. I have enough money saved up for the parts and a paint job. "It runs solid," I finally offer. "Thank you, Viktor." I still despise the guy but at the same time, how can I not thank him for this?

"You have earned it." He gestures toward the garage where the Aston Martin's engine hums. He must have started it. "I told you, I hold up my end of a deal. Always."

He's right. This is business, not personal. No need to feel guilty over accepting fair pay for work completed. Still, a part of me does, because I know he also hits his wife.

The other part is excited to finish up with the Aston Martin, pack my stuff up, and drive back to Sisters for the weekend to worry about nothing but working on my 'Cuda in the garage. *My* garage. My favorite place in the world. I haven't been back in months.

With that in mind, I abandon my car and stroll into the garage to shut off the engine. "You shouldn't have this running until I say so. I still have some last-minute things to do on it."

Viktor chuckles. "That is what I like about you, Jesse. You are not afraid to tell me the truth."

Well, that may be a bit of a stretch, considering I think you're a douchebag. And I fucked your wife.

"You have two hours to finish up what you need to before a truck arrives to load it and take it in." He closes the distance between us and extends his hand. "It has been a pleasure."

I accept it; I don't have any other choice. But the entire time I'm wondering if he hit her with this hand or the other.

Sliding his sunglasses down over his forehead to settle on the bridge of his nose, Viktor gives me a small salute and then heads to his truck, slamming the back shut on his way to the driver's seat. The Hummer comes to life and he guns it down the driveway.

I check my watch. Two hours. He should have checked with me before he made arrangements with the body shop. I need at least three.

A bastard. Right to the end.

———

I toss a wave at the driver as the flatbed pulls away, the Aston Martin loaded on the back of it. The guy was happy enough to admire Viktor's other sports cars for twenty minutes while I scrambled to finish.

Heaving a sigh of relief, my gaze settles on my new car again. *Damn . . .* I smile. It'll take me three hours to get back to Sisters and I'm more than ready to go. On my way to put away the tools and clean up, I pull out my phone to text Alex. Her car's in the driveway, but she never stuck her head out into the garage once. That, or I was too busy rushing to get the work done to notice.

When I've put everything away and she hasn't responded, I decide to use the doorbell for the first time.

Three tries later and no answer, I start to get worried. The last time I saw her, last night, she was being pulled by the neck into the house, about to let that asshat have her body. That's why I walk through the mudroom, past the bathroom—which is as far as I've ever gone inside this house—and continue to the door that leads into the main house. It's unlocked.

"Alex!" I holler as I pull it open. The huge kitchen—probably the size of my apartment—sits in dim light on the other side.

And I wait for an answer.

When I don't get one, I call again, "Alex!"

"Jesse?" comes a groggy answer.

"Shit, I'm sorry." No wonder she didn't come to the door. I must have woken her up.

"It's okay." Soft footfalls pad against the floor somewhere unseen. "What's wrong?"

"Nothing. I just . . ." Do I tell her what I want? I already basically laid myself out on the line last night, making her all kinds of promises about her life with me. A broke-ass twenty-four-year-old mechanic. "I just wanted to say that I'm done. I'm heading out."

"Already?" She peers out from the far side of a cabinet across the kitchen. "Okay. Well . . . I guess I'll talk to you sometime? Maybe see you at The Cellar?"

"Yeah . . . I guess." So, this is it? I was kind of hoping that we'd both say "fuck it" and dive into each other in some epic made-for-film union. Is she feeling the same way?

A small smile touches her lips. "Is that your new car I saw you drive up in?"

So she *has* been watching. Which means she probably wasn't sleeping. Just avoiding me. "Yeah. You wanna come see it?"

"Some other time, maybe." She adjusts her posture.

And winces.

Alarm bells go off inside my head. "What's wrong, Alex?"

"Nothing. So, this car, what kind is it again?" She tries to divert my attention. The problem is, now that I'm paying closer attention, I also notice that the left side of her mouth looks swollen again.

I march through the kitchen in my work boots until I'm standing a foot in front of her. "What the hell happened to you, Alex?"

"It's okay, Jesse. Really," she says, dipping her face away. Everything about her stance—arms folded over her stomach, shoulders curled in, huddling into a corner—suggests otherwise.

I slam my fist against the wall switch and the kitchen's suddenly flooded with light. Reaching forward with both hands, I clutch her chin as gently as possible and turn her face back toward me.

To see that the left side of her mouth is indeed swollen again, and an angry red bruise colors her cheek.

"Did Viktor do this to you?"

She tries to turn her face away but I won't let her. "He was drunk."

"And?" I don't mean to bark at her.

"And he can get a little rough during . . ." Her face flushes. "When he's been drinking. I don't think he actually meant to hurt me." She hesitates. "He wanted me to remember the feel of him while he's gone."

"Jesus, Alex." My gaze can't help but drop. If her face looks like this, what did he do to her body? I can barely see straight, my vision blurring with rage. "You need to see a doctor."

She shakes her head.

"We need to call the cops and have him arrested."

"No!" She tempers her voice. "It's not that bad and it's over. I'm not going to relive it."

"Yeah, until the next time."

"It's never been this bad before. It only happened because I wasn't . . ." She pauses again, her eyes flittering to mine before dropping again, finishing, "*receptive* enough."

I say nothing. Her hands fold over mine and guide them away from her face. But she doesn't let go, squeezing past me and taking backward steps through the kitchen toward the garage, pulling me along with her. "Come, show me your car."

"Fuck my car, Alex! I'm leaving the stupid car!" Or seeing how fast it accelerates as I ram it into his prized collection.

"Take the car. You earned it." She steps forward and her hand lifts to graze my jawline. "It made you so happy. I saw your smile when you first came."

"And do I look happy right now, Alex?" Seeing her face like this makes me want to punch a wall.

She tugs at my hand. "Come on, please?"

My legs automatically unlock and follow her along, my grip of her hands tightening. She takes slow, even steps. Like it hurts her to walk. "Are you hungry? Would you like something to eat? A sandwich?"

"No! I don't want a damn sandwich, Alex," I mutter, shaking my head at her. She doesn't say another word as I follow her into the mudroom and out into the garage, grabbing her coat for her on the way.

"It's really nice." Her eyes sparkle as they settle on the car sitting in the driveway. Probably the same way mine did. The lust has dulled considerably in the past ten minutes, though.

"I'm leaving it."

"No you're not, Jesse." Her eyes widen. "Viktor was excited to give that to you. He'll consider it an insult."

"I don't give a rat's ass what he thinks." My gaze rolls over his cars—his "babies." "What a fucker." A steel pipe propped against the wall catches my attention. Without thinking, I let go of Alex's hand and march toward it.

"Jesse, what are you . . ." When I start heading toward the

Ferrari, holding the pipe like a bat, she figures it out pretty quickly and starts to run. "Jesse. No! Please!" She cries out in pain and I turn to see a grimace contorting her face. I instantly lose my momentum. The pipe clatters to the ground with a hollow ring.

"Please don't do anything stupid, Jesse," she pleads, her face flushed. "Just take your car and leave. If you don't, he'll start to get suspicious and ask questions. I don't want him asking questions. Not about you. I'll be fine, until I can figure something out."

This girl just doesn't get it. "It doesn't have to be like this, Alex."

She looks up at me, a sad smile tainting her lips. "Maybe it does, for me. For now." Her fingers lift to smooth over the light stubble on my chin, the scratching sound somehow soothing to me. She sighs. "I should probably lie down. I have eight days without Viktor, at least."

"I don't want to leave you alone."

"I'll be fine. I'm used to being alone."

"Not like this, you're not." My eyes inadvertently glance down to see a dark bruise on the top of her left breast. What did that asshole husband do to her? It doesn't matter right now. I know exactly what *I* want to do. "Can you handle packing a bag?"

TWENTY-FOUR

WATER

NOW

"Can I buy the quilt in the window?" the middle-aged woman asks, her green eyes glued to Dakota. I understand why. Dakota oozes charisma—she's a natural, exotic beauty, wrapped in simplicity. She's wearing a blue-and-white maxi dress today, with just enough jewelry to make her look glamorous without even trying.

"Yes! You may." Dakota practically sashays over to the window—it's as if she puts on a show for customers sometimes—and pivots the hanger to turn the quilt's front inward. "This is made by our very own Ginny Fitzgerald."

"I've seen them at the quilt fair before and a friend of mine has one. They're all very distinctive. This one, though," her brow pulls together in thought, "I don't think I've seen one with anything besides the tree and landscape before."

"Perfect. Water will ring it up for you," Dakota says, climbing up onto the window display ledge to begin removing it. I automatically adjust my stance and wait as the woman walks down the aisle, credit card in hand.

"My daughter will love this for her room."

"I have one of Ginny's quilts on my bed. It's pretty," I offer as I swipe the card through the manual credit card machine—something else that Dakota hasn't gotten around to upgrading yet.

She sighs. "Yes, well, my husband and I are divorcing and I can't afford to pay the boarding costs for my daughter's horse. She's absolutely devastated. I hope this little gift might make her a bit happier."

I hand her the receipt. "How old is your daughter?"

"Twelve. She's been obsessed with horses since she could barely talk. One of her first words was 'ors,'" the woman reminisces, a faint gloss coating her eyes now. "My ex-husband bought her the horse for her eighth birthday—without consulting me, of course," she rolls her eyes, "and now he refuses to help pay for the cost to keep it." She tucks her wallet into her worn leather purse, the straps cracked where it hangs off her shoulder. "He needs his money for his new *girlfriend*."

While this woman is divulging way more than she needs to be to a complete stranger, the wheels in my brain are churning. This feels far too coincidental to be ignored.

"If you don't mind me asking, how much are you paying to board your horse now?"

"Eight hundred dollars a month!" she exclaims. "And plenty of places cost more."

"Whoa." How much could Ginny get away with charging?

"I know. I looked into something cheaper, but they're all full or at least a forty-five-minute drive away. You'd think with all the ranches around these parts, I'd be able to find something nearby. I just don't know what to do. We're staying with my mother right now, on the south end of Sisters, until I can figure things out. But I can't see how I can take care of a thousand-pound animal on top of my daughter and me."

"How much were you looking to pay?"

She looks at me with a questioning frown.

"I may know of a ranch. A really good one that I think would price reasonably." I pat the quilt. "This lady's ranch." I hold my hands up cautiously. "I can't promise anything, but *maybe* it could work."

She bites her lip. "Zoe would be so happy. She's been crying for days, since I broke the news to her. My name is Teresa, by the way."

I grab a piece of paper and a pen.

And cross my fingers that I'm right about Ginny.

———

Amber pulls up to Roadside, a western-themed bar on the side of the highway just outside of town. It's modeled after an old red barn, and apparently it's the best place to have some fun around here.

Before I open my door, I smooth my hair down against the right side of my face one last time. Amber helped me style it so both my scar and the short patch of growth on the underside are covered.

"You look great," Amber assures me as we make our way toward the set of black double doors under the wide covered porch. I don't believe her, but I bite my tongue.

"Hi, Dean." She flashes him that wide white-toothed smile that she has perfected. It suits the fat curls in her hair and her outfit. With her tight blue jeans and a fitted plaid shirt and cowgirl boots, she looks every bit like a western-themed china doll.

I'm dressed the same—with Amber's guidance—but I don't think I look anything like a doll.

"Hey there, Amber," the beefy guy offers, one of his cowboy boots settled on the rung of his stool, his black leather hat sitting low on his face.

Everyone knows Amber Welles.

Much like everyone seems to know Jesse Welles.

"And . . . Water." He scans my ID and then looks at my face, his pale blue eyes sparkling. "Cool name." He hands it back to me and we step into an all-wood interior—the walls, ceiling, and furniture all made of golden oak—decorated with countless strands of colorful Christmas lights and fake blow-up cactuses. Even the air carries a hint of a woodsy smell, though it's competing with beer and sweat.

The upbeat twang of a country singer comes from a stage at the far end. The live band is loud and everyone's voices are raised, creating a buzz of laughter and conversation.

"I can't believe he ID'd you."

I frown. "Why wouldn't he?"

"Because I went to school with Dean and he knows I wouldn't sneak an under-ager in." She smirks. "I think he just wanted your name. Don't be surprised if he comes around later to talk to you. I heard he's single again."

I hazard a glance over my shoulder to see the giant bouncer chatting up another set of girls coming in. He's attractive; I'll admit that much.

Nothing like Jesse, though.

"Happy birthday, Bonnie!" Amber cries out, reaching out to hug a short blond girl with plump, man-made curls to match hers and a tiara in her hair. I'm assuming because it's her birthday, and not because she normally wears a tiara. Though, based on what Dakota alluded to about Amber's friends, maybe she does.

The table that this Bonnie girl is sitting at—a long, solid picnic table of glossy light wood, in a row of similar picnic tables—is full of girls who look like Amber and Bonnie and guys who look like Dean. Many of them ease out of their seats to come around and give Amber a hug, as if they're seeing each other after a long absence. Given that Amber works more than she socializes, that's probably true.

Amber reaches out and takes my arm, pulling me into the friend fold. "This is Water." She begins introducing everyone. I'm lost by the second or third name, though everyone there instantly grabs on to mine with comments about how "unusual" and "cool" it is.

I simply smile and nod and say, "Nice to meet you," all while trying to keep my hair from falling back off my face. They all take their seats again and someone's boyfriend hands me a glass of beer.

Do I even like beer?

I quietly watch Amber and the others squeal and giggle and chatter on, their eyes roaming around the bar, pointing out people they know from high school who either still live in the area or, like many of them, decided to come back for the long weekend. Some of their comments are benign; many are laced with gossip. "Remember when she . . . ?" "I heard that he . . ." The kinds of whispers and attention that I don't want directed at me.

So I stay quiet and drink my beer, the cold, fresh liquid pouring down my throat with relative ease. I do like beer after all.

"Amber . . . you didn't tell me your brother was back in town." Bonnie's eyes are wide as she stares behind me. Like a well-timed orchestra, every head in my row turns to the door—mine included—to see Dean and Jesse facing off.

"He just got back," Amber says, not sounding too thrilled.

"Who's he with?" a redhead—Kerry or Terry or Tory—asks, as Jesse pushes through the doors with a guy on his heels. A guy who, even wearing a plain black T-shirt and fitted jeans, doesn't seem to fit with the sea of jeans and cotton in this place. Maybe it's the flashy gold watch on his wrist.

"Don't know. I've never seen him before. Must be a friend from Portland." Amber's eyes are on her brother's friend as they head toward our table. "I guess we're going to find out."

Bonnie is on her feet instantly—as fast as she was when we approached, if not a little faster. "Jesse!" She throws her arms around his shoulders.

He obliges her with a small smile and "Hey, Bonnie," his arm curling around her waist.

Amber leans in next to me and drops her voice. "They dated back in high school for a bit."

"Really?" My chest burns with envy as I watch her finally pull away but not step back. "What happened?"

Amber takes a drink, her eyes flickering between her brother and his friend. "Same thing that always happens. I guess my brother got bored and dumped her. She's a nice girl."

"And he doesn't like nice girls?" While Bonnie introduces herself to his friend, Jesse's eyes scan the table. Until they settle on me.

Amber leans in until she's whispering in my ear. "He's never been into the rich, entitled girls. Don't get me wrong—Bonnie's nice and she's one of my best friends, but she's spoiled and she can be fake sometimes. They were a bad fit from the start. Clearly she still has a thing for him."

Almost on cue, Bonnie tosses her long locks over her shoulder and throws her head back to laugh over something his friend said, her eyes on Jesse.

Yes, clearly.

I guess the question is, is he *still* not into rich, entitled girls?

That makes me wonder if, with my diamond necklace and my sparkly dress and one ridiculously high heel, I once fit that description.

Aside from a quick glance my way, Jesse seems into their conversation. I try not to watch, but it's impossible. That is, until his friend comes back from grabbing drinks at the bar and catches my eye. He stares at me until I duck my face into my beer, feeling my cheeks burn.

Several people around the table try to strike up a conversation with me with a "Hey, Water . . . ," followed by a question. I answer them the best I can, with a smile.

And, always, a lie.

As my lies start piling up faster than the people filtering through the door, I begin to get uncomfortable. I can't be honest with these people. I can't be honest with anyone except the Welles family, Ginny, and Dr. Weimer.

I excuse myself to grab a glass of water at the bar because the beer is making me feel light-headed. If I was ever much of a drinker, I definitely am a lightweight now.

"Hey, Water." A wall of chest and bright blue eyes meet my gaze when I turn around. "We didn't officially meet. I'm Dean."

"Hi," I say with a nod, stepping back so I don't have to tip my head back and risk my hair falling.

"You having fun?"

My gaze drifts around the rustic bar, taking in the various animal horns. "Yeah. I like this place."

"You from around here?"

Good question. I don't know, though I have to assume not, seeing as I haven't run into a single person who recognizes me. If I say no, then I have to get into a long conversation of lies. So I settle on, "I am now."

He eases a boot on the bar rail. "I'm surprised I haven't seen you before. I would have remembered you."

Just as I start to shrug, someone shoves me from behind and I tumble into Dean, my face mashing against his chest. He ropes one strong arm around my shoulders while the other stretches out somewhere behind me. "Hey, watch it or you're out of here," he warns the guy.

I hear a mutter of "sorry" behind me as I peel myself off of Dean's body, quickly adjusting my hair that got pushed back.

Not quickly enough.

"Holy shit." Dean stops my hand in his, a shocked frown wrinkling his forehead. "What happened to your face?"

The person standing just behind Dean turns at his words and now stares at me. I feel the bartender staring at me. And others. Others are staring at me, at my face.

I finally manage to yank my hand from Dean's grasp and swipe my hair forward to cover the scar.

That's when Jesse appears. "Don't you ever fucking grab her

like that," he growls, edging in between us, forcing me to take a step back.

"I didn't grab her. And get the hell away from me, Welles, or I'll kick your ass out and there's nothing your daddy can do about that." As if Dean wasn't using his full size before, he suddenly appears larger, looming over Jesse. They may be the same height, but where Jesse is lean and muscular, Dean is broad and bulky. I don't see how Jesse could win against that. And I don't want to see him try.

I reach up to settle a tentative hand on Jesse's arm, the tension in his body surging into my fingertips. "It's okay. I'm fine." Embarrassed and ready to go home, but fine.

He adjusts his stance slightly, peering down at me over his shoulder. "You sure?"

"Yeah, she's sure," Dean answers for me.

I think I hear Jesse's teeth crack against each other, his jaw is clenched so tight.

To me, Dean offers, "It's too bad about your face. You hide it well, though."

I'm not sure if he meant it as an apology or a compliment, or if it was really just a dumbass comment, but the next thing I know, hands are seizing my shoulders and pulling me back, and Jesse's taking a swing at Dean. His fist slams into the big guy's jaw, sending him back a step. Dean's elbow knocks a tray of fries off the bar and onto the floor.

It must hurt, because it takes him a moment to face Jesse again. When he does, rage is burning in his eyes. "George!" he hollers to the bartender, who immediately picks up the phone. Throwing Jesse into a headlock, Dean leads him out, the crowd parting for the two angry men.

The hands that pulled me back earlier fall from my arms. "Sorry about that. I didn't want you getting in the mix."

I turn to see the guy Jesse walked in with beside me. "Thanks."

"They need Licks here, right?" He nods toward the scattered fries.

I frown. "Licks?"

Jesse's friend stares at me for so long, an unreadable look in his eyes, that I begin to get uncomfortable. Finally, I hold my hand out. "I'm Water."

"Right." He takes my hand. "Luke."

"Luke," I repeat. "Nice to meet you. Are you from around here?"

He shakes his head. "Portland. On my way to Boise tonight, and I thought I'd stop in Bend and see Jesse for a bit."

"Do you know him well?"

"I guess you could say that, yeah. We lived together."

Lived together? He must know Jesse *very* well. I know this is prying, but I'll blame it on the beer if anyone accuses me of being nosy. "Do you know why he moved back to Sisters?" And why he and Sheriff Gabe were fighting last night?

"Uh . . ." Luke drops his gaze to the floor, as if he's searching for an answer there. "I think he just missed being home."

I can't tell if Luke doesn't know the real reason or if he's lying. "I can understand that. It's beautiful here."

"You like living here?"

I smile. Finally, a question I don't have to lie about. "Yeah, it's a great place."

"Really? I wouldn't have—" He cuts off abruptly, a frown zagging across his forehead. "I need to go. Uh . . . I'm going to go outside and wait for the cops with Jesse." He grimaces. "Bartender called them."

"Crap . . ." Jesse's going to get into more trouble with his dad. Because of me.

Why would he even do that?

"Maybe I'll see you around." Luke heads for the door, his steps quick.

After a brief visit to the restroom to make sure my hair is all fixed, I head back over to our table to hear Bonnie say, "I thought Dean and him were over all that."

I sit down beside Amber, who's not bothering to hide her scowl. "Over what?" I ask.

"Something that happened to Dean's best friend, Tommy, back in high school."

Tommy . . . "The kid who was stabbed?"

Amber lifts a questioning brow at me and then clues in. "Dakota told you."

"Yeah." I give her a sheepish shrug.

"I didn't say anything earlier because I didn't want you to worry about having Jesse next door after . . . you know." She snorts. "Funny, I figured Dakota was too stoned in high school to even know what was going on."

"Did you say Dakota?" The redhead rolls her eyes. It's obvious that everyone at this table shares Amber's opinion, though some are more catty about it than others.

"I'm going to get some fresh air," I tell Amber. Maybe I can help by talking to the officer about what happened.

She sighs, dragging herself up. "Yeah, I guess I should come with you and see if my brother's in handcuffs. I'm sure my dad's here by now."

I spot the sheriff's emblem on the white car as soon as we step outside. Jesse's sitting on a step under the watchful eye of a police officer, his elbows resting on his knees, glaring at Dean, who's talking to the sheriff.

"Do you know what set him off?" Amber asks.

"I'm not sure." Did it even have anything to do with me? Or was I just an excuse for Jesse to pick a fight? Is he that kind of guy?

We watch as Dean nods to Sheriff Gabe and turns back toward us. His eyes catch mine briefly but he ducks his head and keeps marching, until he disappears into the bar. I'm guessing Dean isn't as interested in knowing me as he was earlier.

With a holler and a wave from Sheriff Gabe, the other cop leaves Jesse and his friend sitting on the curb and drives off.

"I guess he's getting off for that," Amber says as we watch Jesse and Luke climb into Jesse's car. "Probably easier for everyone." She sighs. "I'm heading back in."

Sheriff Gabe looks over at us, his lips pressed into a firm line. "I'm actually going to ask your dad for a ride home."

Amber frowns. "Aren't you having fun?"

"Yeah, I am," I lie. "I'm just tired."

She shrugs, giving my arm a squeeze. "Okay. See you later."

I make my way over to the sheriff's car. "Could I get a ride? In the front, preferably," I add with a smile.

He dips his head. "Sure, Water. Come on."

The farther away we get from the bar, the more I relax. His police radio keeps going off until he turns the volume dial all the way down. "I'm not supposed to be on duty anyway," he explains, adding softly, "though I don't really know what that means anymore."

"You should take a vacation. I'd love to recommend somewhere, but . . . you know."

His head nods slowly, but his solemn mask never cracks. It doesn't seem as though he finds my attempt at amnesia humor funny. I can guess that he didn't enjoy having to bail his son out tonight. "So how come you wanted to leave? You weren't having fun?" Sheriff Gabe finally asks.

I think about that question as the tick-tick-tick of the turn signal fills the silence in the car. "Not really," I admit finally. "I just didn't feel like I fit in there. Amber's friends are nice and all, but . . . I don't know. Maybe it was too much for me."

Maybe I would have enjoyed myself had I been with Jesse.

Or maybe I'm just more of a loner.

He chuckles. "Amber's friends can be too much for *me*. Amber always was the social butterfly growing up. She didn't mind the attention at all."

"I feel like I'm so different from her in that way. Maybe I wasn't before, but I am now." I pause before adding, "Thanks for not arresting Jesse tonight. I think that was partly my fault."

He nods once but doesn't ask any more questions. I've probably created enough work for him as it is. "Wouldn't have done anybody any good."

"Will you get into any trouble over that? You know, with voters and letting your son off and stuff."

His forehead furrows deep. "This is my last term. I'll be resigning after this. Retiring, technically."

"Really? The way Ginny and Amber talk about you, I thought you were meant for that shiny badge."

"Doesn't hang quite right on me anymore."

The rest of the drive is silent.

It isn't until I'm sitting alone on my back balcony, taking in the canopy of stars, that I really think about what happened tonight. I trail my finger against the long ridge running down my face. How many more times will I hide this scar, only to surprise a guy who might otherwise think I'm pretty?

Who will then pass me by once he discovers that I'm not?

I sit back and wonder if I'll be able to find someone who sees beyond it. It's just a scar, right? A blemish on the outside.

And a confused girl with no past on the inside.

Mostly, though, I sit and wonder about the guy next door. I wonder where he is right now, because he's not in his garage.

And that makes my heart heavy with disappointment.

TWENTY-FIVE

JESSE

THEN

It's just after ten by the time I turn into the driveway. I take the potholes extra slow for Alex's sake, but I can't avoid them completely. Her fingers curl around the door's molding with each bump.

She argued with me when I told her where I wanted to take her, but after I promised that it would be fine—that no one would see her like this—she relented, throwing together an overnight bag. I pulled her BMW into the garage and then I helped her into my car, a wary eye on the cameras. I didn't want to bring it up but she must have read my mind, because she told me that she knows how to delete footage and Viktor never checks anyway.

So, just like that, I left Portland behind, with Alexandria Petrova in my passenger seat. I didn't even go home to grab a change of clothes, because I wanted to get her as far away as I could, as fast as possible.

I round the house, passing the sheriff's sedan that I hoped wouldn't be there but knew probably would.

"There's a police car in your driveway, Jesse," she says slowly.

"I know. It'll be fine, I promise. And it's not a police car. My dad's the sheriff." I keep heading down the narrow path toward my garage. I call it "my garage" because my granddad used to own this property and he left that building to me. Sure, it's on my parents' land and they cover the electricity bills, but the space within—to work, to sleep, to be happy—is mine. No one's going to go against a dead man's wishes. Not even the sheriff.

An outdoor spotlight appears in my rearview mirror and a moment later, a figure steps out from the sliding door off the kitchen, flashlight in hand. It takes three minutes to walk from the house to the garage and he's already on his way.

I hit the automatic button to the double door that I keep with me at all times and roll into my big, beautiful garage. Under other circumstances, I'd be floating on a euphoric high right now—pulling my dream car in here for the first time.

But right now, I have a beat-up girl in the passenger seat and if my father sees her looking like this, no one's going to be happy. Hell, he'll probably haul me in for questioning. It wouldn't be the first time.

I unfasten her seat belt for her. "We've gotta move quick, okay?"

She nods and picks up her purse. I grab her bag from the backseat and then run around to the passenger side to help her out. Thank God the garage's entrance is angled toward our neighbor's house—an old hermit lady who'll be locked up in her bed by now—or he'd see right in here.

In seconds I have the back door unlocked. I guide Alex up the narrow stairs and into the small attic apartment, the air cold and stale. "Here, just sit still. Or better yet—" I lead her to the stripped bed, the bedding sitting neatly folded. My mom must have been in here. "Lie down. I'll come back soon."

She eases herself back until she's lying on my bed, staring up at me, her eyes wide with panic. "Please don't tell him, Jesse. I don't want to explain this to anyone." I'm guessing that if she'd known my father was a sheriff, she never would have agreed to this.

"I won't. Promise. Just don't move, because this floor will creak." I lean down to kiss her forehead, adding with a whisper, "And he doesn't believe in ghosts."

One side of her mouth—the good side, the one that's not swollen—curves up in a smile. "Thank you, Jesse."

I don't want to leave her but I do, heading back downstairs to find my father—Sheriff Gabe Welles—scanning the interior of my car, an open bottle of beer in his hand and another one tucked under his arm. He doesn't drink much and when he does, it's only one or two. "Hey, Dad."

He glances up at me. "Hey, Jesse. Your mom didn't tell me you were coming home this weekend."

"Last-minute decision." I watch him as he quietly circles the car, his hand sliding over the body. Without a word, he holds out the extra beer and I take it. Neither of us is a big talker. "So you finally got it."

"Drove it off the lot today."

He smiles to himself. "So that sparked your last-minute decision." A pause. "How much?"

"Just under sixteen." That's what the papers say. Do I think it's accurate? Probably not. That, or Viktor's a rich fool with more money than he knows what to do with. Rebuilding the engine on a car like the Aston Martin wouldn't be cheap, but there's no way it's worth almost half a year's net salary for me.

"You had that kind of money saved up?" I don't miss the suspicion in his voice. It's the same suspicion I've faced for the last ten years, since my friends and I got picked up for lifting a six-pack of beer from the local gas station. Of course, I've done plenty of regrettable things since then, too, in his eyes, but it seems that I also can't do anything right anymore. I went to school and got a full-time job. I pay my bills on time. I stay away from the kind of idiots I hung out with in high school. I don't think it'll ever be enough.

Then again, considering I'm driving what may or may not be

a stolen car, and I have another man's wife hiding upstairs, maybe I'm still doing a lot wrong.

"I've been working hard. And I just rebuilt a DB5 engine for this rich asshole. He paid me well." Not a lie.

"Huh . . ." He holds his hand up. No need to explain further. I toss my keys to him and, leaning into the open driver's-side window, he cranks the engine. Even though that rumble is far from the smoothest I've ever heard, it still gets me excited. I hear the release on the hood pop and move to prop it up. We come together in front of the car, arms crossed. The Welles Men pose, my mom always calls it. There's an old picture of my granddad, my dad, and me—at maybe ten years old—standing in a row right here in this garage, in front of my dad's Mustang, our arms crossed in the same way.

"What does it need?"

"Dunno. I'll find out this weekend."

He nods slowly.

"Where's Mom? Amber?"

"Hospital. Your mom's there for a long stretch and Amber's pulling nights with overtime."

Perfect. "Amber's still going to Europe?"

He sucks back on his beer bottle. "So she tells us. We'll see." If my twin sister actually goes ahead with this idea of hers—to travel the world for a year—I'll probably be the most surprised. She's always played the role of small-town sheriff's daughter effortlessly, charming the right people, smiling for the cameras, weighing her decisions carefully to ensure she doesn't make one that might look bad for my dad. She thrives on being the center of attention in our small universe, and in high school, she was just that—Rodeo Queen, class valedictorian, and the winner of several state championships in horseback riding. She could have applied to almost any program at almost any school, and yet she chose to stay close to home. A part of me thinks it's because she doesn't want to become a tadpole in the ocean.

Taking off and wandering around the world alone just isn't something she's cut out for.

I suck back the rest of my beer and then cut the engine. "I'm heading to bed, Dad."

He frowns. "This early?" He glances at the clock on the wall, which somehow keeps working even though I don't remember ever changing the battery. Granted, I've always been a night owl and it's only ten thirty. Still, his cop radar is always on.

"I've been working nonstop. I'm beat." I give my eyes a good rub, not just for effect but because I really am exhausted.

He nods to himself. "Right. Glad to see you doing well, Jesse. Make sure you check the damper on the woodstove." He turns his flashlight back on and picks his path down the road, heading toward home. I watch him for a while. He's in his mid-fifties, and he'll be sheriff until he loses an election or is forced out. I think he was born to wear that badge. He's good at it, too. Gabe Welles is revered as hard-nosed and righteous, the kind of man who wouldn't balk at questioning his own son for attempted murder when two pieces of shit pointed their fingers his way.

Hitting the garage door—we're four miles from the closest neighbor besides Ginny Fitzgerald next door and yet I always lock up—I leave the hood up and shut the lights, wanting to get back to Alex.

She's exactly where I left her, hugging the edge of the mattress. Asleep.

On nothing more than a mattress cover, in a cold, dank attic, Alex curled up into a ball and fell asleep. She probably didn't sleep a wink last night or today. If she's like me, she hasn't slept well since last Sunday.

I don't want to wake her to make the bed, so I instead dig into the cedar chest in the corner to find my grandmother's favorite blue-and-red checkered blanket. I was only eleven when my dad's mother died. My granddad, in good shape until the day he succumbed to a massive heart attack, decided to turn the attic space into an apartment for himself. Previously, we had all lived together in the main house. Given my parents' work schedules, the arrangement worked well for taking care of Amber and me when we were kids. But granddad wanted nothing to do with living in the house with teenagers.

I cover Alex with the blanket, hoping she doesn't mind the wool texture. Then, after quickly washing up in the small bathroom in the corner, I start a fire in the woodstove, turn off the lights, and edge into the old brown Barcalounger, the only piece of living room furniture left in here and a rickety piece of shit that squeals in protest with my weight. I don't want to assume that Alex would be okay with waking up next to me in bed.

Leaning back slowly, I get as comfortable as I possibly can. And then I close my eyes and listen to her low, shallow breaths.

"Jesse."

My head springs up with a deep breath of panic. Alex's face appears in my blurry vision. I guess I managed to fall asleep in this old chair after all. Now I feel worse than when I sat down.

"Come." She takes my hand and tugs me until I get out of the chair, leading me to the bed. It's still dark out, but the fire casts enough glow.

"Wait, let me get the—"

"No, this is perfect. Really." She's still whispering. The girl who drives a BMW Z8, and wears probably two years' worth of my salary on her finger, curls up on an unmade bed with an old wool blanket and says it's perfect.

I don't think I'll ever judge another person based on a first impression again, thanks to Alex.

Grabbing a pillow, I dump my keys and phone onto the nightstand and slide into the other side of the double bed. Alex stretches the blanket over my lower half and then presses up against my shoulder. I instinctually lift my arm and she doesn't waste a second tucking herself up against my body, resting her head on my chest, her palm over my racing heart.

To say I'm turned on would be wrong, because Alex is hurt and all I want to do is hold her until she feels better. But I feel at ease. And I want her to be at ease too, here in my world, where there is plenty of room for her, where I won't let Viktor hurt her.

I can't say who drifts off first but when I do, it is with a sense of contentment that I don't ever remember feeling before.

———

My ringing phone beside my head wakes me up. It takes me a second to recognize where I am, and another to notice Alex lying next to me, still asleep, her pale blond hair draping her face like a curtain. At some point she detached herself from my chest but she's still molded to the side of my body, keeping me warm. The fire went out long ago, leaving us with the one electric baseboard heater and a chill in the air.

"Yup," I croak, unable to manage a whisper, my deep voice too groggy first thing.

"What happened to you?" Boone's voice asks at the other end.

Giving my eyes a good rub, I stare up at the pitched ceiling, gathering my wits. Morning light streams past the gauzy orange-and-yellow striped curtain, showing me the detailed webs of several spiders up in the ceiling beams. I should probably clear those out before Alex notices them. "What do you mean?"

"You left work early and I never heard from you again. What was in NoPo?"

I sigh. It's hard not to jostle the bed when I get out but I do my best, tiptoeing over to the window, giving my body a good stretch. "My payment."

"You serious?"

"Yup. Decent shape, too." I'm torn. Three hours driving that car here and I know I'm never letting it go, though I probably should.

"Sweet! Why didn't you bring it home, then?"

From my vantage point, I can see the Fitzgerald ranch next to me, the black iron grates in the first-floor windows that apparently I inspired. I used to spend a lot of time over there as a kid, running with the horses. Things changed in high school, though. Now I wouldn't be surprised if the old bat has a gun loaded, ready to shoot me on sight. My relationship with Ginny is a lot like the one with my dad: no matter what I do, I'll never get back in her good graces. And I didn't even do anything to her. "Had some things to finish up at Viktor's and then headed straight for my parents'. Gonna work on it all weekend." Rustling behind me has me checking over my shoulder. Alex, changing positions, but from the looks of it, still out cold. Either way, I don't want to wake her up. "Listen, I've gotta go. I'll see you tomorrow night."

When I hang up with Boone, I make my way into the bathroom. Another cramped space, with poor lighting, a small tub, and a toilet that sometimes runs. The door doesn't even close completely. All fine for an old man whose focus was on function versus style. Perfect for a young guy who doesn't really care about much else besides a bed and a shower. Not nearly adequate for a woman like Alex and the kind of life she's grown accustomed to living. I want her to leave Viktor, but why do I assume she'll leave him for me? For this?

With a heavy exhale, I peel off my clothes and switch on the shower, waiting for the water raining down from the low-pressure head to get hot before climbing in. I know she says she'd trade all her money just to be happy, but would she really? Isn't that a green-grass statement that only the rich make? She didn't come from money, but she married for it; she admitted as much.

When I'm done, I dry off and cover my lower half with a towel before slipping out into the apartment. I'm halfway across the floor to my dresser for one of a few changes of clothes I left here when I hear her call out in a cute, sleepy voice, "You really wanted that car, didn't you?"

I keep walking until I reach the dresser, while prickles run up my spine, knowing her eyes are on the tattoo of a '69 Barracuda across my back. At least I can blame the cool November air for the goose bumps she's giving me right now. "I don't need much," I murmur, fumbling through the drawers for a change of clothes.

"I've thought about getting a tattoo for years."

"Why don't you?"

She chuckles. "I could never decide what to get."

I check the mirror above the dresser, which gives me a perfect view of the bed and her. "How are you feeling?"

She lifts her arms over her head and winces. The swelling on her lip has gone down, but the bruise across her cheek is darker, angrier. She pauses, arms resting above her head, simply staring at the ceiling above for a moment. "I think I may hurt more today than yesterday," she mumbles, the grimace fading but not disappearing. "But I can't remember the last time I slept this well."

"It's the fresh mountain air. You're not used to it."

Deciding that I probably shouldn't simply drop my towel in front of her—though it's nothing she hasn't already seen—I pull a pair of boxer briefs up under the towel before tossing it to the rocking chair. Another glance in the mirror catches her watching me intently, her cheeks flushing. I quickly yank on some jeans and a long-sleeved shirt, knowing it's going to be chilly out there.

"Are you sure we shouldn't have you looked at? I can wake my sister up. She's a nurse, remember?" That would go over well. She'd be phoning my dad in five minutes flat. *Look what your son is involved with now!*

She shakes her head. "I'll be fine. I just need to take it easy."

"Okay, well, I'm going to raid my parents' fridge for breakfast before I run to get the parts I need. Anything you want? Besides blueberries, of course."

She grins. "You remembered."

"Of course I did. You got me to eat fruit. It's a miracle."

A soft giggle escapes her lips. "I don't think I'm very hungry right now." She yawns. "Maybe coffee. Two-and-a-half milks and one sweetener, please."

"Two-and-a-half milks and one sweetener."

"Yes, please."

"Right." I repeat it twice before I give up and write it down on a scrap of paper, knowing I'll screw it up. I doubt we even have sweetener in the cupboard.

On impulse, I cross the attic floor to the bed and lean down to lay a kiss on her forehead. Her fingers graze my throat as I pull away.

"Hey, Jesse?"

"Yeah?"

She smiles up at me. Even with a bashed-up face, she's beautiful. "Thank you for bringing me here."

"I'll be back soon." I lay a second quick kiss, this time on her cheek, and then I leave.

My parents' house is eerily quiet when I step through the sliding door. My dad's already gone—not surprising. He's normally at his desk at the main office in Bend by six a.m., even when he goes in on weekends. I know Amber's asleep in her room, because her red Mini is parked in the driveway. She won't be up until close to dinnertime.

I set the coffee to brew and start rifling through the cupboards and fridge, looking for something that can pass for breakfast. After my grandma died, we operated under very much a "fend for yourself" environment of packaged foods and order-in for a few years, my parents struggling to adjust without the extra help. Thanks to those days, I've grown partial to frozen pizza pockets for breakfast, a habit I haven't been able to break.

My mom started making more of an effort around the house about the same time that I hit rock bottom, my bad choice in friends getting me detained for questioning, with attempted murder charges looming. I didn't do it, of course. I tried to stop it. But for those twenty-four hours, while waiting for Tommy—a mouthy jock who didn't deserve to get stabbed—to pull through, while my supposed friends were both pointing fingers at me, my mom sat in this very kitchen, a constant flow of tears streaming down her cheeks. Asking over and over again where she went wrong with her son.

That's what Amber told me, anyway.

Now all I see in the fridge is fresh fruit and vegetables, some high-end cheeses, yogurt, and weird-colored bread. Fresh steaks ready for the grill. Alex would know what to do with all this stuff. Not that I'd ever let her cook this weekend.

Even though she said she wasn't hungry, I load a plate up with some fruit and cheese and yogurt. Miraculously, I find sweetener in the cupboard, which I add after making her coffee. I move fast. The last thing I want is to discover that Amber has suddenly become a light sleeper and have her appear in the kitchen.

When I climb the stairs to my attic apartment, I discover Alex cocooned in that wool blanket. Asleep again. I set everything down on the nightstand next to her and then, grabbing my keys and wallet, I head out, locking the door behind me.

———

It's almost four o'clock when I hear the water running upstairs.

She slept all day. I know because after I raced out to Bend and back with a trunk full of parts, I kept checking in on her. With me, normally, hours go unnoticed when I'm in my garage. With this car sitting in front of me, I'd expect those hours to turn into days. But I watched that damn clock on the wall all day long, creeping up the stairs several times to make sure she was okay.

She says she's fine and I can't see anything besides what's on her face, but I'm still worried. How long can a person sleep?

"Alex?" I take my time climbing the steps, my footfalls extra heavy so she hears me coming. When I get to the top, she's standing in front of the small side window, an awed smile brightening her injured face.

"It's even more beautiful out here than I imagined."

I come up behind her, probably too close but I can't help myself, and look out the window to see what she sees—snow-capped mountain peaks, the sky smeared with shades of pink and purple from the setting sun. "You should see it here in the summer."

"And look!" She points to the old woman's two horses, grazing on a bale of hay by the barn. "I wish I could go see them."

"Maybe another time." I very gently brush the strands of hair off her face. "Feeling better, Sleeping Beauty?"

She dips her head to hide the coy, crooked smile. "Starting to. I'm going to take a bath, if you don't mind."

"I don't. It's nothing special in there, though, Alex." Definitely not like her house. Or an eight-hundred-dollar-a-night hotel room.

"It's perfect. Really. I just need some towels and I can't reach them. Can you help me?"

"Right." The storage in there is odd, the only cupboards running along the high side and eight feet up. I follow her in and then maneuver around her in the tight space to dig out the fresh towels. "What's that?" I ask, watching her sprinkle white granules into the bath.

"Epsom salts," she explains with a shrug. "It helps."

Sounds like she's been here before, even though she says she hasn't. Gritting my teeth, because she doesn't need to hear my complaints—her body is complaining enough right now as it is—I hand her the towels and then slip out around her.

She shuts the running water off. "Did you get any work done on your car?" I glance back to see the door open a sliver and her slowly easing her shirt up over her head. Numerous black bruises—as if from fingers digging into flesh—mark her back and waist.

"Yeah, brakes and a good tune-up," I mutter, yanking the fitted bedsheet over the mattress. I hate knowing she was with him at all, but to see proof like that? I keep my head down and make the rest of the bed, listening to the sound of her naked body slip into the water.

Since seeing her cowering in the kitchen yesterday, I haven't had a single thought about her besides getting her somewhere safe. Not in the long car ride here, not lying in bed next to her last night, not even while in the shower.

Now, though . . . I can't claim that anymore. Which means I probably need to get the hell out of here. "Hey, I'm going to head back downstairs to work on—"

Her phone begins ringing.

A splash of water sounds. Alex, sitting up. "Is that him?"

I check the screen. "Unknown."

There's a long pause and then, "That's him. Can you please bring it to me?" The sound of the shower rings scraping against the metal rod tells me she's drawing the curtain. Closed or open, I can't say. Either way, it's a see-through material.

I push through the doorway, trying to keep my eyes up and toward the glow from the small window above the tub until I'm close enough to focus on just her face.

She reaches out to take the phone from me, splashing drops of water on my arm. "Stay?" Bright reddish-brown eyes plead with me.

With a nod, I sit down on the floor, my back pressed against the outside of the tub. And I listen.

"Hello?"

The harsh tone blasts through from the other end and, though I can't pick up the words, I know it's him.

"Yes . . . No . . . Yes . . . I'm fine." He talks for a minute straight and she simply listens. "Okay, Viktor . . . Okay . . . Love you too . . ."

My stomach clenches.

"Yes, in a few days. Good night." She hangs up. The phone appears in front of me, her hand extended over my shoulder. "Can you please take it before I drop it in the bath?"

I do, her wet fingers slipping over mine in the process. "What'd he want?"

"Nothing. Just checking in, I guess." She sighs. "I was just beginning to relax, too."

I turn, just far enough to see her from the neck up. "Still glad you came?"

She manages a smile. "Yes."

Although I shouldn't bring it up, I can't help it. "Do you regret the night in the hotel?"

I don't move as she shifts closer to me, until her head rests on the edge of the tub, just inches from mine. "I don't regret that night, Jesse, and I never will. I just felt incredibly guilty for doing it because I knew it was wrong. It's . . . When I married Viktor, I truly believed it was forever. I never thought I would end up being this person who sleeps with another man. And yet, here I am, only four years later. A cheating wife."

"An abused wife, who's been cheated on countless times herself, and who was hurt and angry," I correct her.

"That's an excuse, not a reason." A hollow-sounding laugh escapes her lips. "I guess we're all capable of doing bad things. I was just being self-righteous, thinking I might be above that."

This hollow, cynical version of Alex that I'm seeing now . . . this is what a guy like Viktor has made her into. "Do you *still* feel guilty?"

She toys with the collar on my flannel shirt, her wet fingers grazing my neck, sending shivers down my back. "I still know it's wrong."

And I know that if I don't leave right now, I'm liable to do something to take things too far. And I also know that she'll let me.

———

"I can't remember the last time I had a pizza guy deliver to my door," Alex says between mouthfuls. "And I've definitely never sat on the floor like this."

I smile, propping up the layer of pillows around her back for her. I found some in the old cedar chest and then grabbed a bunch from my mom's living room. "They don't normally deliver this far, but they do it for us. Amber and I used to sit around the fireplace like this when we were little kids, in the winter. We had these long metal pokers, and we'd melt marshmallows and then make S'mores."

"Hmm . . . S'mores. I've heard about those."

"You've got to be kidding me. Seriously?"

She giggles, tucking a strand of melted cheese into her mouth. "My mom stepped off a plane from Russia when she was twenty-four, to begin working sixteen-hour days, seven days a week. I wasn't raised on Western culture's traditions." She rests her head back to share my oversized pillow, the smell of her freshly washed hair erasing my appetite for pizza.

"What were you raised on?"

A faint smile touches her lips. "She used to tell me fairy tales before bed. About fences made of human bones and witches that killed little ducklings." Her face scrunches up. "Horrible fairy tales. They gave me nightmares."

It's not funny but I can't help laughing, which gets her laughing, which gets her wincing and touching the side of her face.

I slip my arm under her shoulders and pull her to my chest.

"I'm going to leave him, Jesse. I'm going to tell him that I know about the cheating and it's not working out. I don't want his money. Maybe if I agree to just walk away empty-handed, he'll let me?"

Somehow, I doubt it. "How do you think his ego will take it?"

"I don't know." She tips her head back, her big eyes peering up at me. "I'm kind of scared, but . . . I figure, what can he do, really?"

That depends. The more I think about Viktor and his dealings with stolen cars, the more worried I get for Alex. I don't know much about that world, but I have to think he's got more at stake than chump change. Otherwise, why would the risk be worth it? "What do you know about Viktor's business dealings? The non-legit ones."

She purses her lips, as if afraid to admit that she has even suspected anything below-board. "Viktor keeps that stuff to himself and I don't ask. I've met Rust. I've met some of his other business partners. Most of them are Russian. We even hosted a garden party last summer and had them over, with their wives. I cooked this whole big spread of things that Viktor used to have growing up in St. Petersburg. He grew up in a wealthy home. Anyway, they all seemed nice." She rolls her eyes. "Although we went through a lot of vodka that night." She pauses. "Why do you ask?"

"Just wanted to make sure you don't know anything that he doesn't want to get out."

She shakes her head. "No . . . For once, I'm happy to be the oblivious wife."

And so am I. Because the oblivious wife is the harmless wife. "So, where are you thinking you're going to go?"

"I don't know yet." I look down at her face to see the flames dance within her eyes as she stares intently at the woodstove. "This should be easy, right? People pick up and start over at thirty and forty years old, with kids and everything. I'm only twenty-two. I should be able to chalk this up to a bad mistake of my youth and move on. But I don't know where to begin. I have nothing besides what he's given me."

"It's all just stuff."

"You don't get it!" Her voice rises with frustration. "Look where we are!" She throws a hand up in the air. "In this cute little secluded apartment at your parents' house that was just sitting here, waiting for you. I have no family to run to. No real friends that I can count on. I have *no one*."

Tucking a strand of her hair behind her ear so I can see more of her face, I whisper, "You have me."

She pulls the wool blanket up around us and, roping her arm around my waist, she rests her head against my chest and squeezes me tight. I want to squeeze her back—I want to do more than just squeeze her—but I'm hesitant, for so many reasons beyond just her injuries. So, I settle for weaving my fingers through her long hair.

"That night in the hotel . . . now that I know what it *can* feel like . . ." Her voice drifts. When she speaks again, it's with a hesitant whisper. "I want to feel that way again. With you. I just can't now. Not until all this is sorted out."

"I'll wait."

We lie among the fluffy pillows, listening to the fire crackle, smelling the burning leaves—I stuffed a few handfuls into the woodstove, just because I love the smell of burning leaves.

Her breathing evens out, her heart beats steady against my side.

I absorb all of it.

As I fall fast and hard.

———

"What's down here?"

"If I tell you, then it's not a surprise."

"And you're sure your family won't come out here?"

"Yup. My mom and sister are in comas and my dad's at some charity police force luncheon. Besides, no one's been down this way in years." I ease the Barracuda down the old, uneven path. Normally I wouldn't think to drive it down, but it's too far for Alex to walk while she's still healing. And I really want to see her dip her fingers into a lake for the first time.

Up ahead the water is sparkling in the noonday sunlight. The blue skies are what I miss most about home. Portland always feels gray in comparison.

"A lake!" Alex turns, her own eyes now sparkling brighter than any sun rays on water.

I shrug. "You said you've never been to a lake."

"And you actually remembered . . ." She doesn't wait for me;

she climbs out of the car and begins walking toward the sandy clearing where my sister and I used to set up for the day, back when we'd come out here to swim in the summertime.

I follow her, the wool blanket that she can't seem to part with tucked under my arm.

"This is just . . ." Her words drift. She stands at the water's edge, wrapped in my old gray-and-taupe flannel jacket, inhaling the crisp air, her eyes taking in the trees and mountains facing us. "This is me. This is what I want. I could trade it all today, for this. Has that ever happened to you? Have you ever stepped into a place and just known that you were meant to be there?"

"Kind of."

She glances over her shoulder at me, waiting.

I pick my path toward her, unfolding the wool blanket out as I approach. From behind, I wrap the blanket and my arms around her slender body, pulling her into my chest. "One night, I got out of my car to help this girl with a flat tire. I didn't know it right then, though. But I was meant to meet her."

She tips her head back to set a light kiss on my jawline, sending my blood racing through my body and my arms tightening around her.

A flock of snow geese that were resting across the lake suddenly take flight, their wings flapping against the water, kicking up splashes that glimmer in the sun.

Alex smiles. "That water must be cold."

I release her from my grip long enough for her to dip her red-painted fingertips in. She pulls back immediately with an exaggerated shiver.

"See that stream over there?" I stretch an arm to point out the small branch coming off the lake. "It's fed off the mountain thaw. So is this lake. There's kind of a funny story to it. The stream runs all the way down into our neighbor's property. Our neighbor, Mr. Fitzgerald—he's gone now—didn't like it so close to their barn. For years, he'd try to stop it. My granddad would help him. They'd dump gravel and dirt. One year, they built a dam. But every single spring, the water would find its way onto the Fitzgerald property." I chuckle, remembering the two old men standing over the stream, scratching their beards in wonder. "Finally they just gave up and let it be. Realized there was no stopping it. The water was going to go where it was meant to go." I feel a smile touch my lips. "My granddad used to tell us that story every spring, when we came out here after the thaw. Of course, it wasn't just a story to him. He turned it into a life lesson about telling the truth. I had a problem with lying when I was little," I admit, sheepishly. "He said the truth is like that water: it doesn't matter how hard you try to bury it; it'll always find some way back to the surface. It's resilient."

I feel her body relax into my chest. "I really like that story. I want to be like water, too. I want to be resilient, to go where I'm meant to go."

I graze her cheek with my nose. "You're here, aren't you?"

She gasps and pulls away to turn and face me, excitement sparkling in her eyes. "I know what tattoo I want now."

———

Beans. I assume that's his nickname, given he's tattooed the letters on his knuckles. Otherwise he's a dumbass.

A dumbass whose wary eyes drift between the two of us, frowning every time they land on Alex's bruised cheek. "What are we going with today?"

Alex's bright eyes are full of determination. "A tattoo." Once she decided that this was what she wanted to do, there was no convincing her otherwise, banged-up body and all. Luckily we're the only ones at Get Inked—a small but reputable shop in Bend.

He smirks—we are in a tattoo parlor, after all—and then asks, "Do you know what you want it to look like?"

"I was thinking something to do with water. Like a symbol or something."

"Hmm . . . Can't say I've done one of those. Let's see what we can find." With a fast flick of his hand, he turns his oversized monitor to face us. He hits a few keys to open up a search engine for "water symbols." All kinds come up.

Alex immediately zeros in on a circular symbol with waves inside. "That one." She nods. "Here." She touches the right side of her pelvis, where I imagine her panty line might run.

"Are you sure about this?" I ask in a low voice. "What about . . ." What is Viktor—the guy who dictates what she does, what she wears, her hair color, everything—going to say about a permanent mark on her body? And without his permission.

She sets her jaw with defiance. "Yes."

"All right, then. Let's get this show on the road," Beans mutters. To him, it's just another design to etch into a body. To her, it's a decision she is making without consultation with or authorization from Viktor. A decision made by her, for her.

To me, it's Alex making a permanent mark on her body with something that represents us, even in an indirect way. And the idea of that makes my chest swell.

After printing out the symbol and filling in all the required paperwork, Beans leads us into one of the rooms and instructs Alex to lie down. "You'll need to roll your pants down and push your shirt up," he says, while removing the needle from its sterile packaging.

"You sure you want that there? It's going to hurt," I warn her.

"I can handle it." She eases herself up onto the table and lies down, adjusting her clothes as instructed, the dark bruises over her midsection and hips glaringly obvious under the bright lights.

She definitely can handle it. She's already handled so much more. As dainty and fragile as Alex appears, she's a lot stronger than I've given her credit for.

Beans turns around and falters at the sight of her bruises, shooting a glare my way.

"He didn't do this to me," Alex says, reaching out for me.

"None of my business. I'm just here to ink you," Beans mumbles, transfer ready.

I hold her hand and her gaze the entire time—through every wince and every teeth clench, every smile—as Beans carves a small round symbol into her body. And when he's done, I refuse to let go.

"I'm not taking you back to your house tonight, Alex," I announce, blocking her entry into my Barracuda.

She frowns. "But we have to go back. You have work, and I—"

"I'm not taking you back there until I have to."

She stares at me for a long time, and then she nods. "Okay, Jesse."

WATER

NOW

"You should go visit Amber," Ginny suggests from her perch, a purple-and-blue quilt stretched out on her lap.

"I tried. She's sleeping." I'm pretty sure she has a hangover from last night at Roadside, since I saw Meredith driving in with her car, followed closely by Sheriff Gabe. "Why?"

"Because your fidgeting is giving me a headache."

I slide my hands under my butt. "Sorry." I've been torn between preparing Ginny and surprising her, knowing that neither will go over well. When Teresa phoned this morning to ask if she and Zoe could come out at two this afternoon, I decided on something in between. That's why, when I hear the crackle of tires on loose gravel, I blurt out, "So I have something to tell you." I'm not even looking at her as I continue. "I met a nice lady at the store. She told me that she was selling her twelve-year-old daughter's horse because . . ." I relay the situation in a quick, planned speech that I practiced several times in the mirror. "It's just the two of them and you don't have to say yes, but I figured you could use the money and you could make this little girl very happy. She's been crying over her horse for days." When the red Honda Civic rounds the corner, I add, "This lady bought your quilt. The latest one, with the horses on it."

I dare to glance at Ginny once before I get up to meet Teresa and her daughter, Zoe, a pretty, wide-eyed girl with wavy brown hair. The expression on her face is completely unreadable.

But she hasn't reached for her broom yet, so I guess there's that.

———

"Two hundred a month for her own stall, plus any veterinarian bills. And she has to use my veterinarian." She lops on a spoonful of mashed potatoes—I made the real kind; not that awful boxed stuff—and then takes a helping of a pot roast that I thought I'd try out. "And it's just her and her mother on this property. No one else. Not this useless hunk of an ex-husband, not any coaches or trainers. Just those two."

I nod. I had already figured as much and warned Teresa. She seemed fine with it, and was impressed with the barn and the land. And Ginny, as cranky as she can be, seemed to take to Zoe right away, asking her questions about Lulu's habits and which stable she might prefer.

I thought that I might get whacked over the head with that broom, but when I left her on the porch to make dinner and read a bit, she was unusually quiet and content. "So, can I call her after dinner and tell her? I know Zoe's probably waiting anxiously."

Ginny studies the meat on her fork intently as she chews a mouthful and swallows. "It was a stable hand."

I frown.

"He was in his late twenties. A big, burly man. But soft, like a teddy bear. Earl was his name. He worked for my dad for three years, one month, one week." She twists the fork around. A bead of gravy drips down and hits her plate. "Four days. I was about that girl's age when I first met Earl. I was in those stables every single day, rain or snow, it didn't matter, helping to muck out the

stalls and care for the horses. We had so many back then, it was hard to keep up." She frowns at the meat. "At first, he just said hi to me. Asked how school was. I was an odd child—wary of people, even then—so I kept my distance. Eventually, though, he became a friend. He taught me how to climb trees. That's what won me over. He was an excellent tree climber." She finally eats the piece of meat, her jaw moving slowly, precisely. "After . . . my daddy did most of the work around here, with my help. It was *a lot* for just the two of us. I'm no idiot. I know that what happened to me isn't common and that I could have a thousand stable hands through here with no issues. It doesn't change the fact that I can't ever be around another one."

"Yes." I bob my head rigorously to emphasize my agreement.

"That Zoe girl, she really loves horses. She lit up around our Felixes." Ginny's narrowed gaze follows the horizon out over the mountains. "My daddy always said that I lit up around the horses, too."

———

What is it about this blanket?

I wouldn't describe it as soft. In fact, it's almost abrasive. Yet, leaning against a pile of cushions in front of the burning wood-stove with a book from Amber, and wrapped within my checkered wool blanket from The Salvage Yard, I feel more contented than my limited memory can recall.

Perhaps I feel particularly cozy given the thunderous storm outside. Apparently we're sheltered from the kind of rain that the east coast of Oregon gets, thanks to the mountains, but we don't get away completely. The radio station playing at work today called for everything from catastrophic winds to clear skies in the span of an afternoon. Dakota and I made a bet—loser buys coffee. I, of course, chose clear night skies, both because I like to take in the stars from my balcony before I go to bed and because Dakota always buys coffee for both of us.

I'll definitely be buying the coffee tomorrow.

A bolt of lightning zags through the sky outside and my attic apartment fills with light. The booming crack of thunder comes almost immediately after. And then the old brass lamp that shines over my book pages cuts out, along with the one other light I have on in my apartment.

Unease begins to slide down my back. The fire glow provides enough light to guide me to the kitchen drawer, where I know that there is a flashlight. It's not big, but I can find my way around the apartment with it.

Another loud crack of thunder has me diving to the window to check the Welles property. There's always a spotlight shining on one corner of their house—bright enough to cast a light to the fence line, emphasizing Meredith's promise that I can come to their door at any time, day or night. Now, though, it's as if that guarantee has been snuffed out. I don't know that I could even make it to their house without tripping and injuring myself, the darkness is so consuming.

I look out the other windows. I even unlatch all the deadbolts and chains that I use every night and open the door. I meet only black nothingness.

That, and a cold, mean rain that pelts my face and dampens my shirt. Pushing my door shut, I relock the door and wrap my chest with my arms. I guess I'll just have to wait it out. Taking my seat by the fire again, my blanket pulled to my chin and my knees pulled to my chest, I watch the flames lick the glass panel of the woodstove.

When footsteps pound up the stairs outside and someone knocks, I'm on my feet instantly, moving for the door. There are only a few people it could be—Ginny or one of the Welleses—and they'll be getting soaked out there, so I begin unlatching the deadbolts again.

But then my hand falters. That voice in the back of my head adds another person to the list of possible visitors: the faceless man who showed himself to me once in a dream. Who hurt me terribly. I know it's not realistic and yet, as I see the doorknob wiggle, a part of me panics.

A fist pounds against the other side. "Water! It's me!"

My heart skips a beat.

I'm safe.

I fumble with the remaining locks and throw open the door, ushering in Jesse.

"Hey," he says through a shudder. "Are you all right?"

"Yes. Why?"

"Oh, just because . . ." He lifts a hand to rub the back of his head. His hair's so short that it barely messes it. "The power's out. I don't like when the power's out."

"I'm not sure I do either," I admit. "How long do you think before it's back on?"

"Honestly? Depends on where the break is, but it could be all night." Flashes of lightning fill the room, and I can see that his flannel jacket and the T-shirt underneath are drenched.

I have the urge to find him something to change into, but nothing I have would fit him. My closet is full of hand-me-downs from Amber and Meredith, along with a few basic things from the secondhand shop in Bend. I forced Amber to go in. She wasn't crazy about the idea but I enjoyed paying for some clothes with my own money, even if they weren't new.

"Well, I guess we'll just have to wait it out, then." I wander back over to my spot by the woodstove and wrap myself up in my blanket, hoping he'll stay. I like not being alone right now, but more than that, I like the idea of being with Jesse.

Without a word, he grabs another log, the handle squeaking as he opens the woodstove and feeds the fire. Hungry, the flames flare, casting a brighter glow and illuminating Jesse's profile, his eyelashes long and thick.

I instinctively reach up to my scar, my index finger running along the thin ridge. I'll never have an appealing profile, not from my right side, anyway.

When the tiny door screeches shut, he pulls his jacket off, exposing his T-shirt beneath, the front of it wet. I'm suddenly thankful for the relative darkness, as it affords me the chance to gawk at the ridges on his stomach without being too obvious.

"Don't like the furniture in here?" he murmurs, stretching his jacket out on one of the wicker chairs—a skeleton now that I've confiscated the cushions for my nest.

"I do, I just . . ." I frown. "I felt the urge to lie on the floor, I guess. It makes me feel cozy."

"Does it?" His eyes drift over the pile of cushions that I lean against. "Well, in that case . . ." He kicks off his running shoes and then dives down next to me. Tucking his shoes under the woodstove, he adjusts the few stray pillows and lies back, stretching out his long body.

From my angle, higher and slightly behind him, I can watch him shamelessly.

And I do.

"Was this ours?" He nestles his head against the cable-knit pillow.

"Yeah. Your mom's very generous." Meredith's spring cleaning involved bringing perfectly good bedding and blankets and books over to my door—things to dress up the space, give it life, she said. Some of these things still had price tags on them. "Do you want tea?" I reach for the mug I was drinking. "I can't make you one right now, but you can have mine if you'd like."

I feel his eyes on my face and I wish we were facing the other way, so the shadows could hide what I don't want him to see. Finally, he drops his gaze. "I'm not a tea drinker."

"Coffee?" His single nod answers me. "Let me guess . . . black?"

The muscle in his jaw pulses. "What made you think that?"

I shrug. "Just a guess. You look like a black-coffee drinker."

"And what does a black-coffee drinker look like?"

"I don't know. I don't know why I said that. I guess you remind me of someone who drinks black coffee." Now I sound even more stupid. "I watch people a lot, wondering what makes them who they are." I watch what kind of food they load onto the conveyor belt at the grocery store, and what they order at Poppa's, the local greasy diner that serves the best coffee in town. I watch the way some people dart across a busy main street while others wait for the light so they can use the crosswalk; the way some parents offer annoyed shushes to their children's incessant chatter while others provide calm answers; the way a group of women will sit at a coffee shop table, their eyes circulating, their words laced with critical comments, while at the next table another group sits, oblivious to anyone else and just enjoying one another's company. I watch and I wonder what makes people who they are. Is it the sum of learned behaviors and experiences? And if they, like me, can't recall those experiences, would they still do those things in the exact same way? Or would they deviate?

How similar am I to who I once was? Would I have gotten excited stepping out of a thrift shop, my arms loaded with someone else's castaways? Would I have willingly cooked meals for a crotchety old lady who doesn't have the words "thank you" in her vocabulary?

Would I have turned my judgmental nose up at a "free spirit" like Dakota?

I think about these things. I think about the fancy dress and the diamond jewelry I was found with, my platinum-blond dyed hair, and how that girl ended up shoveling horse shit out of stalls. And loving it.

"That makes sense," Jesse finally offers.

I giggle. "No it doesn't. You're just trying to make me feel better."

The tiniest dimple pokes his cheek. "You look like a two-and-a-half-milks, one-sweetener kind of coffee drinker."

"That sounds ridiculous." He must be mocking me now. "I'm one cream, one sugar." That was how the first cup Amber ever delivered to me in the hospital was made. I realize now that I've never tried anything else.

He shrugs. "It was worth a shot."

A comfortable silence hangs over us. "Are you happy to be back home?"

A slow nod answers. "It's where I belong. Nothing I want in Portland anymore."

Not even that girl you wanted to marry?

He reaches forward to pick up my journal, lying on the floor between us. "What's this?"

"Just . . . uh . . ." I fight the urge to grab it out of his hand as he flips it open to the latest page, where my pen is tucked in. "It's nothing, just a journal I need to keep for my psychologist. She's hoping there will be a pattern or maybe it'll trigger something."

I see "blueberries" in my circular handwriting and know that he's on the latest page. I haven't been keeping up with the process as well as I should.

"Why'd you cross my name out?"

Heat crawls up my neck. "Because that response was tainted."

"Tainted?" Amusement dances along his profile. "I tainted blueberries?"

"You gave me the blueberries. Of course the first word that enters my head is going to be your name."

"Right." He flips through the other pages. "My sister's helping you with these?"

"Yeah, sometimes. Your mom, too. Sometimes I quiz myself. Though it's not quite as effective."

When he reaches the page where I've written "Baby = Impossible," he stops. "Is it? I mean, is that what my mom told you?"

I'm surprised he's asking me this so bluntly—but then again, he doesn't seem like a small-talk kind of guy. And for some reason, I don't mind talking about it with him. "No. She said the exact opposite, actually." My hand shifts to rest on my abdomen of its own accord. "I would have been about seven months pregnant by now." I've caught myself doing the math often. Usually when I'm walking along the stream, or watching the horses trot by. Imagining what it would be like to raise a child out here. "I think I really wanted this baby."

"I guess that one wasn't meant to be," Jesse offers softly. He lifts the pen, making a spectacle of clicking the top several times.

I playfully pull my blanket to my face to cover my nervous smile, equal parts curious about and wary of what he's going to prompt me with. I've found that Amber relies on cues from our surroundings as a resource. Meredith's a little more creative, throwing out things like "Barbie doll" and "gymnastics," things that may relate to my childhood. Both treat the exercise as a light, unchallenging way to help me.

A prick in my gut tells me that Jesse may not take that approach.

"Tire."

What? Wait. Meredith told me he's a mechanic. I guess that makes sense. "Flat." I watch him scribble the words down, his pen strokes long but neat. The knuckles on his right hand are red and bruised. I assume from punching Dean.

"Hotel."

Hotel . . . Hotel . . . Hotel . . . "Bed?"

My cheeks heat as I watch his hand scribble the words down. Not because there's anything unusual. Because the second word that popped into my head after "bed" was "Jesse."

"Water."

"Yes?"

"No . . . I mean, 'Water.'" I hear the smile in his voice.

"Oh! Tattoo. Your sister's already done that one."

"Why tattoo?" he asks softly, his eyes on the page, his hand ready to write.

"I have one, right here." I tap my pelvis, drawing his attention to it. Heat spreads through my legs and thighs instantly.

"Okay. The second word that comes to mind. Water."

I close my eyes and let my mind go blank. *Water . . . Water . . . Water . . .* "Stream." Like that stream that runs behind the barn. I sigh. "I think my new life is bleeding into my thoughts. That's not going to help this exercise much."

He says nothing for a moment. Then, "Tattoo."

"Water . . . No! Wait." I reach out to touch his arm, to stop him from writing that down. "That's too obvious."

The bicep muscle beneath my fingertips tightens, but he doesn't move. "Okay. What, then?"

Tattoo . . . Tattoo . . . Tattoo.

Jesse.

I can't even think straight anymore, with him here. "I don't . . . next word," I demand, flustered.

"Scar."

"Ugly." I didn't really mean to blurt that out. There are plenty of other words that I could use—ones that don't make me sound weak and whiny and quite so vulnerable—but I can't deny that it's the first thing that popped into my mind.

The pen sits poised over the paper in his frozen grip for long seconds, as both shame and anger swirl like an angry cloud within me. It's one thing to fear that you're ugly; it's an entirely different thing to acknowledge it out loud to another person. Especially when that other person is a guy who you seem to be developing a crush on.

There's really nothing he can say: agree with me and kick me while I'm down, or try to argue with me, knowing I won't believe him.

He tucks the pen into the spine and closes the book.

Probably the best option.

I quietly watch him get up and stoke the fire with another log, opening the vent to let more heat in. I'm expecting him to grab his shoes and jacket and say good night, but he doesn't. Instead he lies back down beside me, but closer this time, the itchy checkered blanket that I have cocooned myself within the only barrier between us.

He takes a deep breath and closes his eyes.

"Why did you punch that guy at the bar?"

"I didn't like the way he was touching you."

I watch, waiting for him to say something else. I watch until his chest begins to rise and fall at a lower rate and his full lips just barely part. Until I realize that the damn boy from next door has fallen asleep in my apartment.

———

It takes me a few moments to realize that I'm no longer on the floor. The last thing I remember is listening to Jesse breathe. I guess I fell asleep.

That means Jesse carried me to bed.

Thanks to the pre-dawn light streaming in through the sliding door, I can see that he's not here now, though the fire is burning bright, as if someone just fed it. My alarm clock is flashing big bold red numbers at me, so the power's back on.

And my journal sits beside it.

I reach over and open it to the last page, with Jesse's narrow scrawl, his last entry:

Scar = Resilient.

TWENTY-SEVEN

JESSE

THEN

"What the fuck are you doing, Jesse!" Boone hisses, his eyes darting from the living room to my bedroom, where I left Alex with her bags.

"Did you not just see her face?"

"Yeah, I did. I also know who did that to her. Make her go to the hospital, the cops. Convince her to ditch the asshole. But don't shack up with her in our apartment. Jeez . . ." He pushes his hands through his gelled hair, sending his perfectly styled long waves into disarray.

"I tried. She won't do any of that. But she *is* going to leave him."

He blows a mouthful of air out, his hands resting on his hips. "I hope you're right. For both your sakes. And mine, since I'm your roommate and it'll be hard for me to deny that she was here if Rust ever hears about this."

"*No one's* going to hear about this. She'll lay low. It's just for the week, man. I promise. We'll figure something out after that. Just . . . no visitors during that time. Especially not Priscilla."

"Fuck, you think?" He shakes his head and goes to his room, Licks on his heels.

When I open the door to my room, I find Alex standing in front of my mirror, her pants and shirt pulled away as she inspects the fresh tattoo on her pelvis. "It's not too much, is it?"

My heart begins to race at the sight of her long, slender torso, bruises and all. "No, it's definitely not too much." I step in close behind her, my hands covering hers where they hold her clothing back. "Do you like it?"

"I love it."

And *I* love the way her tongue curls around that word. The way her eyes flicker to mine in her reflection when she says it. The way she's watching me in the mirror now.

I hate bringing it up, but I have to because I'm still worried. "What do you think Viktor's going to say about it?"

She turns toward me, her hot breath skating across my neck. "He'll never find out." She's making it damn near impossible for me to restrain myself around her, especially when she does things like that. Still, I keep my hands firmly in place.

"I like what you've done with your room."

I know she's teasing me. "You know that saying, 'I rolled out of bed'? Well . . . I do, every day. Literally."

Her eyes skate over the small, sparse space—white walls, a single dresser, a mattress on the floor. Just like my above-garage apartment, this place is perfect for a twenty-four-year-old guy who needs a bed to fall into. Thinking back to the small part of Alex and Viktor's home that I saw—designer-decorated and custom everything—almost makes me laugh now.

But she says she wants *me*. And right now, *this* is me.

The question is, will she still want this when she's free of him?

———

"Damn . . ." Boone moans, leading our way through the door and tossing his keys on the rack. "I could get used to this."

I chuckle as I kick the door shut behind me, the delicious smell of whatever Alex is cooking today—beef and herbs and definitely Italian—making my stomach growl. We step into the kitchen to find her stirring a pot of tomato sauce on the stove. A strainer full of limp spaghetti sits over another pot. If the pile of dishes is any indication, that sauce didn't come out of a jar.

"Hey, Alex," Boone and I chirp in unison.

This is the third night we've come home to a set table and Alex in the kitchen, Licks faithfully waiting at her feet. And all I did to deserve it was make a grocery run with a list on Sunday night. Boone's right—I could totally get used to this.

"I finally see how Licks earned his name," she announces with a giggle, sticking a sauce-covered wooden spoon out for the bulldog that sits by her legs. He goes after it immediately, his long tongue slurping up every last drop until it's just wood. "I think he'd lick the grain right off the wood if I let him." She tosses it into the sink.

"Time for a run," Boone announces, slapping his thigh on his way to his room to change into his running gear. The dog doesn't move. I have to nudge him away with my leg as I step up behind Alex.

"You know you don't have to cook and clean for us, right?" I wrap my arms around her waist and dip my face into her neck to inhale the scent of her skin. I'm addicted to the smell and feel of her. It's what gets me through long days at work, just waiting until I can come back and be with her again.

"I know I don't. But I like doing it, and I know you two appreciate it." Shutting the stove off, she twists in my arms to face me with a smile. Her lip is back to its normal size and the purple in her cheek is fading to green. "Besides, I had enough of my schoolwork and reading." Alex has had to skip her classes this week, on account of her face, but she's made a few friends who she's been emailing for assignments.

Taking a deep breath, I look down at that mouth. Wanting to kiss it so badly. "I'm going to jump in the shower, 'kay?" And not just to wash off the garage. Sleeping next to Alex for the past five nights has been both heaven and hell. And a lot of cold showers.

I feel her eyes on me the entire way down the hall to the bathroom, passing Boone on the way, leash in hand.

"Licks!" The dog's collar jangles the way it always does when Boone's hooking the leash around him. "Come on, Fatty." I glance over my shoulder to see the dog hanging from under Boone's arm, having refused to abandon Alex's side. "You've ruined my dog!" Boone hollers, throwing a wink at Alex before heading out the door.

I'm still chuckling in the shower when Alex steps into the bathroom and shuts the door behind her. I watch her through the glass shower enclosure as she flips the lock. "Is everything all right?"

She pulls her shirt off and tosses it to the floor with my clothes.

We haven't so much as kissed up until now. I wasn't expecting this.

I'm instantly hard.

Her jeans come off next, followed by her lacy black bra and underwear. And then she climbs into the shower behind me, a shy smile touching her lips.

Before I have a chance to fully turn around, she edges up behind me, sliding her arms around my waist. Soft lips land on my tattoo.

And then her delicate hand reaches down.

With a low moan, I close my eyes and tip my head back, letting the shower spray hit my face.

"Look at me," she whispers.

I turn to face her, and within seconds she's on her knees and taking me into her mouth. In the back of my mind, I worry about her lip but, peering down at her, her heated eyes locked on mine, I don't see any hint of pain there. All I can see is how much she actually wants to do this for me.

It's not even a minute later that I'm balling my fists to keep from grabbing the back of her head as I ride the waves of pure fucking ecstasy. I'm barely coherent when she stands, close enough that her chest presses against mine.

Trailing kisses from my throat to my mouth, she murmurs, "I've wanted to do that for so long."

My fingertips skate across her belly, across the scab forming over her tattoo, until my hand rests on her inner thigh. But I hesitate.

"I have three more nights with you, before I have to face reality." She reaches down and guides my fingers in for me. "I know what I said, but I can't wait. I've never been this happy before, Jesse," she whispers against my mouth.

Neither have I. I punch the faucet, shutting the shower off. I need to be inside her tonight but that's not going to happen in the shower. With towels draped around our dripping bodies, we stumble across the hall. I ease her down into my bed and then, pulling the towel away, I take a moment to just drink in the sight of her perfect, lean body. The bruises on her body are mere yellow spots now. Barely noticeable. But that tattoo . . . it's downright sexy.

Her eyes graze over me as I drop my own towel. I'm already hard again. With her, I think I always will be.

She's right. We have three more nights together before I have to let her go. Even if for only a day or two, before she comes back to me. I've seen what Viktor can do to her and the thought that letting her go long enough that he might do it again makes my stomach churn.

He fucked up. This is on him. He was given an angel and he tried to break her wings. But she's strong. Resilient. And now she's all mine. I don't give a damn what anyone thinks about that.

"You'll tell me if it's too much, right?" I say, slipping a condom on.

She lets her legs fall apart in answer.

I don't hesitate again.

"We're meant to be together," she whispers into my ear, moving with my body, our arms and legs and heated breath a tangled mess.

There are no tears tonight.

———

"Miller actually asked me what was wrong with you. Like, he wanted specific details."

"What'd you tell him?"

Boone shrugs, his eyes flickering over Alex, leaning into my side on the sectional. "Told him you had a stomach thing."

I smirk. I know what that means. The jackass told the garage that I had the shits. I'll be the butt of Tabbs's and Zeke's stupid jokes all of tomorrow. Totally worth it, because I spent an entire day in bed with Alex, memorizing the sound of her giggles as my fingers slid over her curves, her freckles. Kissing away her fading bruises. Falling deeper into this swirl of emotions with every minute that passed. Her sweet, caring, strong spirit is an intoxicating fog; it's so easy to get lost in it and dismiss the reality that looms.

And that's exactly what we did. We got dressed only a couple of hours ago, after Alex insisted she wanted to make dinner and then study for an upcoming test.

"Okay, Alex. You ready for the next question?" Boone's been flipping through the reproduction chapters in Alex's anatomy textbook, reading out random quotes to make her blush and me laugh. I've caught myself forgetting who Boone's uncle is and his connection to Viktor several times tonight, instead picturing the three of us living here together. *It could work*, I keep fooling myself.

He frowns. "Alex?"

She's staring at the television, her mouth parted slightly, her face white as snow. "I know her."

Boone and I share a glance. "Who?"

"That woman." She points at the news broadcast where a picture of a dark-haired woman in her mid-thirties sits next to a picture of a man. "I mean, I've met her. She came to our house last summer for that garden party. Her husband is one of Viktor's friends."

I wasn't really paying attention to the TV before. Now, though, all three of us are glued to the screen, listening to the reporter's monotone voice as she explains that this woman and what the police believe to be her lover were found shot to death in a hotel room, her wedding ring still on her finger. Police have detained her husband as a prime suspect, with evidence that places him at the scene of the crime.

When the camera flashes to a picture of the suspect, a tall blond guy with the same hardened look as Viktor, Alex gasps.

I reach out to smooth a comforting hand over her back. "I'm sorry, Alex, I—" The reporter's closing remarks freeze my tongue:

"Authorities suspect Pavel Federov of having ties to Russian organized crime; however, this particular incident appears to be a case of domestic violence."

Russian organized crime.

Holy shit.

Boone quietly sets the textbook down and then heads to his bedroom, Licks on his heels.

But so am I, kicking his door shut behind me. "Tell me that Viktor isn't with the fucking mob."

He doesn't turn around.

"Boone!"

"I don't know for sure, all right!"

"No. Not all right! Are you fucking kidding me? Why didn't you tell me?"

He spins on his heels to face me. "That's not exactly the kind of thing you talk about. And it's not like they carry around business cards to announce themselves." He lowers his voice.

"Look . . . I'm just starting to work my way into Rust's circle. You don't just stroll in there, unannounced and uninvited."

"Rust's 'circle'?" I make air quotes around the word. "Are you telling me that *Rust* is Russian mob? What the hell have you gotten me mixed up in? What are *you* getting mixed up in?"

"No! Rust is not *with* them. He's got several businesses—two that are legit, one that technically isn't . . ." This is the first I'm hearing that Rust may not fully be aboveboard either. "And he's making a ton of money that I want in on. That's all. Some of his connections may be to guys like Viktor."

"And Viktor is mob." It's not a question.

"I don't know one hundred percent, but it's probably a safe bet to assume so. Look, I hear shit! They have a lot of business conversations around that table and they have no fucking clue that I might understand what they're saying."

Nausea burns my stomach as panic sets in. I rebuilt a car for the damn mob. I've had the wife of a Russian mobster in my bed for the past six nights. Dropping my voice, because I don't want Alex to hear, I ask, "Is he capable of something like that?"

Boone's mouth opens but he doesn't speak right away, like he's trying to choose his words. "I've heard that he has a bad temper."

Would finding out that his wife is leaving him set it off? How about for the twenty-four-year-old gearhead who he hired to fix his engine? "Why wouldn't you warn me?"

He shoots a finger at me. "I *did* warn you. More than once, remember?"

"No. Not about this, you didn't."

"Dude, what the hell was I supposed to say? I told you about the stolen cars, didn't I? That should have been fair warning that Viktor's not some office chump who will roll over for the guy screwing his wife."

"Fuck you, Boone. You're an asshole." I march out of his room, slamming his door on my way.

Alex is sitting on my bed, her cheeks wet with tears. "I didn't know. I swear, I didn't. I'm so sorry."

I drop to my knees in front of her, taking her hands in mine. "You have nothing to be sorry for."

"What have we done?" she whispers, her eyes pleading with me. "He's going to kill us."

"No he's not, because he's never going to find out. That couple on TV—they were probably being stupid about it. That's why they got caught. We've been careful. You haven't even left the apartment since Sunday. No one knows you're here except Boone, and he's not going to say a thing." Boone's the one who brought me into the fold. I'm sure he doesn't want to go down with us.

She dips her forehead into mine. "He's not going to just let me leave, is he?" The defeat in her voice squeezes my heart.

"We'll figure it out. We'll get you away from him. I promise."

That night, I hold her tense body against mine as we both stare out the window, not speaking, not sleeping.

And I feel it.

Everything has changed.

TWENTY-EIGHT

WATER

NOW

"The usual, Water?" Lauren asks with a smile, reaching for two large Styrofoam cups.

"No. Not today."

The short, apple-figured cashier and daughter of Poppa—the owner of Poppa's Diner—freezes midway. She prides herself on knowing what the regulars want. Now she's looking at me like I've thrown a wrench into her weekday routine and irreparably damaged her flow.

"The usual for Dakota," I quickly correct. "But can I have a large with," I cringe, "two-and-a-half milks and one sweetener?"

She cocks her head. "Honey, a what?"

I have to repeat my order three times before Lauren gives up and slides a carton of milk and a few packets of Splenda across the counter with a black coffee. "I'll just screw it up."

After paying, I shift over to an open table to mix my coffee, inhaling the delicious scent of bacon and home fries. Everyone and their children and their grandchildren have eaten at Poppa's, a staple in Sisters for sixty years this summer. The white-haired man behind the grill opened the place when he was twenty-two years old and still works seven days a week, double-time on weekends, when the town packs the small place. Even now it's buzzing with light chatter, half the tables occupied by the retired population.

"Excuse me." I look up to find an older woman with short auburn hair standing opposite me. "Are you Ginny Fitzgerald's cousin?" Her blue eyes glance over the right side of my face and I can see her mentally adding a check mark next to "giant scar." Whoever gave her my description didn't neglect to mention that. I wonder where it was on the list of my identifying features.

"I am."

Her face softens. "I'm glad to meet you. My name is Hildy. Ginny and I used to be best friends."

"Really?" I can't keep the surprise from my voice. Ginny had a best friend?

She chuckles. "Yes, for most of grade school and into high school. We were going to move to Seattle together, the summer after we finished our senior year."

"Were going to" obviously means that they didn't.

Hildy doesn't elaborate on the reasons why, but she doesn't need to. "I went anyway, and then met my husband, and got married. Then I had children and we just . . . we lost touch." Her brow pulls together in a way that tells me she genuinely feels bad about that. "I've thought about her over the years, but you know how it is. Well, I suppose you're still too young to lose touch with people, but you'll understand one day."

I stifle my derisive snort. *Lady, you have no idea how out of touch I am.*

"Well, didn't my granddaughter go on about the amazing ranch where she just brought her horse, Lulu, for boarding. I didn't put two-and-two together until she started describing the barn and the corral. I realized I had been there before. Plenty of times, actually."

"You're Zoe's grandmother?"

Her head bobs up and down. "She's a good girl, that Zoe. Too bad she has a schmuck for a father." She pauses. "I would like to come visit Ginny when Zoe and Teresa go again. Do you think Ginny'd be okay with that? I'd love to see her. Talk to her again."

"I'm sure I can talk her into it." Ginny could use a friend. One that doesn't walk on all fours and harbor fleas.

"Thank you so much." She reaches out to pat my forearm, and my chest instantly fills with warmth. "My daughter said you were a kind girl. Ginny's lucky to have you."

I watch Hildy leave Poppa's, her words clinging to me. *Ginny's lucky to have me.* I've always thought of it as the other way around.

I finally dare take a sip of my coffee.

I don't believe it.

Jesse was right. I *am* a two-and-a-half milks and one sweetener.

Or maybe I just want to be?

———

"What are you drawing now?" I lean over Dakota's shoulder to peek at her sketchbook, watching her black pen fill in a frog's belly with steady strokes.

"Tina wants to get this on the back of her neck for her eighteenth birthday, to symbolize her transformation," she explains, leaning against the counter on an elbow, her chin propped in her palm.

Tina is Lauren's daughter, and Poppa's granddaughter. I'm guessing by "transformation," she means Tina's extreme weight loss. The high school senior has apparently lost eighty-five pounds in the last year through diet and exercise. "How's Poppa going to feel about that?" Tina serves at the diner on weekends. I've only said hello to him in passing once or twice, but he doesn't rub me as the kind of guy who wants his staff displaying neck tattoos.

"Well, rumor has it Lauren got knocked up at eighteen and they had trouble identifying who Tina's father is, so I would think a tattoo won't be a big deal to Poppa. But Tina can deal with that. Or Lauren."

Another few months and I probably won't be able to look at a single person in this town without having to push their dirty laundry out of my line of sight. Dakota doesn't gossip with malicious intent, the way Amber's friends seemed to. She simply has an archive of information that she shares liberally with me.

"They'll know who enabled her, though." My eyes drift to the dream-catcher tattoo that stretches across the top of Dakota's back from shoulder to shoulder, on display thanks to a black tube top and a sleek ponytail. She has several more on her body, all similar in style and all designed by her. Dakota's sketches are distinctive—curvy pen strokes, with tribal undertones. Most depict what she calls "spirit animals," something Dakota seems very into. I thought this was a tie to her own native heritage but apparently she's been studying spirit animals and their meanings for years, adopting other tribal beliefs and traditions and adding her own unique flare.

"Do you want to annoy the woman who makes our coffee every morning?" I remind her.

She smiles, her teeth all the more white against her dark complexion. "She'll still love me."

I chuckle on my way over to the old cedar chest that's serving as a table and begin tidying the stack of blankets. Dakota's laissez-faire attitude is a refreshing change from what I deal with from Ginny. Nothing seems to ruffle her. Not even the fact that we haven't had one customer step in in the last hour and she probably doesn't need to be paying me to stand here. "It's a weekday. Everything's slow on a weekday," is her only response.

"You know that you could charge people money for those designs," I suggest.

"I know." She hums softly as her hand slides over the paper. "Hey, do you have any tattoos?"

"I do. A small water symbol, right here." I pat the right side of my pelvis, silently wondering what I was wearing—or not wearing—when I had that done.

There's a long pause. "You should let me design one for you." The end of her black pen is tapping rhythmically on the counter.

"What did you have in mind?"

She frowns. "I'm not sure yet. Frogs are tied deeply with water, but it doesn't feel right for you. Your aura," her fingers swirl with her words, "says resilience and agility."

Resilience. There's that word that Jesse wrote in my journal. Every time I hear it, I smile.

"But your spirit hasn't spoken clearly to me just yet. I've heard mere whispers."

"And what do the whispers say?"

She continues working away at her frog sketch. "That your soul is scarred but it will survive, once it finds what it is searching for. There's great inner conflict. I see that, too."

A shiver runs down my back. Some people—Amber included—would probably roll their eyes at Dakota's ramblings, writing them off as airy and weed-induced and borderline creepy. But I would be happy to sit here until her uncanny skill can shed some light on my spirit.

The door jangles, pulling me away from thoughts of my aura and right into the dark eyes of Jesse Welles.

My heart leaps.

I haven't spoken to him in days, since the night of the storm. His car has been sitting in his garage, but he hasn't come out and I haven't had the nerve to venture over. I'm afraid that I may wear out my welcome. Instead, I've sat in my nest of pillows every night, staring at his words in my journal, hoping to hear his footsteps up the stairs.

"Hey." The side of his mouth kicks up in a smile as he strolls down the aisle, coming to a stop a few feet away from me, sliding his hands into his jeans pockets.

I feel my face burst with heat at the simple word. "Hey. What are you doing here?" Jesse doesn't seem like the kind of guy in the market for recycled art.

He juts his chin across the street. "On break and grabbing coffee." His T-shirt reads "Hart Brothers Forestry."

"Did you find a new job already?"

"Through a buddy I went to school with. They need help clearing after the forest fire. It's good money. And it's temporary."

"No mechanics jobs available yet, I guess?"

"Nope." He takes the folded blanket from my hand and drops it on the pile for me. Glancing behind me, he offers, "Hey, Dakota. How's it going?"

She doesn't answer immediately, still leaning against the counter, her chin in her palm, staring at Jesse. Almost *through* Jesse. And then it's as though invisible fingers snap in front of her, because she startles. "Hi, Jesse! It's good to see you."

A horn honks from just outside the store. It's a big green truck with "Hart Brothers" stamped into the side and a young guy sitting in the passenger seat, his hand slapping the side of the door as if to the beat of music.

Jesse gives my waist a light squeeze. "Gotta go. Just wanted to stop by."

"See you later?" The question's casual enough.

"Yeah, I'm around."

I watch him climb into the back of the truck cab. Wondering what the hell "Yeah, I'm around" means. That I'll see him because he's around and, by default, I may literally *see* him? Or should I go visit? Or maybe he'll come visit? Or . . .

"He has feelings for you." Dakota's eyes have that dreamy look in them. "Deep, consuming feelings. The kind that dominate your thoughts and control your decisions. And feed your soul."

My stomach leaps to my throat, her words sparking something inside me. Hope, that's what that is. And it's silly. "We barely know each other, Dakota."

Her wide mouth spreads into a smile. "And yet you *know* each other. Your spirits are . . . entwined."

"Did you smoke something while you were tossing the trash out back?" I exclaim.

That smile simply hangs there for a few seconds. And then she starts to giggle.

———

Lasagna—one of Ginny's favorites—is cooling on the stove when I first hear the rumble of Jesse's car. I practically jump out of my chair and run to the window in time to see him pull into the garage and cut the engine. The door slams and a moment later, he strolls out to the edge of the garage.

And then he turns to my window.

The lights are off in here so I doubt he can see me, and yet he stares for so long that I perhaps think he can.

"I'm around," I mutter, repeating what he said earlier. Before I can chicken out, I grab two plates and slice into the lasagna with a spatula, heaving sizeable pieces onto them. Covering them with foil, I take the stairs down faster than I normally would, afraid that Jesse will disappear into his attic.

He's leaning against the back wall, his arms folded over his chest, simply staring at his car when my foot hits the concrete floor. "Does it look different than it did yesterday?"

He smirks. His work clothes are dirty and I see a small scrape on his arm. I'm guessing he's going to be getting into the shower soon, a visual I don't need to be having right now.

I hold up the plates. "I thought you and your dad might like dinner." Dakota's voice rings out loud inside my head. *He has feelings for you.*

"Thank you." He takes the plates and our hands touch briefly.

And that strange sense of comfort I keep feeling around him washes over me in a wave. Regardless of what my mind has decided to protect me from, my senses are telling me that Jesse is safe. That Ginny is wrong about him.

Ginny.

"Shit." I glance up at the wall clock and see that I have exactly two minutes to get the lasagna to the table. "I've gotta go. See you later?"

"Yeah, I'll be here. Or upstairs."

I make it to the porch with exactly ten seconds to spare and Ginny's already waiting in her seat. "Your favorite. There's enough for a few meals here."

She frowns. "It's missing a quarter."

"Yes, it is." I load her plate and mine, and then take a seat and stab at it, starving.

"Well?" Ginny's staring at me now. "Where did it go?"

"I thought Sheriff Gabe and Jesse might like a piece, so I brought it over."

"To Gabe?"

"Nope." The *p* in the word pops out of my mouth, and then I shovel a piece of lasagna in my mouth and level her with a look.

For once, she doesn't answer, deciding to mimic me and fill her mouth with food, either because it's that good or she's intentionally shutting herself up. Ginny's answers are usually more logical and palatable with at least a seven-second delay.

That's why I wait until she has another mouthful before I say, "I met a Hildy today." Ginny's eyes flash with instant recognition, so I know that her childhood best friend hasn't been forgotten, even after almost fifty years. "She would really like to come visit you."

She chews slowly, her hazel eyes looking past me, to the fields, to the mountains, to years ago, when things were different for her. Finally, she swallows and says softly, "That'd be nice."

Ginny is surprisingly chatty for the rest of our meal. She tells me about the time she and Hildy went to the rodeo and saw the sheriff at the time fall off his horse walking down Main Street, an empty flask of whiskey in his hand, the contents already poured down his gullet.

I catch myself smiling, and not because of the story.

Maybe we're both lucky to have found each other.

———

"Jesse?"

I fold my arms against the chill. The big storm brought with it milder weather, but the evenings are still on the cool side. He's not in the garage, so I knock on the door in the back. He did tell me to come by. Kind of. And he did tell me that he might be upstairs.

So I try the handle. The door pops open. A familiar smell fills my nostrils immediately, but I can't place it.

"Jesse?" I call into the open space. I get no response, but I hear the low voices from a television. Climbing the stairs, I find Jesse sprawled out on his back, in bed. Asleep.

I should feel like I'm intruding, but I don't. It's a cozy space, made entirely of wood, and almost as sparse as my attic. The only light comes from the TV, save for a night light plugged into the wall near the stairs. The floor creaks loudly as I step across it to turn it off.

"Hey," comes a groggy voice from the bed, and my heart swells instantly.

"Sorry, I didn't think you'd be asleep already."

He groans out loud. "I just drifted. Cutting down trees all day sucks ass."

He hasn't moved and doesn't look like he has any intention to do so. "Okay, get some sleep, then." I shut the TV off and move to pull his bedspread over him.

I freeze when a hand skates up my forearm, gently, slowly, his calluses scratching over my skin as his fingers slip up the sleeve of my sweater. But they stop at my elbow, waiting. For my permission, maybe? I give it to him by sitting down on the bed.

"Stay."

My stomach tightens. What does he want from me? Or expect? Because I don't know if I can give it to him.

But I also know that I don't want to leave. "Like last time?"

"Just like last time," he assures me.

My heart is pounding as I lie down. His hand slips out from my sleeve and then his arm lifts beneath my back, pulling me closer to him, until I can't help but curl into his chest. To hear his quick, shallow breaths.

I catch movement from his hand in the sparse light only a second before a finger grazes my hair, my neck, my chin.

The edge of my scar.

My right side is lying against his chest but he gently prods my head up, until I'm facing the ceiling and he has access. I swallow hard as he trails a finger up and down the length of it.

"I read what you wrote in my journal," I finally offer into the silence.

He doesn't answer, making two more passes along the scar with his finger, as if memorizing the feel of it. And then his hand settles gently on my neck as he leans in, until wet heat from his mouth skates across my skin.

He kisses my scar.

I close my eyes, the sensation stirring a ball of emotions deep within my stomach that I don't understand but are raw and crippling in their intensity. The tears begin to spill from my eyes.

Jesse stops but he doesn't pull away, simply pressing his forehead against my scar, his thumb stroking back and forth against my neck soothingly as the tears continue to fall.

Until I drift off.

————

I'm faintly aware of an alarm going off somewhere nearby, and then I feel someone leaning over me, the scent familiar and warm. Cracking my eyes open a sliver, I see the ridges of Jesse's chest. I automatically reach for him, curling my hand around the back of his neck, pulling him down into me . . .

Kissing his throat like it's the most instinctual thing in the world for me to do.

It isn't until he slaps the alarm clock that I fully wake up and realize what I'm doing. I pull back with a gasp. "I'm sorry."

He props himself up, his elbows on either side of my head, cradling me. His dark eyes are twinkling.

"It just felt so . . ." I feel myself frown, searching for the right word. "Natural."

"In general? Or with me?"

"Not in general." I pause, hesitating. "Why do things feel so natural with you?"

He shifts to run the backs of his fingers over my cheek, his eyes dropping to my mouth. "Do they?"

"Yeah. You must remind me of someone. I feel like I know you."

He smiles. A sad smile. "Maybe you just *want* to know me."

"Maybe."

"Maybe," he echoes, his thumb drifting over my bottom lip, first over the faint scar left by the attack, and then over the full length, each sweep dragging an exhale from my lungs until my breathing is ragged and my body starts to ache in a familiar way, a way I know I've experienced before. I just don't remember when.

I'm about three seconds from begging him to kiss me when he leans down and closes his mouth over mine.

And the alarm goes off again.

"Fuck," he mutters, dipping his face into my neck. "I have to go."

Checking the clock, I see that it's ten minutes after eight. "So do I. The horses need to be let out."

His mouth closes over my throat to kiss it gently, and I can't help the moan that slips out.

"You're killing me," he whispers—so soft that I barely hear

it—and then he lifts himself up. I stand and watch as he peels his shirt off for a clean work shirt from his dresser. It gives me a chance to see the muscular curves in his shoulders and back. And the tattoo stretched from shoulder to shoulder, which I recognize right away as his car. "What came first, the car or the tattoo?"

I hear his smile as he answers, "Tattoo. I got it when I was sixteen."

"Your parents allowed it?"

"Fake ID."

Of course. Stepping closer, I dare reach up to run a finger around a tire. "You really wanted that car, didn't you?"

He freezes with his shirt held in front of him, a hiss that sounds a lot like "Jesus" slipping from his lips. I'm not sure if it's my words or my finger that he seems to be reacting to. He turns to face me, his eyes searching. Begging, almost. "I did really want this car." He says it like it's a confession, like it's something to feel guilty for. I watch his Adam's apple bob with a hard swallow as he steps into me, the heat from his bare chest radiating off him like the woodstove I curl up next to each night.

With a hand around the back of my neck, he leans in to kiss me, this time without hesitation, without caution.

With urgency and passion. And fear.

Just as suddenly, he breaks free. Gripping my hand, he leads me down the stairs, past the car, to the edge of the garage. "I'll talk to you later, okay?"

I smile, waving, until the tail end of his car disappears around the corner of the house.

That's when I notice Meredith sitting on the deck with a mug in her hands. Watching.

My cheeks flame immediately. What must be going through her head right now? She knows what happened to me. She knows I was carrying some man's baby only months ago. Would she approve of me being with her son? Would she want him mixed up with someone with my past, given his own?

I give her a quick wave—because it would be rude not to—and then I rush toward the barn, a nervous sickness rolling in my stomach the entire way, as if I've been caught doing something wrong.

Which is ironic, since everything about Jesse feels right.

———

"Zoe asked if we could change this sign," Ginny says from atop her stepladder, unhooking the dust-covered horseshoe that reads "Peaches." She holds it within her palm for a moment, studying it, before adding, "I guess I'll need to go into town to get a new one carved for Lulu. Ironwoods is still open, right?"

I don't answer. I *can't* answer. Not because I don't know—I drive by the iron and millwork shop every day on my way to work. It's because my mouth is hanging open.

"Well?" she snaps, turning to find me gaping at her. "Should I waste my time going all the way into town and dealing with those gossipers if it's not there?"

I smooth my face and continue spreading fresh hay in Felix the Black's stable. "It's still there."

The ladder squeaks with her descent. "I don't really have any-where to keep these." Her rubber boots scrape the ground as she sets the old horseshoe on a small shelf. "But I don't want to toss them out. We need someplace to keep these things, if we're going to be taking any more down."

Taking any more down? We'd have to do that only if . . . a slow smile stretches over my lips. Only if Ginny allowed more horses here again. "I'm sure we can come up with something," I say, my voice trembling with exhilaration. For Ginny, because this is a big deal. A *huge* deal. I keep my head down because I don't want her to see the sheen coating my eyes.

The wall she has built, enclosing her in a self-prescribed solitary confinement, may finally have a structural crack in its foundation.

"Hello, Ginny," Meredith's smooth voice calls out.

"I thought you were working all night. Shouldn't you be asleep?" Ginny answers.

"Soon." I turn in time to see Meredith step into the barn, the circles under her eyes darker than usual. "I just had an . . . unusually difficult shift. I need to decompress a bit. Hello, Water. I hope you had a good night's sleep."

"I did." I feel my cheeks heat again.

"Good." She nods, a secretive smile on her thin lips. "I was thinking that the two of you should come over for dinner tonight."

"What for?" Ginny honestly looks perplexed.

Meredith shrugs. "To eat. To talk. To spend time together. I thought it'd be fun. I mean, I'm not the best cook, but I . . ."

"You're right. You're not." Ginny's head shakes with force. "No, I don't think that'll work. Felix is old and blind and won't know where I am."

"So bring him along."

"I like Water's cooking."

"Yes, I hear she's a good cook. Maybe she can help me." Meredith winks at me. "Gabe really appreciated the dinner last night."

"That's right. The lasagna. It needs to be eaten tonight and there's not enough for everyone." Now Ginny's just lobbing over excuses at Meredith.

"Actually, we're saving that for tomorrow because I won't have time to cook. I'm going to the rodeo, remember?" I pipe up.

Ginny glares at me. I sympathize with her; I really do. But she's only alienating herself. Before I got here, the woman had dinner conversations with a dog. For years. Every single night. How does someone not go insane without human companionship?

I shoot a responding glare back at her, if only to keep the grin from my face—that would irritate her more—as I say, "We'd love to come, Meredith. What can we bring?"

"Just yourselves. And Felix, I guess. I'm sending Amber out

later for groceries. Jesse said he'll be home by six." With a knowing glance my way, she says, "I'm going to catch some sleep now,
so I don't cut my hands off with a kitchen knife tonight. I'm excited. It's been a while since we had a family meal."

A family meal.

Because that's what we all are. A family.

Meredith leaves as quickly as she came. Ginny doesn't utter a
single word in the five minutes it takes me to finish up with the
stall. "I need to get a shower before work," I say, propping the rake
against the wall. "So, I'll come get you when I'm back. We can
head over together?" I stroll past Ginny, feeling her sharp glare
skewering my back.

"Have I ever told you about the time Meredith cooked dinner
and gave everyone food poisoning?"

I stop. "Is that really true, Ginny?"

She pushes the broom across the floor, muttering, "It will be
after tonight."

———

The pent-up excitement that's been building inside me all day,
that began heating my body when I heard the Barracuda pass
by the house on its way to the garage, finally bursts as Jesse steps
into the Welleses' kitchen.

"I thought we'd have dinner together since we're all home
tonight," Meredith announces, standing next to me, chopping the
last of the parsley while I stir the pot.

My heart flutters as his dark eyes settle on me. "And Water's
making it?"

"I think that's for the best, don't you?" Ginny mutters from
the corner, where she's stitching her latest quilt.

Amber and Sheriff Gabe both snort.

"That was one time, Ginny!" Meredith exclaims with exasper-
ation. "And it was the salmon, not my cooking. And you weren't
even here!"

Amber and I share a secret look and smile. I got a text from her around one o'clock, presumably when she woke up, begging me to come by early to cook because Meredith decided that making paella for dinner would be "adventurous." Apparently, Ginny's comment on food poisoning wasn't so far-fetched after all. The last time Meredith felt "adventurous" with a casual dinner for friends, two people ended up in her hospital with food poisoning.

"We know." Sheriff Gabe comes up behind to place a kiss on his wife's cheek, a rare sign of affection that's heartwarming to see. Then he leans over and mock-whispers to me, "We're so glad you're cooking tonight, Water."

Laughter fills the Welleses' kitchen. I realize that it's the first time I've seen them all together, ever.

"Could you set the table, darling?" Meredith says to Jesse.

He rounds the counter to squeeze her shoulder. "Sure, Mom." On his way to the sink, I feel his hand graze my back. It's so quick, I write it off as an accident.

"I can't remember the last time we set this table," Sheriff Gabe says, helping his son by placing the cutlery.

"It sure looks different." Ginny's eyes finally lift to scan the kitchen—a fusion of modern and country, with stainless-steel appliances and smooth granite countertops mixed in with plenty of wood grain and bull horns mounted on the wall. "I haven't been here since your daddy died." She purses her lips together. "He was a good man."

Jesse takes the seat next to me, pulling my chair out when I come to sit. Ginny sits across from me, next to Amber, looking wary. Of the food, the plates, the faces. The change from eating alone to sharing meals with me on her porch was hard enough.

I catch Meredith's eye and nod toward the door, where Felix sits outside on his haunches, peering in.

"Oops! We forgot someone." She pushes open the door, letting in the dog—who's not quite so mangy or scrawny now that

Ginny has taken to brushing him daily and his diet isn't limited to dried-out chicken.

Ginny's bobbing knee immediately quiets.

"Wine, anyone?" Meredith holds a bottle up, taking her seat at one end.

Amber shoots a stern look of disapproval. "Mom, it's Tuesday."

"It is," she agrees, tipping the open end into her glass. "And tomorrow is Wednesday, and the next day is Thursday, and one day you'll learn that none of the names really matter. What matters is that you make the most of every day while you still can."

A solemn silence falls over the table.

"Your mother lost an eight-year-old girl last night," Sheriff Gabe explains, watching his wife take a generous sip of her wine.

She stares hard at the glass. "I keep thinking that I could have done something differently." Her hoarse whisper cuts through the room and settles in a painful knot at the base of my throat. It's a pinprick next to what she must feel. What any surgeon must feel, stepping into a day with hope and ambition and a wealth of skill, only to lie down at night having witnessed that sometimes none of that matters.

"I'm sorry." Amber reaches over to squeeze Meredith's shoulder.

I wish I knew what to say to comfort her. Instead, I push my chair out, making a move to at least fill people's plates.

"Sit back down," Ginny barks, standing fast enough to make Felix scamper back. "You cooked." Grabbing the serving spoon, she starts digging into the pot.

"Oh, thank you, but that's too—" Amber begins, her hand up in protest as Ginny dumps enough for three people onto her plate.

"No it isn't. You need to fatten up. So do you." She scoops a heap onto Meredith's plate. Mine follows. "And you."

She sticks her hand out. "Pass your plate on over here, Jesse."

I think that's the first time I've ever heard Ginny call Jesse by anything besides "that damn boy."

We all stare at one another, wide-eyed, until Amber quickly starts a conversation about the upcoming rodeo weekend. That segues into tales about the Welles and the Fitzgerald families, and soon the room is filled with laughter. Even Ginny cracks a few smiles.

And I can't help but beam.

When we've all eaten what we could, Sheriff Gabe and Jesse start collecting dishes. "How was it?" I ask Jesse. In one corner of his plate, a pile of chopped vegetables sits, having been picked through. "That's right, you don't eat vegetables," I tease. But then I pause. We've never eaten together before, so how would I know that?

"I've been trying to get him to eat them for years, but it's useless," Meredith jokes. "Unless they're stuffed in pizza pockets."

"Right. Pizza pockets." That's it. Meredith *has* made comments about his poor diet in the past. I must have just assumed that included avoiding vegetables.

———

Meredith and Gabe sit in the gray Adirondack chairs just outside, drinks in hand, talking quietly, as the sun sets over the mountain range.

"This was a great idea, Meredith. Thank you," I say, pulling my sweater around my body against the evening's chill.

"Yes," Ginny echoes, her lips puckering. She slaps her thigh, beckoning Felix to follow. "You coming, Water?"

My eyes wander to the lit garage, the black car pulled in, its hood up. Jesse's phone rang when we were cleaning up the last of dinner and he headed back there. "In a bit."

"Suit yourself." Felix trails Ginny as she makes her way along the foot-worn path, evidence of the long-standing connection between these properties.

"Did you get enough of the leftovers?" Meredith asks. "We never seem to finish them."

"That's because they're never that good," Sheriff Gabe mumbles.

She smacks her husband across the arm playfully.

"I did. Thanks." I glance over again in time to see Jesse step out, looking over at us. Is he waiting for me? Or am I just hoping for it? "I need to go ask Jesse for some help. Something for Ginny."

"What exactly—" Sheriff Gabe begins to ask but then stops, Meredith's hand on his wrist.

"You have a lovely night, Water."

"You too. And I hope you get some sleep tonight." I begin taking steps but then hesitate. As pleasant as tonight was, Meredith's earlier words still linger in the recesses of my mind, her own silent struggle weighing on me. "For what it's worth . . . you saved me. You may not be able to save everyone. But I'm standing here because of you."

A tear slips from her eye. "You saved yourself, Water. With your strength and your determination. You are such a strong girl."

With a slight nod of good night, I walk toward the only other place I want to be.

———

We stand side-by-side, staring at the old piece of barn board that we found tucked inside one of the empty stables, Jesse with a hammer in one hand. "Are you sure she's going to be okay with this?"

"Yes. No. Yes." I bite my lip with a touch of worry, tapping the horseshoe against my thigh.

He shrugs. "I guess she'll learn to be okay with it, if she's not right away."

"Right. And we can always put them back if she's really mad."

"Right."

I hold the horseshoe up. "Start here. That way we can fit them all in."

He shifts to stand behind me, his arms circling me from either side as he takes over holding the shoe, fitting a nail into the hole and hitting it with the hammer to fix it into place. "Like that?"

I smile. "Exactly like that."

He slides a finger around my ear, tucking my hair back, exposing my scar, before leaning in to kiss my temple. It's like a silent communication, telling me that he knows it's there, he sees it, and it won't deter him.

He grabs another shoe and nail.

"Does it really not bother you?" I ask. "You can tell me the truth. It bothers *me*. A lot."

He sighs, moving back to stand with me just like before, lining the next shoe up. "Not in the way you think it does."

"What do you mean?"

"It's a constant reminder to me." He pauses as he hangs another shoe. "That someone hurt you like that."

"They did," I admit. "And they've gotten away with it."

"Maybe they haven't. Or won't."

"What do you mean? Your dad would have told me if they found someone, wouldn't he? From the sounds of it, the case is dead."

He's quiet as he hammers a third shoe into the board. "Maybe life will punish them."

"Yeah. Maybe. But by that logic, life could have been punishing me for something I'd done."

"No." Jesse drops the hammer and grabs my shoulders, his eyes penetrating mine. "You didn't deserve this. Okay?"

I nod. "I'm not hurt anymore. I'm fine now. It's just a scar."

His voice softens. "Are you? I mean . . . are you happy here?"

Am I happy?

I am lost and yet somehow found.

I am afraid and yet somehow comforted.

I am drifting and yet somehow . . . home.

A smile stretches over my lips. "Yes, I think I am."

His hands drop to slip into mine, his fingertips curling around mine, squeezing tight. "Good."

It's late by the time we've nailed all thirteen shoes to the board and I've brought the horses in for the night. Ginny will see this in the morning. I wonder how she'll react.

Jesse leads me by the hand toward his garage. He didn't need to ask and I didn't need to even consider it, although each step closer fills me with a mixture of excitement and trepidation. This is all moving so fast, and yet Meredith's words resonate with me. Yes, this is a Tuesday. And what if it's the last Tuesday I ever see? Or the last Tuesday Jesse ever sees?

It's such a morbid thought to have, and yet thoughts like that will forever linger in my mind. They are a part of who I am now, an invisible scar.

Dakota is right. My soul is scarred.

I step into Jesse's apartment to find a low fire crackling in the woodstove. It's mid-June and probably unnecessary now, and yet I'm happy for it. "What is that smell? I know it's wood, but it's . . ." My voice drifts as I inhale deeply. *It's so familiar.*

"Leaves. I like the smell of them burning." Jesse pulls me down with him into a pile of pillows.

"Copycat," I tease. He reaches across me for something behind my head and flutters fill my stomach. As he produces a long metal stick with a fat marshmallow speared onto the end, I stare at him crouching in front of the opened stove, flames dancing in his dark eyes, his strong arms held steady, waiting patiently for the marshmallow to brown.

"I can't promise you that I'll like it," I warn.

He fumbles with some plastic in the corner. When he settles himself beside me, the melted marshmallow is now surrounded by two flat cookies and a chunk of chocolate. "I can promise you that you will."

I open my mouth for the gooey sandwich and he feeds me between laughs, as crumbs scatter and drips of chocolate and marshmallow cover his fingers, my chin, my shirt.

"You're right. It's a bit messy, though," I admit, watching him lick chocolate off his thumb.

Wishing he'd kiss me again.

His left brow arches. "What?"

I inhale, gathering my courage, and reach for the hand against his mouth. I pull it to mine, stealing the last drops of chocolate from his knuckle with my tongue.

Drawing a long, low hiss from him.

He must finally decipher the silent plea in my gaze, because the next thing I know, his hand is cradling the back of my head, his mouth is closed over mine, and I'm sinking deep into a tailspin of heady emotion.

And fear.

Crippling fear that makes me break free of his lips, because somehow I know with certainty where we're heading tonight if I let it happen.

Jesse's intense gaze settles on me. "I get it. We don't have to go any further."

"No. That's not . . ." That's the thing: I don't *want* to stop. I'm ready for this with Jesse. What I'm not ready for are any demons that may choose tonight to resurface.

"What do you want? Right now, from me," he whispers against my mouth.

My breath catches. Has he asked me that before?

Or have I only wished that he has?

I swallow against my ball of nerves. "I don't want to be afraid."

Understanding flickers in his eyes.

He kisses me again.

And again.

And again.

Mercilessly, until my lips are sore and my tongue feels tangled and I've memorized the taste of his mouth. And then he whispers, "Afraid?"

A breathless "no" escapes me.

His free hand slowly slides under my shirt, unclasping my bra, to smooth over my breasts, the touch gentle and caring. Almost reverent. Cool air springs goose bumps as he lifts the material up and over my head. Just like he kissed the scar across my face, he now leans down and skates his lips across the unsightly five-inch scar on my stomach where Meredith had to remove my spleen.

"Afraid?"

I curl my arms around his head as his lips drift up, leaving a wet trail over my skin on their way back to my mouth. "No."

When his fingers snap open my jeans button, stealing a few of my heartbeats, he pauses to watch my face, a silent question in his eyes. He unfastens the zipper and slips his callused hand down, his thumb rubbing absently across the exact place where my tattoo sits, his hand resting on my pelvis. Where my hand has rested so many times, thinking about the fragile life that resided in there for such a short time.

My body responds to the feel of his hands, welcoming it.

"Afraid?"

I shake my head and tug at his shirt. Reaching back, he yanks it over his head and tosses it aside, giving me a chance to take in his olive skin and lean muscles. I focus on tracing their lines as he slips the rest of his clothes off. And helps me with mine.

I can see how much Jesse wants me—scars and damaged past and all—and it ignites my blood, hot enough to chase all fears and demons away.

There is no pain, tonight, as Jesse pushes into me.

There are no horrid flashes, no menacing whispers.

No demons.

Only a strange, euphoric sense.

As if I'm exactly where I'm meant to be.

TWENTY-NINE

JESSE

THEN

I know something's wrong the second I step into the apartment and Licks swaggers to the door. For the past five days, the bulldog's been too attached to Alex's leg to greet anyone.

The sinking feeling has already settled in my stomach by the time I walk the seven steps to the kitchen, to find a still-warm casserole sitting on the stove. I know before I reach my room that Alex is gone, leaving nothing but a note in her curvy handwriting:

> Jesse, I've gone home. I need some time and space to think. —A.

"Fuck!" I throw my keys at the wall. This morning, when I kissed her goodbye before leaving for work, I saw the fear in her eyes. I should have expected this.

"It's probably for the best, man." Boone leans against my door-frame. Normally we drive in together, but I left in my own car this morning, not waiting for him. I haven't said two words to the guy, still too pissed.

"The hell it is," I mutter, scooping up my keys and heading for the door.

————

My thumb sits on the buzzer for a good twenty seconds before the gate crawls open.

She's waiting for me at the front door, her arms hugging her chest. "You shouldn't be here."

"You just took off."

"Viktor comes back tomorrow. I have a lot to do." Her wide eyes scan the driveway, the road, the trees, as if someone may be watching. She was never worried about that before, spending hours in the garage with me. "Grocery shopping, laundry, I have to get his dry cleaning . . ." Her voice trails off as I close the distance, stepping well within her personal space; so close, she's forced to tip her head back to meet my gaze.

"You just took off," I repeat.

Tears spring to her eyes and she blinks them away. "We can't do this anymore."

"You mean just for now, right?" When she doesn't answer, my gut clenches. "Have you forgotten what he did to you?"

She shakes her head, taking a step back. "That's the thing—I haven't forgotten *anything* that he's done to me. I wish I could. I wish I could forget every lie, every slap, every insult. I wish I could forget how stupid I was to marry him."

"You *can't* stay with him, Alex. It's too dangerous!"

"No, Jesse. This"—her hand flies back and forth between us—"*this* is too dangerous! You even being here right now is too dangerous." Her bright eyes flare with anger, such a rare sight. "What if someone drives by and sees your car? There's no good reason for you to be here. You said we aren't being stupid, but *this* is us being stupid!"

I trap her against the door with my arms on either side of her, afraid she's going to run inside. "*You're* my reason for being here."

"And that reason is what's going to get us both hurt. Or worse," she whispers. Her hands push against my chest.

Pushing me away.

"Just because that friend of his reacted the way he did doesn't mean Viktor is capable of the same." Even I don't believe those words as they come out of my mouth, but I'll say anything right now to convince her to come home with me for just one more night. We can talk. We can figure this out, together.

"I met that guy, Jesse," she says, her voice wobbling with fear. "I sat next to him in a lawn chair and talked to him about buying organic pork instead of regular pork. He seemed like a normal guy. A nice guy. He brought his wife her drinks and had his arm around her most of the night, and I remember wishing my husband was like that with me. I wasn't afraid of him. I'm afraid of Viktor. I think a part of me always has been." A bitter laugh escapes her lips. "What did I honestly think I was going to do? Tell Viktor I want a divorce, pack a bag, and move in with you? He isn't the kind of man who will accept that. And if he even suspects that something has happened between us, he wouldn't let you off."

"I'll deal with it."

"No, Jesse. It was one thing when I thought it might earn me some bruises. But this . . ." She grits her teeth. "I'm going to leave him. But it may just take a while. And I need to be smart about it. That means you need to go, now. *Please.*"

"What if he hurts you again?" I can't keep my voice from cracking.

Her fingertips find my mouth, a soft smile settling on her lips. "I won't give him a reason to. I'll be fine, Jesse. Don't worry."

She disappears behind the heavy door and the deadbolt clicks.

Deep down, as much as I hate it, I know she's right. I shouldn't have shown up here like this.

If I don't smarten up, my feelings for her are going to get her hurt.

———

I step out from the can to find a line of greasy mechanics standing at the edge of an open bay door, the cold late-November temperature flooding the garage.

The engine's purr is unmistakable.

"Nice work," Tabbs offers as I settle into the open space between him and Zeke, the freshly painted silver Aston Martin sitting like a show car smack-dab in the middle of the parking lot.

I barely glance at it, too busy staring at the woman standing behind it.

She's hidden, disguised as the rich trophy wife of a Russian mobster again—her cotton-candy pink coat a bright spot in the cold, overcast day—but I see the real girl underneath.

I haven't heard her voice or touched her body in three weeks. It's been agonizing.

"Welles!" My head snaps to Miller, standing with a sharply dressed Viktor. "Get over here."

Shit. I close the distance to them and Miller promptly leaves, as if he's not privy to the conversation we're about to have.

"Hello, Jesse." Viktor's accent sends prickles down my spine. "What do you think of the car?"

"Looks incredible. They did a good job on the bodywork. Still running well?"

He strolls toward it—and Alex—forcing me to follow. "Yes. I wanted to take it out for one drive before parking it for the winter." He pauses. "I have another job for you, if you are interested. It is for a friend of mine. A time-sensitive restoration."

I keep my gaze to the ground, afraid I'll get caught staring at his wife. "What does that mean?"

"It means that when the car arrives, it must be restored quickly."

"What kind of car?"

"Those are details for a later date."

Fuck. Here we go. I'm no idiot, especially now that I have a better understanding of who Viktor really is. We're not talking about a pet project in his garage anymore and I don't want to be in this guy's pocket. "I'll pass. But thanks."

"I will give you some time to think about it. The payment will be significant." He reaches a hand out for Alex. She comes without hesitation, close enough for him to lean in and kiss her right in front of me. I turn my attention to the car, my teeth cracking against each other. And yet I can't help but inhale, desperate to fill my nostrils with her perfume again. The scent of her has long since disappeared from my sheets. "I should go away more often. I came back from Russia to the woman I first married," he says. Then, "Think about it, Jesse." He rounds the car, leaving Alex to climb into the passenger side on her own. She does so without so much as a glance at me.

It's as if we don't even know each other.

Boone appears next to me as they speed away, my eyes trailing them. "What'd he want?"

"He wants me to rebuild another engine, for his friend this time. I said no. It sounds shady."

"It is." He pauses, and I wonder if he's going to elaborate. He's been out with Rust a lot more lately, working his way into "the circle." "The cars that need work are lower-risk and therefore cheaper to lift. He can flip them and then sell them for a ton of money without the buyer knowing that a week before, the car they're buying was a hunk of junk sitting under a tarp in a storage garage. Most of the time, the owner doesn't even know the car is gone before its wheels are rolling across foreign soil."

"Smart, if he has some idiot to do the work for him."

"Yeah. His last guy is doing ten to fifteen for robbery. I guess he was hoping to rope you in as the replacement."

"Did you know?"

"Just found out. I would never have brought you to The Cellar without telling you what he really wanted. I swear."

"I don't want anything to do with it."

Boone nods slowly, his eyes in the direction that mine are, the direction in which Alex just disappeared. "She's scared. That's what that was."

I sigh, because that's all I can do. "Yup."

"For what it's worth, I'm sorry." He slaps my back once before walking away.

A painful knot forms in the base of my throat.

Because I know that I've lost her.

She's never going to leave him.

THIRTY

WATER

NOW

I nearly stumble over my own two feet when I round the corner to find Ginny sitting in the truck.

She holds up a horseshoe. "Lulu needs her own sign."

"Okay . . ." I climb in and crank the engine, unable to keep my gaze from wandering over to her wide-brimmed hat and the oversized purse tucked under her arm.

"What?" she snaps.

"Nothing, it's just . . . you're actually going *into* town?"

"Well, not if you're just going to sit there all day, holding the steering wheel."

I put the truck into gear, avoiding a confused-looking Felix who simply stands in the middle of the driveway, like he doesn't know what to do with himself without Ginny there. "How long do you think it will take to get that engraved? I can drive you back right after. I'm sure Dakota won't mind."

"I have some errands to run, anyway. They'll take me a few hours. Maybe you can drive me back over lunch."

"Errands?"

"Yes, errands." She sets her jaw and I know I'm not going to get any more out of her. So I tune the radio and settle into the drive.

And think about Jesse. Since that night last week, we've been alternating between apartments for the last few nights. Thank God he left my apartment early this morning. I'd hate to think what would happen if Ginny caught him strolling down my steps. Though she seems to have warmed up to him a bit since she saw what he helped me with in the barn. She didn't even comment on the fact that he needed to be in her barn in order to do it.

As we approach the main street, I notice her hands curl tighter around the straps of her purse, until her knuckles are white. "I can go with you to do your errands, if you want, Ginny."

"I'm not a child."

Okay . . . "Don't forget, Hildy's coming out with Zoe tonight, after school."

She shakes her head, mumbling, "The girl thinks I'm senile."

———

"Who's that?" Meredith nods toward the small woman standing next to Ginny, their backs to us as they watch Zoe and Lulu trot past.

"That's Hildy. She and Ginny were childhood friends."

By the time Zoe and Hildy drove up in Hildy's black sedan an hour ago, Ginny had changed out of two different outfits, swept the porch, given Felix a good brushing, and was sitting stiff on her swing, her arms folded in her lap.

I couldn't tell if she was nervous or excited. I suspect a bit of both, though she wouldn't admit it to me.

Seems there was nothing to be worried about, though. One minute out of her car, Hildy was hugging Ginny and Ginny was letting her.

"I hear Ginny went into town today. I never thought I'd see the day."

I chuckle. "Yes. She had 'errands.'" I air-quote the phrase. I

honestly don't know what she spent her time doing. Aside from
the engraved horseshoe, I drove her back empty-handed. I think
maybe she just wanted to rejoin the land of the living, if only to
wander among them for a few hours.

"You wouldn't believe how much of a fight that stubborn
mule put up over the gallbladder surgery. I didn't even know
something was wrong until I saw her hunched over outside the
barn. Apparently she'd been having digestive issues for years.
And even after the gallbladder attack, she still refused surgery.
Honestly, I think it was me telling her about you, and my sug-
gestion to have you move here, that motivated her to go in at
all."

"That's . . . crazy."

She sighs. "That's Ginny."

"Well, Zoe asked if her friend could board her horse here. If
Ginny agrees—which I'm pretty sure she will—then she'll have
an excuse to go back into town for a new horseshoe."

"Huh." I turn to find Meredith with her arms folded over her
chest, smiling at me.

"What?"

I get a tiny head shake in response. "Come on. We're going
to grab dinner at the rodeo. Jesse can meet us there." She ropes
an arm around my shoulders. "You two have been spending a lot
of time together."

If, by a lot of time, she means every moment that we're not
at work, then she'd be right. I honestly didn't think that anyone
had noticed, but I guess I was wrong. I duck my head as I feel my
cheeks begin to burn.

"And you haven't had any issues?" She hesitates. "I'm asking
as your doctor, not as a nosy mother."

"No issues." Nothing but hours feeling like I've fallen and
somehow landed in my own private heaven.

"Good. I'm glad." Her words are encouraging, but the worried frown over her brow has me second-guessing her.

———

The crowd explodes with hollers and cheers as the bull charges through the gates, bucking through the air like he's on fire and desperate to put himself out, the rider somehow staying on his back.

"This happens every June?" I ask as I take in the bleachers, hundreds of locals and tourists filling them.

"Yup. One of the busiest weekends of the year for Sisters." The way Gabe says that, he doesn't sound at all enthused. We're sitting near the front in special seats. One of the perks of being part of the sheriff's family.

I guess I'm classified as "family" now.

Meredith sits on the other side of Gabe, in deep conversation with Mrs. Green, the town councilor. The topic of conversation appears serious by the stern frown in Meredith's forehead. If I had to guess, it's about building a bypass around the town. That or maintaining the curbside appeal of Sisters. Meredith holds a lot of pride in this town. When we first drove through it, I never noticed the dented trash cans and cracked curbs, but now that I'm a "local," I've seen what she has complained about.

Amber stands down in the front row, talking and laughing with another girl. Both of them look done up like dolls with their fat curls and their wide-brimmed embroidered hats, their smiles dazzling.

"That's this year's Rodeo Queen," Gabe explains. "That was Amber, a few years back. When she was little, she used to sit on my shoulders and stare at the girls. She was determined to win and so she did."

"Right! Dakota mentioned something about that."

A buzzer goes off just as the bull finally achieves his goal and bucks the rider off, rearing on him. The rider's quick, though, landing on his feet and darting out of the way, his hands stretched in front of him. Several guys run into the arena to help corral the bull.

"How's your first rodeo?" The smell of mint hits me a split second after hearing his voice spikes my heart rate. Jesse slides into the bleacher next to me, his leg pressing up against mine from hip to knee.

"Interesting." My breath catches as he curls his arm around my shoulders, pulling my temple into his lips for a soft kiss.

I guess Jesse has decided that we're going public.

He leans forward. "Hey."

"Jesse." Sheriff Gabe's eyes graze over his son's arm but he says nothing else, turning his focus back to the bull pen.

The crowd roars as the voice announces the second bull over the speaker and it charges out, this one bigger and bucking even more fervently. I should be watching the show and yet I can't. I've lost interest. The entire event—whatever it is, ten seconds? Thirty seconds? A minute?—continues in the background as I absorb Jesse's body heat against me.

Amber's not watching the rodeo anymore either. She's now staring at us intently, her wide eyes skittering between us and her parents, then back to us, finally to settle on her brother, a mixture of shock and worry and hurt on her face.

I probably should have said something to her. I just didn't know how to explain it.

Other than I'm falling hard for her brother.

THIRTY-ONE

JESSE

THEN

"Jesse?"

My heart jumps at the sound of her voice.

I haven't seen or talked to Alex in weeks.

"Hey . . . hold on a second." A quick glance around the garage confirms that no one's paying any attention to me. But Miller will bust my balls if he catches me on the phone. "Hey, Boone—I'm taking my break now, in case anyone's looking for me."

He sees the phone in my hand and nods. "Got it." We're at least on regular speaking terms lately.

A light drizzle falls. Not enough to soak me but enough to be annoying. "Hey. Is everything okay?" An image of her curled up in a dark corner in her house, bruised and battered, hits me and I grit my teeth.

"Yeah." There's a pause. I hear the hesitation. "Can you meet me?"

"When?" I check my watch. It's three. "I have another couple of hours at work, but I can cut out if you need me to." Miller can dock my pay. He can fire me. Right now, I don't give a shit.

"Tonight, then."

———

The white Christmas lights coiled around a fake palm tree ahead are impossible to miss. I pull off the road and into the parking lot of the restaurant, thirty miles outside of Portland. I know why she chose it.

Her husband's unlikely to find us out here together.

I ignore the hostess standing at the door because I saw the Z8 parked around back, so I know Alex is here, somewhere. It takes a lap around the surprisingly large restaurant to spot her white-blond hair at a small table in a corner, concealed from the entrance by a giant Christmas tree.

"Sorry I'm late," I offer.

She looks up at me, startled, and I instantly remember how much I like Alex's eyes. I can see by the dark circles that she hasn't been sleeping well. Her face wasn't as drawn before, either. She's lost weight. "Jesse." It's almost a whisper, it's so soft. "Hey."

I want to kiss her. That wedding ring is staring back at me, though, and in my worn jeans and boots, there's no doubt to anyone around that I'm not the one who gave it to her. I slide into the booth across from her and stretch my legs out to hug the outsides of hers. It's cramped, so I have an excuse.

She doesn't pull away.

"Have you been here a while?"

She swallows, and her gaze drops to the empty sweetener packets covering the closed menu lying on the table. "Since I called you."

It's after seven. That means she's been sitting here for four *hours.* Something's wrong. That much is obvious. "Where's Viktor?"

"Out for *business.*"

"So not much has changed."

She shrugs. "He hasn't hurt me again."

"Yet."

"I haven't given him a reason to."

What the fuck does that mean? I'm running a few scenarios in my head, and they all involve her doing things that make me want to scream. "And the tattoo? What does he think about the tattoo?" My voice is full of bitterness. I'm sure he's seen it by now.

"He liked it, actually." She pauses. "I told him that I went out with a few girlfriends from school and we all got one done." Her voice drops an octave. "I said it was a surprise. For him."

Well, now I'm just pissed. "It wasn't for him, Alex. It was for you." *For us.*

Before she can speak, the waitress strolls by. "You thinking of ordering food, darling?"

Taking a deep, calming breath, I answer "Yeah" for both of us, knowing that Alex probably hasn't eaten. I may be angry, but I'm also starving. I had just enough time to race home to shower and change. I don't bother opening the menu. "Can you bring me a burger? No toppings. And what do you have with blueberries?"

The waitress sighs, looking at the ceiling. "Pie, cheesecake, mousse, ice cream—"

I cut her off. "Good. Bring one of each. And a beer for me. Do you want one?"

Alex shakes her head. I watch the waitress walk away and then return my focus to Alex, ready to push her. I need her to remember how happy she was with me.

Because I was so damn happy with her, and now I'm miserable.

"How's school?"

She shrugs. "I just finished the semester. But . . . I'm not going back in January."

"Alex—"

"How's Boone? And Licks? Are you going home for Christmas?"

I heave an exasperated sigh.

She reaches across the table to curl her fingers around mine, her eyes pleading with me. "Can we not talk about me for to-night? Please?"

I want to argue. I want to demand that she tell me everything and promise me that she's okay, even though I know she's can't possibly be okay with him.

But I merely nod.

Denial it is.

———

The overhead lights are shutting off, a polite signal to get the hell out.

"You ready to leave?"

She shakes her head but stands, sliding her pink coat on over a short black dress. *Damn*, how I've missed seeing her long legs.

I climb out of the booth and offer her my hand. "We don't have to go right away."

She takes it and we exit, hearing the distinct lock of the deadbolt as soon as we step outside.

"Come on, this way." It feels so natural, Alex's hand in mine as we stroll through the cold, dark parking lot, snowflakes drifting down from the dark sky.

An invisible but palpable barrier between us.

I did what she had asked. All through dinner, we talked about everything but Alex. I bit my tongue against the urge to ask her if he's yelled at her, slapped her, touched her, been inside her. All the questions that have kept me tossing and turning at night for weeks, I kept in.

I don't think I can handle the answers.

And every time I opened my mouth to urge her to leave him, I promptly shut it.

When we reach my car, I pull open the passenger-side door and guide her in. Ducking into the driver's side, I start the engine and rev it, hoping to quickly crank up the heat. I leave the lights off, though. I'm not ready to leave, either.

"How are you liking the car?" She reaches forward and runs her fingertips along the dashboard.

And I wish those fingertips were running over me again. Prickles run down my neck with just the thought.

"Still love it," I admit, turning the radio down before reaching into the backseat for the red-and-blue plaid blanket that I now keep there. When I start stretching it over her legs, her eyes light up. "I hate that I do, but . . . I do. It's what I've always wanted." Viktor found me a car with a solid engine and an interior in mint condition. "Found" being the operative word. Everything looks legit paper-wise. I'll bet money that my father ran the VIN when I went home that first weekend, but I haven't heard a word about it since. I can't be certain that someone's not missing a 1969 Barracuda. That's the thing with these old cars—they're not stamped with their VIN codes, so unless there's some identifying marker on them, they're as good as gone when a guy like Viktor gets his hands on them. Plus, with his legitimate car sales business, I'm sure he has the connections to get ownership documents created.

"It's okay." She reaches out and grasps my forearm. "You're happy with this car. That makes me happy." She pauses. "Fuck Viktor."

I've never heard her swear before. It makes me smile. "Fuck Viktor," I echo, rolling my head to take her face in. I find beautiful russet-colored eyes with a thousand questions swirling in them staring back at me.

She pulls the blanket to her nose. "Smells like your apartment. Like the woodstove."

Like the night we curled up together in front of the woodstove, in the blanket, I want to remind her. But I don't think she has forgotten. I sure as hell haven't.

The last lights on the restaurant shut down, leaving only one dim security light shining down on the side entrance. A moment later, the waitress who served us appears, pulling the door shut behind her and darting to her car.

And we're now completely alone.

I can't hold back anymore. "Are you ever going to leave him?"

"Yes, I *am* going to." Her gaze drops to her hands. "It's just not that simple anymore."

"Yeah, it is. Pack your stuff up and file for divorce on grounds of his cheating on you."

"You mean like I cheated on him?" she whispers.

"This is different and you know it, Alex. He doesn't give a fuck about any of them. But you and me—" I cut myself off.

Silence fills the car.

"Why'd you want to meet up with me tonight?"

Alex's mouth opens to say something but she stops, as though she can't get the words out. "I miss you so much, Jesse."

My gut tells me she was going to say something else, but it doesn't matter. What she did say makes all the long nights lying in bed alone, bitter that she gave up on us so easily, disappear from my thoughts. It makes my heart start pumping and all my resolve vanish. I reach over and grab her around her waist with both hands, using my strength to lift her over the console and onto my lap, blanket and all. Not caring about Viktor or the ring on her finger or anything else except having this girl's mouth on mine again.

She doesn't resist, climbing onto my lap to straddle my thighs, her dress sliding up around her hips. I bury my face in her neck, inhaling her scent. I'd kill to cover my pillows with it again.

I don't even notice the cold anymore, too focused on her as she undoes my fly. The hesitant girl from the hotel is long gone, and this one is tugging my pants and boxers down, her chilly hands warming up as they reach inside. I slide my hands under her dress to find the lacy tops of her nylons—the sexy kind that stop high on her thigh instead of going all the way.

My favorite kind right now, because they mean easy access.

And I can't wait anymore.

Hooking one arm around the back of her waist and shoving aside her panties with a finger, I sink into her.

And let out a pained groan as she lifts her body off me. "We need a condom. Viktor refuses to use them, and who knows what he has been with."

"Seriously?" The guy not only fucks around on her but risks her life like that? Not that I should be talking right now because I was ready to go bareback with her, but at least I know I'm clean. I fish a condom out of my back pocket and throw it on in record time.

She slides me into her again.

And then I don't give a shit about Viktor or anything else.

———

I pull up alongside the BMW as Alex adjusts her clothes, wishing I could just take her home with me. "What now?"

She pauses to take a deep breath. And sadness slithers back into her gaze. "Now . . . Have a Merry Christmas, Jesse." Leaning in, she lays one last sweet kiss on my lips, before exiting my car.

THIRTY-TWO

WATER

NOW

"The hummingbird."

"Good morning, Dakota," I offer, placing her coffee down on the counter in front of her. I have no clue what she's talking about.

She waves a sheet of paper. "That's your spirit animal."

"A bird?"

She smirks. "A tiny, tireless bird who will fly thousands of miles to get to its nectar, who will appear dead at night, and then full of life in the morning. They're the only birds who can fly backwards, did you know that?"

I shake my head, transfixed.

"In the spirit world, the hummingbird represents so many things—hope . . . persistence . . . miracles . . ." The passion in her voice is contagious, and I feel my own excitement swell. "Vitality . . . resilience."

There's that word. The one Jesse wrote in my journal. The word that calls to me.

"This," she thrusts the paper out, "is what I see when I look at you."

My jaw hangs open as I take in her creation—a medley of swirls and pen strokes, the detail intricate and precise. It's a black-ink sketch of a hummingbird in flight, only its feathers are curled to form droplets of water.

In a word, it's beautiful.

"Dakota. This is . . ." I can't stop staring at it. "It's incredible. Thank you."

"You should get it right here." She taps the back of my left shoulder.

I nod. "That's exactly where I'm going to get it."

"I think Jesse will like it."

I feel her steady gaze on me and I hazard a glance to see the small smile she hides behind a sip of her coffee. I haven't admitted anything to her about Jesse and me yet.

"I picked up dinner at Poppa's last night and overheard Tina talking about how the sheriff's son and the Crazy Tree Quilt Lady's cousin were seen cuddling at the rodeo."

I blush. Of course. This town really does love the sheriff's son.

She flashes that alluring smile. "Surprise him with a tattoo. I know a great tattoo shop in Bend."

———

I begged for the darkness to swallow up the pain and it listened, wrapping me in a cold embrace.

"Tell me who the father is," that voice—full of anger and hatred—demands.

My baby. What's going to happen to my baby? Panic ignites, somewhere deep inside me.

"Tell me!"

My mouth moves to form the words; the same words I've said over and over again. A chant. "Just some guy."

I feel pressure seizing my chin and cigarette smoke wafts closer. "Who is he?"

"Just some guy . . ."

"Come on . . . Did you really think I would let some guy fuck my wife and get away with it?" The glint of a blade flashes.

"Just some guy . . . bar . . . just some guy . . . bar . . . just some guy . . . bar . . ." I whisper. I won't give in. I won't give him a name. The tip of the blade pierces my skin at the temple. I'm too weak to scream, even as I feel it slowly tearing into my face, the agony bringing tears to my eyes. I won't tell, I won't let anyone hurt him—

"Wake up!"

My eyes snap open to find Jesse's face hovering over me, his hands on my shoulders, shaking me hard.

I'm gasping for air.

"You're with me. Jesse. You're safe." He smooths his hands over my face, wiping away tears that must have sprung in my sleep. A worried frown mars his beautiful features. "You kept saying—"

" 'Just some guy,' " I whisper through ragged breaths. "I think I just had a flashback."

Jesse's jaw clenches. "What was it?"

I shake my head slowly, desperately trying to grab on to the bits before they slip back into oblivion. "A voice. And a smell. Cigarettes. He kept asking me for a name." I reach up and touch my scar. "He wanted a name. He cut me because I wouldn't give it to him." Burying my face in Jesse's bare chest, I inhale deeply, trying to rid myself of the acrid tobacco smoke that still somehow taints my subconscious.

Did you really think I would let some guy fuck my wife and get away with it?

I gasp. "I'm married. My husband did this to me." I push away from Jesse but he grabs hold of my hands.

"Do you remember why?"

Why?

Why?

Why would my husband do this to me?

Tell me who the father is.

"Oh my God." My stomach tightens. "Because it wasn't his baby. I wouldn't tell him whose it was."

Dr. Weimer was right. I had an affair.

Jesse's hands around mine slacken. Even in the pre-dawn light, I can see the deep frown. "Are you sure?"

"Yes." My palms find their way to my empty abdomen, a longing ache spreading through my chest. Somehow, I'm sure.

Jesse scoops me into his arms and lets me sob against his chest. But I feel the growing tension in his body. When I hazard a glance at his face, I find him glowering at the ceiling.

What must he think of me?

THIRTY-THREE

JESSE

THEN

I barely hear the trance music this time, though its steady beat throbs in my chest.

I haven't been back here in almost two months. The only reason I'm here now is because it's New Year's Eve and Boone said Viktor would be here.

I'm praying that means Alex is, too.

Boone hands me a drink, which I have no intention of touching. I need my wits about me, or I'm liable to do something stupid. Like kiss Viktor's wife in front of him.

We cut through the thick crowd of drunk, rich assholes, and I narrowly avoid a martini on the shirt and pants I bought for tonight. At first I felt like a chump at the store, but now that I'm seconds away from seeing Alex again, I'm happy I bought the tailored outfit.

Except, she's not here.

I take in the table, spilling over with the usual guys and a few new ones, plus a slew of young, pretty girls, some of whom may very well be paid escorts. Priscilla is in the mix, attached to Viktor's side, his arm draped over her shoulder, his thumb absently grazing the top of her tits that are practically falling out of a plunging neckline. He's making no attempt to hide his philandering, which makes me think that Alex isn't due to arrive anytime soon.

But wouldn't he make her come tonight, of all nights?

Unless he's bashed her face in again.

"Happy New Year!" Rust stands to pat his nephew's back as if he hasn't seen him in months, though Boone's been out with him almost every night lately. I have a feeling Miller will be out of a job come spring. "Jesse!" He offers me his hand.

I put up with two minutes of small talk before I excuse myself to use the restroom. Really, to text Alex.

I'm at The Cellar. Where are you?

She hasn't returned the three texts that I sent her since the night at the restaurant. This time, though, she answers almost immediately.

I'm not feeling well so I stayed home.

Dread swells.

Did he hit you?

I'm fine, Jesse.

A moment later:

Have a Happy New Year.

Fuck that.

I round the corner and nearly plow into Viktor.

"Jesse." That snakelike smile greets me. "Where are you off to in a rush?" A slight slur twists his words.

I force my jaw to unclench. "Another club. I promised some friends I'd meet them there for midnight," I lie. I always was a good liar.

"You should reconsider. We have a few extra girls here tonight."

"Too rich for my blood. I like the low-maintenance ones."

He stares at me for a long moment, as if weighing the truth to my words. I'm expecting him to bring up the car rebuild he wants me to do, but he only chuckles. "You are an odd one. Have a good night."

I speed through the crowd without a second glance back.

———

I've been buzzing the gate for ten minutes now and she's not answering. When I see her run out the front door in her pink coat and head for her car, I know Alex isn't willing to deal with me here. Not with Viktor in the same city. That's fine, as long as she's willing to see me.

I tail her BMW for ten miles, until she finally pulls into an empty park in a wooded area. I'm out of my car and pulling her door open before she has a chance. "What happened?" I demand, taking her face in my hands. It's even more drawn than before and pale, but otherwise, it's unmarked.

And yet the fear in her eyes is unmistakable.

"What's going on, Alex?"

Tears begin to stream down her cheeks. "I'm pregnant."

Two words, whispered so softly, punch me in the stomach. "Jesus." I didn't expect that. I take a few steps back, inhaling the cold air. It's too cold to be out here without a jacket and gloves, but I barely feel it. My eyes automatically drift down to her stomach, though I can't even see it, buried within her jacket. "Does Viktor know?"

She shakes her head. "When he heard me throwing up my lunch today, I told him I have the stomach flu. That's why he didn't make me come out to The Cellar tonight."

"I . . ." I struggle for what to say.

"I'm keeping it." Fierce determination flashes in her glossy eyes.

I nod slowly. Of course she is. I'll bet she's going to make an incredible mother, too. I think I'm in shock. In the back of my mind, I keep thanking God that we used condoms every single time we slept together, or I'd be losing my shit right now.

But I don't bring that up.

"Viktor doesn't want to be a father, does he?" I remember her telling me that.

She opens her mouth but it only hangs there, whatever words are sitting on her tongue left unspoken as hesitation swims in her eyes. Finally, she says, "He's never going to find out." She pauses. "Viktor is always handing me cash. *Lots* of cash. For groceries and bills and shopping. I've been saving it all since I found out. And I've been quietly selling off some of my jewelry and designer stuff. I should have enough to cover rent and basic necessities for the next two years, if I live really cheaply. I'm just going to leave a note and tell him that I've had enough of his cheating. I can't risk confronting him and having him hurt me. Not now. A legal divorce will have to come later."

I breathe a sigh of relief. "How long have you known?"

Her steady gaze answers me before her words do. "About a month."

That night at the restaurant . . . she knew. That's what she wanted to tell me but couldn't. "When are you leaving?"

"In the next few weeks, before I start to show."

As if things weren't hard enough for her before, now this? I crouch down in front of her. "Are you afraid?"

"Terrified," she whispers, her eyes searching mine, an unreadable look in them. Like a soft plea, only not quite.

"Where are you going to go?"

"I don't know yet. I'm definitely leaving Portland. Probably Oregon. Viktor can't *ever* find out about this baby."

I don't blame her. She'd have the asshole in her life forever, then. Even if he doesn't want kids, he seems like the kind of guy who would keep tabs on it.

But . . . far away from Viktor means far away from me.

My heart sinks.

"Why didn't you tell me before?"

"I don't want to drag you into this," she admits. "I wish things could be different for us." She sighs and then tunes the radio, just in time to hear a crowd cheer from wherever the station is broadcasting. "Happy New Year, Jesse," she whispers, saying my name in that way that sends shivers down my back. Leaning down, she skates her lips over mine, the very same hesitant way she did the night I stopped to change her flat tire for her.

I guess some may say that it was the flat tire that changed me. But, really, it was Alex.

"Don't go," I hear myself blurt out. I can't lose her.

I think I'm in love with her.

"I don't have a choice."

"Yeah, you do. Stay with me."

A sad smile touches her lips. "You know that won't work."

"No, not in Portland." It's all so clear to me now. "In Sisters, in my apartment. Viktor's not going to find you there. I know it's not much, but you said you were happy there. So *be* there, with me."

"But . . ." A deep furrow creases her forehead. "What are your parents going to say?"

"Don't worry about them. I'll deal with them. The garage is mine anyway."

She scoops my hands within hers, pink from the cold. "Things have changed, Jesse. I'm having a baby."

"Yeah, I haven't forgotten," I mutter.

She pauses, frowning. "You'd take me, even if I'm carrying someone else's child?"

"Yeah. I guess I would." Am I crazy? Maybe. But the truth is, I'll take her however I can have her.

"Jesse, it's . . ." She hesitates and then clamps her lips shut, as if to stop herself from saying whatever she was going to say. Tears well in her eyes and she nods. "Okay."

Relief and happiness slams into me, and that's how I know this is the right decision.

Shutting her door, I climb into the passenger seat and take her hand.

And we begin making our plans.

THIRTY-FOUR

WATER

NOW

The second she flicks on the high-frequency needle, I tense.

I remembered that sound, and the pain associated with it.

And then a thrill courses through me.

Because I *remember* that sound, and the pain associated with it.

"The outline is the worst part, I promise," the artist—a young part-Asian woman named Ivy, her ears filled with silver rings—says as she begins tracing the transfer of Dakota's design on my right shoulder.

I grit my teeth against the sting, trying not to move as the needle pierces my skin.

"I don't get tattoos," Amber mumbles, her gaze roaming the gallery on the wall. "It's permanent. Why would you want to put something on your body now that you'll just regret later?"

"Not everyone regrets their tattoos," Ivy interjects, her own full sleeve of them on proud display.

"I won't regret this, Amber. Besides, my scars are permanent too. At least I'm choosing something beautiful."

"I guess . . ." Amber squints, leaning in. "Is that a man's—"

"Yup." Ivy doesn't even need to glance back to know which tattoo Amber's referring to.

Amber folds her arms over her chest and dips her head sideways to examine it more intently, her long brown hair hanging in a shiny curtain. "I can't say I'll ever be able to look at an elephant again without thinking of this."

"You see a lot of elephants, do you?" I don't miss the sarcasm in Ivy's voice. And, thanks to the mirror on the wall, I also don't miss the judgmental look she throws Amber's way. It's similar to the one Amber settled on her the second we stepped into Get Inked, the Bend tattoo shop that Dakota recommended.

"No, but I will when I go on an African safari next year," Amber answers lightly. She's being nice enough—she always is—but I sense the invisible barrier between the two of them. On the other side of that barrier is my warm, considerate friend. Not just anyone gets to hurdle it, though.

"Huh . . . No kidding." Ivy's tone changes quickly. "I've thought about doing that before."

"It's really expensive. The African safari alone is going to cost me close to ten grand."

"Yeah?" I see the smirk curving over Ivy's lips. "That's not too bad."

"It is when you add traveling through Europe and Asia, too."

"I backpacked through Europe when I was nineteen."

"Oh, I'm not backpacking."

I feel like I'm watching a pissing contest but with girls. "I think you two should go together," I suggest, more because I need a distraction from the pain in my shoulder than anything else.

"Don't make me laugh when I'm inking you," Ivy murmurs. I get nothing more than a high-browed glare from Amber.

A few minutes of silence pass. "So the almighty sheriff's daughter doesn't remember me, does she?" When Amber frowns, Ivy elaborates. "We went to the same high school. You were a year older than me."

"No. Can't say I do. Sorry."

And that's the end of that conversation, though I suspect much more could be said.

Its takes another thirty minutes to finish Dakota's elaborate design. I let my thoughts drift to last night's revelations, thanks to my dream. I'm still shaken up by it and, though Jesse says that whatever I did before doesn't matter, I could tell by the frequent frowns and hard gazes this morning that he's troubled by it.

For the first time since meeting Jesse, I'm relieved to get some time and space from him. Because if he decides he doesn't want this thing between us to work . . . the very idea makes me break out in a panic.

And that tells me that I'm falling in love with him.

When the buzzing finally stops, Ivy holds up two mirrors, one to reflect the one from my back. I can't help the grin from spreading. "It's beautiful."

The last time someone held up a mirror in front of me like this, that's not a word I would have used. But Dakota's creation—a symbol of resilience—doesn't resemble Jane Doe.

This symbol represents all that I am, right here, sitting in this chair.

Today.

Alive, and living my life, regardless of whatever ugly mistakes I may have made in my past.

"Wow," Amber mumbles, walking up closer. "It actually looks nice."

"You ready? I'll even do it for half off," Ivy jokes, flicking the needle on and letting it buzz before shutting it off again. She dresses my shoulder with gauze—upon which, of course, Amber interjects, telling her that she's doing it wrong.

Leading us into the front foyer, Ivy reaches over the desk to grab a sheet. "Okay, here are the instructions. Make sure you—"

"I'm sure it's pretty straightforward." Amber snatches it from her grasp.

Ivy's flat stare makes me want to laugh. "You can call here if you have any questions." She points to the card that she has stapled to the top of the bill. "And if you want me to do any more, just call ahead and ask for me specifically. I can give you an appointment."

"You stealing my client again?" a booming voice echoes.

"Shut up, Beans. She's new here."

Beans? Like the vegetable? I turn to see a guy in his mid-twenties with a long goatee and a shaved head.

"Is that what you told her?" he says, his eyes on me. "I remember you."

"No . . . Not likely." I shake my head. There's no way.

Is there?

"That's what he says to all the pretty girls," Ivy warns.

"No. I remember you. You came in a few months back—in the winter, I think—and I did your tattoo. But . . ." His head dips to the side and he frowns. "You didn't have that scar back then."

I glance at Amber, feeling my eyes widen. Is this really happening?

"Prove it. What's the tattoo?" Amber tests.

"A round symbol, on your pelvis."

"Water." It's barely audible as it escapes from my mouth.

"Yeah."

My blood doesn't know whether to drain from my face or race through my limbs, and so I end up feeling both faint and hot. If I was really here, then. . . . "Did you photocopy my license that time, too?"

His mouth curves into a frown. "Yeah. We always do."

There's a paper in this shop with the old me on it.

I lunge for him, grabbing on to his arm. "Can you please find it? I need that photocopy."

"What for?"

"Just, please . . ." I beg, tears springing to my eyes.

His eyes shift to Ivy. "It'll take me awhile."

"If you want, I can have my dad, the sheriff, here in fifteen minutes to help you do it," Amber says, holding up her phone. "Of course, he'll probably close you down for the rest of the day. Maybe tomorrow, too."

Beans doesn't look happy, but he holds up his hands in a gesture of surrender.

I trail him as he rounds the desk and, using a key hanging from a chain affixed to his pants, he opens the filing cabinet. "Date? Name?"

"Just look for my face."

He stares at me for a long, hard moment before simply nodding to himself. His fingers begin rifling through the pages and I'm temporarily distracted by the letters tattooed on his hand.

Beans = knuckles.

Oh my God.

It was a clue. Dr. Weimer's exercise wasn't pointless after all.

"Are you okay?" Ivy asks, stepping in to take my elbow as my knees wobble.

I can't manage more than a nod in return.

It takes only five minutes to find my past, fit neatly on an eight-and-a-half-by-eleven-inch sheet of paper.

"You were here in November," Beans says, holding up the paper in the air.

I feel Amber's hand settle on my back as I reach for it, my own hand trembling as I look at the black-and-white face staring back at me.

"Alexandria Petrova," I read out loud, swallowing against the rising nausea that threatens as I hear myself say it for the first time.

I know that name.

It's there, inside my head. I can *feel* it—my real name—trying to break free of its shackles.

I scan the rest of the information. "I'm twenty-two. I lived in Portland. There's an address. Right here. This is where I lived," I

choke out. I could drive there. I could go right now and find . . .
what? "Why can't I remember any of this?"

The truth is right here. Am I not supposed to have some great
epiphany now? Should this not trigger something? Why is my
brain still denying me?

Somewhere in my haze, I hear Amber ask, "Do you remember if she came in with anyone?" I've forgotten that Beans and Ivy
are even in the room.

"Uh . . . yeah. That's the license plate number, written on the
bottom. I took it down because you were pretty banged up when
you came in. You said he didn't do it, but I wasn't sure."

My eyes snap to Beans. "*He?* Who was I with?"

"Uh . . . the guy driving the car."

"Can you be a little more specific?" Amber demands, at the
same time that Ivy smacks him in the arm and mutters, "Come
on." She's obviously picked up on the fact that something here is
very wrong. "What did he look like?" Amber presses.

"He looked like a guy! Hell, I don't remember. You two left in
in a black car. Old-school muscle car, you know?"

My hands go for my throat, which is starting to close up.

No, it can't be.

"A Barracuda?" I manage to get out in a hoarse whisper.

"Yeah. I think that was what it was."

His words feel like a solid punch to my chest.

———

"My dad will get the truth out of him—I swear it, Water. I
mean . . . Alexandria. I mean . . . Oh God." Amber's hands shake
as she races up the Welleses' driveway, nailing each pothole with
her little red Mini in her rush.

I'm not crying. I'm not talking. I'm barely breathing, my chest
laboring with each inhale as I frantically claw away at the recesses
of my mind, looking for Jesse in there. And all I can keep thinking
is how stupid I am, how he's been right there in front of me. This

entire time, my heart was trying to tell me what my mind still refuses to: I didn't know someone like Jesse.

I knew *Jesse*.

I knew the smell of his skin, the taste of his mouth, the sound of his voice, the feel of his dark gaze on me.

"Why?" I whisper.

"We're going to find out. I promise." Amber reaches out and takes my hand, squeezing it as she continues racing down the driveway. She looks green. I doubt I'm much better.

By the time we pull around to the back of the Welleses' house, heading for the two figures standing by the garage, I can barely feel my body. My hands open the door, my legs hold my weight, my muscles pull me out, but none of it registers. All that registers is that the guy facing me, with his arms folded over his chest and a smile on his face, knew who I was all this time.

And hid it.

Who does something like that?

A guilty person, that's who.

The question is, what is he guilty of?

"Water! How was the movie . . ." Jesse's voice drifts.

For just a second, time seems to hang still, as my heart pounds with a slow, aching rhythm against my chest, as I stare into those intense dark eyes that drew me in from the first moment I saw them, when he stormed into my hospital room under false pretenses. That was no accident. Jesse was there to see me.

His face pales. He knows that I know. I see it.

"Don't you mean Alexandria?" Just a whisper, and Jesse flinches from the impact.

He pushes his hands through his hair. "I . . ." He swallows hard as he grapples for words. "I was going to tell you tonight. I swear."

"Why not five months ago!" Amber screams. "What is wrong with you? How could you do something like this to her? To Mom and Dad!"

Jesse's eyes ignite with rage as he lashes out at Amber. "You have no fucking clue what you're talking about, Amber."

"No?" Tears stream down her cheeks. "Well, how about you enlighten us? I'm sure Dad would love to know that you've been lying all this time."

I hear them but I don't see them, my gaze glued to Jesse's face. "Did you do it?"

Four simple words. And only one answer that won't kill me right here where I stand.

"What?" It takes Jesse a few seconds to figure out what I'm asking, and then his face screws up with horror. "No!" he yells. He takes a step forward and I instinctively take three steps back.

No . . . that's right. It was my husband who did this to me. I wouldn't have been married to Jesse without his family knowing. But that leaves . . .

"Oh my God." I clutch at my stomach as the pieces from my dream click together. "You were the other guy. The one I was protecting." The father of my baby.

His throat bobs with a hard swallow and I have my answer.

"Can I please see that?" Gabe takes the photocopy of my ID that flitters between my fingers, hanging like a loose thread next to my thigh. He's strangely calm.

"Dad! He knew her. He's been lying to us this entire time!" Amber cries out.

"No, he hasn't." Meredith suddenly appears, walking around me until she's at Jesse's side. Where did she come from so suddenly?

"You knew?" Amber asks the question I can't, her words a punch to my windpipe.

Meredith's crystal-clear green eyes settle on me for a long moment. "We've known all along."

"*We've . . .*" Turning to Gabe, I watch him drop his gaze and squeeze his eyes shut. Just like he did that first day in the hospital. I realize now that that wasn't from the sight of me. That was guilt.

Meredith edges forward, one arm still around her son, her free hand reaching for me. "We did what we thought was best, for your safety *and* for our son's."

All this time. They let me linger in this purgatory, building a new life that would never be real, wondering who out there would want to hurt me so badly.

Wondering what I had done to deserve this.

"Did you know who did this to me?"

Jesse's eyes never leave my face, but I watch Gabe and Meredith, the exchange between them . . .

They know.

A new hollowness takes over my insides, one borne of betrayal.

"We never thought your memory lapse would last this long," Meredith calls out, her eyes glossy with tears. "And then you started getting settled in here, and you were doing so well in your new life. We couldn't figure out *how* to tell you. And then you and Jesse . . ." Her brow pinches together. "Seeing you together again, and so happy."

Together *again*? "What do you . . . You met me before?"

There's a long pause before she nods.

This can't be happening. I stumble backward, the urge to vomit overwhelming.

"Water, just wait."

"It's not Water," I choke out. "Water isn't real. She never was."

Away. I need to get away.

"Alex!" Jesse shouts, his voice cracking.

I don't stop. I run toward home—or whatever it is now—not caring about tripping or my leg buckling or anything except surrounding myself within a set of walls. I see Ginny standing halfway between her house and the fence line.

Without thinking, I run to her.

"How much did you hear?" I ask between sobs. I didn't even know I was crying.

She heaves a shaky sigh. "Enough." Her arm reaches around my shoulders in a very non-Ginny way; a way that I need right now. "Come on."

She leads me up her stairs, across her porch.

And in through her front door.

THIRTY-FIVE

JESSE

THEN

"Don't be nervous. They're going to love you." I give her hand a squeeze as we cut a path up to my parents' house, the thin layer of snow crunching under our boots. The sheriff's car sits in its usual spot, my mom's sedan parked next to it.

Alex and I have kept in close touch through texts these past two weeks, as we finalize plans. When she mentioned that Viktor would be heading to Seattle on business for the weekend, I told her to pack a few bags. And then I called my mother, to make sure that my parents would be home.

I haven't figured out how I'm going to break the news to them—that they'll have a tenant on their property beginning next weekend. I guess I'll let them fall in love with her first. It shouldn't be hard.

I'm pretty sure it took me only one night.

Of course, the whole "and she's pregnant with her husband's baby" topic would complicate things. I'm just going to have to lie and tell them that it's mine. I'm still not sure if I'm ready to admit to them that she's married. She made sure to leave her ring in her purse.

My mom greets us at the sliding door into the kitchen, in jeans and a sweater, looking nothing like the esteemed surgeon and every bit like the mom who used to bring Cheez Whiz sandwiches to me on those lazy summer days while I sat perched on the workbench, watching my granddad tinker with his Ford truck.

"It's so nice to meet you, Alex." My mom squeezes Alex's shoulder in greeting, her smile broad and genuine. Besides the odd friend of Amber's that I dated—and inevitably got bored of—my parents have never met any of my girlfriends. When I told her I was bringing Alex up to meet them, there was a good five seconds of dead silence on the receiver.

"This is Jesse's father, Gabe," my mom says, sliding her arm around my dad's waist.

"The sheriff, right?" Alex says, taking his extended hand.

"Just Gabe around these parts." He's smiling. It's rare to see him smile, period, and damn near impossible when it has anything to do with me.

"It's too bad Jesse's sister, Amber, isn't here to meet you, but she's working."

Alex's eyes flicker to me. "I'm sure I'll have a chance to meet her sometime soon."

"Please, sit." My mom gestures to the table, a platter of nachos and salsa out. One of Mom's specialties.

Maybe Alex can finally teach that woman how to cook.

———

"Your parents are so nice."

I throw an extra-large log into the woodstove. "They really liked you. I could tell." I could also tell that my mom is dying to interrogate me.

"Are they still going to like me when they find out?"

I glance over my shoulder in time to see Alex's hand smooth over her abdomen. It still doesn't feel real, that there's a human being growing inside her. I try to picture what she's going to look like lying on the floor in those pillows with a big, round belly.

With Viktor's kid.

I'd be lying if I said it didn't bother me at all. But it should bother me more than it does. "They'll be fine with you. They probably won't like *me* too much for a while, but . . ." I sigh, holding a marshmallow above the flame to brown. "It won't be the first time I've disappointed them."

"You know, you and your father are a lot alike. You're both very quiet, but with this calm, strong presence. You look a lot alike, too. Those eyes . . ." I feel her gaze on my profile. "I've always loved your eyes."

"Are you telling me you have the hots for my dad? Do I have to worry about you alone here for the next two months?" I'm not moving back until March. Alex is worried that both of us disappearing around the same time will look suspicious. I think she's being overly paranoid, but I've agreed to humor her. Gives me more time to find a job around here, too, where mechanic jobs are hard to come by.

I catch the pillow she flings at my head with one hand and toss it back, chuckling. "We're alike in some ways. Very different in others. You should have heard the fights we had. I was a bad teenager," I admit. "I made his life hell, but he was hard on me, too."

"That's because he loves you so much, not because he doesn't. I'm sure that, when the time comes that you really need him, you'll be able to count on him."

"I wouldn't bet on that." I really needed him when Dirk and Ian tried to pin Tommy's stabbing on me, and yet I was the first one that my dad threw into the back of his cop car.

I'm not bringing that story up tonight, though. That's one for another day.

Alex pulls the plaid wool blanket up around her body. "You're lucky you have a father like that. It's better than indifference. Or nonexistence. Maybe if my father was in my life, I wouldn't have ended up with a man like Viktor."

"Or maybe your father was a scumbag like Viktor, and you were better off not knowing him," I interject, though I know that's not her point.

"Maybe," she concedes. "Well, I for one am looking forward to getting to know your parents. I like them a lot already. They're both so calm. I want to surround myself with calm people. Not volatile ones, like Viktor."

"Here." I sandwich the melted marshmallow between the chocolate and the graham crackers. "Stop talking about my parents and eat this. Welcome to Western culture."

I feed her a bite. A tiny, appreciative moan escapes her and, when she licks the melted chocolate off her lip, my heart starts racing. I haven't so much as touched her leg in weeks.

I'm dying to be with her again.

"Before I forget . . ." She rolls to her left and grabs the strap of her tan messenger bag. "Here's the money I saved. We should leave this here with my things." We filled my trunk with bags of clothes and basics she wanted to bring with her—towels, bedding, some things to cook with that she said would only collect dust if left with Viktor.

I test the bag's weight. It's heavy. "You want to leave this much money in here?"

She shrugs. "I figured it's safer here than in Portland."

I smile. "Yeah. Probably." This is pretty much the safest place around.

Her bright eyes roam the space. "This little attic has so much potential. I was thinking we could . . ."

I just nod as she goes on about curtains and tables and all the things she wants to do to the small space, watching her lips move.

"The crib can go over in that corner. We'll have to get rid of that chair, but I want to anyway. It's a bit old. Jesse? Why are you staring at me like that? Are you listening to me?"

"Not really. You can do whatever the hell you want with this place."

A playful smile curls her lips. "Oh, good! Because I was thinking that there's not a lot of space, so we'll need to convert the garage downstairs into more living—"

I steal a deep kiss. "You can do whatever the hell you want with *this* place, but the garage is off-limits. God knows I'll need it with a screaming baby in here," I correct, and then kiss her again, tasting the chocolate and marshmallow residue.

She breaks away and bites her bottom lip with worry. "Are you sure you want to do this? Because you don't have to. You can still back out."

I glare at her. "Back out?" She just doesn't get it. I'm not ready to say it out loud yet, but there's no doubt about it. The fact that I can't wait for next weekend, and I know that the next two months will be the longest of my life, proves it.

I'm in love with Alex.

"I just . . . I know what it's like to feel trapped. It's utterly suffocating. I don't ever want you to feel like that."

In all honesty, I've been terrified these past two weeks. It has nothing to do with worrying that I don't want this. I'm terrified that I can't be what she needs me to be.

But I'll never admit that to her. She needs me to be strong, and I *want* to be strong for her.

As strong as she is.

"Is it just my hormones or is it boiling in here?" she suddenly exclaims, unzipping her sweatshirt and peeling it off to reveal a plain, long-sleeved shirt underneath. She may not be showing yet, but her boobs are getting bigger. If Viktor stopped to really look at his wife over the past few weeks, he would have noticed.

"No, it's boiling. I built the fire nice and hot. And opened all the vents."

"God, why?" She kicks off the blanket with a scowl of confusion.

I shrug. "Best way to get a girl to strip."

She stops to stare at me, probably to figure out if I'm being honest. And then she falls back into the pillows, laughing. That deep, infectious sound that makes me dive into her mouth.

She doesn't hesitate, tangling her tongue with mine to give me another sweet taste of chocolate.

I can't wait anymore, sliding her shirt up and over her head.

"Gentle. They're sore."

I have her bra off in a matter of seconds. I'm just about to show her how gentle I can be with my mouth when a knock sounds on the door at the bottom of the stairs, followed by my mom's holler of "Hello?"

I roll onto my back with a groan. "Stay right here."

My mom's waiting in the garage, her arms loaded with one of the winter duvets. "I don't want you and Alex to get cold overnight."

I stifle my smirk. "Thanks, Mom."

Her eager eyes flicker up the stairs. "Where'd you meet her?"

Should I be honest? "On the side of the road. I fixed her tire and she kissed me."

My mom starts chuckling. I'm not sure if she believes me. "I really like her." She pauses. "You're serious about this one, aren't you?"

I nod. "Yeah, Mom. She's it."

This is the start of the rest of my life.

———

The trance in the background tells me that Boone is at The Cellar.

"Have you talked to Alex lately?"

I hesitate. "No." Boone doesn't know we're talking. He sure as hell doesn't know about the pregnancy or my plans to pick her up tomorrow night and take her to Sisters for good.

"Are you lying?" There's an edge to his tone that I don't like.

"No. Why?" I snap.

I hear his rushed breathing, like he's walking fast. Suddenly, the music is gone and I can hear him clearly, though he's talking low. "Look, I don't know what the fuck is going on. Viktor was supposed to be here tonight to meet up with some guy, but he told Rust that he had to deal with a problem at home and it was going to take all night. Apparently this was an important meeting. It's not like Viktor to miss this kind of stuff."

My heart has just gone from normal to spastic in a span of two seconds.

"And then Albert was talking—"

"Who the fuck is Albert?"

"The big blond guy who's always with Viktor. Anyway, Albert just got a phone call from Viktor. He was talking in Russian and you know my Russian's not great, but it sounded like he was trying to calm Viktor down. And then he started giving him directions to this old logging trail he knows about, in the interior, off Highway Twenty. He was saying it's a far drive but it'll be safe. He said nobody goes there this time of year." Boone pauses. "Albert told Viktor that he'd drive out in the morning and clean up. Maybe I'm just paranoid, but . . . something in my gut doesn't feel right."

I'm ready to throw up the late-night pizza pocket I just inhaled. "Did he say where this logging trail was?"

"He did, but it was hard to follow along. Something about some burned-out woods and a totem pole?"

I know exactly where that is.

I'm in my car in under thirty seconds, racing for Black Butte, hitting redial over and over on my phone. But it just goes to her voice mail.

THIRTY-SIX

WATER

NOW

I stare at the swirl of steam that rises from the cup of tea next to me, with no intention of drinking it. "You didn't know?"

Ginny settles herself into her creaky rocking chair with a sigh. "No, Water. I had absolutely no clue." It's the tenth time she's said those exact words. Because it's the tenth time I've asked. She stretches her quilt over her lap and picks up her needle. "Do you think I would have had any part in it, had I known? Do you know me to be a liar?"

"No," I whisper, hugging my knees to my chest as my eyes roll over the cramped den inside Ginny's house. If I had to guess, I'd say that the myriad of pictures, the figurines on the shelves, the western-print curtains—everything in this room—have remained exactly where Ginny's parents first placed them.

But I also know Gabe to be a hard-nosed, black-and-white, follow-the-law-to-the-letter kind of man. The kind of man who threw his own son in jail. And Meredith . . .

"Why would they do this?"

Ginny's needle stops weaving through the fabric. "What exactly did Meredith say, again?"

"That they were protecting me. And Jesse."

Ginny's head shakes. "That damn boy. He just can't keep himself out of trouble."

A fist pounds against the door, making me jolt.

Ginny merely peers over her glasses at the front door.

A moment later, Gabe's voice booms. "Ginny? Open the door! I need to speak with Water."

Water.

That name now sounds almost as ridiculous as Jane Doe.

"What would you like me to do?" she asks.

"I can't," I whisper, resting my face on my knees. "Not right now." For months, all I waited for was even a shred of my past. Now I have the chance to know *everything* and I'm not sure that I'm ready for it.

She rubs her jaw in that stubborn Ginny way and then, setting her sewing down on the table next to her, she edges out of her seat, stepping over a lazy Felix, to shuffle toward the door. "She doesn't want to speak to you right now."

"I'll explain everything."

"You should have done that months ago, ya hear?"

A lighter thump hits the door. "Alex, *please.*" That's not Gabe. That's Jesse, pleading with me, stealing a few of my heartbeats as I imagine his head pressed up against the door.

It's followed quickly by, "Ginny . . . open this door or I'll break it down."

She snorts. "Good luck with that! You'll just cripple yourself, old man." When Ginny had the bars put up on all her first-floor windows, she also had a large two-by-four barricade installed on the inside of her doors. No one's breaking into this house unless they have a ladder to get to her second floor. "Now get the hell off of my porch before I call the police and give the town something to talk about."

"I *am* the goddamn police, Ginny!" he barks back, his patience and normally calm demeanor finally lost.

"Then act like it and arrest yourself and that damn son of yours for what you've done."

"Just let me explain."

"Oh, you'll get your chance, don't you worry. But you can sit out there and stew for the night." Her slippers slide across the worn wood plank floor as she shuffles back to take her seat.

"They know you don't have a phone to call the police," I mutter. Neither do I right now. Mine is sitting in my purse in Amber's car, where I left it.

"Don't matter." She goes back to rocking and sewing, as if she can't hear the heavy footfalls back and forth across the front porch.

"How long do you think they'll stay out there for?"

She doesn't miss a beat. "All night." She gestures with a nod up at a picture above the old piano in the corner. A boy of maybe nine stands in the center of the barn, his cowboy hat on, a long stick in his hand and his shoulders pulled back. Dark eyes pierce the person behind the camera. "That's Gabe, there." She chuckles. "After Earl attacked me, I mostly stayed in my room. Stopped going down to see the horses for . . . a good three years. Being in that barn was too hard.

"Every day, Gabe would track down my father and ask him when I'd be back. He didn't understand at the time. My father just kept telling him, 'Not today.' But people talk around this town and I guess Gabe must have started hearing things. What things, I can't imagine because I didn't tell anyone anything. I refused to talk to a soul about it. I guess they just started making things up on their own.

"Anyway, one morning, my father came down to the barn and he found little Gabe pacing up and down the center of the aisle. When he asked him what he was doing, Gabe told him he was on guard for bad guys. That was in June, just after school let out, and every single day for that summer, Gabe paced up and down.

"Eventually, I started going down to the barn again. I missed being around the horses. I couldn't breathe, those first few steps inside bringing the demons with them. But then I saw the path Gabe had worn into the floor. If you look hard enough today, you'll still see it." She turns her focus back to her quilt. "I don't think Gabe could be anything other than what he is."

She flips the quilt around on her lap and reaches for her signature black tree, already cut out and ready to be stitched on.

"Why the tree?"

She doesn't answer right away, her focus on positioning and pinning it in place, and I finally assume she's ignoring me.

"It was one of the first days of warm weather after an unusually cold winter. I was fifteen, and I decided I'd pull my bike out of the garage and go for a ride down the road before dinner. Just to the other end of our fields. It'd be too dark if I waited until after." She switches out the red thread on her needle for black. "I didn't think anything of it when I saw Earl's truck pull over on the side of the road ahead of me. I didn't think anything of it when he told me that he had found the perfect tree to climb nearby . . ."

I hug my knees tighter to my body, listening to Ginny reveal to me what I know she hasn't told another living soul.

"When I realized what he wanted—what he thought I wanted—and I tried to run . . . he got *really* mad. Irrationally so. Turns out he wasn't such a kind, nice man, after all. He had a very dark side." She pauses. "It wasn't until he was about halfway through that I noticed the big white oak tree watching over us. So I started focusing on that, instead. On its height, and its bare branches. Pretending that I was just lying in the grass on any regular spring day, and that if I watched closely enough, I'd get to see it wake up; I'd see the leaf buds sprout." She shifts a pin out of the way of her needle. "It made it easier to deal with."

"What happened to Earl?"

Her nostrils flare with a deep inhale. "He just stood for the longest time, staring at me as I lay in the grass, crying, a dazed look on his face. Then I watched him head toward his truck. I thought he was leaving. I wasn't in any shape to pick myself up and run. But he didn't leave. He reached into the back of his truck," Ginny makes the hand motion as if reenacting it, sending shivers down my back, "for some rope. I thought that that was it. I was a goner. He was going to kill me right there, under that big tree. He walked past me without a word, slung the rope over his shoulder, and began climbing the tree, all the way up to the first branch. And then I watched him hang himself from it." Her mouth crests downward in a frown. "He was an unstable fellow. History of mental illness. Of course, my father had no idea about that when he hired him. But I guess when Earl's own demons went to sleep and he realized what he had just done to me, his guilt got the better of him."

"Oh God, Ginny . . ." I mutter softly.

She goes on. "When time for dinner came and went and it started getting dark, my father came looking for me. He found my bike and the truck on the side of road. It wasn't hard to spot a two-hundred-and-forty-pound body swinging from the tree. That's how he found me. Lying under that tree.

"I guess you could say I lucked out. There was a very brief police investigation. I refused to give them any details. I figured they didn't need more than what they had between the body and my medical report from the doctors. There was no point. Earl was dead. They couldn't punish him. The most unfortunate thing about the entire situation is that the great big tree—that gave me my escape, that helped serve justice to the man who wronged me—never did bud any leaves that year. Or any other year. It just up and died. White oaks aren't common in this part of Oregon anyway, so the fact that it was even growing out here was something. And then to just die like that? Unheard of."

I say nothing.

"I never forgot that tree. When I had trouble falling asleep because I couldn't shake the memory of him, I'd close my eyes and picture the big oak."

"And then you started making quilts with it."

She nods. "I found out that winter that my daddy took a chainsaw to it, cut it down. That was his way of dealing with the memory. But I wanted to keep it alive, to pay my respects to it for giving me solace that day and for so many nights after. I only ever meant to make one, but I found it strangely therapeutic."

I take in the tidy stacks of boxes lining the far wall, three high and stretching the entire length of the wall, identified with color names scrawled across the front. All filled with material for her quilts. Hundreds more, probably. "Why don't you ever give it any leaves?"

Her hands stop and she looks up at me with a baffled expression. "Because it is a dead tree, Water. It will *always* be bare. It'll never be that oak that grows big and beautiful and changes colors in the fall, ever again. Not in this life, anyway."

I nod slowly. "Right." Is Ginny really talking about the tree anymore? Or is she talking about herself? Is she the lone tree that died that day, and now watches the world from a distance? The thing is, Ginny's not dead, far from it. She's just been afraid.

"I think the buds are there. You just need to look harder to see them."

She opens her mouth to say something but hesitates, as if changing her mind. "You should stretch out on that couch and get some rest. You'll need your energy to deal with them tomorrow."

"Or I could just hide out in here forever," I say, half-jokingly, my eyes on the black bars that protect me from the outside.

"You will not." Ginny's stubborn jaw sets. "I won't allow that. You'll find out what that boy knows and then you'll decide what you want to do."

"What if I don't want to know?"

"It's too late for that, now. The truth has found its way to the surface, like it always does, eventually," she answers, matter-of-factly. "You'll never be able to trust any of them again if you don't just face this—and, whether you like it or not, they're your family now. They're going to be in your life for a long time. You have to trust your family or you have nothing.

"Besides, I've seen the way you look at that boy. Since the very first day. Those feelings didn't sprout the moment you walked onto this ranch, and they'll survive *because* you came to this ranch. If you're lucky, you'll come out of this never needing a dead tree to save you. Promise me you'll hear them out."

"I will," I promise.

A bit softer, she says, "Go on now. Lie down and sleep."

I figure that's her way of telling me that she's done enough talking so I do as she says, expecting that I won't ever fall asleep. But when I close my eyes, I feel the weight of the day start tugging at my consciousness. "I'm really glad I met you, Ginny," I say into the silent night as I drift off.

I think I hear her say, "Not as glad as I am to have met you, girl."

I can't be sure, though.

———

Moisture against my cheek wakes me up, followed by several urgent pokes. Cracking an eye, I find a snout in my line of sight. It takes me a second to find my bearings and remember I'm at Ginny's. In another second, I remember why, and the hollowness in my chest instantly appears. "You want out, Felix?"

He begins prancing and lets out a whine. The curtains are drawn shut, so I have no idea what time it is, but it feels too early. I give my eyes a rub and then, pushing off the quilt that Ginny must have draped over me at some point, I sit up.

Ginny's still sitting in her rocking chair, her quilt stretched across her lap, her eyes closed. Asleep.

Felix whines again. "Shhh . . ." I warn, not wanting to wake Ginny up. "Come on." I get up and head toward the front door, inhaling deeply as I prepare for what may be waiting just outside. Did they give up and go home?

Felix whines a third time and, when I turn around, I realize he's not following me. He's beside Ginny, his chin resting on her lap.

I half-expect her to reach down and swat the dog away. But she doesn't stir. Something's wrong.

"Ginny?" The old wood floors creak under my weight as I quickly backtrack. Reaching out, I give her shoulder a shake. Her head flops to the side and then forward. "Ginny!" I grab her wrist, searching for a pulse. It's there, but it's weak.

I need help. I need a phone and an ambulance and . . . I need Meredith and Amber.

I struggle with the barricade, finally getting it off and the door open. Stepping out into the pre-dawn light, I find Jesse and Sheriff Gabe perched on either side of Ginny's porch swing, each wearing the startled look of someone dozing off and then suddenly wakening.

"Help!" is all I can manage, my fear for Ginny overpowering everything else.

———

It's weird, being a visitor in the hospital I considered my home for almost three months. My first home. I experienced so much confusion, so much panic, so much fear within these beige walls. Now, I sit in an uncomfortable white plastic chair in the waiting room, experiencing them all over again, except this time for someone else.

We've been here all day: Amber sitting on one side of me, Jesse on the other, and Gabe pacing the room. All of us silent, with dark circles growing under our eyes. Avoiding what felt unavoidable only twenty-four hours ago. Still, I can't imagine being here alone, without them, right now.

Amber has attempted conversation a few times but I've reciprocated with only two-word answers, losing myself in the emergency cases walking through the door—everything from children with fevers to open forehead gashes. Jesse seems content just to sit beside me. He drifted off a few times, falling onto my shoulder.

I didn't push him away. I didn't want to.

I'm on my feet the moment Meredith emerges, taking slow, even steps toward us. She's trained to give news—both good and bad—to families, with minimal emotion. As a result, I can't guess what she's coming to tell us, her face an unreadable mask.

Until she slumps into the chair across from me. That's when I know.

"We found a sizeable tumor inside Ginny's head. That's what caused the herniation in her midbrain, which put her in a coma. We've relieved some of the pressure in her head. But . . ." Her voice grows hoarse. "It's unlikely she's going to wake up and, if she does, we expect that she will be severely disabled."

What? "No . . ." My head shakes back and forth. "She was fine last night. She was talking to me and yelling at them," I throw a loose hand toward Jesse and Gabe, who stands beside him now. "She was fine."

Meredith nods. "She was. And now she's not. Sometimes that happens with these kinds of things."

"Is the tumor cancerous?"

"We're still running tests."

"And you had no idea? Wasn't she here just a few months ago?" Gabe presses.

"For her gallbladder," Meredith snaps. "We weren't doing CT scans of her brain."

Silence settles over our small group, and I try to process this. Ginny is a part of my life. A foundational pillar. I feel like everything's about to topple.

"But . . ." Jesse rubs my back with his hand. "No. She needs to come home and make her tree quilts and feed Felix and see the barn that's going to be full of horses and complain about Jesse's car being too loud, and . . ." Tears stream down my face. "She needs to come *home.*"

"I wish I could give you a—"

"She'll wake up." I wipe both eyes with my palms and set my jaw stubbornly. "You didn't think I'd wake up, and I did." Meredith gives me a solemn nod.

"Can I see her?"

Meredith takes a deep breath, sharing a glance with Gabe. "Come on, I'll take you."

I turn to Amber. "The horses need—"

"I'll go bring them in. Feed the dog . . . all that." She pulls herself to her feet, passing her parents without a word.

I follow Meredith as she leads me through the ICU, the sterile smell, the low buzz of machines and voices, the long, monotonous halls, all sparking my earliest memories.

"She'll have some bandages on her head, but otherwise she looks fine," Meredith cautions as we enter the room. The machine beside Ginny beeps rhythmically. The sound used to be a lullaby for me.

"Visits are supposed to be kept to ten minutes, but I'll ask them to leave you alone."

"Thanks." It sounds hollow but that's all I can manage, wandering over to the chair beside Ginny's bed.

"I understand that you're angry with us, Water. But please give Jesse a chance to explain. His motivation—all of our motivations—came from a good place. One that meant you well."

I simply nod, unable to process my own personal turmoil right now.

The door closes softly.

And I simply stare at the small, frail woman lying there, unconscious, the lump in my throat growing larger and larger until I can't swallow without tears springing to my eyes.

The reclusive, ornery woman who in reality was brimming with life. Who spent decades hiding behind dead trees and scraps of quilts and an abrasive disposition. If only she had let that tree bud again, maybe others would have had a chance to see it, too.

Reaching forward, I slip my hand within hers. A giggle escapes. "Boy, will you be mad when you wake up and find yourself in here."

And then I bow my head and cry, because somehow I know that Meredith is right, and I'm never going to argue with Ginny again.

———

Jesse and Gabe are still in the waiting room when I emerge, my cheeks sore from the burn of so many tears.

Sickness churning in my stomach, I'm terrified of what this vault inside my head doesn't want me to see. But I also made a promise to Ginny last night, and I intend to keep it.

I settle eyes on Jesse. "I need to know everything. *Everything*."

———

The weathered totem pole stands proud among the trees at the dead end of the road, its paint faded. A shiver runs down my back as I lock eyes with the hummingbird that sits on top, staring down its long, pointed beak at me.

Is that just a coincidence?

"When I was about twelve, a couple of teenagers from Sisters came up to Black Butte to camp. They had a campfire—they weren't supposed to, it was too dry—and it started a forest fire. They died in it. I remember the day the town put this up here as a memorial," Jesse explains, staring up at the totem pole.

"Why did you bring me here?"

He reaches for my hand and I let his fingers graze mine for a second before I pull it away. I don't know how I'm supposed to feel about Jesse right now, except that there must be a good explanation for all of this.

With a heavy sigh, he drops his hand to his side and then begins a slow walk around, his gaze roaming the ground, as if he's searching for something. Finally, he stoops over to pick up the remnants of a cigarette butt, studying it for a moment before flicking it away. "Because this is where I found you."

"*You* found me?" My heart skips a beat as I take in the surroundings again. "Why did you lie?"

"It's a long story." Jesse's jaw tenses. "But you got your wish. You got to start over."

THIRTY-SEVEN

JESSE

THEN

Lifting her limp body up in my arms as delicately as possible, I start plodding through the snow toward my car, trying to hold her steady, my muscles straining against her dead weight. "It's okay . . . You're going to be fine . . . It's me, Jesse . . . I won't let him hurt you anymore . . ." I ramble. I doubt she can hear me but I talk anyway. I need to hear these words as much as she does. I need to believe them.

How the hell did Viktor find out? And exactly what does he know?

As carefully as possible, I slide her onto the backseat, thankful for the car's wide frame. I'm afraid to let her go but I have to, if she has any hope of survival at all. Wrapping the wool blanket around her broken body, I rush to the driver's seat to crank the engine and blast the car's heat. If the severe beating hasn't done her in, the winter cold certainly will.

My hands . . . I hold them up in the dim interior light. Like two slick red gloves, they're coated in Alex's blood. The front of my light gray hoodie—because I bolted out of my apartment too fast to grab a coat—is also covered. A quick glance in the rearview mirror confirms the crimson streaks smeared across my cheeks, where I wiped away my tears.

And I've got a badly beaten girl with ties to Viktor in my backseat.

Shit.

I can't just show up at the ER with her, can I? There'll be too many questions that I can't answer. What if she dies? I just . . . My brain is a jumbled mess. I know she needs helps, but . . . I just . . . I can't think straight. My hands tremble as I reach into my coat pocket for my phone, to do the only thing I can think of, because I'm in way over my head this time.

He answers on the second ring. "Jesse?"

"Dad?" My voice cracks over that one syllable. "I really fucked up this time."

"What do you mean?" His tone immediately takes on that authoritative edge. Normally, I clam right up when I hear it. Not this time, though. "It's Alex. She's . . . hurt. Bad."

"What? Where are you?"

"Near Black Butte. I have her in my car and I'm heading toward Bend." I throw the car into gear and, pinning my cell to my ear with my shoulder, I maneuver out of the dead end and head back, struggling not to speed too much for her sake. "I don't think she's going to make it."

"You shouldn't have moved her. *Exactly* where are you? Pull over. I'm calling an ambulance."

"I'm not sure that's a good idea."

"What the hell do you mean?" he snaps.

"It's not that simple." *Fuck.* Alex used those exact same words with me once. "Alex's husband did this."

He exhales loudly. "Well then, we'll have him arrested. But first we need to get her to a hospital."

"He's Russian mob."

"*What?*" My dad seems winded, like he's walking fast. "Jesus, Jesse. How the hell did you get mixed up with that!"

"I'll explain everything later. Right now I just need her safe."

"Did this happen because of you?"

I shake my head.

"Jesse!"

"I don't know! Just, please, Dad. Please help me." I don't know if he even hears that last plea, my voice is so hoarse, this engine so damn loud.

"The old tannery. How far away are you?"

"Maybe ten minutes."

———

Those ten minutes feel like an hour. I half-expect the entire Deschutes County police force and handcuffs when I get to the run-down building on an isolated side road, abandoned for years. A single set of tracks leads me around back, to where the white cruiser sits with a prominent green star emblem on the door. My dad's marching toward me.

"Holy . . ." He winces as he looks in the backseat.

"I know."

"Shut your car off and pull her out. Lay her down here." He points to the ground on his way back to his car.

I'm not going to argue with him, so I push my seat forward and scoop her up.

Another light, gurgling sound slips through her lips and I have to grit my teeth to keep the sob from tearing out of me as my dad calls our location in over the radio. "Just hang in there, Alex. Stay with me."

As much as I don't want to, I lay her down in the fresh bed of snow.

"Get out of here, now. Take this." He pulls the blanket away from her body.

"But it's cold out here. She needs it."

"Does it have your DNA on it?"

Both of ours. All over it.

My hesitation answers him. He thrusts it into my hand. "Take it. Drive this car right into the garage. Bag everything on you, bag the rags, the blanket. *Everything*. And stay there. Don't give anyone a reason to pull you over, Jesse. Go! Now!"

With one last glance at her, I dive into my car.

A blurry kaleidoscope of blue and red lights races past me about twenty seconds after I pull onto the main road. "You can survive this, Alex," I whisper. "You're strong."

I'll take whatever's coming to me, but only if she survives.

————

"Your language skills aren't too bad after all." My hand runs through my damp hair. The small hot-water tank went cold long before I got out and now I'm sitting on my bed, shivering.

I hear a soft "fuck" slip through Boone's lips. "Bad?"

"Yeah." I don't want to say much more over the phone. "I'm going to stick around here for the weekend. I'll be back for work on Monday." It's the last place I want to be, but I need to face whatever's coming to me. Me suddenly disappearing will only raise suspicions. "I don't know what he knows."

"I'll keep an ear out. Take it easy. And I'm sorry. I could see how much . . ." He drifts off, probably as paranoid as I am right now.

I hear his unspoken words. "Yeah. I did. Thanks, Boone. For tonight." If he hadn't been there, if he hadn't called me . . . she'd already be dead. "Watch yourself, too."

I hang up with Boone and am left sitting on my bed, wearing only a towel, staring at hands that were covered in Alex's blood only hours ago, my stomach a mess of nerves. I followed my dad's instructions, stripping off my clothes and bagging everything, and then wiping up the small pool of blood in my backseat. Now all I'm left with is time. Time to play out how different things could be for her right now. I can't be blamed for pulling over to help a woman out with her flat tire. That choice was a good one, an innocent one. But every choice I made after that . . . I could have told her that her muffler was damaged and walked out of that customer lounge. I could have parked my ass on the couch and watched baseball instead of going to The Cellar that second night. I could have said no to the Barracuda that Viktor dangled in front of me. I could have left her to Triple-A when her gas ran out. I could have not given her my number; I could have not gone to the hotel . . .

So many choices, and I kept picking the wrong one. All because I let a faceless girl kiss me on the side of the road.

Then again, maybe it never really mattered, what I did or what choices I made. Maybe the truth is that we were meant to find each other. A simple truth that would have kept finding its way to us, no matter which path I tried to turn down.

No matter how deep I buried the feelings she sparked within me with one damn kiss.

If you wait long enough, the truth *always* finds its way. Just like that stream. Just like water.

Alex is my truth.

I toss a few logs into the woodstove and then fall into the pillows still scattered around it, watching the flames devour the wood. Trying desperately to remember all the things she wanted to do to this place to make it her home.

She would have been so happy here.

———

"Jesse!"

My dad is crouching beside me. In the window beyond him, I see stars sparkling in the black Oregon skies. Nothing but glowing embers remains behind the glass in front of me. I've been staring at the woodstove all this time and I didn't notice the fire go out.

"How is she?" My jaw hurts from clenching my teeth the entire day.

Silence hangs through the air, and I hold my breath against the answer I expect to hear.

"She's still alive. I don't know for how long. I don't know how, but—"

Air sails from my lungs. "Can I go see her?"

"No, Jesse." He shakes his head to emphasize his point. It's an old habit of his, and that's when I know it's serious. "She's still in the OR. Your mother's doing everything she can."

Jesus. My own mother is operating on her. "Does Mom know?"

"All she knows right now is that it's an attempted murder investigation and it needs to be kept confidential. I'll have to tell her sooner or later, though. Especially if Alex survives. Your mother's met her. She knows what she looks like." He adds softly, "What she looked like."

"What do we do now?"

He stands, and begins pacing around the room. Another Sheriff Welles tic. "We get rid of everything. Your clothes, the blanket, all traces from your car."

"Bleach?"

"No, we need something with oxygen. Luckily your mother has an affinity for stocking hydrogen peroxide. We have a few bottles." I guess there's a benefit to having a sheriff for a father. Especially one intent on discrediting CSI. "And then you're going to tell me everything, Jesse. From beginning to end. Every last detail. No lies. I need to know that I went against e*verything* I stand for for a good enough reason."

I nod solemnly. "Thanks, Dad."

The muscles in his jaw tighten. "If she dies, he'll get away with it. By moving her, we've lost evidence. The case has lost credibility. *You* will be the prime suspect if there are any links at all."

My forehead falls into my hand. "I know. I just . . . I saw her and I couldn't think straight. I still can't. I just want to hide her from him."

"Do you know how lucky you are that you were never booked and fingerprinted with that whole Tommy mess? If you had been, Crane would already be busting down the door."

That's one complication averted. But it's far from the only one. Viktor's friend, Albert, would have driven out to Black Butte by now. He would have seen that she's not there. What happens then? "Things may still get worse, Dad."

———

Encircled by a small ring of stones, with dark smoke swirling into a black sky for no one to see, my father—the righteous sheriff of Deschutes County—and I burn all evidence that I was ever near Alex.

And I tell him every last detail.

Including how much I love her.

———

"Welles!"

I try to hide my scowl as I peer out from under the hood of the Honda I'm working on. "What?"

"Don't 'what' me," Miller barks. "Go outside. Mr. Petrova's waiting for you. Now."

My stomach tightens. Taking a deep breath through my nose, I toss my wrench on the table—earning Miller's sneer—and then make my way through the side door, feeling Boone's eyes on me the entire time.

I still don't know what triggered the attack, or what Viktor managed to get out of Alex before he left her there. I've been waiting nine days, my heart pounding every time I step into my apartment or walk out to my car, expecting to find Viktor or Albert or some unfamiliar face waiting for me. Couple that with the agony I feel as Alex lies unconscious in a bed in St. Charles Medical Center—she's defied all odds to make it this far, but she's still not out of the woods—and I'm basically a disaster.

When my father gave me a rundown of all her injuries—how Viktor raped her, how she lost her baby, how she'll have an unsightly scar running down her face for the rest of her life if she lives—I sat in my car, ready to find and kill Viktor on sight with my bare hands.

But I *do* know that Viktor thinks the evidence of his crime is gone. Boone went back to The Cellar with Rust the next night. Viktor was there, fingers twitching and eyes roaming. Definitely on edge. Boone kept his mouth shut and sucked back his vodka while listening to Albert confirm in Russian that, yes, he drove out in the morning to clean up.

That a mountain lion had gotten to her body.

And, yes, he cleaned up. Not a trace left.

Boone's certain he heard—and translated—correctly.

The only reason Boone and I can think of that explains Albert's lie to Viktor is that he assumes a mountain lion *did* in fact get to her but Viktor will lose his shit if her body isn't burned or buried. Mountain lions are rare in those parts, but I'll gladly take Albert's lie if it keeps Alex hidden. So far, it seems to have worked.

Still, as I approach the gold Hummer sitting outside and the murderous son-of-a-bitch standing next to it, those naturally cold eyes on me, I have to wonder if I'll end up in a field somewhere soon, too.

"Hello, Jesse."

"Viktor." I make a point of pulling the rag from my back pocket and rubbing my greasy hands in it, to avoid any potential handshake he offers. In truth, as much as I hate this monster in front of me, I'm ready to piss myself right now.

"I wanted to extend my offer to you once more. My friend's car is arriving this weekend. He's willing to pay well for the restoration."

What? That's what this visit is about? It takes me a moment to gather my wits. "Not interested."

He smirks. "You like working all day in a garage, having that . . ." he says, muttering a Russian word, "bark orders at you? You could have what I have, if you make the right decisions now."

I did have what you have. Because I made all the wrong decisions. And it didn't matter, because he still fucking stole it from me. "I like my eight-to-five job. Simple. No stress. That's all I really care about. You should ask Tabbs or Zeke. They're both good with engines. I'm sure one of them could help your friend out, and they've got mouths to feed."

I'll bet he gets what he wants by being able to predict people. The way he's sizing me up now, I don't think he predicted a second rejection. He probably doesn't know what to do with it. "And what if you lose this job?"

Is that a threat? I shrug. "Then I'll get another one. I was thinking of leaving Portland anyway. The rain's getting to me. Thinking San Diego may be more my thing."

He offers a flat smile. "I had hoped you were more ambitious than this."

"I'm not." I swallow hard and then force out, "But thanks for thinking of me." The vile aftertaste burns in my mouth.

"I will not be making this offer again."

"I understand."

His lips twist with disdain. "I wish you luck in your *simple* life." He says the word with disdain, and I catch the light bruising against his knuckles as he reaches for his car door. Evidence, right there. Fading. Soon it will be gone.

Why did you do it? What do you know, Viktor?

The brief glimpse I get inside shows me Priscilla sitting comfortably in the passenger seat, her eyes sparkling as she takes in Viktor. She thinks she's hit the jackpot. I never liked her, but I feel sorry for her now. She has no idea what's in store for her.

Not until the Hummer's taillights disappear around the corner do I let out the breath that I've been holding. Maybe he doesn't know about Alex and me. But, then, what else would have triggered such a violent attack? Did he find her note and figure out she was leaving him? There's no way he'd do something so savage just because she's pregnant.

My phone begins vibrating in my pocket. I see my dad's name on the display and Viktor vanishes from my thoughts in an instant.

"Yeah?" I suck in my breath again and hold it, waiting for the words that I've been dreading for nine long days.

"She's awake."

"Seriously?" I stumble over to lean on the closest car, a mumble of "thank God" slipping through my lips. "And?"

There's a pause. "And right now she doesn't remember a thing."

I feel my brow pull together. She doesn't remember the attack? "I guess that's good, right?" Nobody should have to live with those kinds of memories.

"No, Jesse. You don't understand. She doesn't remember a *thing*. Nothing. She doesn't even know her own name."

———

Alex sat in that very chair just over two weeks ago. Now my mom occupies it, her face drawn and dark circles hugging her eyes.

Staring at me as if I've lost my mind.

"You want us to do *what*?"

"Don't tell her." It's a simple request.

"She doesn't have a brain injury, Jesse. She's going to start remembering things on her own soon enough."

"Then let her remember on her own terms. When she's ready."

"We can't just leave her adrift like that. The poor girl is completely lost! You should see the look in her eyes. She doesn't even know her own name!"

"And she also doesn't remember being raped and cut up and beaten to an inch of—"

"I don't need the list. I'm well aware of everything that her *husband* did to her, Jesse," she snaps. My mom didn't take the news that I was having an affair with a married, pregnant woman too well. I could have lied and told them that the baby was mine, though I don't know how much that would have helped. Luckily for me, though, she thinks Viktor should be executed on sight.

My mom sighs. "Why did you two let it get this far? I mean, this man is obviously a maniac and I can see why she wanted to get away from him, but how is hiding all of this now any better? What if she wants to press charges?"

"She won't."

She pauses. "This isn't the first time he's hurt her."

I shake my head. "It's just never been this bad before."

"What about her family? Won't someone be looking for her?"

I shake my head a second time. "She doesn't have anyone but me. *Us.*"

My mom shares a look with my dad, who leans against the patio door, his face as drawn and tired as the rest of ours.

"There are things that you cannot know, Meredith."

She answers him with a glare. Apparently that's been their main method of communication since my dad told her who she was struggling to save, right before he put a gag order on her. She still has no idea who Alex's husband is—his associations. She'd never sleep again and she sure as hell wouldn't ever let me out of her sight. My dad's not willing to put that kind of stress on her.

"Look, Mom. If she starts remembering things, I'll tell her everything—I promise."

"And if she doesn't?"

The entire drive back to Sisters after my dad's phone call, Alex's words kept springing into my head. By the time I pulled into my parents' driveway, I was sure this had to be an omen. "If she has a chance to start over fresh, then we should let her have it. That's what she wanted. A fresh start. This might be it. You did say this is psychological. So maybe this is her instincts, burying everything she doesn't want to remember."

"But that would also mean she doesn't want to remember *you*, Jesse," she says softly.

Maybe she doesn't. I don't know what Viktor knows, or why he did this, but I have to think it has *something* to do with me. Maybe Alex would rather be free of me, too.

I keep that worry to myself as my mom shakes her head absently. "I just don't see how this can work. Or how it will end well. I mean," she frowns, "she had deep feelings for you. I saw it the second she walked through this very door. Just being around you may bring everything back."

"Then I won't be around her." It kills me, just saying that, but if that's what it takes, then I'll stay away.

"And you certainly can't pick up your relationship with her." My mom's voice takes on that stern tone that she rarely uses. "It's one thing for your father and I to deceive her, but there's no way you can carry on like you did without telling her the truth."

Would she even want that? If she doesn't remember me, if she didn't feel trapped and utterly alone, would a girl like her fall for me a second time? I grit my teeth against the possibility that the answer is no. "I'll stay away from her, I promise. I'll stay in Portland."

"Does this husband of hers know about you two? Does he even know who you are?"

"No." I steal another glance my dad's way. We agreed that Mom doesn't need to know about the work I did for him, or about the probably stolen car I'm driving. My dad hit the roof when I admitted that. "Just give this a chance, Mom. Please. She may remember everything in a few weeks' time, but at least she'll have a bit of peace until then."

"I don't know, Jesse." My mom rests her forehead in her hands. "What if she wants to press charges against her husband?"

"Then I will help her," my dad says. He and I both know what that means. Right now, my dad can control the investigation. He can keep it low profile. But a deeper investigation and charges would mean potential disaster for him and me. It might uncover all kinds of things, including my ties to her. What if Viktor admitted to it all, including where he dumped the body? How, then, would anyone explain the fact that the body was found somewhere else? By Sheriff Gabe Welles. The father of the guy who was having an affair with the victim, the accused's wife?

More than likely, Viktor wouldn't admit to a damn thing. But what he would learn is that she survived, that she was clearly moved, and that my father happens to be the guy who found her.

It stirs up way too many questions that my father can't answer without either perjuring or incriminating himself for his part in all this. I don't know if he grasped the full extent of these consequences when he picked up that radio to call it in. I have a hard time believing he didn't. He's never been one to make rash decisions.

Maybe Alex was right. I guess when it came time, I really could count on him.

"And if, by some chance, she still doesn't remember anything three months down the road?"

"Wouldn't that be the best thing for her? You don't want her ending up like Ginny Fitzgerald, do you?"

"Ginny's a special case," my mom argues, her lips pursing with wariness. "But realistically, the hospital won't carry the financial burden forever. Where does Alex go when they release her?"

"I have some ideas." Gabe gazes out the patio door, his shoulders sagging as if burdened by a weight.

His eyes locked on the Fitzgerald garage.

THIRTY-EIGHT

WATER

NOW

I can't stop staring at the grassy clearing, bathed in late-day sun and smattered with purple and yellow wildflowers. A perfect setting for a lazy stroll, or a picnic.

Or, apparently, to leave a person to die.

"It was dark, and there was snow everywhere, but . . ." Jesse's gaze drifts over the field, his eyes blinking rapidly. "This is where I found you. I still can't shake that memory."

I've listened to Jesse unload invaluable information—day by day, from the moment we met until the agreement he made with Meredith and Gabe to keep me in the dark—for hours.

Catching little flickers, little feelings.

Like bits of things on the verge of escape.

It's as if I needed to see the overall picture before I ever had a chance to begin fitting together all the tiny pieces of this thousand-piece puzzle.

"So, I was moving to Sisters anyway?"

Jesse swallows hard. When he speaks again, his voice has turned gruff. "That weekend. You were going to leave him a letter and then walk out the gate. I'd be waiting for you at the end of the road, where the cameras wouldn't catch my car, in case he checked the footage."

"And I told you it was Viktor's baby? Why would I lie?"

Viktor.

The name presses against its confines in my brain. The more I hear it, the more I think it, the closer it is to breaking out. The one demon that I probably want to remain in the steel trap.

"You didn't lie, technically. I never asked you. I just assumed it was and you didn't correct me. We used condoms every single time and I figured you were on birth control. But I never asked. The first night we were together, you were so upset. I just tossed the condom without checking it." He shrugs. "It must have torn. But I don't know."

"But why wouldn't I just tell you? If I cared so much about you, why wouldn't I want you to know?"

He shrugs. "You said something to me one night about not wanting me to feel trapped, and how if it wasn't working out, not to feel obligated. I think you didn't want me feeling like I was stuck. That pretending it was Viktor's baby would give me an out."

So Jesse thought it wasn't his kid, and yet he was still willing to take me away from that mess.

"And my husband found out that I was pregnant with someone else's baby." It's still not making sense. "But how did he know? How did *I* know it wasn't his?"

Jesse bends down to pluck a flower, to twirl it in his fingers like I've seen his sister do. "I've never been sure of what Viktor knew, or what caused this. I figured either he found out you were leaving him or he found out about us. As for *how* he knew that the baby wasn't his . . . My old roommate, Boone, called yesterday. You met him at Roadside, remember?"

I nod. If what Jesse tells me is all true, then that guy is the other reason why I'm standing here today. Now I know why he was acting weird around me. I think I owe him a hug, at least.

"I never bothered telling Boone that you were pregnant before. But I told him yesterday. The first thing he said was that it couldn't be Viktor's because the guy couldn't have kids."

I frown. "How on earth would he know?"

Jesse rubs his forehead, like he doesn't want to admit the rest. "Boone's been fucking around with a girl named Priscilla, who Viktor knew *very* well." He doesn't need to elaborate. "According to Priscilla, Viktor refused to wear any protection with her, because he assumed she was one hundred percent his and he knew for a fact that he was one hundred percent sterile."

Priscilla . . . Priscilla . . . "Pink."

He pauses, regarding me with a smirk. "Yeah. She used to wear bright pink lipstick."

The word association game may work after all.

Nodding slowly, I play my responses back in my mind. Baby = Impossible. That's why I said that. Because it was impossible for me to have a baby with my husband.

Jesse simply stares at me through those intense eyes, for so long that I have to drop my gaze. "So, we were going to have a baby together?"

"Yeah, we were."

Despite everything, my heart swells with that knowledge. "This is all just . . . crazy."

He kicks a stone lying in the grass. "Trust me, I know. It was so hard—first to stay away, and then, when I moved back, to still stay away. You kept saying things and doing things that you've done before. I was sure you were going to wake up and start remembering. Half of me wanted you to so we could pick up where we left off, but the other half was terrified that you wouldn't want me anymore. None of us thought your memory problems would last this long. I almost told you a hundred different times, but then I thought you might not ever talk to me again." Wet eyes plead with me. "Please don't hate me, Alex."

Alex.

So weird. Can I ever be his Alex again?

"And don't hate my parents. They only went along with it because I told them it's what you wanted, and that was after days of fighting."

"But how could this be what I wanted?"

"I can't explain it. It sounds so stupid when I try to explain. I wish you could just remember."

A painful knot pops into my throat. "So do I."

He hesitates. "Do me a favor? Close your eyes for me."

Without a second's thought, I do. That's the thing about Jesse. I've trusted him from the beginning. Even now, after all of this, I still trust him.

I sense him stepping in close and I swallow.

"That night on the side of the road, in the pitch black, you stood this close to me." I feel his breath against my mouth. "We'd never met, you couldn't even see my face, and yet you leaned in and kissed me." He skates his lips across mine, so tenderly. Almost cautiously. It sends shivers across my back and makes me believe for a moment that we've never kissed before.

"And you asked me if I was happy in my life. You asked, if I could just escape my bad choices—"

"And start over fresh, would I?" My eyes flash open as the words slip out of my mouth unbidden. "It was raining," I whisper, an image of the faceless stranger from my dream appearing in my head. Not the one who threatened me.

The one who saved me.

It was Jesse.

I gasp, tears of shock and excitement and relief welling in my eyes. "I remember that. I remember you."

His strong arms rope around my waist, pulling me tight to his body. Part of me wants to push him away, but I don't have the strength to do anything but melt into his chest, accept his comfort, and cry softly against him.

Droplets land on my forehead that I know aren't mine. "I was afraid I'd lose you; that what he'd done to you would take you away from me forever," he explains in a husky voice, ripe with emotion. "I couldn't handle the idea of that."

A long, quiet moment stretches out, my sobs the only sound in the vast open field.

And then a new worry blossoms. "What about him? Is he really not looking for me?" Do I want Viktor to keep thinking I'm dead? Do I want him to get away with what he did? It's probably the safest option. What would he do if he knew that I survived?

Jesse steps back far enough to see my face, his hands finding their way to either side of my jaw. "This past April, Viktor was racing his Aston Martin around the slick roads and lost control. He crashed it into a telephone pole." He pauses. "Viktor is dead. He got what he deserved."

I don't know exactly why, but that news buckles my knees. Jesse's arms dive down to catch me by the waist, pulling me back into his chest.

"That's when you moved back, isn't it?" When Jesse pulled up behind Ginny's old broken-down truck. And rescued me.

I close my eyes and let him press his forehead against mine. "I just couldn't stay away from you for another day."

"Where do we go from here?" I hear myself whisper. I doubt I can stay away from him either.

Jesse's grip around me tightens, as if he's unwilling to let me go. Ever.

————

"I think I still wore Velcro-strapped shoes the last time I was in this house," Jesse muses, gazing over the shelf of horse figurines. There must be fifty of them.

"It hasn't changed. Just a little more cluttered," Gabe admits, sifting through stacks of papers on the kitchen table. For what, I'm not sure.

I fold my arms over my chest, taking in the boxes and bags. In case of the end of the world, Ginny could hole up here for weeks. "How is she?"

"No change." Meredith sits down in the very chair that Ginny occupied last night, the creak from its worn frame cutting into the awkward silence.

We've shared a lot of quick gazes and two-word answers since Jesse drove me home from the field where I was supposed to have died five months ago. Where the old me *did* die. I'm so tired— both emotionally and physically—from the last twenty-four hours, and yet I doubt I could sleep.

Meredith picks the unfinished quilt off the floor, where it had fallen when the paramedics moved Ginny. Stretching it out on her lap, she frowns. "Huh. I've never seen this before." Holding it up for us, her finger touches the low branch on the right-hand side. "Do you know why she did this?"

I smile, taking in the tiny green leaf bud that sits there. "No." It's my secret with Ginny. I'll take it to my grave.

"Here it is." Gabe lifts a manila envelope up from the dining room table with my full name—Water Fitzgerald—written across the top in block letters and a stamp that reads "Tilden Law Office."

Jesse and I share a frown.

"I ran into Ward Tilden a few days ago. He told me that Ginny'd been in there to revise her will," Gabe explains, handing it to me.

I tear it open. Sure enough, it's dated last Wednesday, the day that Ginny went into town.

Jesse leans over my shoulder to read with me as I scan the pages. It's a fairly straightforward legal document.

That says Ginny is leaving everything to me.

The house, the farm, the 1,018 acres of land, the Felixes.

Everything.

I feel the color drain from my face. "Wait . . . but . . . I didn't expect this, or want it. That's not why . . ." That's not why I loved Ginny like she was my family.

"We know." Meredith smiles, a tear rolling down her cheek. "And so did she."

———

"So, Ol' Mr. Fanshaw showed up on my doorstep today." I pause.

And wait for the old woman to sit up and start ranting about being swindled out of her land. But she remains still, her eyes closed, her face peaceful. The same way she's been for the past week. I've visited her every day, sitting here for hours until my voice grows ragged, relaying everything that Jesse has told me, as well as small things that I think I remember, and all the tiniest flashes that have stirred my subconscious over the past few months. All the things that have started to make sense now.

Jesse has sat with me every night on the porch swing—along with Felix the dog, parked at my feet—and highlighted all the ways that I'm the same person.

And all the ways that I'm now so much stronger.

I can't be angry with him, or Meredith and Gabe. Maybe I should be, maybe I need my head examined by Dr. Weimer yet again, but I've been through too much to be angry about something that they did with only my best interests at heart. And I believe they really did have my best interests at heart.

Jesse . . . My blood still races when I see him throw a leg over the fence. My chest still swells when I think about how much he must care for me.

And my heart now aches when I think about how much he risked for me.

He saved me long before the night I almost died; that much I'm sure of. Maybe one day I'll remember exactly how.

I take Ginny's weathered hand in between mine. The heart monitor catches a blip—three beats that are much faster than the rest—before it slows.

And then stops.

One long, everlasting beep cuts through the room and a giant ball forms in my throat.

"It's time to go see your big white oak in full bloom again, Ginny."

———

I watch Jesse park beside Ginny's big, yellow truck from my perch on the concrete steps outside of the hospital. I guess it's *my* big, yellow truck now. Everything of Ginny's is technically mine, a concept I haven't given any thought to.

All that's been cycling through my head since I called Jesse is how much I need him here.

Here, right now.

Here, in my life.

Just as he always seems to be.

Here. For me.

He runs up the steps two at a time to take the seat beside me, his body wedged next to mine. The Hart Brothers work shirt he wears smells of fire—a comforting mix of burnt bark and leaves. I close my eyes and inhale deeply.

It reminds me of all those nights together by the woodstove, wrapped up in a wool blanket. The ones I can remember as Water and the ones I can't as Alex. But I know that smell.

It's Jesse, and it feels like warmth, like contentment. Like love.

We sit in silence as the sun drops down behind the mountains.

And then I slip my hand into his. "Let's go home."

To exactly where I'm meant to be.

"It's nice to have the stream back." The long snake of water runs through the corral, sun glittering off it. Amber was right; it was nothing but an indent in the dirt by August of last year, the summer heat emptying it completely.

And yet it has found its way back again this year.

Jesse answers with a kiss against the corner of my mouth, draping his arms over the newly mended fence on either side of me as a line of horses gallops past, enjoying the first warm day of spring. All eight of them—the Felixes, Lulu, and their five new friends. We have another two boarders coming next week, and most weekends are busy with owners and little girls like Zoe coming to ride their horses.

The ranch has come back to life.

A clatter of metal rings through the quiet, followed by Gabe's curses and Jesse's low chuckle. "I should probably go help him before he fucks that engine up."

"No bickering." I watch Jesse's back as he heads for our garage, to where the rusted and inoperable pea-green '67 Mustang sits, its round headlights peeking out. It's Gabe's pet project, now that he has retired. Meredith insisted that he find one because she was afraid she'd strangle him otherwise.

Gabe's sudden retirement last fall caused quite the stir in town. The only reason he gave was that he was ready to do some fishing with his son. The Welleses and I know the truth. Though Gabe himself has stood by the idea that what he was accomplice to was for the best—for my safety, Jesse's safety, even Boone's safety—and that Viktor did get what he deserved, I don't think he'd been comfortable wearing that badge ever since.

So, now he occupies his time puttering around his property and mine, fixing fences, fishing, and "helping" Jesse rebuild engines. The Mustang will be the fourth classic that Jesse has rebuilt and then sold, though Gabe is keeping this one. The others Jesse has finished for his friend Boone to sell. Boone has already sworn up and down that it's all legit. Gabe would probably come out of retirement just to arrest Jesse if it were anything else.

Jesse glances over his shoulder at me, flashing a sly smile my way. He knew I'd be watching. I've never been good at *not* watching Jesse.

Not even as Alexandria Petrova.

I remember.

It's still only bits here and there, but almost each day unlocks a new puzzle piece of my past. Some good memories, some not. Long days of school and cleaning houses with my mom. My mom, with her worn hands and tired smile. The roses that would be waiting for me on the kitchen counter of Viktor's Seattle condo, with a card; the swirl of curiosity and excitement that hit me when I saw them, thinking how lucky I was that I had attracted the attention of such a handsome, successful man.

I remember his face, his light blue eyes. I didn't see the cold calculation behind them. The first day that I remembered Viktor, I remembered him in a good light. A kind light.

It's unfathomable how deep the real truth can become buried in the human mind.

It was around August that I woke up in the middle of the night—Jesse's arm slung over my stomach, my own hands pressed against my womb—that I remembered the day I sat on my bed in Portland, waves of nausea and fear and excitement coursing through my body as I stared at the two blue lines in the display window of the pregnancy test.

Because I knew then that it was Jesse's baby. The condom *had* broken. I remembered noticing the sizeable tear when I cleaned up the hotel room, before leaving the next morning.

In October, on the day that Jesse and I moved into Ginny's old house, the landline phone rang for the first time, a loud trill echoing through the newly remodeled house.

And I remembered how Viktor found out about the pregnancy.

It was a fluke, really. I'd never even thought about removing our home phone number from the doctor's office files; I'd always used my cell phone to contact them. I never thought that the obstetrician might call the house line and leave a message on the answering machine about my coming appointment. I never thought that, while I was upstairs, fitting myself into that sleazy blue sequined dress for the last time, worried that Viktor would notice my swollen breasts, he was downstairs, listening to the message.

I remember my heels clicking against the spiral staircase as I descended, to find Viktor waiting for me at the bottom, a simmering rage like nothing I'd ever experienced before radiating off him. But the demons from that actual night still remain safely locked in their steel trap, which I am grateful for.

Pulling Jesse's flannel jacket around me—I guess I should just call it *my* flannel jacket now because I wear it so much—I head toward the barn, smiling at the nice new red roof on it. It matches the ones that we put on the garage and the house.

The day that Ginny revised her will to leave everything to me, she also went to the township office. For years, Meredith and Gabe had urged her to sell off some of her land; she didn't need a thousand acres. She had refused though, just like her father before her.

So, when the land assessor appeared in the driveway one day a few weeks after Ginny died, to discuss the parcels she wanted to sell, we were all quite surprised. And relieved. I really don't need a thousand acres of land, but I would never have sold so much as a square foot of it had Ginny not approved.

The land was snapped up by Chuck Fanshaw's family almost overnight, leaving me with enough income to pay for some much-needed work around here, and then some. The messenger bag of money that Jesse pulled out one day—that I had squirrelled away for my escape—made finances even easier.

With a sigh of contentment, I grab the paintbrush and begin climbing the ladder. I knew this would be an ambitious under-taking when I explained it to Jesse, given the size of the barn and the fact that I'm not overly excited about heights. Or being on ladders.

None of that swayed me, though, as I took to the west-ern-facing wall with a brush and a can of black paint a week ago. It took three days, from dawn until dusk, to finish the body, its bare limbs spanning as far as twenty feet on either side of the trunk. It turned out better than I had anticipated.

But it's the splotches of red and orange and yellow and green blending together that hold my attention, especially at sunset, as the last streams of daylight hit the barn before disappearing behind the mountain range, casting a spotlight on the tree's beautiful leaves.

———

The mind, it can be a deceitful thing.
But it is no match for the heart.

ACKNOWLEDGMENTS

A brand new series, with new characters, new lives, new plots. What a scary notion. As much as I loved writing the Ten Tiny Breaths series, everyone needs a change. I think this new series is a good change for me as a writer. I hope that it's a good change for you as a reader.

Burying Water was an ambitious story. The shift between past and present, alternating POVs, and two people falling in love twice was a lot to take on. Too much, at times. But I did it, and I have many people to thank along the way.

To my readers and the bloggers, for your continued support, especially as I embark on a new fictional world. This is about as opposite to *Five Ways to Fall* as you can get, but I hope you still feel that it is authentically me.

To Nicole Jacquelyn and Papa Jacquelyn. Though I'm planning a trip to Portland and Sisters, Oregon, next year, I have yet to visit either. That means I had to rely on those who actually live in Oregon. Thanks to these two lovely, helpful people, I was able to build two settings with some degree of authenticity (though I've made up the shops and restaurants). Papa Jacquelyn was actually the one to suggest the small town of Sisters, and the second I looked it up, I knew it was exactly what I was looking for. Thank you to both of you for helping me to bring this book to life.

To doctor, fellow writer, and agent sibling, Darin Kennedy, for one of the most disturbing phone calls I've ever had. I knew Ginny would have to go, but I wasn't exactly sure how. And Water . . . that poor girl's medical condition got worse and worse the longer we talked!

To K. P. Simmon, publicist extraordinaire. We're coming up on two years, buddy, and you haven't fired me as an author yet. This bodes well for me.

To Stacey Donaghy, you continue to surprise me with your knowledge, your patience, and your willingness to put up with my skinny wrists and my strange shopping requests. Best. Agent. Ever.

To Sarah Cantin, for surviving another book with me. I know my writing process is painful at best, and yet you stick with me, helping me shape the characters and plots into something special; something that people may want to read. I already know you're an incredible editor. I'm starting to wonder if you're also a glutton for punishment. Either way, I'm completely aware that I am one lucky writer to have you for an editor.

To my publisher, Judith Curr, and the team at Atria Books: Ben Lee, Ariele Fredman, Tory Lowy, Kimberly Goldstein, and Alysha Bullock, for another brilliantly packaged book.

To Paul, Lia, and Sadie, for your love of premade food and low expectations for a clean house.